"I'm sorry," he murmured. Whether he was sorry for what he'd done, or what he was about to do, he couldn't say. Without thinking, he leaned forward to taste those pink lips, the sweetness of her amazement.

The smack never came; it was as if she were a fly in a web and he was the terrible spider who had caught her. He pressed his lips to hers. She jumped as if shocked, her mouth opening, and he fought himself not to take advantage.

Not to push this strange moment into shattering. He kept the kiss tender, her chapped lips all but breaking his heart.

Carefully, as if she were a horse that might spook, he touched her cheek with his fingertips, and when she didn't shy away he slid those fingers around her neck, cupping the heat of her skin, the pounding of her heartbeat in his palm.

There was a vibration in her throat and he felt it in his mouth, in his hand, and he knew she was moaning. Crying slightly, because she hated herself right now, hated that she couldn't resist him. And the devil in him loved that. Lived for that.

He should have done this earlier, cut through all the bullshit negotiation and bullshit communication, and gotten right to this.

Because sex he understood. A woman's soft groan reverberating against his tongue was all the communication he needed.

Can't Hurry Love

Molly O'Keefe

BANTAM BOOKS
NEW YORK

Can't Hurry Love is a work of fiction. Names, characters, places, and incidents are the products of the author's imagination or are used fictitiously. Any resemblance to actual events, locales, or persons, living or dead, is entirely coincidental.

A Bantam Books Mass Market Original

Copyright © 2012 by Molly Fader
Excerpt from *This Can't Be Love* by Molly O'Keefe copyright © 2012 by Molly Fader

Published in the United States by Bantam Books, an imprint of The Random House Publishing Group, a division of Random House, Inc., New York.

BANTAM BOOKS and the rooster colophon are registered trademarks of Random House, Inc.

ISBN 978-0-345-52561-1
eBook ISBN 978-0-345-52562-8

This book contains an excerpt from the forthcoming book *This Can't Be Love* by Molly O'Keefe. This excerpt has been set for this edition only and may not reflect the final content of the forthcoming book.

Cover design: Lynn Andreozzi
Cover photograph: George Kerrigan

Printed in the United States of America

www.bantamdell.com

9 8 7 6 5 4 3 2 1

Bantam Books mass market edition: August 2012

For Pam Hopkins,
who had faith and confidence
when all I had were dirty diapers.
Thank you so much.

Can't Hurry Love

chapter
1

Victoria Schulman was hugging his horse.

If that wasn't enough to piss a man off, Eli Turnbull didn't know what was. That she was doing it in one of those fussy satin shirts only made it worse.

The woman was tiny, a paisley-covered speck against his horse's wide black head. Eli had some inclination to worry about Victoria—about her thinness, and the dark circles under her eyes—but he ignored it.

And he felt bad bullying a woman who clearly needed not only a good meal but someone to take care of her. But every time he tried to be nice—thinking about honey versus vinegar and all that shit—something about her would just make him crazy.

Like, right now, her shoes. They were red and they had bows.

How in the world could she put on those shoes and say "Yeah, I'll be a rancher"?

Honestly, he wanted to be nice, but she was just so ridiculous.

"You need boots if you're going to be in here."

His voice cut up the distance between them and she stepped away from his horse.

Not very nice.

Instead of flinching, she lifted her chin as if they were about to box. He'd give her points for foolish courage, but foolish courage never helped anyone.

"I . . . ah . . ." She glanced down at the silly shoes on her feet. "I suppose you're right."

He stepped across the wide aisle between the tack room and the stall where he kept Patience, his mare. Victoria didn't back away. Her hands flexed into fists for a moment, but then she spread them wide and ran them down the edges of her skirt.

Her efforts at control were totally ruined by her eyes. Their navy-blue depths betrayed her interest. He felt her gaze travel across his chest, his arms. Felt it linger at the base of his throat where the sweat ran down his shirt.

She tried to act nonchalant, she really did, but she failed.

"Ah . . . Ruby said you were looking for me," she said.

"It's nine. I was looking for you at seven this morning." Okay, that wasn't nice either, but he couldn't resist pointing out how terribly unsuited she was for this place. For this job she'd taken on.

"I have a son, Eli. I can't drop everything when you need me."

Biting his tongue, he opened the stall to lead Patience into the aisle.

"Careful," he said when Victoria stumbled out of the way.

She glared up at him as if she knew what he was doing, how he was trying to bully her.

He gave a smile another shot.

"Oh, you can stop the act, Eli. I know you're mad."

"I'm not mad."

"Eli, it's not like I'm doing this to hurt you." The brief touch of her hand against his back, like lightning over the high pastures, lit him up from the inside.

This time he shied away, feeling the burn of her hand under his skin.

"Of course not. You're taking over the ranch because you have a deep and abiding love of the land."

"Is that so hard to believe?"

He looked pointedly at her hair, pulled so tight from her face, that stupid ruffled collar, her stick-thin legs beneath the hem of her skirt. Those ridiculous shoes.

"Yes."

Two hours ago he'd had a plan for this conversation; now he had to get going, and Victoria was wearing those stupid shoes and he was angry when he'd intended to be nice.

"Fine. All right. Look, Eli, we both know I have no clue what I'm doing with this ranch, but I want to learn. I want . . ." She took a deep breath and squared her shoulders.

Oh crap. She was going to reveal something now. Something that was supposed to make him feel bad, make him want to help her.

Don't, he wanted to say. *Don't hand me any more weapons to use against you.*

"I want to be good at this."

"Because you've failed at everything else?"

Color rose in her cheeks and he smiled in the face of her shame. Through convoluted means she'd gained control of this ranch that should by rights be his, and he just had to correct the mistake. Which he could do, right now.

"I was looking for you this morning because I can make you an offer."

"For what?"

Be. Nice. "For the ranch."

"I'm not—"

"Two million."

"Dollars?"

Ah, the Scarecrow was cute when she was confused.

"A year from now when the ranch is out of escrow

and you're begging your brother to sell this place, you won't get that kind of offer. And two million dollars will buy a lot of security for you and your son."

That pushed her back on her heels.

"You . . . there's no way you have that kind of money."

To his ears it sounded like she was wavering, and his heart pounded hard in his throat. This was it. His hands went numb.

"I can get it by tomorrow. Then you can go back to throwing parties and buying curtains and whatever the hell else it is women like you do."

Oddly, she smiled. And for a moment, surrounded by sun-shot dust motes, he saw the girl she'd been years before, when her father had forced her to come down to this ranch for the summer. Sweet and out of place, she'd followed Eli around like a shadow, even though she was older. She'd been game, always game. And he'd liked her. A lot.

But when she'd arrived at the ranch a few months ago when Lyle Baker was dying, he'd been unable to find any of that girl in the pinched, angry, and scared woman she'd become.

A woman who hadn't even recognized him at first. She'd looked down at him as if he were a servant. A slow and clumsy waiter.

He didn't want to see that girl now, not when he was doing his best to crush the woman under his boot heel.

"Do I seem so useless?"

"You know the answer to that."

The barb sunk deep but instead of curling in on herself, she stood up straighter and somehow, he realized too late, he'd galvanized her.

"I'm sorry, Eli—"

Sorry? His guts twisted. "Didn't you hear me? I said two million dollars."

"Two million dollars won't buy me any pride. Or self-respect."

"And when you fail at this? How much pride are you going to have then?"

"I'm not going to fail."

He laughed at her then. Right at her. And that smile faded, replaced by the most ridiculous determination. The most asinine belief in herself. It was like watching a house cat trying to be a tiger.

"Not if you help me. I'm uninformed, Eli. Not stupid. And I want to learn. I want . . . I want—"

"To be good at this, yeah, you said." He managed to dismiss all of her good intentions, all of her noble and brave efforts, with a curt wave of his hand.

Victoria Schulman, the society widow, who had lost her fortune, had just turned down two million dollars. And Eli was back in the same position he'd been in for the past ten years of his life—throwing money at a Baker who just wouldn't take it.

Damn it.

He slipped a padded blue saddle blanket over Patience's back while she sidestepped and shook out her mane. Heaving the saddle on next, he fumed. Victoria was still standing there. Still expecting his help. He put his knee in Patience's belly as he tightened the saddle cinch. If only every woman in his life were this easy to manage.

But the truth was that Victoria had given him the tools to make her fail, to ensure her defeat. The poor woman had been too honest; she couldn't even hide her desire for him . . . her curiosity. The way her eyes clung to his body for just a moment too long.

Between his own father and Lyle Baker, the man he'd worked for half his life, Eli had learned everything he needed to know about being a cruel, self-serving bastard. He'd never had a reason to use those lessons.

Until now.

He would wear her down until she begged him to take the ranch.

Victoria felt naked, utterly skinless in front of Eli. She'd said all she could to convince him of her good intentions toward the ranch and the land. She didn't know how else to sway him, and yet he seemed unswayed.

He slipped the bridle over his giant horse's head, tucking the bit into her mouth, clucking when the horse gummed at him.

It was as if Victoria were totally invisible and after being invisible to every man in her entire life, she'd had enough.

"Where are you going?"

Eli tipped his hat back off his eyes and she forced herself not to look away. Those eyes were like sunlight on a mirror. Too bright. Too sharp.

"It's Saturday. Auction day for the Angus herd. Up in the north pasture."

"Today?" she asked and he nodded, leaning past her. The smell of him—sunshine and sweat, horse and dirt—eddied around her, making her dizzy with a terrible hunger.

In the early days of their courtship, Joel had called her femininity delicate. And he'd loved that; said her weakness had made him feel strong. Like a protector. So, like any good idiot, she'd cultivated it. Until she was treated like glass, which was fine in public, but boring in private.

Their sex life had been respectful, she told herself.

And if smelling Eli Turnbull made her feel as if she'd been missing out on something in all those years of quiet and plain missionary position, well, then, add it to the pile of disappointments.

She watched his muscles flex and bulge under his brown-and-white plaid shirt as he lifted a shovel that had been tucked into the corner of the stall.

Over the last few years of her marriage, all she had seen Joel lift was his martini glass and the occasional disapproving eyebrow.

"The herd is mine to do with as I will. Said so in the will. I just have to split any proceeds from the sale with Luc."

"How . . . how many are you selling?" Not that she knew how many there were, but she had to try.

"All of them."

"My father has only been dead for three months and you're selling off his pride and joy?"

"Yep."

"That's . . ." She stopped. Her laughter was a surprise, like finding something she'd lost so long ago she'd forgotten all about it. Lyle Baker had been a terrible father, a wholehearted son of a bitch, and throwing stones at his bastard daughter had been his favorite pastime. Selling his pride and joy seemed like a marvelous idea. "Awesome."

Eli's green eyes slid over her, over her face and eyes, the two thin collarbones revealed by the ruffled shell she wore, her breasts, small hills against the silk, and then away.

Light-headed, she had to put a hand on the stall door for balance.

"I'd like to go with you." It seemed like the rancherly thing to do.

"You want to learn how to be a rancher; you can start at the beginning."

"Great." Joy surged through her and she fought the urge to clap her hands with excitement. "I'll come—"

"You'll stay," he said, handing her the shovel. "And muck stalls. Like any good greenhorn."

"No." She pushed the shovel back at him.

"You want my help?"

The shovel dangled between them.

"This is a test?" she asked.

He shrugged, his smile gleaming with ugly victory.

She yanked the shovel out of his hand. "You have nothing to teach me about embarrassment, Eli. You think you're punishing me. You think you're teaching me a lesson about something, but trust me, you smug bastard, there's nothing I don't know about degradation. I'll muck your stalls. I'll do whatever you think I need to do—"

"That's right."

She leaned in close, her anger a bright flame in her chest, lighting her up in a way she'd never experienced before. As if a pilot light had exploded in her furnace.

"But I'm still your boss."

For a beautiful moment Eli was blank-faced and silent, and she knew she should regret angering the one person she needed as an ally, but it was just too delicious.

She smiled as the skin beneath the scruff on his cheeks got red. He swung himself up onto his horse in one smooth, effortless motion.

Her body turned to pudding. Did he have to be so . . . big? Masculine? It made her feel . . . small. And to her great shame, damp.

"I want every stall in this barn cleaned up by the time I get back."

And then he was gone.

She stood there, in her inappropriate shoes, holding a shovel that smelled like poop, and smoldered.

He might have won this battle, but he didn't know who he was up against. After years of lying down, of capitulating, of surrendering before she even realized she had something she wanted to fight for, she was filled with an unholy hostility.

There was a war's worth of lost fights inside of her. And if Eli was going to stand in the way of what she wanted . . . well, she smiled, he'd better brace himself.

She was a woman who was just beginning to realize how scorned she truly was.

chapter
2

"*Hey, Mom.*" *Jacob,* Victoria's seven-year-old boy, stepped into the quiet barn two hours later. "Where are you?"

"In here. The last stall."

Using her wrist, she pushed back the lock of hair that was flopping into her eyes, and smiled as he walked through the great blocks of sunlight that streamed down onto the dirt floor from the high windows. The horses in this corner of the barn all lifted their heads, shaking back their manes, as if they knew him. And they probably did.

Jacob snuck in here every chance he got. Despite his allergies, his asthma, and her explicit precautions.

Eli's horse's stall, the last of the ten, was almost done. Victoria's hands were sore, red, and blistered and the smell of horse poop wasn't going to leave her nose anytime soon, but she'd cleaned out all of the stalls.

Tony, one of the hands not involved with the auction in the north pasture, had shown her where the pile for the dirty straw was. He'd helped her kick fresh hay down from the loft and had managed not to laugh at her surprise that haylofts really exist. He'd even found her a pair of boots—stinky black rain boots that were cracked and faded and made her feet sweat as if she were in the jungle. But they were better than her Chanel ballet flats. In the end, as she'd expected, he'd offered to help, watching her with about as much skepticism as one man could muster. And maybe it was because of that skepticism that she told him she was fine.

And she was. The shoveling was harder work than she'd done in forever, but holy hell, it felt good.

It felt good to do something after years of pacing. Of worrying. Of doing nothing but wringing her hands.

"What are you doing?" Jacob asked, coming to stand in the open door of the stall. He was wearing his favorite Spider-Man shirt for what was probably the fifth day in a row, judging by the spots on the front. And his socks had given up the fight of clinging to his thin legs and were slouching around his ankles. Sort of like everything in Texas during August, they had just wilted.

"Mucking stalls."

"Mucking?"

"Getting rid of the horse poop."

"Mom," he said as if it were his job to let her know what a mistake she was making. "That's so gross."

"Tell me about it. Did you bring the stuff?"

He lifted a plastic bag, and she knew in her heart of hearts that this little revenge plot was silly.

She should rise above it, but she was so damn tired of rising above everything. Her husband's betrayal, the public scorn. Eli's very private scorn.

She was going to wallow in some base and silly behavior. And wouldn't you know it, wallowing felt good, too.

"I think you're supposed to wear gloves, Mom." He pointed at her red hands.

"They didn't go with my skirt." Her joke fell flat and he just stared at her. He wasn't used to a mother who joked. It made her heart hurt, thinking of how cold she'd been, how paralyzed by fear, for so much of his life.

She touched the curl over his ear. His hair was longer than she'd ever let it grow before, almost down to his shoulders. He looked bohemian, as if he'd never spent a minute in her company, and she kind of liked it.

What she didn't like was the downward curve to his lips, the slump in his shoulders.

"Jacob? You okay?"

"I was just . . . I was just wondering when we were going back home."

"Home?"

"New York City."

She felt her jaw drop, her eyes open wide. How in the world had she not explained this properly?

"Honey." She rested the shovel against the wall and crouched down in front of him as best she could in the knee-high rubber boots. "You're starting school here next month."

"I thought that was just until you got Grandpa's will all figured out."

"It's figured out, Jacob. We don't have a home in New York anymore."

"What about Toronto with Uncle Luc?"

"We were just staying with him. That's not our home either."

She blinked and took a big gulp of air, wondering what kind of protest Jacob was going to throw her way. And wondering how she was going to muster up the energy to put it to rest.

"You mean we live here? At the ranch?"

She nodded and slowly, to her great relief and delight, he started to smile.

She laughed. "I guess that's okay with you?"

"Totally okay. It's awesome! But what are you going to do?"

For good or bad, the Crooked Creek Ranch was hers now. Well, sort of. Her brother had been given the ranch in their father's will three months ago. But he had no interest in this land.

And Luc had suggested that she run the ranch for him until it was out of escrow, at which point she intended to buy it.

Not that she knew a single thing about ranching. But she wanted to learn. Needed to. Because she'd utterly failed at everything else in her life, and this place seemed like her last chance to make a home and a future for her son.

But the only way that was going to happen was through Eli Turnbull. And it was pretty safe to say that Eli Turnbull hated her.

He'd made his intentions to buy the ranch very clear and now she was standing in his way, which was a very uncomfortable place to be.

But she wasn't giving up. She'd done enough of that in her life.

"I am going to run the ranch."

"Isn't that Eli's job?"

"Eli is the foreman." Like his father and grandfather before him. Eli had roots in this land that were twisted and tied up with her own. "But the ranch belonged to my dad and now it belongs to Uncle Luc, and I'm going to run it for him until you and I can buy it next year."

"Wow." She tried not to preen as he looked at her as if he'd just noticed her superhero cape.

That right there, the pride and wonder in her son's eyes, was worth all of Eli's disdain. She'd muck a hundred stalls if that was what it took to have her son look at her like that.

"But . . . what about our friends?" Jacob asked, and just like that the pride, the cape, the wonder—it all vanished.

"What about them?" *They're not our friends,* she wanted to say. *Not anymore. Not after what your father did. Not after how they treated us.*

"We're not going to see them again?"

"We'll make new friends."

Her son's shoulders curved forward again and she waited for his next question, but he was silent.

Unused to his silence, she cocked her head to see his face.

"Jacob?"

"Do you miss Dad?"

It took a long time for her to get her breath back.

Jacob didn't talk much about Joel, and the grief book she had on her bedside table said that was okay. But Victoria hadn't gotten to the chapter about what to say when the kid started to talk.

"Do you miss him?" she asked, because that seemed like a self-help-book kind of thing to do.

Jacob tilted his head and his eyes, so big and dark, the best thing he'd gotten from his father, looked far too old.

"Not really." She blinked with surprise. "Is that bad?"

Ahhhh . . . maybe? Honestly, she should have finished that damn book by now.

"He just . . . he worked all the time."

She nodded, stroking Spider-Man on his sleeve. "I know."

"Did he love me?"

"Of course," she gasped. Not that she had any proof she could hand him, anything she could point to and say "See, that's what a father does when he loves his son." But she couldn't let her baby believe otherwise.

"Then why—?"

"Daddy got into a lot of trouble with people," she said quickly, hating the thought that her son would attach anything Joel did to his own small shoulders. That he would feel any responsibility for his father's sins made her ill.

Crouching down in the dirt and hay, she cupped his cheeks, ran her thumbs over the tender rosy skin.

"Because of the Potzie thing?" he asked.

"Ponzi," she corrected, stroking back his hair, her heart cracking right down the middle even as she smiled. She'd tried once to explain a Ponzi scheme, but Jacob just didn't understand. Truth be told, she didn't either. She didn't understand why Joel had started it, how he'd kept it going knowing he was stealing from people, and why he hadn't just gotten out when things had started to fall apart. "He tricked a lot of people and he was scared and embarrassed."

"Because he lied?"

"Yes. He owed a lot of people a lot of money."

"That's why he killed himself?"

Bile and grief kicked up stones in her stomach, sending lumps into her throat. For a moment she saw the blood splattered against the den's plum silk wallpaper, and the smell, hot and coppery, flooded her nose.

The gunshot had woken her up that night. And she'd raced through the penthouse, past Jacob's room, right to the closed door of the den.

She'd made a lot of mistakes in her life, but opening that door had been one of the worst.

Jacob's hands twitched in hers and she grabbed onto his fingers, probably squeezing too hard. She usually did. But he was all she had to hold on to, the only thing she knew she'd done right.

This boy was Joel's gift to her, and because of that she had to make peace with what he'd done. The anger and fear of being widowed in such a violent way, of being hounded by the press, of being yanked by her hair out of the ivory tower she'd lived in, was nothing compared to her wonder in this boy.

She had to remember that. Every day she had to balance the scales in her head. When he'd been sick in the hospital nearly a year ago, it had been easy to keep the balance. But now that he was better, now that life had moved on, everything was harder.

"Did he love you?" The question put a hook in her stomach and yanked, and for a moment she couldn't breathe for the pain. This was how Eli had wanted to make her feel with his cruel comments, but he had no idea how hard he would have to work to succeed.

"Yes." She lied. Right to his face, she lied.

"Do you miss him?"

"I miss having someone to talk to." Not that Joel was a great talker. But now that her brother was gone, she was so alone here on the ranch.

"You have me."

She smiled. "I mean another adult."

"Like that Dennis guy?"

Earlier this summer she'd gotten caught up with a con artist trying to steal money from Luc and his girlfriend, Tara Jean Sweet. Victoria had been gullible and desperate, easy pickings for a man like Dennis. When things didn't work out the way he'd hoped, Dennis had shown up at the ranch and had held a gun to Jacob's head before Luc and Eli had managed to disarm him. And the memory of that night was so embarrassing that she felt her skin crawl. Her stomach turned at the thought of how Jacob's life had been endangered because she was so dumb.

"No, honey. Dennis was a mistake."

Jacob stood inside a bright square of sunlight streaming in through the high windows. His skin was translucent in the light; she could see the blue of his veins, the beat of his heart. "Are you going to get married again?"

"No." That, at least, was one thing she could bank on. She didn't have that kind of love inside of her anymore. That kind of faith and trust and compromise. It all just cost too much. "It's just you and me, kid. Now, you want to help me finish this horse's stall?"

"Yeah!" he cried and tipped over the plastic bag. Two

big pouches of the rose potpourri that Ruby, the house-keeper, loved came tumbling out, along with a big heart pillow with hearts and the words "Home Sweet Home" embroidered on it.

She ripped open the potpourri and started scattering it across the fresh hay.

As far as revenge went, it was pretty silly. But imagining Eli's fierce face when he saw the rose petals all over his precious horse's stall made her smile.

And her smile made her son smile.

And that was reason enough for anything.

Cresting the low bluff over the north pasture, Eli swung down from his horse and counted the trucks in the green valley below. Twelve of them. He saw Jones, who'd be acting on behalf of the Triple L, Lou from Spring Creek, Oscar from Los Camillos. Quite a few people he didn't recognize, who'd probably come down from Oklahoma. But all of them were here to take away a piece of the in-famous Crooked Creek herd.

The far green and brown hills were dotted with cattle as far as the eye could see. Nine hundred lots. Half heifers born of stock known for its fertility, easy births, and resilience to infection. Two dozen certified studs, most of them bred from Lyle's first stud, that award-winning beast on which he'd spent a fortune.

A hot wind blew up from the south, rustling through the grasses that had gone dry and yellow in the last weeks of summer. And the wind seemed to be whispering, *What the hell are you doing?*

Selling the herd was going to ruin Victoria. Without the income of the cattle she wouldn't be able to pay the taxes on the land. She probably didn't even know that.

Christ, how could she refuse two million dollars?

If he got rid of this herd, he didn't have a job and he didn't have access to the Crooked Creek breeding equipment.

Without the equipment the next part of his plan wouldn't get off the ground.

What am I doing?

The clop-clop of horse hooves behind him made him turn. Uncle John's arrival was a mixed blessing. He didn't stand for people feeling sorry for themselves, among other things. And Eli was feeling very sorry for himself.

"Well, now, boy, is this the day of your vengeance?" John asked, coming up over the hill on that blue gelding he loved. No one would say it to his face, but Uncle John needed to lose a couple ten pounds. Even on his six-foot, six-inch body, the man was getting big. But when a man's sixty-five with no wife, no kids, more money than God, and no one around to tell him what to do, Eli supposed he could do what he wanted. And Uncle John wanted to eat chicken wings for breakfast.

No matter the soft belly, though, Eli's uncle fit the landscape. He was hard and tough, and larger than life.

"*Our* vengeance. Today is the day of *our* vengeance," Eli corrected, feeling the stir of his misgivings settle down. Nothing like having a teammate to make a man feel better when things were going to shit.

Uncle John laughed, heaving himself out of the saddle. And once he was on the ground, he slapped Eli's back so hard that it reverberated through his body like thunder, shaking loose what was left of that doubt. "That's my boy."

Eli wasn't, not strictly speaking. Yet in all of the ways that mattered, Uncle John was more of a father to Eli than his own father had ever been. Eli had never had much reason to feel like a kid, even when he'd been one. But standing next to his uncle, in the shade of his large smile, he felt small. And just a little—just enough—cared for.

Emotion rolled itself into a ball in the back of his throat.

"Oh man, you're gonna start crying, aren't you?" John said. "I always told Mark you were more like your momma than us. We shoulda beat you more."

Eli laughed at the old joke.

"You just roll out of bed?" Eli took in his uncle's slap-dash look. "You've got coffee all over your shirt. And"—he reached out a hand to pick up the jelly-covered crumb of donut that was stuck to his collar—"Uncle John, the doctors told you to lay off the fried food."

"Donuts ain't fried, are they? Besides, Janet keeps giving them to me every time I go to the coffee shop."

"Then stop going to the coffee shop."

"Well, now, you know if I did that, Janet would probably die of a broken heart."

Uncle John was a rock in a river; everything rolled off his back. Eli threw up his hands—there was no winning.

John had left the ranch as a kid, and had worked some years roughnecking on oil rigs along the gulf until he had enough money to buy land and build some rigs of his own. Now he had more money than any man in faded denim and a dirty shirt should. Truth was, Eli wouldn't have a chance of getting back the Crooked Creek if it weren't for his uncle and all his money.

"I guess you're right," Eli conceded.

"Damn right I'm right." John pulled off his hat and swept his hand through what was left of his haywire, sweaty black hair. "Question is, why the hell are we meeting up here, when the auction is down there?"

"Jared the auctioneer knows what to do. I'd just be in the way."

"Yeah, and I suppose it's got nothing to do with all

those questions everyone down there is going to have about why Lyle Baker's trusted foreman is selling off the entire herd."

"No one down there is going to ask. Half of those trucks belong to men who want to stick it to Lyle Baker's ghost as best they can. I'm going to get low-balled all damn day."

"But no one thought it would be you getting in the first shot."

"Well, I'm not selling the entire herd. I've kept about fifty head, heifers mostly. A couple of bulls."

"Why?"

Eli tipped back his own dusty and sweat-stained hat and grinned into his uncle's florid face. "Steak."

It wasn't the whole truth, but it was a truth his uncle would like. And he did—his laughter echoed down through the valley.

Eli smiled, but his guts twisted with doubt. He squinted up into the sun, feeling as though the ground, so sure under his feet a few hours ago, had turned to quicksand.

"She turned down our offer, didn't she?" John asked, and Eli nodded. "Son of a bitch, those Bakers are stubborn. Ten years we been making offers—"

"Maybe I'm not making the right arguments?" Eli asked.

"Is there a better argument than two million dollars?"

"If there is, I can't think of it."

John's eyes chased him down, held him still. "You're not giving up, are you?"

Eli stared at the same green hills he'd been staring at since he was born. The land his entire family had been born on. And this . . . this was the only land he wanted. But Christ, it was wearing him down trying to get it back.

"Of course not."

"Maybe you want to try that again so I'll believe it?"

He couldn't. The words just wouldn't come out of his mouth, crushed down by all of the frustrations of his life, and of his father's life before him. Getting back his family land was a chain around his neck.

"I've worked for that family my entire life, for what? Half the proceeds of a herd I practically built? I pay rent on my own damn house!"

"Not after today. You'll make enough to buy back the house."

"That's not the point, Uncle John."

"Then why don't you tell me what this little temper tantrum is about, son."

Eli shut his mouth, chastened like a child.

John wouldn't understand; he had the money to do what he wanted. All Eli had was this damn herd and a bunch of plans he couldn't even get off the ground.

John sighed. "I know you staying on as foreman has made it hard for you to get your breeding business started. But I've told you, breeding isn't any way to make money."

"I don't need to be rich, Uncle John. I just . . . I just want something of my own. Free and clear."

Uncle John's big hand settled on his shoulder and Eli flinched.

"When you were ten years old, you know what you said to me?"

Eli shook his head, words caught behind the emotion in his throat.

"You said the Crooked Creek Ranch felt like home. The only home you ever wanted. And I thought you were just a little kid, mimicking what you'd heard your daddy and me talk about, but you kept right on saying it. Got to the point where you knew this land better than your dad ever did and sure as hell better than any Baker. I'd watch you take that old dun out along the fence line, and you'd be gone for a week, checking the fence, camping out along the way, missing school, missing out on everything a boy your age was supposed to be doing—"

"Come on, Uncle John—"

"No, you need to know that I see you. I see what you've done. You are a part of this land. And yeah, I want it back, but I want it back for you, boy. It's your birthright."

It was a powerful one-two punch: the word *birthright* and his uncle's steady affection. His unflinching support. "But I need to know we're in this together," John said. "That we're a team."

Victoria would cave sooner or later. She wasn't made for this land, or this work. Eli was closer than ever to getting the land back. He just had to be patient.

"We're a team," Eli said, forcing himself to feel what his uncle wanted him to feel.

"Now, about that breeding business you're cooking up—"

"With the sale of the herd, I'll have money to get a couple of stallions from Los Camillos."

"What about equipment? The barn down at your place is in sad shape."

"I can use the equipment at Crooked Creek and they've got plenty of empty stalls. Lyle was fine with it when he was alive."

"If you need money, I know there's oil out there beyond the house. One drill and we could live like kings."

Eli shot him a look over his shoulder. This was an old argument, and it hadn't changed for a decade. Eli didn't want any wells on his land.

"What do you need more money for?" Eli asked.

"You can never have too much money. And frankly, I got a bone to pick with that land; seems a Turnbull should get more than saddle sores from it."

"No drills."

"Fine, a loan. You can go see my lawyer—"

It would be so easy to take it. If he were a different man, maybe he would. Maybe it wouldn't matter. But for some reason, he couldn't take any more of his uncle's money. Not for his own personal stuff. "You're already paying for Dad, Uncle John. I'll be all right after I sell this herd." More than all right—his bank account wasn't going to know what hit it. Even after buying his home and the ten acres around it and a couple of horses.

"Seems to me you've got a problem. If there's no herd, she doesn't need you."

"The thought had crossed my mind."

"Of course, if she doesn't have a herd, she doesn't need land." John pushed his hands into his back pockets. "After what her husband did to her, she might just be desperate enough for cash to sell some of that land she doesn't need."

Eli smiled, catching the old coyote's drift.

Suddenly, selling the herd not only put some much-needed cash in his pocket, but it also put Victoria in a position to sell him back his land, a few acres at a time.

The same way his family had lost it to the Bakers over the years.

He grinned and turned to watch the auction down in the valley.

"Good thing I'm a patient man."

At twilight, Eli rode Patience back into the barn on Crooked Creek, satisfaction a light in his chest, guiding him home. The auction brought in a million five. Split in half with the Baker estate, that gave him three quarters of a million dollars. And that . . . that gave him limitless possibilities. He had his eye on the land on the other side of the creek. He could start a hay crop. Get the combine fixed. Fix the barn on his property so Patience could bed down in her rightful home.

Maybe get another mare in addition to the studs he was planning on buying. That Palomino over at Los Camillos was a total beauty.

Inside the barn, the cats mewed quietly from their various homes. Horses nickered in welcome, heavy hoofs hitting the dirt behind the green-painted stall doors. There was a strange smell in the air, something flowery.

Maybe money made the world smell like roses.

He smiled at the thought. Money made him dumb. Probably good he'd never had any until now.

But he slid open the door to Patience's stall and the flowers . . . that smell . . . it wasn't in his head. It was in the hay. Dried roses and cinnamon sticks crunched under his heels. It was that potpourri crap, scattered all over the fresh hay.

Behind him, Patience snorted, throwing her mane. She didn't like it any better than he did.

But the indignity didn't stop there. On the far wall, the splintered wood was adorned with a glittering Christmas wreath and in the corner, like a fat white cat, sat one of Ruby's embroidered pillows from the couch in the den.

"What the hell?" He picked it up, the fabric soft under his rough fingers.

"Home Sweet Home," it read, surrounded by big pink hearts.

Victoria had done this.

She'd mucked the stall and then covered it with this . . . crap.

He picked up the shovel and got rid of the hay, because he knew Patience wouldn't sleep with the strange smell.

And in the solitude of the barn, in the dark hushed shadows, with only his horse as a witness, he couldn't quite stop the smile that tugged at his face.

Potpourri.

As far as pranks went, this was a good one.

chapter
3

In Victoria's life, bad things happened in dens. Not just suicide, but systematic marital betrayal. Dens were worse than strip clubs or whorehouses. The password-protected computers in the mahogany-paneled rooms were more damaging than a lap dance or a smear of lipstick on a white collar.

In the dark nights after Joel's suicide, when the lawyers and accountants were stripping her home down to the studs before selling it out from under her, she wished her husband had just been caught with a whore or two. An orgy of strippers—male and female. A cow, if need be.

It would have been better than what he had done.

And he'd done so much of it—from the Ponzi scheme to the suicide—in the den, which she had so lovingly and diligently decorated with his taste in mind.

Dens were bad, bad places.

And her father's was no different, perhaps worse. Because it was the den belonging to the first man who'd betrayed her.

Sunday morning, she stood in front of her dad's closed den door, the wall of the hallway against her back.

It wasn't as if he'd be in there. And it wasn't as if she hadn't been in there since he'd died. But the room . . . the room was so him.

And now it was hers.

She wondered if the old man was rolling over in his grave. His useless bastard daughter was running his precious Crooked Creek. Not that she'd really been running much of anything these past weeks.

It was time to change that.

The doorknob was cool under her hand, the door heavy against her shoulder. The air inside was stale, smelling of her father's cigars and Old Bay Rum even after all this time.

The décor was atrocious. Cowhides, serapes, deer heads staring down at her. It was right out of a tacky Western-themed bar.

"Thinking about redecorating?" The smell of Chanel No 5 and cayenne pepper preceded Celeste Baker. The hot spice in the air stood at odds with the coolness in the woman's voice.

Celeste Baker, Lyle's ex-wife, had for some totally incomprehensible reason decided to stick around after her son had left the ranch a month ago.

Out of habit, Victoria wanted to believe it was to see her fail. It was not as though Celeste had any reason to want her to succeed. Victoria was, after all, the daughter of Lyle's mistress, born just eighteen months after Luc.

But for whatever reason, the imperial Celeste, in all of her regal beauty, had thawed toward Victoria in the last few months. Maybe because Celeste seemed to believe that the mistreatment Victoria and Luc had received at Lyle's hands as kids was somehow her fault for leaving him when she did.

A ridiculous notion, but to her great shame Victoria did nothing to assuage that guilt.

Which only made her more uncomfortable around the woman. When Celeste was judging her, Victoria knew where she stood—directly beneath the former fashion model. Now that Celeste had decided to like her, of all things, or if not like her, at least support her—well, Victoria was totally adrift.

One more thing in her life that she couldn't count on staying the same.

"It could use it," Victoria said, striding across the wide plank floor as if there were no trepidation in her heart about this room and her place in it. "It could use a match."

"The whole ranch could. The only thing worse than the décor is the architecture."

Well, on that they were in total agreement.

Victoria didn't even hesitate as she pushed the rolling chair away from the oak desk and sat on its worn fabric seat as if she belonged there.

A spring poked her butt as if to argue.

Celeste sat in one of the black leather club chairs set up across from the desk. In the day's brand-new light, she looked like one of those paintings of the Madonna. Serene. Lovely. Her complexion like milk.

Despite her two showers, Victoria still smelled like horse poop.

"When do you leave?" Victoria asked, when the silence pulled taut between them.

"Today. I have a reservation at Big Sky Resort for the week."

Victoria sighed in nostalgic bliss. Spa weeks. She remembered those.

"Mud baths? Tell me there will be mud." The mud baths had been her favorite and she tried not to sound like a kid asking for candy, but it was hard. It had been over a year since she'd even gotten a pedicure, much less sat in mud.

"And seaweed."

"Oh! Seaweed wraps, with the plastic wrap and the hot towels?"

Celeste smiled like a cat with a mouth full of cream, the bitch. "If it's a good spa, I certainly hope so."

"Well, for your sake I hope it is."

"You could come."

The idea was like a whisper from her old life, as if someone had left open a window and the memories of better times came swirling in on a breeze.

She'd been a princess, spoiled and pampered, sitting in mud and wrapped in seaweed, and for a few years it had felt so damn good. She'd been so deeply infatuated with the spa lifestyle that in the years before Jacob was born, she'd thought of opening a spa. She'd even picked out property in New Jersey. At one point she'd been so excited, she'd told her best friend, Renee, about the idea.

And Renee had laughed and told their entire circle of friends about it as if it were a joke. As if Victoria herself was the punch line. And Victoria had been young enough, and insecure enough, that she'd tossed the dream aside.

But that was so far behind her it was as though it had happened to another person. And going back or wanting to go back was like a betrayal of every person her husband had robbed. Every life that had been ruined so that she could sit in mud.

It was ludicrous when she thought of it like that.

"I can't," she finally said. "I just . . . can't."

Celeste nodded, smiling sadly. "I know."

Celeste blew on whatever was inside the steaming crimson bowl she carried and then set it on the edge of the desk.

As the scent of eggs, bacon, cheese, and sour cream filled the room, Victoria's stomach roared like a bear coming out of hibernation.

She jumped, startled and embarrassed. It had been a long time since her body had made itself known. Between her husband's suicide, and the resulting fallout, and Jacob's sickness and hospitalization, she'd begun to consider the feeding and bathing and clothing of her body as chores that needed to be checked off her list.

But suddenly . . . she was hungry.

Celeste arched an elegant silver eyebrow. "You can have this." She pushed the bowl across the desk.

"You're eating it." Victoria stared at the scrambled eggs with bacon and cheese. Little green flecks of chive sat on the mountain of sour cream on top. She couldn't even imagine Celeste eating something like that.

"Ruby made it; I couldn't say no."

Couldn't say no? Celeste?

"Go ahead," Celeste urged.

There was a voice in her head telling her to reject the offer. To pretend that she wasn't hungry. To pretend that she was fine despite the fact that her stomach was a speaking bear. That was the old Victoria.

"Thanks," she said and grabbed the bowl, scooping up the dollop of sour cream sprinkled with cheese. It melted in her mouth, salty and tangy, and she nearly groaned.

It tasted like colors, like explosions of yellow and orange and creamy white.

When had she stopped tasting things?

Celeste smiled, and Victoria didn't even care that the Queen was laughing at her.

"So? How is the ranching business going?"

Again, the lie surfaced on her lips. *Fine. Just fine. Everything is great.*

But it wasn't.

She stood on the edge of another failure, and pride hadn't ever helped her. Ever.

"Eli sold the entire Angus herd yesterday," she said. "I told him I wanted to learn how to ranch, how to do this . . . well, and he made me muck out the stalls."

"Muck—"

"Shovel shit." The words felt good in her mouth, round and then sharp at the end. She should do more swearing.

Celeste's lips pursed slightly and Victoria mined through the eggs for a big chunk of bacon and then groaned at the taste. Salty and meaty, with a hint of smoke. Pink, it tasted pink, tinged with black. So good. Food was so good sometimes. She'd forgotten.

"He hates me." She was talking with her mouth full, and even that felt good. "And I don't blame him, but this land is mine now and I don't know what to do with it."

"Well, it seems to me Eli might not be the best person to talk to."

"He's run this ranch for years, his father before him, and his father before that." She shoveled more eggs, finding chunks of tomato like buried treasure.

"Yes. I know." Celeste crossed her legs and ran a hand over her perfectly behaved silver hair, from crown to nape. "And I suppose if you want to learn how to be a cowboy, or . . . I don't know . . . shovel shit, he'd be a wonderful person to talk to."

Victoria choked on her eggs in her delight in Celeste's cattiness. If there was anything Celeste was good at it was being a snob, and as a recovering snob herself, Victoria relished a little backslide into bitchery.

"But I can guarantee you that Lyle didn't ask Eli how to run his business."

Victoria sat up straighter, catching on to Celeste's way of thinking. Being the recipient of Celeste's smile was like getting blessed by the pope—Victoria felt suffused with purpose.

She took another bite of breakfast and started opening drawers to the big desk, stopping when she found an old-fashioned Rolodex. Rifling through the cards, the white paper worn and frayed under her fingers, she pulled out the ones that might be helpful to a woman in her position—bank managers, accountants, lawyers.

"I need to talk to the accountant. Arrange a meeting with Randy Jenkins. There's probably someone at the bank who—"

The soft click of the door closing behind Celeste as she left the den sounded like a door slamming.

Victoria stared at the shut door.

Once upon a time she would have thought that she'd done something wrong. That Celeste was mad at her. And she would have gone out of her way to figure out what the problem was and then try to fix it.

She'd stopped humming early on in her marriage because Joel had found it disruptive.

Victoria took another bite of eggs and wiped her mouth with the back of her hand.

Feeling gloriously unmannered, she went back to her Rolodex and the task of becoming a rancher.

Monday morning Victoria walked into Randy Jenkins's Dallas law office with all the enthusiasm of the freshly converted, the born-again.

Look out, Crooked Creek Ranch; I'm ready to make some decisions.

About what, she didn't know.

"Good morning, Victoria," Randy said, coming around his desk to shake her hand. The mid-morning Texas sun blasted through the floor-to-ceiling windows and hit the polished surface of his desk. She squinted against the glare and shook his hand.

"Hi, Randy." She smiled into his nondescript face. He had all the trappings she'd come to associate with lawyers. The wire-rimmed glasses that probably cost more than they should. The dark suits, the red ties. The too soft hands.

Where Randy was different, however, was in the eyes. There was none of the raging judgment there that she was used to from the Manhattan lawyers prosecuting her husband's estate. Instead, there was an almost apologetic eagerness. Probably because Randy's son had knocked Luc unconscious on the ice last month. It was an accident, but it had ultimately put an end to Luc's NHL career. Either way, Victoria was ready to pretend that eagerness was all about her.

"I assume you're here to start paperwork against Eli Turnbull?"

"That . . . what?"

"Eli sold the herd on Saturday." Randy turned back around the desk, reaching for a file.

"I know."

He stopped mid-reach, gilded by the sun flowing in from outside, and she felt the cold breeze of insecurity. "You know?"

"He was given control of the herd in the will. Remember?"

"Not so he could sell the whole herd. We could argue intent, and frankly, there's a case for sabotage—"

"Sabotage of what?"

"The ranch?"

"He wants to buy the ranch." She managed a weak little laugh, despite the hard lump in her throat.

"I know. Trust me, Eli's made his intentions clear. But your family has been adamant about not selling it to him or his uncle."

"His uncle wants the ranch, too? What is it with these men?"

"Eli's uncle, John Turnbull, is a man of some means. He is the bank account behind Eli's offers."

"But how does selling the herd sabotage the ranch?" She tried to connect the dots on her own, but she didn't even know where all of them were. And suddenly there seemed to be a lot more than she'd ever dreamed of.

"Much of the valuation of the ranch is based on that herd. And since your brother intends to give the controlling interest of Baker Leather to Tara Jean Sweet—"

"He does?"

"You didn't know?"

"Clearly." Randy Jenkins with his bland face was too easy a target for all of her embarrassment and anger, so she let him have it. "I don't know anything, Mr. Jenkins. That's why I came here today. To learn something."

Randy blinked and then sat carefully behind his desk, as if his office was suddenly filled with land mines.

He gestured for her to sit across from him and she did, forcing herself not to clutch her nearly empty purse like a life jacket. It was the last of her Coach bags, the leather frayed at the edges and the straps getting sticky from use.

She crossed her legs at the ankle, tucking them underneath the chair, and cultivated stillness. If there was one thing she knew how to do, it was keep her shit together while bombs were raining down from the sky.

In the face of her calmness, Randy relaxed.

"Your brother called a few weeks ago to ask about the legalities of giving Tara Jean control of the leather portion of the inheritance once it's out of escrow."

"That seems reasonable; she's earned it."

"Well, between losing controlling interest in the leather business and the herd, that leaves your brother with only the land and the house." He paused, as if checking to see if she was keeping up.

Once again, she felt the need to explain the difference between uninformed and stupid, but then she realized all she'd done so far was prove how in this case they were the same thing.

"When he sells the land—"

"We're not selling the land."

For a moment he just blinked at her. "You intend to stay there?"

"When the ranch is out of escrow, I intend to buy it—"

"How? You have no money. No job. Thanks to your husband, no bank in the world will loan you money."

She refused to be beaten. Refused.

"Look, I know I don't have much money, but it's not like my brother is going to charge me market value."

"I'm not making myself clear." He sighed as if he were talking to a child, and Victoria wanted to scream. "You can't afford to keep that house, or that land, without income. There are taxes. Utilities. Owning that much land costs money."

In a heartbeat she realized what a fool she'd been. All this time she'd thought she was building a home with stone and concrete, only to find out it was feathers.

She took tiny sips of air around the crushing pain in her chest. She clutched her hands together to fight the numbing cold in her body.

She had a home. She had her son. There were decisions to make and she would make them. Bit by bit she pulled herself together—her pride, her hope, the intelligence and strength no one seemed to credit her with—and she cobbled it all together with some righteous anger. Righteous anger that had no target.

"What do you suggest I do?" she asked.

"Your brother has given you free rein to act on his behalf when it comes to the ranch. I suggest you sell the land to Eli."

And there was her target. That man had made her shovel his horse's poop, while he sabotaged her family's ranch.

"I'm not selling him anything more than he was granted in the will," she said.

"But the land he's most interested in across the river is only a hundred acres."

"Nothing. Not one acre."

There was a universe of disapproval in the click of his ballpoint pen, and she realized she was staring right at the difference between stupid and uninformed.

"Unless there's no other way to make money from the land," she quickly amended, searching out a plan in her fevered brain. "I would imagine that if Eli is interested in the acreage across the creek, then others might be, too. And I would imagine that if a few people want to buy it, in this market, even more people would be interested in renting it—"

"Leasing." He ran a hand down his tie. "It's called leasing."

"Fine. I'll lease the land." Without the herd, what did she need with a thousand acres?

"That is a great idea." Randy's approving smile was like a pat on the head, uncomfortable and condescending, but a relief nonetheless.

"Do you handle that or do I need to talk to a realtor?"

This at least was familiar. One thing she knew was realty. And however many miles separated Manhattan and Crooked Creek, realtors were realtors.

"Realtor."

"Do you have one you recommend?" She pulled her phone from the purse at her feet, intending to type in whatever information he gave her. She missed her iPhone. She really did. But the lawyers had deemed the monthly plan too expensive.

"Cheryl helped us with my father's land when he passed."

A card slid across the desk, pushed by Randy's manicured fingers. Those hands were so like her husband's that she paused, starting to doubt the sense of this plan. What did she know, really? About anything? The old demons had their claws sunk in deep and it was hard work shaking them off.

Forcing herself to feel confident, she picked up the card. It was real in her hands, substantial, something she could use to climb and crawl toward higher ground.

She slipped it into the pocket of her light cardigan, where it glowed and pulsed with possibility.

chapter
4

Eli waited a week after the sale of the herd until the last of the paperwork was done before going to see Victoria. That morning the broker he'd hired to handle the sale had called to tell him that the money had been split and Eli could expect to see his half in his account within two hours.

So at noon on Friday, he was at the front door of the Crooked Creek Ranch, shaking the rain off his slicker, before walking in.

"She's in the den," Ruby told him, rearranging the cards in her hand without looking up, as if the game of gin rummy she was playing with Jacob was the most important thing in the world. They sat at the kitchen table as a summer storm pounded on the windows beside them.

"The den? What the hell is she doing in there?"

Ruby shrugged and picked up a card from the pile on the kitchen table. "Running things."

Eli smiled slightly at the thought. There was nothing for her to run. He'd made sure of that.

He didn't care to examine why being a jerk to this woman filled him with a strange goodwill, a foreign satisfaction. He'd never in his life taken such pleasure in the face of another person's failure, but there wasn't a bit of regret in him.

It had to be because of her shoes.

He leaned over Jacob's shoulder and rearranged the boy's nine of spades so that he could see he had gin.

"Hey!" Ruby cried as the boy slapped his cards on the table with a whoop.

Smiling, Eli walked down the dark hallway, listening to the thunder roll across the land, shaking the foundations of the house.

Inside, he was all sunshine. He was rainbows and blue skies.

The door to the office was cracked open and he knocked while pushing the door wide.

Whatever he'd been expecting—maybe interrupting her while she painted her toenails, or waking her up from a nap—was not happening in the office. In fact, it was totally the opposite.

"Nope, no, that'll work," she said into the phone she had cradled between her ear and her shoulder. She pulled the top off a black marker with her teeth and turned toward a big aerial map of the ranch that used to be framed in the front hallway; now it was tacked to the wall behind the desk.

Right into the wall. As if the den were a dorm room.

He entered and shut the door behind him.

"Fifty acres closest to the west access road. Got it. How much? That's great. Thank you, Cheryl."

She dropped the phone and set it on the desk, and then with that big black marker put an *x* over a portion of the map. The portion by the west access road. She made a series of notes on a Post-it and then slapped the Post-it on top of the *x*.

There were five *x*'s on the map.

"What the hell are you doing?"

At the sound of his voice she turned, and he was confronted with a new version of Victoria Schulman. First of all, that mean little bun she usually wore at the nape of her neck had, in the week since he'd seen her, migrated into a sloppy knot on the top of her head, with a white pencil growing through it. She looked like a genie.

The black circles were gone from under her eyes, as though whatever had been keeping her awake at night had decided to leave her alone.

And her skin, which had looked gray and pale, was now . . . pearly. Pink lit up her cheeks as if she were a girl again.

All of this was strange and slightly nerve-wracking, but what really made him nervous was that she stood there, a smear of black marker and what looked like ketchup across her cheek, smiling at him.

For some reason, the hair at the back of his neck whistled out a warning.

"Well, I was wondering when you'd come find me. My brother called this morning. It seems Matthew Pierce at First National was fairly surprised by a deposit of three quarters of a million dollars in the ranch account."

"Your family's part of the sale." He crossed his arms over his chest, his eyes drawn to the map over her shoulder. The land he'd come in here to buy had one of those black *x*'s over it.

"Yeah, let's talk about that sale." She tucked the black marker in the topknot on her head, picked up half of a grilled cheese sandwich, and dunked it in a puddle of ketchup.

"Not much to talk about. It's over," he said, strangely transfixed by the sight of her licking a drop of ketchup off the sandwich before taking a huge bite.

"So I gathered." She was talking through a mouth full of food, a woman who had once told him it was rude to wear his hat in the house. And then she groaned. Not like she was in pain, or even simply enjoying a good sandwich. She groaned with pleasure. With sensual pleasure, like someone was licking her where it felt best. He'd never thought she might have that kind of groan in her and the surprise of it made his blood thick, his skin hot. "You know I've never had this?"

"What? Grilled cheese?"

"And ketchup. It's the ketchup that changes everything."

He tended to agree but he kept his mouth shut.

"What are you going to do with the hands, now that there's no herd for them to handle?" Her question surprised the hell out of him, because it was the right question to ask and he hadn't given her that much credit.

Maybe he should have.

"We still have fifty or so head. We'll train the quarter horses with them."

"So you can sell them, too?"

"No point in keeping 'em." She was trying so hard to wear her father's big rancher hat and it just didn't fit her. She wasn't made for this life, this conversation. Refraining from smiling wasn't usually a problem for him, but right now it wasn't easy.

"So, do you need all the men to train ten horses?"

"I've given two weeks' pay to the full-time guys; the seasonal workers I've paid up in full. We're keeping Phil and Jerry."

"Jerry? The old guy?"

"Jerry is sixty years old and has arthritis. If he doesn't work here, he doesn't work anywhere."

"Oh." She paused, those midnight-blue eyes working hard to see into him. "You know, I just can't decide if you're an asshole or not."

He couldn't fight the smile anymore and it burst across his face like biting into an orange. As fast as it was there, he put it away, but she saw it and slowly, despite the animosity that snapped and popped between them, she smiled, transforming her face, filling the pinched corners of her lips and eyes with a womanly lushness. She was, suddenly, vibrant.

And he was instantly, painfully aware of her. Of the joy she seemed to be unleashing on the world. She used to be that way before her father and, Eli supposed, the rest of her life had quashed it.

He was oddly happy to see that joy return.

But then she schooled her features back into the pinch.

"What about you?" She took another bite of sandwich, oblivious to the ketchup in the corner of her mouth.

"What about me?" He couldn't take his eyes off that ketchup, the pink of her lip.

"What are you going to do here with no herd and no men?"

"You want to fire me?"

"I didn't say that. But Randy Jenkins thinks I could sue you. Over that sale."

For a moment he was dumbstruck. A lawsuit? "The control of the herd was granted to me in the will."

"I know, but he was talking about reasonable intent and sabotage—"

"Sabotage?" He stepped farther into the room, his temper beginning to smoke. "I told you about the sale and you said, 'Awesome.'" He was deliberately snide and she put down the sandwich, brushing crumbs off the tips of her small fingers. She dabbed her mouth delicately with a napkin.

"There's no case," he insisted. "And you know it."

Some of that pink blanched from her cheeks. "Why'd you do it?" Her gaze was so level that he felt, briefly, ashamed. Not because he'd sold the herd, but because of that nasty trick in the barn—she deserved better than shoveling manure.

And he knew all too well what it felt like to deserve better than what you were given.

But he didn't have any answers for her. None that she would like anyway.

She looked at him and then back at the desk—a tell, if

ever there was one. "You know," she said, and he nearly rolled his eyes. The woman had to learn to not talk so much; every time she opened her mouth she just handed out secrets like they were dimes. "I learned a lot of things from my marriage—"

He lifted his hand just to shut her up.

"This used to be Turnbull land. Your great-grandfather was the foreman."

"I . . . I didn't know that."

"Your great-grandfather started that leather business and he bought some acreage. And then more. My great-grandfather couldn't hold his booze, or the land, and he just kept selling it below value. My grandfather tried to buy some back but your grandfather refused. And then my grandfather started selling off more acreage."

"None of that is my fault. If there's anyone you should blame it's your relatives . . . not mine."

Ah, she'd just leveled him with her upthrust chin. Really, someone should warn her about that foolish courage. She was going to get herself in trouble.

"Yeah, well, anytime things got tough for a Turnbull a Baker was there with a lowball offer to buy some land, until there wasn't any left."

"So you're carrying around a hundred-year-old grudge?" She made it sound as if he'd been wasting his life trying to get back this land.

"I don't expect you to understand, Victoria—"

"Stop it. Stop it right there." All the girlishness was gone, and standing there in her genie bun was one pissed-off woman. She planted her hands wide across the desk and leaned toward him. "I won't be marginalized, Eli. Not anymore. I've spent the last week getting myself a pretty good education in the business of managing this land, and let me assure you, you have no idea what I do or don't understand."

Was it weird that he was turned on? It was. He cleared his throat and looked away.

"Explain it to me, Eli. Go slow if you want, but I promise, I'll understand."

"My family lost it, your family wasted it—I just want to do right by it. Do you understand that?"

Slowly, she nodded. His stomach shook with nerves and adrenaline.

"So you're here to make an offer?"

The checkbook stuck in his back pocket and he had to tug it free. "I want to buy back the ten acres of land my house sits on and some of the land adjacent."

"Your house is not a problem. But what other land are you interested in?"

He stepped around the desk up to the map and his arm brushed the bare skin of her wrist. For a second the softness of her skin registered, as well as the smell of flowers under the sharp tang of ketchup. She was a cotton ball of femininity—insubstantial, but sticky. Impossible to brush away.

The glossy black pile of hair on top of her head seemed precarious and shiny and he had a painful desire to tug it free, to see how she looked all undone.

He should apologize. Not just for that stunt in the barn, but for everything he'd thought about her. Every ungenerous and cruel comparison he'd made in his head.

"Which land?" She stared at the map, rubbing at the wrist he'd touched.

He pointed to the fifty acres across the creek with the big black *x* across it.

Well. Crap.

She stared at Eli's blunt finger, with the cracked nail and split skin, right smack dab in the middle of the land she'd leased to the McDougals, and realized she was not a creature cut out for revenge.

Silent grudges she excelled at. Passive-aggressive snobbery was her specialty.

Revenge she just didn't have the stomach for.

As of ten minutes ago she'd been fine with it. Had relished it even. All week long, she'd gone to sleep each night imagining what Eli's face would look like when she told him that the land he wanted was gone. But then he came in here and talked about wasted opportunities and wanting to do right, and all the revenge in her heart rolled over on its back and died.

She stopped rubbing her wrist, the sensation of his touch gone, though its effect on her still zipped around in her blood.

The storm outside put electricity in the room and it was as if she could feel him in the air. She stepped away, but the sensation stayed. She couldn't run from him.

"Well? I'll pay you a fair price." Those grass-green eyes were so focused and intent it was as if everything he had, and everything he was, was at play in this moment.

Unable to look away, she started to shake her head. His eyebrows clashed under the wide brim of his hat.

"I'm . . . I'm sorry, Eli. I've leased that land."

"What?"

"I've rented—"

"I know what a lease is. To who?"

"The McDougals."

He swore loudly, glanced back at the map, and took his finger away from the wall. "All of these *x*'s?"

"Leased."

It was as if someone had left a door open in the room, letting in an ice-cold draft—that was the power of his anger. He turned on her, every muscle in his lean body tensed, his hands in fists at his sides.

She tried not to shake in the face of his emotion, at

being the unholy focus of all that anger. But it was impossible. So that she wouldn't look like the coward she actually was, she lifted her chin. Which for some reason seemed to make him more angry.

"Is this a joke?"

"You tied my hands, Eli. When you sold that herd you took half the value—"

"I know what I did."

Of course he did. He'd set out to ruin her family. Ruin her. A brush fire eradicated any sympathy that might have lingered in the tiny vessels of her heart. And it definitely took care of her fear. Now she felt nothing but the strength born of righteousness.

"I have no intention of leaving this ranch." Her anger inflated her body. She was three times her size, towering over him. "I told you that."

"I just never thought you'd screw me like this."

She could only gape at him. Was every man so blind, so stupid? "Likewise, Eli."

He stared at her, right into her, and for a second she couldn't breathe for the pain of it, the intimacy. And as much as she wanted to look away, she didn't. She stared right back, right into him where he'd shown her his secrets. His disappointments.

Which were not so different from hers, if he could just see that. They both wanted to be useful, do the right thing. They could bury the grudges between their families right now. Right here. If he could understand that, then maybe they could move on from here. As friends. Co-workers.

And if the skin of her wrist burned for more, that was her problem.

"You don't belong here!" he said, and she leaned back against the desk, slightly light-headed with hurt. She should stop being surprised by the malice of men. Of this man.

"And it's not your place to decide."

He looked back at the map, the skin of his neck red, the muscles in his jaw practically bouncing against his skin.

"We're not done here, you know that, right?"

"Yes, we are, Eli. You just need some time to see it."

Thunder shook the room as he walked out, his long legs in dark denim eating up the distance between her and the door. He didn't glance back, didn't even pause, and he threw open the door so hard it ricocheted back and closed behind him as he stepped into the shadows of the hallway.

She collapsed backwards into the chair, feeling like a popped balloon. The grilled cheese didn't seem half so inviting and she pushed it away.

What was done was done, she thought, spinning to look up at the map. She imagined, all things considered, that her father would be proud of her in some way. She'd made a strong business decision, thwarted an enemy's plan, and in essence had done exactly what he would have done.

Somehow, the thought didn't make her feel any better.

chapter
5

Celeste was in crisis. Or rather, that old woman staring back at her in the mirror was in crisis. Sixty-three. Yesterday. Using her fingers she lifted her eyebrow practically up to her hairline, pulling the crepey skin of her eyelids as taut as she could.

In the mirror, they still looked crepey.

And her neck. Good Lord, don't get a woman started on her neck.

The facials and acid peels, the Botox injections and oxygen treatments just weren't cutting it.

She was getting old.

This week's facials had taken care of the dry skin, the sunburn across the edge of her nose, and the giant gaping caverns of her pores. But it hadn't, as promised, turned back time.

She would not panic. Honestly, panic was for younger women. And gerbils. But neither was she going to be resigned.

A floorboard squeaked and the dining room door thumped just as Jacob's laughter burbled through the house. For a second she nearly closed her eyes to better hear it. Longing was a tender ache in the back of her throat.

But then the door opened with a bang and Jacob was screaming through the room, howling with laughter as he made a lap around the dining room table.

"Jacob." She turned away from the black lacquered mirror over the sideboard. "I don't think your mother—"

"Where'd you go, varmint?"

Victoria came in through the door, pretending to be some kind of Wild West sheriff. Celeste had been gone for only a week, seeking the fountain of youth in deluxe spas and resorts across northern Texas, but the woman in the doorway, with the messy hair and pink cheeks—that woman was a stranger.

Certainly not her husband's daughter.

At least not a version she'd ever seen.

"Oh, hey, Celeste." Victoria pulled herself up short and all that lovely spark in her eyes—the liveliness of her entire body—dimmed. It didn't go out, not the way it used to. The few times she'd seen Victoria as a girl, all Celeste had to do was step into a room and the kid would shut down as if her plug had been pulled.

And it was terrible—an awful truth that sat in her stomach like a walnut shell—but for a few years there, Celeste had relished that power. She couldn't hurt her ex-husband, who had wounded her over and over again, but she could take all of her spite out on that little girl who flinched whenever Celeste looked at her.

So much to feel guilty for. So much.

"When did you get back?" Victoria asked.

"A few minutes ago."

"Well, you certainly look well rested. I guess it was a good trip to the spa?"

"No, to be honest. It was the worst one yet. Every meal was terrible. Ruby is a better cook than the chef they're paying a fortune. As if mushrooms were the only facet of spa cuisine he cared about."

"Ewww," Jacob cried and she turned to him, her heart aflame with love for the little guy. At some point in her distant past, she'd wanted more kids. A dozen of them.

"I know," Celeste agreed. "Mushrooms are gross."

"Well, my heart bleeds for you and your subpar spa week." Victoria's sarcasm was new and different, and Celeste laughed.

"Even the mud was bad."

Victoria pulled a face.

"You look well," Celeste said. "You've gained some weight."

The moment she said it, she knew it was the wrong thing to say. Victoria put a hand to her still flat tummy and her eyes slid over to Jacob, who had stopped paying attention and was climbing under the table.

"It's a good thing," Celeste said, trying to dig herself out of the hole her mouth had put her in. Funny how she didn't have this problem with anyone else in the world. Just her ex-husband's bastard daughter. "You were way too skinny before."

Oh God, she thought. *That was worse.*

It was as if she wanted to undo the weeks she'd spent trying to get Victoria to eat.

"Yes," Victoria finally said with a laugh. "You're right. I was."

Celeste attempted a smile, and her sand-blasted skin pulled at the effort.

"How is the ranching business going?"

"Well, I'm in the land-leasing business now."

Celeste tried to lift an eyebrow, but the Botox made it impossible.

"You all right?" Victoria asked, and Celeste waved off her concern.

"Yeah, you look funny," Jacob said, his head poking out from between two ladderback dining chairs.

First old. Now funny. Aging was an abomination.

She excused herself so she could go back to her room and panic like a gerbil.

*   *   *

Wednesday morning, the skies opened up again and Eli brought the horses in from the paddock through sheets of cold, miserable rain. Rain plunked onto the wide brim of his hat, dripping off onto his yellow slicker. September had come in like a bitch and stayed that way, but the land could use it, so no one complained.

"Let's go, girls," he told the two ponies who balked at being led. They were nervous in the rain and he had to stroke their necks. Hum in their ears.

And the two big stallions ran in tense circles in their pens until he came and tucked them back into their stalls.

Lucky and Patience followed on their own.

"No, wait—" he said, just as Lucky shook her mane, spraying Eli with horse-scented water. He ducked as best he could, but he still got it all over his face.

"Perfect," he muttered. "Just perfect." He shrugged out of his slicker and hung it up on the hook outside the tack room, tearing the lining in his haste and frustration.

Angry, he shoveled feed into the bags hanging outside the horses' stall doors.

They all got hungry in the rain.

The orange tabby curled around his boots and he scratched her between the ears before shooing her into Phineas's stall, where she'd keep the big bay from freaking out during the thunder.

With the money from the sale of the herd he'd gone on a shopping spree, and yesterday he had bought two studs from Los Carillos. Along with Patience and Darling, they would be the backbone of his new business. He'd ordered supplies to repair his barn, splurging on some new tools even.

But it hadn't been enough to lift the dark edges of his terminally bad mood.

Victoria Schulman was a blight.

Worse, he would venture a guess, than all the other Bakers who had screwed over all the other Turnbulls—because she did it in stupid clothes. And she felt bad about it. It was so obvious she regretted leasing out that land and if he were a smarter man he might have exploited that little fact, but instead he just got pissed off and insulted her.

The rain kept on and the barn was as dark as midnight, so he ducked back into the tack room to flip on the lights. He'd put a desk and a landline in here years ago, and he sat down in the hard chair and pulled out his calendar.

The day's work waited for him. The endless care and management of land and animals that weren't his, that would never be his. For years he'd worked this job thinking of the future when it would all be his. And that had made the sting of being a Baker employee bearable.

But looking down at that calendar, with all the same notes on it—he needed to make sure the stone wall behind the house held, last time it had rained like this the old fence had melted and mud had flooded the kitchen—he felt empty. Useless. Victoria had robbed him of the land and his pride in it. His pride in himself.

And that really pissed him off.

Wallowing in his anger and misery, he didn't hear the commotion out in the stalls until he heard the laughter.

Jacob was out with the horses. Again.

Usually he ignored the kid when he snuck into the barn early before school, but today Eli was so frustrated, he stood up from his desk and stepped out of the tack room. Lucky, the sweetest mare he'd ever worked with, was gumming the boy's hand. Jacob fished in his pocket and grabbed another slice of apple, which Lucky hoovered up quick as a wink, and the boy chortled with delight.

The sound was so foreign in this barn, among the animals and the silence, that everyone came out to investigate. The cats were roaming the long hallway, the horses hung their heads over their doors. Jerry stood in the entrance to the riding arena.

"Does your mom know you're in here?" Eli asked, shattering the mood. Jacob jerked away from the horse, dropping the rest of the apple slices into the dirt.

"Ah . . . no."

Eli nodded but didn't tell the kid to leave. He pointed to the horse sniffing Jacob's hair for more apples. "You like Lucky?"

"That's her name?"

"Yep." Eli stepped forward and patted the horse's soft muzzle. "When she was just a foal she got struck by lightning—"

"Noooo."

"Yep. And see here?" He pulled on Lucky's bridle and the horse turned her head, showing off the gray hair in her mane. "She's been gray ever since."

"Are you telling the truth?" Jacob's eyes were narrowed as if he could see a lie if he just looked hard enough.

"Swear to God." He crossed his fingers over his chest for good measure. "She got hurt not too long ago, stepped in a groundhog hole and twisted her ankle."

"You gonna shoot her?"

Eli started and Lucky spooked at the motion. He whistled low and soft and curled his hand over her ears as if to prevent her from hearing.

"Why would you think that?"

"My dad told me you have to kill animals that are hurt."

"Well, not here," Eli said, thinking that the man's suicide suddenly made more sense. "Here we make sure they get better."

"That's good. Are you like a hospital?"

"No. I just really like Lucky."

The boy's smile was like a lightbulb in the dim barn, and Eli found himself smiling in kind. "Me too."

"Well, you should meet her properly." Eli had a pretty good gut feeling that Victoria would hate him showing Jacob the barn and the animals. Doing it to spite her made the sourness of losing to a Baker every damn time he tried to get his life started very sweet.

Lucky's stall door creaked open and he led her out into the hallway. "Careful," he murmured, and the boy leapt back.

Jacob dug around in his pocket again and Eli thought he was going to pull out another apple, but instead it was an inhaler. The boy shook it and then took a puff. Waited a second and took another puff.

"Are you sure you should be in here?" he asked, watching the kid's thin little rib cage lift and expand.

"I'm okay," he said. "I have some allergies, but it's no big deal."

He wondered if Victoria thought it was no big deal. The boy had been through a lot lately. That night two months ago when Tara Jean's old boyfriend had shown up drunk and with a gun, he'd scared the bejesus out of everyone when he'd tried to hold Jacob hostage.

Victoria tended to watch over her son like a hawk. And he hadn't known the kid had asthma and allergies.

"Can I ride her?" Jacob asked, which wasn't unexpected.

"Have you ever ridden before?"

"No." Points to the kid for telling the truth.

"Would your mom be mad?"

He could see the boy wrestling with his instincts and finally his shoulders slumped. "Yeah. She'd be really mad."

Perfect.

"You can't ride Lucky," he said, and the kid nodded

as if he'd expected that. "On account of her leg. But you can ride Patience."

"Really?" The boy was all hope and eagerness. A youthful mix of everything Eli hadn't felt in a long, long time. The boy was in no danger, not with Patience, and Eli would be walking right beside him. And suddenly it wasn't just about pissing Victoria off, though that was a bonus.

Jacob was a seven-year-old boy on a Texas ranch. He should ride a horse. In fact, the more Eli thought about it, all he was doing was righting a very big wrong.

"Really."

He shuffled Lucky back into her stall and brought Patience out, then led her and the boy—who leapt and jumped beside him—into the riding arena, where the rain pattered against the roof and the swallows made their homes in the rafters, and his fight with Victoria got personal.

Victoria stood on the back verandah and watched the rain drip off the roof. She blamed Celeste and the constant rain for the fact that she couldn't stop thinking about a mud bath.

If Crooked Creek were a spa, she'd put the baths right here. She'd dig them right into the cement floor of this porch, in the open air, but protected by the roof. The view of the rolling green and beige hills, the poplars down there by the creek—it would be dramatic and different.

Perfect.

She took another bite of the yogurt and grapes Celeste had pushed into her hands this morning. Ruby had stirred lime zest and honey into the yogurt and it was so freaking delicious. Like candy.

She started to take another bite but stopped herself.

She was looking for Jacob so she could give it to him, but the boy was nowhere to be found.

"Have you seen Jacob?" she asked Ruby, back in the kitchen, where it smelled like coffee and toast.

"No," she said. "He's probably in the barn again."

The bowl screeched across the tiles of the countertop.

"How many times do I have to tell him to not go in there by himself?"

"He's a boy." Ruby shrugged. "And there are horses in there."

"That's the problem!" Horses with giant hooves that could crush his little bones with no trouble at all. Dust that could clog his compromised lungs.

"Eli's in there," Ruby said, and that did not allay her fears one bit.

In fact, the memory of all that anger on his face quickened her steps. When she reached the front door, she threw on a slicker and the cracked black rain boots she'd claimed as her own.

Leaping over puddles, her head bent to better deflect the rain from her eyes, she ran across the lawn to the closest door—to the riding arena—which was connected to the barn.

Using both hands and all her strength she threw open the door and hopped inside, shaking the rain from her jacket and hair. Wiping her eyes she looked up, and her heart stopped.

Past her brother's workout equipment, which had been shoved toward the sloping walls of the building, was a big black beast and on top of that big black beast, looking so tiny, looking as fragile as a tender green seedling pushing out of black dirt, sat her son.

His eyes wide in terrified wonder.

And beside him, clucking softly at the horse, smiling up at her son, was the devil.

Eli Turnbull.

She ran across the dirt floor, the sound of the rain pounding on the roof camouflaging her steps until she was right next to them, and the horse shied away at her sudden movement. Eli lunged forward, following the horse's skitter. Jacob gasped and clutched tighter to the saddle in front of him.

"Christ, Victoria, don't you know better than to sneak up on a horse?" Eli's eyebrows knit together as if she were the one making a mistake.

"Get. Him. Down."

Eli stared at her for a moment as if to argue, and because anger was making her wild, she wanted him to argue, so she could smack him.

"Mom," Jacob said as Eli lifted him from the horse. "It was my idea."

"I'm sure it was." Her mother's gaze ran over him, her hands following, checking for injuries, seen and unseen.

All she saw was fear, hers and her son's. She turned back to Eli, because while she knew she was scaring Jacob, this was all Eli's fault, and he stared back at her as if he had his doubts about that. "Go inside, I'll talk to you later," she ordered her son.

"Mom, it was fun. I'm fine. Patience is—"

"Go. Inside." She didn't even look at him.

"The hospital was practically a year ago—"

"Hospital?" Eli asked.

"Jacob." It was her lethal-mommy voice. The one that meant business, that might—if pushed—lead to a grounding, the taking away of his toys. If he didn't leave now, she was scared down to her core that she might spank him, out of fear and worry and anger. "Please go."

He ran away and she turned herself into a blade, pointed right at Eli Turnbull. His strength, his virility, the beauty of his lips and eyes only sharpened her rage. What did he know of worry? What did he know of sickness and hospitals? What did he know of bedside vigils?

"What the hell do you think you're doing?"

"He wanted to ride." The shrug made her crazy. Insane with anger. "I didn't see the harm in it."

Of course he didn't.

"He was never in any danger," he said. "I was here the whole time. You're on a ranch, for crying out loud, Victoria."

"My son has allergies, asthma. Eight months ago he was in the hospital with pneumonia from H1N1."

He blinked, stunned into silence. "I didn't know."

"They thought he was going to die. They told me that. To prepare for the worst." Tears burned in her eyes at the memory of that night, of hugging him close, whispering in his ear not to leave her. Eli's face blurred and doubled.

"I . . . I didn't know." He had the good grace to sound ashamed, but it was too late.

"You knew I wouldn't like it, didn't you? You put him on that horse because it would make me mad. To get back at me for leasing that land?"

After a long moment, he nodded, his eyes never leaving hers, and she didn't bother to hide the pain. The gasp of shock that this was how low he'd go.

She blinked and the tears ran down her cheeks, clearing her vision, and she saw suddenly what needed to happen.

"You're fired, Eli."

chapter
6

Eli couldn't believe her. Didn't believe her. But that hard look in her eyes, unearthed by the two tears making tracks down her face, brooked no argument. Panic was a cold snake down his spine.

"Come on, Victoria, don't you think you're overreacting?"

"About Jacob on that horse? Maybe. But you involved my son in this . . ." she waved her hand between them, her lips curled in distaste, "thing between us. And I can't . . . I can't forgive that, Eli."

"Victoria." He caught her hand, panic making him reckless. His instincts told him to stop, but this was too much to lose; he needed the barn. The ultrasounds and chute were equipment he couldn't start his business without.

Her hand shook in his. He pressed his thumb to the center of her palm and reflexively her fingers spread out wide. Her soft skin felt like velvet and he traced the lines of her palm from finger to wrist.

Time was nailed to the floor and he absorbed the pleasure of touching her. The shock of her softness, her stunned compliance.

She watched dumbstruck and he held his breath, waiting. Wondering.

Her eyes were wide, her pink lips open, a blush burned onto her cheeks. She was so beautiful in her surprise and his body reacted, his heart pounding.

"I'm sorry," he murmured. Whether he was sorry for what he'd done, or what he was about to do, he couldn't say. Without thinking, he leaned forward to taste those pink lips, the sweetness of her amazement.

The smack never came; it was as if she were a fly in a web and he was the terrible spider who had caught her. He pressed his lips to hers. She jumped as if shocked, her mouth opening, and he fought himself not to take advantage. Not to push this strange moment into shattering. He kept the kiss tender, her chapped lips all but breaking his heart.

Carefully, as if she were a horse that might spook, he touched her cheek with his fingertips, and when she didn't shy away he slid those fingers around her neck, cupping the heat of her skin, the pounding of her heartbeat in his palm.

There was a vibration in her throat and he felt it in his mouth, in his hand, and he knew she was moaning. Crying slightly, because she hated herself right now, hated that she couldn't resist him. And the devil in him loved that. Lived for that.

He should have done this earlier, cut through all the bullshit negotiation and bullshit communication, and gotten right to this.

Because sex he understood. A woman's soft groan reverberating against his tongue was all the communication he needed.

He stepped closer, caution be damned. She wanted him, he'd known that about her for a while, and if he couldn't win the honest way, he'd win like this.

Now he took advantage of those parted lips and his tongue swept inside as he pulled her closer, flush against him. His body, hard and tense and tortured by his own stupidity, cheered at her nearness. Those hard edges he'd expected weren't that hard and she melted against him with a sigh, revealing curves and sweetness that he would never have expected from her tiny, rigid body. It was as if his touch had transformed her.

Her hand clutched at his wrist, her fingernails biting into the skin, and lust coiled in his gut.

That messy knot of hair on top of her head toppled without much convincing, and the silk of it ran through his fingers as he clutched it in his hands.

She was panting in his arms like a quarter horse coming off the track and he stroked her, tried to gentle her, calm her into obedience. But the more he touched her, the more his kisses coaxed her into kissing him back, the more agitated she got. She wanted him and hated him at the same time and the combination was a terrible turn-on, an evil aphrodisiac. His pulse pounded beneath his zipper, and he wanted to strip off that ugly cardigan sweater and that ridiculous frilly shirt and find the woman behind the old-lady clothes.

His hands, the calluses catching on the silk, ran up from her waist to her small breasts and she jerked against him, crying low in her throat.

But then he realized that jerk was actually her pushing against him.

She was saying no.

Sickened by himself, horrified at what he was doing, but even more horrified by what would happen when he let her go, he pulled her tighter. Closer. Kissed her harder. Ignored her every sign of distress.

He needed this job. Needed this place. He couldn't let her get rid of him.

"You want this," he breathed against her mouth, sucking at her lips. He lifted her like she was nothing and arched against her, pressing the erection that pounded in time with his heartbeat against her core. "Don't fight me."

The crack of her palm against his cheek spun him sideways. Her face was flushed, her hair tousled by his hands, her lips damp and stung by his mouth. She was gorgeous and furious. Turned on and pissed off.

"Get the hell off my land, you bastard."

She spun on her heel, running for the door, but he caught her hand, expecting it to slip, like sand, like this whole situation, right through his fingers.

Shame, that old companion, settled around his neck, strangling him. "I'm sorry," he breathed. "I've never—"

"No, you're not." Her eyes snapped with anger, her cheeks flushed red with all her hate. Loathing him brought her to life. When she shook her head, the black curls slid across her shoulders, catching the light. "What the hell is wrong with you?"

Ah. The million-dollar question. He didn't have an answer for that one, never had—not for his father when he was a kid, not for the women who wanted more than he could dream of offering them. And absolutely not for her.

"You're not welcome on the Crooked Creek anymore," she said and walked away, head high, shoulders back. The stupid bow on her shirt fluttering over her shoulder like a battle flag.

What's wrong with you? Victoria laughed and poured herself some more wine. It sloshed a little in the glass, spilling across her father's desk. She used the sleeve of her sweater and part of a land contract to sop it up.

What the hell is wrong with me? *That's the real question.*

She didn't have answers. Inside her head was a mess— a storm with lightning, tornadoes, wicked witches on broomsticks.

Was she so easy to disregard? Was she so insubstantial a person that Eli could simply roll right over her?

Well, the answer was clearly yes. Every man in her life

had done that. Her father. Her husband. That was old damage.

But that kiss, devastating and wonderful all at once, had torn her in two, and what was worse than Eli ignoring her protests was that she had ignored them too, letting him kiss her. Letting him touch her. Letting him bring her dead body back to life.

The bottle, nearly empty, scraped against the desk when she set it down.

The door to the office swung open and Ruby stood dripping in the doorway, wearing galoshes and pink polka-dotted rain gear. "You need to get Eli up here. He's not answering his phone."

"Why?" Victoria stood, grabbing hold of the desk when the office sloshed to the left. *Oops. More drunk than I thought.*

"We got mud sliding down over the verandah. It's coming in under the door into the kitchen and I can't shovel fast enough."

"I'll help."

Ruby sniffed.

"What?"

"You're drunk."

"Hardly."

Victoria held her chin up high. "I can handle a shovel, Ruby. Despite what the world thinks, I'm not totally useless."

"All right," Ruby sighed. "We got gear in the closet and I'll go find another shovel."

As soon as she was dressed like the fisherman on those fish stick boxes, Victoria went into the kitchen and saw the mud pooling on the floor.

Victoria had spent the last ten years of her life in penthouse apartments. This mud slide seemed dangerous. She liked her nature at a distance, and watching it soak the rug under the kitchen table made her feel very poor. Very third world.

Jacob appeared on the other side of the door, his face pressed to the glass. His very muddy, happy face.

"Come on, Mom!" he cried.

Ruby jerked the door open an inch and more mud squeezed through. "Get yourself out here if you're going to help!" she barked.

"Goodness," Celeste said, appearing at Victoria's elbow with an empty mug. "What's happening here?"

"The rain is causing a mud slide."

"What are you going to do about it?" Celeste eyed her yellow slicker as if Victoria had put on a superhero suit and declared her intentions to save mankind.

"Shovel. Want to help?"

"Lord no! Don't we have men around here to fix this sort of thing?"

Not anymore. If Victoria weren't drunk she probably would have felt bad, but the bottle of wine in her blood had convinced her she had been right to kick Eli off of the ranch. Mud or no mud.

"Suit yourself." She found the shovel by the front door and ducked out into the rain that was coming down in sheets. It was falling so hard that her exposed skin felt pierced.

Ruby was scraping and shoveling mud off the concrete verandah, and Jacob was trying his hardest to hold the mud away from the sliding glass doors with a squeegee.

Ruby pointed to the place where the edge of the cement pad was usually visible and Victoria hunkered down, scooping up a heavy, wet pile of mud. And looked around at the sea of mud for a good place to put it.

Immediately she knew she wasn't up to the task. She was drunk, for crying out loud. And the mud was heavy. With nowhere else to put it, she heaved it as far past the hill as she could, only to watch it slide right back down at her.

The rain poured down the gaping tops of her boots and made the shovel handle slippery. Wind blew back her hood, tossing her hair into her face, where it got wet and stuck across her eyes.

But she kept shoveling and throwing the same damn mud.

She slipped. Fell right on her butt. Mud squished between her hands.

"You okay, Mom?"

"What are you doing out here? It's dangerous." The mud sucked at her feet and hands, her butt, making it impossible for her to stand on her own.

"It's just rain, Victoria," Ruby yelled over the sound of the rain.

Just rain. Just mud. Just a ranch she didn't know how to run. Just another man pushing her aside, treating her like she didn't matter.

"Right," she yelled, and grabbed the timber post and heaved herself to her feet. When she shook it off her hands, mud splattered her face, her hair, even Jacob.

"Isn't this fun, Mom?"

Fun? No. Nothing about this was fun. It felt like the rain was laughing at her, enjoying the never-ending downward spiral of her life. Surely Eli had to be the bottom. That kiss had to be her low point. Things could not get worse.

"It's great," she said as she grabbed her shovel from the muck and tried to keep working.

The rain was not helping her body lose the feel of Eli's touch. Like a shadow it lingered on her skin, everywhere he had touched her—her neck, her lips, her breasts.

She felt like a candle someone had forgotten to blow out. Burning, for no good reason.

The memory of that kiss in the arena, that colossal

failure of hers, was sore to the touch, so she turned away from it. Because examining it would only hurt. Her loneliness, her neediness—they were bombs waiting to blow up in her face. Like this summer with Dennis. She'd been so desperate for any kind of attention that she'd believed him—a con artist and liar, who was only using her for money.

And she'd played right into his hands because she didn't know who she was without a man. She had no identity of her own.

The memory burned through her, adding to her self-hate.

She felt so stupid. So foolish, so fucking weak when she was trying so damn hard to be smart and strong. But who was she kidding, really? She wasn't strong. She wasn't smart.

She stepped sideways to catch a giant river of mud gathering force down the small hill to her left, only to lose one of her boots. She tried to put her foot back into the opening, but it fell sideways and when she tried to use her hand to right it, she fell sideways too, right back into the mud.

The last string holding her together snapped.

Pushing herself back up on her knees, she grabbed her shovel and started beating the living hell out of the mud.

"I hate this place!" she screamed while rain and mud splattered up over her face and hair. Her hood fell off and she didn't care. "I hate Eli! I hate men! I hate rain! I hate my life!"

Her arms gave out and she curled over her stomach, crushing her pain, cradling it in her hands as if she could just rip it free.

How could she possibly expect to love her life when every single thing she did was in reaction to something some man did to her? Her father, Joel, Dennis, Eli—all of them acted and she just reacted.

She hadn't had a plan—hell, an original idea—in years.

She was just one of those mice they put in lab mazes, running around, hitting dead ends, frantically searching for a new path, and then when she found it, clinging to it as if it were a divine gift. Until another wall got in her way.

No more.

She sat back on her heels, panting. Suddenly, as if the mud had cleared, she saw what needed to be done.

"Mom?" Jacob gaped at her. "You okay?"

"No!" Ruby yelled, her sarcasm undiminished in the rain. "Your mom's lost it. Totally *loca*."

"We're not doing this right!" She ignored Ruby, getting to her hands and knees.

"Yeah, and what do you know about it?"

"We're reacting to the mud now instead of stopping it." She jabbed her foot into its boot and forced herself upright. She looked around at the hills, the stone fence that had caved to her left, letting in the worst of the mud. If they could shore up that fence . . .

"Jacob!" she yelled and her son jerked, unused to seeing so much wild emotion from her in one day. "Let's go to the barn and get some hay."

"Hay?" Ruby was skeptical. Ruby was always skeptical.

Victoria pointed to the fence, and after a moment the doubt washed away from Ruby's face and she set down her shovel.

"Let's give it a shot."

Victoria helped Ruby carry two bales of hay, her fingers burning under the plastic twine, from the arena to the back verandah. Her back ached, her arms were numb. Her hair made it impossible to see anything, but the mud made the landscape homogenous anyway. All they had to do was slog along until Jacob told them to stop.

"You're at the fence!" he yelled.

With groans Victoria and Ruby dropped the hay, ignoring the splash of mud that surged up over their coats and legs. What was more mud at this point? Victoria slid down the hill toward the shovel she had left by the sliding glass door and then clawed her way back up.

She used the shovel to clear a trench in front of the wall and then kicked the hay bales into the trench before the mud had a chance to fill her little moat. Ruby took the shovel and used the bottom edge as a knife to separate the bales, spreading them out. Jacob jumped on them, pounding them into the hole.

God, as a personal favor, put a cease-fire on the rain and downgraded the deluge to a minor downpour as Jacob, Victoria, and Ruby stood watching to see if the hay would hold back the worst of the mud.

Come on, Victoria thought as the water ran down her back in a cold stream, finally dousing the lingering heat of Eli's touch. She knew it was stupid to have so much of her worth tied up in hay, but that's where she was. All she had left was hay.

And when the hay held and the rain slowed and the mud stopped running in sheets down to the verandah, pride erupted inside of her.

"You did it, Mom!" Jacob cried, and Ruby nodded and Victoria laughed. Really laughed, the sound rolling up from her wet, cold toes, from the horrible memory of her husband's betrayal, from her desperate gullibility with Dennis, the satisfaction of getting the best of Eli and the embarrassment of wanting his hateful touch.

At the sound of her laugh, Jacob jumped, wrapping his arms around her waist. Her feet slipped on the unsteady ground and she fell down hard, her son right on top of her.

But she could not stop laughing. She was drunk. Uncorked. Filthy. And it was so damn great.

Jacob rolled away, flopping beside her.

Victoria grinned at his mud-smeared face and scooched around to make a mud angel.

"I was just kidding before, but you really have lost it." Ruby picked up the shovel and half slid, half walked her way back down the hill.

Jacob stayed with Victoria, his love so powerful it warmed her, even as she lay in the cold mud.

"No more reacting, Jacob."

"Okay, Mom."

As of this moment, she would no longer be a mouse in a maze. No more blind scrambling.

"We're going to make something right here. Right now. For us."

Jacob looked around. "Like a mud castle?"

Starting right now, half-drunk under a low-hung moon, she would build a life from the ground up.

Like all the self-help books she'd read in the last year had told her to, she emptied her body with a long sigh, clearing out her lungs, closing her eyes. She gripped her son's hand and opened up her blank mind to the world. To possibility. And waited for the universe to answer.

Right now, this minute, what do you want more than anything else?

I want . . .

I want . . .

The answer crawled out of her past, a forgotten wish that she'd been too meek to reach for.

Mud.

Her eyes flew open.

And her answer was right there in the moonlight, all over her little boy's beaming face.

Eli slammed his truck door so hard the windshield rattled. In the silence he didn't start the pickup, didn't do anything, really. He stared up at the rain pouring down in sheets and wondered if he was sad. Or angry. Because he couldn't tell anymore.

Fifteen years of this shit and he was just numb.

Losing his job today. His chance at the land. Everything he'd been working for his whole life felt like it was buried under ice.

The knock on his driver-side window made him jump, his heart startled out of its apathy with a heavy thump. In the shadow of the big elm, Caitlyn stood next to the truck, her palm pressed white against the window. Her raincoat hid most of her face.

Her panic was obvious and he quickly opened the door. "What's wrong?"

"I'm sorry, Eli." She stepped sideways, letting him slide out. His feet splashed in a mud puddle. "He just lost it after you left and I know you don't like the drugs—"

Before she was finished he'd started walking back through the twilight toward The Elms, his head bent against the rain. He shouldn't have left those pictures.

The white walls of Mark's room had to stay white, his pajamas blue. The TV in the corner showed John Wayne movies and John Wayne movies only. Caitlyn was the only nurse who could feed him.

Mark was a broken barometer, so sensitive to change that any difference sent him spinning.

Eli pushed through the front doors, nodding to Clark, the night guard, before heading down the dim hallway toward the screaming in the farthest bedroom. He nudged the door open and stepped into the bright artificial light from the ceiling fixtures over the bed. The two new aides—Jim and Eddie, both former high school linebackers—were holding the nearly skeletal frame of the old man against the white sheets of his bed.

"Where's my wife?" The man bowed off the bed as if possessed. "What the hell did you assholes do with her?"

"Christ, man, you're gonna break something," Eddie said. "Why the hell aren't we giving him a sedative?"

"Because it makes him sick." Eli's voice brought the big men around, their faces folded into all kinds of respect. They probably thought he was footing the bill for this place.

He flipped off the bright overhead lights and reached down to turn on the lamp on the bedside table. The gold light pooled across the table and bed, and almost instantly, the old man calmed down.

The bright lights freaked Mark out—Eli didn't know how many times he'd had to tell the staff that.

"Sorry, Mr. Turnbull," Eddie said. "We just didn't want him to hurt himself."

"Fuck you!" the old man said.

Eli smiled, but the old man didn't see and wouldn't care. Eli waved away the two aides. "I got it from here."

"Mr. Turnbull—" Eddie and Jim shared a look. "He's pretty violent—"

"I'll be fine." Eli stepped up to the bed, felt the metal of it against his legs. The light from the lamp sliced him in half, illuminating his hands and legs while shadows covered his face and chest. It looked like he was disappearing, one inch at a time.

"Who the fuck are you?" the old man asked, his runny blue eyes searching the shadows until Eli leaned forward into the pool of light.

There was no sign of recognition. Nothing but distrust. Eli wasn't even aware of hoping it would be different until it wasn't.

Your son.

"A friend," he said instead, because Mark Turnbull had no memories of a son.

"Where's my wife?"

"She left." Twenty-seven years ago. But his father's memory had folded up like an envelope, hiding the last

thirty-five years as if they'd never happened. As if Eli
had never happened.

"Stupid bitch."

Eli hooked his boot around the chair behind him and
pulled it forward so he could collapse backwards into it.
"Stupid bitch" was usually the beginning of a song Eli
knew by heart. But Mark wasn't fighting anymore; he
lay still and trembling against the white sheets, his blue
pajamas skewed around his stomach, his ribs poking
through like the ruins of a shipwreck.

Eli, risking his father's wrath but unable to resist,
reached forward and pushed the white hair off the old
man's face. Tired, he didn't protest, and Eli took a moment to fix his damp collar.

His father's skin felt like paper: too fragile a bag to
hold all the hate and anger and confusion that filled it.

"Why did she leave?" Mark's runny eyes got runnier.
Anger and grief were the only stops left on Mark's emotional train.

Eli's body sagged with weariness.

He'd already had this endless conversation tonight
and he didn't have the heart to hash it out all over again.
His father was stuck in the lowest moment of his life,
the days when Amy had left them.

Eli wondered if he'd share that fate—would he grow
old and senile and live in this moment forever?

"I lost my job at the ranch. And the land," he said,
needing to say the words even though he knew there
would be no reaction from his dad. "I fucked up. She'll
never sell it to me now."

He would have smiled had he been able; he was more
like his father and grandfather than he'd thought. He
couldn't outrun it, he couldn't change it. Despite his every
intention, he was doomed to occupy the same space at
rock bottom as every Turnbull man before him.

He could fix his barn, start the breeding business, and

become the best breeder in all of Texas, and there was a pretty good chance that none of it would matter.

What mattered was that he'd kissed Victoria . . . he'd fucking assaulted her, and ruined everything.

"Where are the horses?" Mark asked, tilting his head toward the lamp where Eli had propped up the pictures of the horses he'd bought with the money from the Angus sale.

But the pictures were gone.

Caitlyn must have picked them up when Mark started to lose it.

Eli had thought the pictures of the horses might bring him some peace, bring him back to himself, even just a little.

Apparently, he'd been wrong.

Mark's eyes were drifting and Eli stood up, pulling the blanket up over his father's thin shoulders. The old man was as small as a kid, so different from how he had once been. In every way. But cataloging the changes was work for a son with something other than duty in his heart.

"My wife," Mark whispered, his eyelids drifting shut. "Where'd she go?"

Mark's breathing calmed down, his eyelids darkened with sleep, his lips fell open, and the snores fluttered out.

When he knew the old man was fast asleep, Eli stood over him and gripped the metal rails of the hospital bed.

"Dad," he whispered, as if trying it out. But it didn't work in his mouth. Tasted like shit.

Eli shut the door to his father's room and walked down the long hallway toward the central nurses' station. The heels of his boots sounded like gunfire in the silence, but there was nothing he could do aside from crawling to be any quieter. So he just walked as if he didn't realize how loud he was. How disruptive.

Caitlyn was at the station, talking to one of the other nurses. A blonde, who smiled quickly when she caught his eye but then gathered a tray and some files and left.

"You got the pictures?" he asked, and Caitlyn's hand disappeared into the pocket of her sweater, only to resurface with the stack of photos.

"Really wound him up," she said, handing them to him.

"I'm sorry. I was hoping . . ." It wasn't even worth finishing the sentence and she knew that.

Her smile changed her plain face into something sweet and kind, wise in ways his brain just couldn't comprehend. Immediately, he felt that tug he always felt toward her.

It was like she was the picture you got when you bought a new wallet. A smiling, round-faced woman, with a kid in her arms. All the love in the world in her eyes.

And the purchase of that wallet somehow bought you the rights to that kind of woman. That kind of life. Normal. Simple. Happy.

Loneliness was a sharp pain in his chest. As if she knew, and she probably did—Caitlyn had a nurse's instinct for people in pain—she grabbed his hand, touching him where he held on to the photos. Her eyes were shining.

"I get off at ten. You want to get a drink? I think I owe you for last time." Her offer was shy despite what had happened last time, or maybe because of it.

They hadn't even made it back to her place after dinner. He'd had her stretched out across the front seat of his truck in the bar parking lot.

He thought about saying yes, but then the memory of Victoria's lips, her agonized surrender against his body—the way he'd forced her into a situation she'd hated as much as she'd wanted—burned through him and he knew he wasn't good enough for any woman right now.

And in truth, if he took Caitlyn out and she ended up across the front seat of his truck, she would be a substitute. His mind would be on Victoria, and he didn't want to treat anyone that way.

Especially a woman as sweet as Caitlyn.

He dropped her hand.

This had been inevitable—it always was. And he didn't have to say anything, not really. Women had a sixth sense about being dumped.

After a moment, after the disbelief, shock, and then hurt crossed her plain face, Caitlyn tossed back her brown ponytail and met his eyes. He could see it was hard for her, that she was nervous about him. She always had been and he didn't know how to change that. How to be . . . softer.

"So this is it?" she said through her teeth.

"This was always going to be casual."

"There's a difference between casual and what you and I . . ." She shook her head as if she'd already gone down this road with him. "Everyone warned me about you, Eli. 'Don't get close. He doesn't like it when people get close.'"

"We had a lot of fun together, Caitlyn."

"Fun?" She arched an eyebrow. "I think you mean to say sex. We had a lot of sex." She licked her lips, as pink as her scrubs, and he felt bad for dumping her at work. "You know, you're . . . great in bed, Eli. You're a freaking sex rock star but you're . . . you're the angriest man I've ever met."

Her laughter was a knife, and to his shame he could tell she was hurt. That he had hurt her without ever meaning to. When he was actually trying to be kind.

"I'm sorry." He didn't know how to make this right. How to make anything right.

"Just go. Just . . . leave."

He shoved the pictures back in his pocket. "Thanks for your help with Dad."

He turned on his heel, flipping his denim jacket's collar up against the rain, knowing that he'd done the right thing. She'd get over it in time, realize what a mistake hanging her heart on him had been.

Stepping out into the rain, he realized that in a world gone to shit, doing the right thing felt good. Made him proud.

And he hadn't been proud of himself in a very long time.

chapter
7

Celeste followed Ruby into the sun-splashed office where Victoria had summoned them bright and early on Thursday morning. Just from looking at Victoria, Celeste could tell something was going on, something . . . big.

Apparently stopping that mud slide last night had lit a fire in Victoria, and now she looked like a jack-o'-lantern, light spilling out of her mouth and eyes. Even her hair glowed.

And the sad truth was, Victoria's happiness was usually a precursor to disaster.

"Uh-oh," Ruby said, sliding a dark look over at Celeste. "Last time she looked like this we got held hostage."

"Please, Ruby," Celeste said as she sat in one of the chairs in front of the big desk Victoria was currently glowing on. She crossed her legs and then uncrossed them. Varicose veins were a constant threat—a shark under shallow waters. "*We* weren't held hostage. *We* were hiding under the dining room table."

Ruby rolled her eyes, indignant at Celeste's efforts to rain on her Mexican soap opera theatrics.

But Ruby wasn't wrong; as disastrously as that Dennis affair had ended, Celeste wasn't all that convinced Victoria had learned her lesson. Women like Victoria were always going to be motivated by men. Celeste knew, because she was the same way. She just did everything in her power to stop herself.

"This isn't about a man," Victoria said.

Celeste arched a doubtful eyebrow.

"I swear." Victoria sighed. "This isn't about a man."

"Well, hurry it up." Ruby sat down into the black leather chair beside Celeste. The sequined Our Lady of Guadalupe on her T-shirt glittered like a holy disco ball in the sunlight. "I have a pie crust in the oven."

Victoria looked down at her desk, at a list she had there. Her lips moved as she read it. And then she shook back her hair and faced Celeste and Ruby.

"There have been some changes here at the ranch. As you probably know, Eli sold most of the cattle a couple weeks ago and laid off many of the cowboys."

"The boy is trying to lose his job," Ruby grumbled.

"Yes. Well, about that." Victoria's smile was self-deprecating. "Yesterday, I fired him."

"Eli?" Ruby asked, and when Victoria nodded, Celeste swallowed her own gasp. This early morning meeting was certainly getting interesting.

"Why?" Celeste asked, and the sudden blush on Victoria's cheeks was damning.

"Personal reasons," she said, folding and unfolding the edge of the list.

"Who will care for the ranch?" Ruby asked, as if the ranch were now orphaned and wandering the desert.

"Well, there's not much of a ranch to care for anymore." Victoria circled to the front of the desk and leaned back against it, crossing her legs at her ankles, a position Celeste had seen Victoria's father assume countless times.

As angry as she had been with Lyle after their marriage fell apart, watching Victoria find her inner Lyle Baker—which was to say, her inner asshole—gave Celeste hope for the girl. Now if they could just get her out of those ridiculous clothes she wore. Her pink blouse was Prada and her black pants were Gucci, but it was as if someone had pointed her in the direction of those labels and blindfolded her. And then she had managed to pick the ugliest, worst-fitting items available by sheer bad luck.

The girl had a gift, truly.

"I've leased most of the land except for about a hundred acres around the house, including the river," Victoria continued. "Eli owns four of the horses in the barn, so they're going to go with him whenever he picks them up. Which leaves us with six. We have about fifty head of cattle left. And . . . we have the house."

"Are you firing me?" Ruby surged to her feet.

"Oh, calm down, Evita." Celeste tugged Ruby back down. "Let her finish."

"No one else is getting fired. Actually, I'd like to offer you an . . . opportunity." Victoria's level gaze nailed Celeste to the wall. "Both of you."

"I don't know anything about cows," Ruby cried. "Or horses. I hate horses."

"I am not fond of them either," Celeste said, in case Victoria had some sort of Band of Cowgirls vision in her head.

"No." Victoria straightened the already straight cuffs of her silk blouse but then stopped herself. "I want to offer you the chance to invest in a business venture."

"In a hundred-acre ranch?" Ruby asked.

"No. In a spa."

Celeste and Ruby gasped together.

The gasps cemented it. The Crooked Creek Resort and Spa was a crazy idea. Victoria had known it the moment she woke up this morning—last night's big dream had looked silly and insubstantial in the daylight.

That's what you get for making a plan under the influence of a handsome man's devastating kiss and a bottle of wine.

But she wasn't going to let go. There was merit in this idea. Merit in her, drunk or not. She had to believe that.

Without it, all she had was some hay in a rainstorm—and she wanted more.

"What do you know about spas?" Ruby asked.

She smiled; with this at least, she was comfortable. "There's nothing I don't know about spas," she said.

"Except how to run one," Celeste pointed out, a tiny blow dart right to Victoria's throat.

"I will hire someone for that. For the day-to-day management. But how a spa should look, what it should create and offer, that I know. The differences between a good spa vacation and a world-class destination—I know that by heart. By touch."

She was painfully aware of Celeste just sitting there, silently judging her. No doubt condemning Victoria and this idea to the pit of bad ideas. She glanced down again at her list—she'd written it last night, had listed all the reasons why she was perfectly suited for this project—and she gleaned some strength from it.

"My life has made me a connoisseur of manicures and salt rubs and mud baths and the environments to which they are best suited. I know what people want when they walk in the front doors of a spa, from the décor down to the staff. And this land, the Crooked Creek, could be something special. The acreage I've saved is the most beautiful in the whole county. The views alone make us different from every other resort in the area. And that's to say nothing of what we can do to this house. We're close enough to Dallas to attract and maintain global interest, but removed enough that we can hit that fine balance between cosmopolitan and rustic. Staff can commute from the city, and esthetician schools there should offer us plenty of hiring opportunities."

"You've thought this out," Celeste finally said.

"I have."

Celeste's silence was like the Spanish Inquisition. And it was on the tip of Victoria's tongue to say, *You're right. Of course this is a ridiculous idea. What could I have possibly been thinking?*

But she bit down on her tongue until she tasted blood.

"Well, I think it's a great idea!" Ruby cried, her eyes alight with excitement. The spa idea grew back its weight and heft. It was solid, once again in the palm of her hand.

"I'm glad you think so, because I would like you to be my chef, Ruby," Victoria said.

"But . . . I . . . I am just a cook. A housekeeper. What do I know about spas?"

"Don't sell yourself short," Celeste finally piped up, breaking the icy façade she'd developed over the last five minutes. "You know food. With some work—"

"Work?" Ruby bristled, casting aside her self-effacing modesty. "Listen to you. What would you even know about food? You barely eat."

"Ruby," Victoria sighed. "Would you like the job? I can't pay you more, not at first, but I will offer you profit sharing." She held her breath.

"Of course. I would love to cook for your spa. We will do great things."

Ruby clapped and Victoria laughed, and suddenly she found herself pulled into the woman's fierce hug.

"I hate to break up the celebration, but how are you going to afford this?" Celeste asked.

Victoria stepped away from Ruby's enthusiasm and support into the chill of Celeste's doubt.

"Don't listen to her," Ruby whispered. "She is miserable and dried up and doesn't know how to have fun."

"Don't you have a pie crust to see to?" Celeste asked,

as imperial as the woman who had terrified Victoria as a child.

"The money from the sale of the cattle will get us started, and the money from the leases that are rolling in should keep us going through the renovations."

"It's going to take more than three quarters of a million dollars and a few thousand dollars a month to change this eyesore into a resort."

"I have some money," Ruby offered, surprising both Victoria and Celeste.

"Stealing silverware again?" Celeste asked.

"Very funny, but no, you sour old woman. I have no children. No husband. I have lived here rent free, so most of my salary has been saved. A hundred thousand dollars."

Victoria gaped at Ruby's generosity. But, as flattered as she was, she wasn't going to take Ruby's safety net. What if this failed? She'd suck Ruby down into the abyss with her. No, if she was going to take money from people, it would be from people who had money to spare.

"That's retirement money, Ruby," she said. "I couldn't—"

"Boob job," Ruby said with a shrug. "I just could never commit."

Even Celeste's perfect face creased into a smile.

"What about me?" Celeste asked. "Will you take my money?"

The question was an accusation and Victoria bristled, suddenly feeling like a beggar at Celeste's door.

"You offered a few months ago to pay for me to go back to school—"

"I remember."

"Well, I was hoping perhaps you would let me have that money and apply it toward this."

"Just to be clear. The 'this' you are referring to is turning this very ugly house into a spa?"

"First-class spa and resort. Canyon Ranch meets The Red Door."

Celeste laughed. "Well, my dear, when you lose your mind you really lose your mind."

Victoria had had enough of the woman's condemnation. She'd been a victim of it all her life and was working hard to shake her low self-esteem. Which was hard enough without Celeste's judgment dogging her every move.

"I'm not kidding, Celeste, and if you don't believe in this project, you can leave."

"I didn't say that. You're just going to have to renovate."

"I know."

"Suites, dining room—"

"Kitchen upgrade," Ruby interjected.

"I know," Victoria said. "All of it. I know. That's . . . that's why I was hoping for the money. But, frankly, Celeste, if you want me to beg, I can find another way."

Celeste lifted her hand and Victoria stopped on a dime, such was the power of Celeste's hands. "You can have the money. And I do believe. I believe in you and this project. I think it's a fantastic idea. I can't think of anyone better suited to the creation of a spa than you, except perhaps me. And that's why this isn't a loan. I want to be your partner."

"A partner?" Victoria gasped. The idea was . . . ludicrous.

"Take it or leave it."

"You come with the money?" she asked.

"I usually do."

"I will never understand white people," Ruby muttered.

"Frankly, Celeste, I find it odd that you want to be a part of this project, since you're acting like it's a colossal mistake."

"I just want to make sure you understand what you're taking on. This idea is huge and not to be taken lightly. And if this is just a reaction to Eli selling the herd—"

"This has nothing to do with Eli."

Celeste licked her lips. "I don't believe you."

"I don't care."

The words hung in the air, faintly smoking with her ire.

Celeste smiled. "If you say so."

"I do. Now, I have a question for you."

"I will not be your masseuse."

"I wouldn't dream of asking."

The question burning on her lips seemed counterintuitive to her needs, but for some reason Victoria wanted her future cut free from the past.

"I want to know if you're giving me this money because you feel guilty."

"Guilty? Me?"

"For my dad and the way he treated Luc and me after you left him."

Celeste's alabaster skin turned pink. Her lips parted, letting out a shaky breath. "Let's say I do feel guilty. You would turn down the money?"

"I . . . no." She wasn't an idiot. "I'd still take the money. But I don't want you thinking you need to do this to make things right. Dad was Dad. You leaving had nothing to do with how he treated me."

For one very strange moment, Celeste's face seemed to melt, transformed by grief and regret and sadness, revealing a human side to her otherworldly beauty.

"The money is yours," Celeste said. "My reasons are mine."

In the end Celeste invested one hundred thousand dollars and in the partnership agreement that Randy Jenkins drew up, that hundred thousand dollars bought her a 25 percent share of the Crooked Creek Resort and Spa. Initially, Victoria worried that even 1 percent would be too much, but in the week that followed, she was astounded to find that Celeste's opinions fell into place with her own.

When it came time for Victoria to show her amateurish sketches of the mud bath verandah, the dining room, the foyer beneath the glass portico, and the small but elegant suites, she'd expected them to be attacked with a red pen.

But the small changes Celeste suggested only enhanced the vision.

And her total revamping of the treatment rooms made for more rooms in the same amount of space.

On Monday, when the first architect they'd consulted came out to look at the house and discuss the project, Victoria showed him their amateur drawings and when the brash Texan sniffed, a smug little smile on his face, Victoria tried to convince herself that the whiff of misogyny that was wafting off of him was all in her head.

"Neanderthal," Celeste said, once the front door shut behind him.

Victoria was delighted not to call him back.

By the time the sixth architect showed up, they still hadn't had any luck. He was a handsome young man with very cool glasses and a borderline offensive attachment to his cell phone.

"Excuse me," he said for what had to be the fifth time since his arrival. They were still in the foyer. He rudely turned away, cell phone pressed to his ear.

Victoria glanced over at Celeste, who shook her head and left, silently inviting her to get rid of the boy once he was off the phone.

"You know what we need?" Victoria asked that night

at dinner. The sun was setting in the wide windows behind them, casting the whole room in shades of pink
and yellow. Jacob, coloring beside her at the eat-in
counter, looked good enough to eat in the late afternoon
light.

She kissed him and he wiggled away. "Come on,
Mom. I'm working."

"Sorry, Mr. Schulman," she murmured and kissed him
again for good measure.

As beautiful as her son looked in the light, the kitchen
did not fare equally well. The terra-cotta and Mexican
tiles that covered nearly every flat surface might have
been slightly fashionable twenty years ago. Now they
were kitschy; the grout was gray and the tiles were
cracking.

Everywhere she looked there was more money to be
spent. More money that was needed to make this plan
work.

"More money?" Celeste asked as if she could read her
mind.

"Besides that."

"You need to pay attention to what you're eating,"
Ruby said, her back to them as she stood at the stove
spooning something green and goopy into bowls. She
wore a pair of red sweatpants with the words *Hot Mama*
across the seat.

"What are we eating?" Jacob asked as the bowl was
slid in front of him.

"Watercress." Ruby wiped her hands on a towel and
tossed it over her shoulder. "Why you want me to make
lettuce soup, I don't know. But it was in the cookbooks."

"Aren't you supposed to puree this?" Celeste asked,
and Ruby glared at her.

"You know, Ruby," Victoria felt compelled to say, because while she'd never been a fan of watercress soup,

this one looked particularly unappealing. "You don't have to change the way you cook."

"You think all those rich people are going to want to come here and eat tamales?"

"If they're yours, yes."

"She doesn't eat them." Ruby pointed at Celeste, who had pushed aside the bowl.

"She's a robot."

Ruby laughed and turned back to the stove, promising a better second course.

"A female architect," Celeste said.

"What?"

"That's what we need. A female architect. Someone who won't just be humoring us. Someone who can share our vision."

It was exactly what they needed. Someone who understood the whole earth mother/sophisticated socialite vibe they were going for. "Yes! Exactly. Girl power," Victoria whispered.

Celeste stared at her. "You can be so odd sometimes."

"I know one," Ruby said, this time placing plates piled high with roasted squash and arugula in front of them. The salads were drizzled with mustard vinaigrette and pomegranate seeds.

"That's better," Celeste muttered.

"You know a female architect?" Victoria asked.

"We all do." Celeste and Victoria shared a blank look, as Ruby pleated and unpleated the edge of the dishcloth over her shoulder. "But . . . I think it might not be a good idea."

"Is she an ex-con?" Victoria asked, worried by Ruby's odd attitude, the worry on her face.

"I don't know any ex-cons. Lesbian?" Celeste asked.

"Celeste!"

"What? Lesbians are wonderful to work with. Very no-nonsense."

"She's not a lesbian." Ruby tilted her head. "I don't think. Though that would explain a lot."

"Then what's with the secrecy, Ruby? Who is she?"

"Eli's mother."

chapter
8

Eli's father had once had a thing for these half-broke Criollo ponies he got from a breeder down in Mexico. And at dawn the morning after Eli's mother had left, Mark loaded his son into the truck, and they set off on a two-day trip down to the southern tip of Sonora, the horse trailer dragging behind them.

After crossing the border, Eli finally gathered up the courage to ask if his mom had left for good. His father's silence was answer enough, and Eli spent the rest of that first day staring out the window at the sun, burning his retinas so that his tears wouldn't fall. He had been eight at the time. Eight-year-old boys didn't cry—his dad had told him that clear enough.

Once they got to the dusty, hardscrabble pocket of land on the flat edge of the desert, Mark and José Ontegna shook hands and discussed horseflesh.

Forgotten, Eli dozed in the truck, his hat pulled low over his eyes. It was tough ignoring the hunger making his stomach growl and even tougher to ignore the bitterness that ached in his muscles. Bitterness over his mom. Over the fact that they didn't have enough money to stop at McDonald's after the peanut butter and jelly sandwiches Mark had made were gone, but they had money for horses.

When the passenger-side door was jerked open, Eli fell

out, barely managing to catch himself against the door before meeting the hard red dust.

"What's going on?" He squinted up at Mark.

His father's face was different. Not angry or sad, but blank. Like extra skin had grown up around his eyes and mouth, armor against showing emotion. He wasn't going to smile. Or cry. Ever again.

"Come on out here. We're gonna break these ponies before we put 'em in the trailer."

The thick, sturdy Criollos stirred in the paddock as if they'd heard Mark's words and started running the edges of the pen, their manes and tails black banners behind them.

Eli had watched his father break dozens of horses over the years and he stepped up to the split wood of the fence, climbing to the top rung, where he planned on watching.

But Mark put a hand in the collar of his denim jacket. "Come on," he said.

"Me? You want me to break them?"

"That one." Mark pointed to the only mare of the three in the paddock. "You're big enough."

Fear and excitement made his spit sour, his mouth a dry cave. That horse was huge and his body felt so small.

"Dad—"

"You a coward?"

This version of his dad wasn't totally unfamiliar—he usually showed up after fights with his mom—but that blankness on his face was terrifying, and Eli knew he couldn't admit he was scared. He couldn't say he was only eight and that his dad was acting crazy.

The tough Mexican vaqueros lined the paddock, shaking their heads, but Dad ignored them.

"You don't leave because something's hard, Eli. You don't get to walk away just because you're unhappy."

That day, getting the beating of his life from a strawberry mare, Eli was given the first taste of what the next twenty years of his life would be like as a substitute for his mother.

His dad wasn't abusive, but he was cold and unforgiving. The crimes he couldn't pardon weren't even Eli's—they were Eli's mother's.

And happiness, starting that weekend, became a rumor. A ghost. A bedtime story other kids were read.

It wasn't as if he was happier after getting fired by Victoria. But a week later, after the sting and the shock wore off and the shame was something he was used to, he did feel lighter. He could stand up straight without the weight of a hundred-year-old grudge on his back.

He owned his house and the ten acres of land around it. He had a barn full of strong, good-looking horses with excellent pedigrees and he still had money in the bank.

This was more than he'd had his entire life. He felt rich with possessions and purpose.

And for the first time in his adult life he could focus on the now. And the now was a lot of work. The now kept him pretty busy.

Sitting up on the roof of his barn, Eli took another nail out from between his lips and hammered in the last of the shingles. Twilight was turning purple around the edges and Eli knew he'd have to head inside soon, but he wanted to finish the roof on the barn tonight.

He had four horses he needed to pick up from Crooked Creek tomorrow. And if he stopped working he'd have to think about seeing Victoria again, about what he would say to try to make what he'd done right, so he just kept working.

Headlights sliced through the growing shadows as a pickup bounced down the gravel road toward his house. Soda, his collie, stood up from the porch and barked. The truck stopped and his Uncle John stepped out, looking for him as he hitched his pants up over his belly. Soda went over for a pat, her tail wagging.

It was about time John came looking for answers. Eli had expected him sooner.

"Up here," Eli said.

John took three steps toward the barn, peering up at him from under his hat. "Fired?"

"Yep."

"Boy, you better get down here and tell me what the hell happened."

"Give me a second." Slipping the hammer into his tool belt, he crab-walked over to the ladder and climbed down. He hoped his uncle had a six of Shiner Bock in the truck. Because what he needed a hell of a lot more than his uncle giving him a hard time was six cold beers.

"You let that woman fire you?"

"Go ahead, make your jokes."

"Boy, you are the joke!"

Eli sighed, preparing himself to weather his uncle's temper.

"Your father drank himself into a stupor every day he worked in that barn and he didn't get fired."

Eli shrugged. "Clearly I have a special talent."

"You hit her?"

"What? No!"

"Well, even that's forgivable with certain women."

Eli stared at his uncle. That had to be a joke.

"What I did was pretty unforgivable. And it's all right that I'm not there anymore. It's . . ." He laughed. "It's fine, actually."

"Fine?" His uncle stepped closer, his wide chest straining at the buttons of his dirty shirt.

Eli felt the bite of his uncle's temper on the scruff of his neck and he stepped away rather than pushing John back. He was just starting to feel good about himself; he wasn't going to go and hit the only family he had left.

"It's not fine. You're a Turnbull."

Laughter burned like bitter medicine in his throat. "And what has being a Turnbull ever gotten me?"

"Don't go ungrateful on me now, boy. We agreed you having that job was our best chance at getting the land back."

"We're not going to get it back, Uncle John! Victoria has leased most of the land."

"Leased? What the hell are you talking about? Since when?"

"Couple weeks ago."

Uncle John's face went white and still, and his big chest panted. Eli grabbed his elbow, feeling him weave.

"Whoa, Uncle John, you need to sit down?"

"What rights did she lease?" he whispered. "Water? Minerals? Someone going to start drilling on our land?"

"I doubt it. She leased most of it to ranchers in the area." Eli led his uncle, ready to sit him down on the wide bumper of the truck, but John slapped his hands away.

"You said she had no idea what she was doing."

"She didn't. But she went out and got one." He told himself it wasn't respect coloring his voice, but Uncle John heard it and gaped at him.

"You *like* her. A skinny bitch from the city and a Baker to boot? Boy, I never thought I'd see the day when you'd so spectacularly fail me."

Eli gaped, feeling like a kid getting hit for the first time by someone he trusted. "I feel nothing for her. I feel nothing for any of it anymore."

"You are giving up."

"I got my own life to worry about; I can't keep carrying the mistakes my family made. It was making me . . ." He thought about that kiss, of her arms pushing against him. The fear and desire in her eyes. The way he ground himself into her softness, like a man without conscience. What kind of man takes advantage of that? What kind of man thinks it's okay to use a woman's desire to his advantage?

Not the kind of man he wanted to be.

"It was turning me into a man I didn't like."

"Who the hell cares?" John cried, sounding a lot like Mark thirty years ago. "Poor you. This is your home. Our home. All the home you ever wanted, remember? Jesus Christ, son, what have we been working toward all these years? This is for you!"

Eli shook his head, wounded by the look in his uncle's eyes, by his words, by the injustice of his disappointment. "Not anymore it's not. Even if I somehow could get my job back, no Baker will sell me the land. Not now. Between selling the herd and . . . this thing with Victoria . . ."

Uncle John rubbed a hand over his red cheeks. "You force her?"

It took him a second to catch on to what his uncle meant by "forced" and he instinctively recoiled, staring at John, wishing he could be offended, shocked at the thought.

But how far had he been, really, from something like that?

"No, but . . . I pushed . . . when I shouldn't have."

"Some women like that sort of thing."

Jesus Christ, what kind of women was his uncle dating?

Eli thought of the prim Victoria, the pride she wore like another ugly shirt. She might have wanted him, but she didn't want him like that. A woman like Victoria wouldn't want something so coarse. So raw.

And she hadn't.

"Not her. Trust me."

"I thought we were a team, Eli."

"Yeah, well maybe it's time to realize we're the losing team."

"Bullshit."

Eli couldn't take it anymore. He couldn't be under one more person's boot heel.

"I don't want all that land anymore, Uncle John. I'm done. If you can't get behind me on this, then maybe you should leave."

"You kicking me off your land?"

"Kicking you off? God, listen to you. No. But I don't want to fight anymore."

"I've lost enough to the Bakers; I'm not losing you, too. I'm still fighting." That gnarled finger of his uncle's jabbed his chest, sunk into his skin like a barb.

Uncle John pushed a six-pack of beer into Eli's arms and then climbed back in his truck. Eli watched, shell-shocked, as the only man who'd been in his corner over the years drove away, leaving him to drink a six-pack all by himself.

It was too dark to keep working on the barn, much to his regret. He had nothing else to do but walk back into the house and wait for the morning to come.

And with it, Victoria.

He turned, the beer in his arms, and was brought up short by the sight of his house in the moonlight. It seemed so much smaller somehow. A toy someone could pick up and take away. He'd added a porch a few summers ago, while Uncle John had shouted advice at him from his seat under the poplars. The summer he turned fifteen, he rebuilt the stone chimney by himself after it had been ruined by raccoons. When his father moved out, he finally fixed the sagging floor in the kitchen that his mother had always complained about.

He'd lived alone in this house for fifteen years, systematically banishing the bad memories, and he'd never felt lonely.

But tonight the sky was so big and the stars were so far away.

Soda's cold, wet nose touched his hand, urging him into action. He cradled the beer under his arm and practically ran up the porch, as if ghosts were after him. With a sigh of relief, he pushed open the door, letting the familiar golden light spill across his feet, welcoming him home.

Soda, all the company he'd ever needed, followed him into the empty house.

"You want this." Eli's breath skimmed over her skin, pulling her nipples into tight beads. She groaned, rolling her body against him, trying desperately to find relief, but her hands were tied over her head and he kept his skin away. His hardness just out of reach.

"Say the words, Victoria," he breathed, licking her lips. "Like a good girl."

His fingers toyed with the damp curls between her legs and she wanted to beg. She wanted to scream with lust and frustration, with the desire that she'd hidden away for fifteen years.

"Fuck . . ." She swallowed, the words so foreign, so ridiculous in her mouth, but she was dying. "Fuck me. Please. Eli."

The callused edge of his thumb slipped into her mouth and she sucked him, arching hard against him, seeking that hand between her legs. Something hard and rough brushed her clitoris and she cried out, shaking.

"More. God. More, Eli."

"No."

She screamed in frustration, breaking the bonds around her hands, and sat up, only to find herself in her dark bedroom, tragically turned on.

Alone.

Again.

Grabbing a pillow from beside her she put it over her face and screamed, flopping backwards. Lust ran thwarted circles in her body, making her crazy. Frustrated. But mostly, embarrassed.

It was just a dream. Just another sex dream wherein Eli debased her and she loved it.

Conscious, there was no way she wanted to be treated that way. But somehow when she fell asleep every night, all she wanted was to be forced to feel something. Forced to admit that under her clothes, under her skin, she was a woman who'd long been neglected.

Between her legs she was wet and sore with frustrated desire, and she curled over onto her side with a moan.

Early morning sunlight pushed against the yellow curtains, filling the room with a dim, milky light. She was going to see Eli today. He was coming to get his horses. It had been nearly two weeks since he'd kissed her and she felt like a different woman. The spa, Celeste's support, Ruby's eagerness—all of it had somehow changed her, given her more of herself than she'd had before.

But that kiss . . .

She knew in her heart that he hadn't kissed her because of any desire he had for her. He didn't *want* her like that.

But that didn't change the fact that she wanted him exactly like that.

The cotton of the tank top she wore to bed was warm under her hands, her nipples ached against her fingers, her breath hitched. It had been years since she'd done this. When she was young, before the ice age of her marriage, she'd taken care of her small aches, the most persistent of her desires, instead of falling into shallow casual relationships.

Marriage to Joel, however, had proven her desires were not that persistent after all. And within a few years she'd channeled all that lonely desire into finding the perfect drapes for the den every spring.

But now it was back with a vengeance; she felt empty and her skin hurt with its need to be touched.

What she liked—the soft touch, the firm squeeze—came back to her in a flood.

Don't do this. Don't think of that man and touch yourself. You're better than that. Better than him.

But in the end she couldn't stop herself. She slipped her hand between her legs and thought of all the dangerous things Eli made her feel.

The horses neighed and stomped in greeting the minute Eli walked into the barn.

"Hello to you, too," he murmured, running his hands over Phineas's star, pulling on his forelock. Lucky snorted and danced in the next stall, and it broke his heart to be leaving her here.

"You'll miss me, won't you?" he murmured. A lifetime spent in this barn and this deaf old horse might be the only creature to care when he left.

Didn't say much for his life up to this point.

He heard the scrape of feet against the hard-packed ground and his stomach flinched in sudden dread. Victoria. It had to be. But when he turned, it was the little boy standing there in rain boots that came up to his knobby knees.

"I'm sorry." Jacob wrapped his hands in the hem of his own shirt, and Lucky stomped and shook her head in reaction to the boy's agitation.

"What are you sorry for?" Eli asked, scratching behind Lucky's ears just the way she liked. The horse immediately calmed, but the boy still vibrated with emotion. Down the way, Darling stomped her feet. Jacob was worse than a storm when it came to agitating the horses.

"I got you fired."

Eli smiled sadly at the boy. "No, kid, you didn't. Getting fired was all my doing."

"But I knew my mom would be angry if I rode that horse and I did it anyway, and I tried to tell her but she wouldn't listen and then she fired you and—"

Eli stepped up and put his hand on Jacob's head, which was so little that his thumb and fingers touched the boy's ears. His silky hair, so like his mother's, sprouted up between Eli's fingers. "Not your fault."

The boy hung his head. "I'm still sorry," he whispered.

For a second Eli thought about warning the boy about the dangers of taking on other people's crimes, about guilt and the burden over the years, but in the end he just gave Jacob's head a little wag and let go of him.

"You taking all the horses?" Jacob asked, jogging to keep up with him as he made his way to the office.

"Phineas, Patience, Darling, and Buddy."

"What about Lucky?"

"Not my horse."

"Who is going to take care of her?" Jacob gasped as if Eli were abandoning the horse on the side of the road.

Eli smiled down at the kid. Maybe he was putting off leaving this place, or putting off going to see Victoria, or maybe he was taking a minute to do something good. Which was practically a trend with him at this point.

"How about you?" he asked.

"Me?" The boy lit up like a bonfire.

"Jerry will handle him, keep him clean. But you're going to need to feed him."

"Oh . . . okay."

"I'll show you what to do."

Ruby put a bowl of her yogurt and grapes sprinkled with granola in front of Victoria and waited for the verdict, a smug smile on her pink lip-glossed lips.

"I think this is the best granola yet," said Celeste, who was sitting beside her at the counter.

Victoria tasted the granola and agreed. Filled with pumpkin seeds and dried cherries, it was crunchy and delicious. After that first considering bite, she dug in with gusto. Torrid dreams and shamefaced masturbation gave her an appetite.

"Where's Jacob?" she asked.

Celeste sighed. "I don't understand why all of a sudden you want to talk with your mouth full."

"He went into the barn," Ruby said, looking out the sliding glass door. "Eli's there, picking up his horses."

Victoria's throat locked down like a prison. She pushed the grapes away.

"Already?"

"His truck and trailer are out by the barn." Ruby pointed vaguely toward the front of the house.

"Amy is coming this morning to bid on the project. Any minute," Celeste said, making notes in the calendar at her elbow.

Ruby turned, staring at them wide-eyed and horrified.

"Is that . . . a problem?" Victoria asked, though she could feel the answer in the air.

"Amy hasn't been back on this ranch since she left, when Eli was eight," Ruby said.

Victoria's stomach twisted, those pumpkin seeds turning into heavy clumps in her throat. "Because Eli always goes to see her in Dallas? Because despite her leaving they have always had a loving and close relationship?" She sounded delusionally hopeful. Perhaps she should have pushed Ruby for more information about Amy Turnbull, but she'd just been so excited about getting a woman down here to look at the project.

"As far as I know, Eli hasn't talked to his mother since she left."

There was a stunned moment of silence before Victoria and Celeste scattered into action.

"I'll call her and see if I can't change the time," Celeste said.

"I'll go get Eli off the property," Victoria added. She pushed her feet into her boots and grabbed a sweater from the rack by the door.

"Victoria?" It was Ruby, her tiny body casting a long shadow down the hallway. "Don't tell him about his mom. I don't think—"

"He'd like knowing the mother who left him was coming back to help turn his beloved ranch into a spa?" Hiring Eli's mother would be a mistake, and she never should have went along with it. Celeste had tried to talk her out of bringing Amy in for an interview, but she hadn't listened. Bringing Amy here was only going to hurt everyone.

"No." Ruby shook her head. "I don't think he'd like it."

"You think?" Victoria slammed the door behind her as she headed out into the morning, determined not to think of that kiss, or her own hand between her legs.

Or what happens to a little boy when his mother leaves him and never comes back.

chapter
9

The barn was warm and it smelled like horse poop and hay to Victoria, bitter and sweet all at once. A few months here and that smell suddenly wasn't so bad. Imagine that. Poop didn't smell so bad anymore.

Eli came around the corner from the office, a white bucket filled with feed in his hands, and beside him was her son, skipping to keep up.

They didn't see her and she watched as Eli poured the feed from the bucket into a black canvas bucket thing hanging in front of a horse's stall. A white horse pushed her nose against Jacob, who looked up at Eli as if he were telling him state secrets.

"Now, Lucky is a pig," Eli said. "If she gets into the grain she'll eat herself sick. Or worse."

"Worse?"

"I had a pony once, got into the grain and ate until she died."

"You're making that up."

"Wish to God I was. But that's what you've got to remember. Hay is fine, but grain once a day." Jacob nodded sagely and Eli kept talking, giving Jacob instructions on what to feed the barn cats and how to keep the dogs away from the manure pile.

Jacob listened carefully, trying so hard to seem older, responsible, all while his eyes glittered with gratitude that this man was taking him seriously, treating him like a person rather than a little boy or an afterthought.

And Eli recognized his gratitude and his need. And he handled it with sure hands.

Victoria stepped backwards into the shadows of an empty stall and pushed her fist against the pounding of her heart. *Not fair,* she thought. Not fair that he could be so kind to her son and so awful to her.

Not fair that he could be exactly what her son secretly needed and what she so secretly desired.

She pressed her head against the splintered wood of the barn wall, her hair catching in the wood, pulling just enough that tears sprung to her eyes.

Since when is life fair? she told herself. *You of all people know that fairness is a fairy tale.*

And that man isn't what any of us needs. Not really.

"Which is why," she murmured, "you fired him."

With that battle cry in her heart, she stepped out into the open, making enough noise so that both Jacob and Eli turned to look at her.

Jacob, bless his heart, managed to look both guilty and defiant, as if she'd caught him hanging out with the wrong crowd again. Which, in a way, wasn't far off.

Eli dropped his hands to his sides and for a moment she got the impression that he was unguarded. Revealed.

So she looked away from him, because her X-rated dreams had made her feel foolish enough. She didn't need to add X-rated daydreams.

"Eli's showing me how to feed the animals," Jacob said.

"That's great."

"I'm just picking up my horses," Eli added.

She glanced at him. "I know."

Looking at him was a mistake, because once their eyes had met, she couldn't turn away. He wore his regret like a neon sign.

Asshole Eli was far easier to deny, far easier to push aside. With contrite Eli, it wasn't going to be so easy.

"Jacob." Eli cleared his throat. "Could you give your mom and me a second? We've got some business to figure out."

"Sure. Will . . ." Jacob blinked up at the cowboy, not even sparing her a sideways glance. "Will I see you again?"

"I, ah . . ." Eli shot her a panicked look and she kept her face neutral. He had started this hero-worship; he could figure his own way out of it. She'd been the bad guy enough in Jacob's life. "I don't know, Jacob."

The honesty surprised her. Joel had told Jacob lie after lie about birthday parties and trips to the park that he had no intention of being around for.

"But . . . but what if Lucky gets in the grain? Or Boots gets into the manure pile? What do I do?"

Eli's smile was breathtaking. Small and slightly unsure of its welcome, it barely flirted with his full lips. "You call me," he said, "and I'll come on over to help."

Jacob used his whole body to sigh with relief, and Victoria couldn't help but smile.

"That's good," Jacob said and then to her surprise he put out his hand. "Bye, Eli."

After a long moment Eli slowly shook the boy's hand and she refused, absolutely refused, to be moved by Eli's surprise. By the softening around his mouth. That he was touched by Jacob's good manners was nothing to her.

"Ruby's got breakfast waiting," she said, pushing her son out the door.

One last wave over his shoulder and Jacob was trotting out of the arena. Within seconds of his departure she wished he were back. Because now it was just Eli's green eyes staring at her across the aisle, shrinking the world down to the two of them.

Her skin remembered with terrible clarity the warmth

of his hand on her breast. The way his body felt against hers, hard and solid. Strong. Like he knew exactly how to bend her and lift her and hold her so he could screw her into oblivion.

She'd never been screwed into oblivion. It would have been novel.

Where, she asked herself, *is your pride?*

"You have everything you need?" she asked.

He nodded.

"I've made sure the accountant will pay you until the end of the month."

"Victoria—"

"You've been, if not loyal, at least here for the last fifteen years. I figured it was fair."

"Fair." He laughed and then shook his head, but offered nothing else on the subject.

She bit her lip to keep from asking what he meant. She liked to collect thoughts on fairness, add them to her library, and his would have been interesting.

"Look, Victoria—"

This was it. The apology. The apology she was going to hurl back in his face. She lifted her chin and drew her sweater tighter around her chest, as if that could protect her from the embarrassment of wanting so badly a man who just wanted to punish her.

"The breeding equipment in the far stall—"

Her ears buzzed. "Breeding equipment?"

He stepped closer and she shifted back, determined to keep him as far away as possible.

At her sidestep, he stopped on a dime, his hands in fists.

"What about it?" she asked, pleased that her voice was firm.

"You have a phantom, four different ultrasounds. A chute, a couple of boxes of gloves and inseminators. Some other odds and ends."

This was all news to her. And mostly Greek. Phantoms? But she wasn't about to look the fool in front of him again.

"What about them?"

"I'd like to buy them. I can give you a fair price—"

She laughed. She laughed right at him and his cheeks got red, his eyes started to glitter. She didn't know whether he was angry or embarrassed, and she didn't care.

"Fair? You? Excuse me if I don't believe you."

He wiped a hand over his mouth. "That wasn't . . . I wasn't always like that."

"A bastard?"

A muscle ticked in his cheek. "You remember."

She swallowed, her body cold and then hot. "If you're talking about what happened in the arena—"

"I'm talking about when we were kids."

Uncomfortable, off her stride, she ran a hand down the front of her shirt, feeling the edges of the buttons like they were stones. It calmed her down, counting those seven buttons. Seven deep breaths. Seven steps back toward control.

"You don't remember?" His voice was rough. As if her not remembering those summers when they were kids hurt his feelings.

"You were nice to me when we were kids. But that doesn't excuse what you've done since then. I don't know what's happened to you over the years, Eli, but the boy I knew . . . I don't see much of him in you anymore."

For years in her other life, she'd lived on innuendo, backhanded compliments, letting rumors do the hard work for her in terms of letting people know how she felt about them. Telling Eli he was an ass, straight and plain, filled her with both anxiety and elation. She felt mean and righteous both at once.

"Me neither."

He shoved his hands in his pockets and her heart dipped in reaction to the very real regret in his eyes.

Eli was a big man—tall and lean through the waist but wide in the shoulders—but right now he seemed small. Diminished.

"You can call around, find out what I should pay you for that equipment."

"I'll do that."

The silence buzzed, growing louder until she wanted to scream just to break the tension, but she didn't. She glued her mouth shut and just stared right back at him until he finally broke eye contact.

As he glanced around at the high windows and stable doors, she sucked in a breath to calm her heart rate. Unclenched her cramping fists.

"I never thought I'd leave this place," he finally said.

"Maybe you should have thought of that before sticking your tongue down my throat."

His laugh was a dry gust of air from his chest. "I should have."

"And you can apologize all you want, but—"

"I haven't apologized," he said, stunning her into silence.

"Well . . . you should."

"I don't apologize for kissing you." He stepped closer and she didn't step away. She knew with uncomfortable certainty that it was this morning's lurid fantasy that shackled her in place.

He kept walking toward her, his green eyes bright, and she just stood there like a dummy, because her inner horndog wanted to be stroked.

"That's not very . . . nice of you." She cringed. *Nice? Oh Lord, help me.*

"No one's accused me of being nice."

He was right next to her, so close she could see that his green eyes were actually hazel. The golden brown rim at the center around his iris was swallowed up by the brilliance of the green.

"But I am sorry I pushed you." His breath smelled like coffee and mints and the barn was tiny again, suffocating. "I'm sorry I didn't listen to you. I'm sorry I scared you."

"Because you were scared." It was an accusation. She put the words in his mouth because she didn't want to hear some lie about how badly he wanted her.

He nodded, and her breath hitched in her chest. Seven buttons. Seven breaths, the plastic cool under her hot fingers.

"You wanted to hurt me. Get back at me." It shocked her how much she needed her words to be true, so she could just climb back into her shell. So she could negate everything she felt for this man. The ice age her body was used to waited with open arms if she could just push that kiss out of her mind.

How the hell had this happened?

For a second Eli wondered if this was maybe a joke. He was supposed to apologize for one of the most foul things he'd ever done in his life, the last in a long line of increasingly foul things, gather his horses, and walk off the ranch.

But instead, he was getting the distinct impression that he should kiss her again.

He should have seen this coming. Of course Victoria would take herself right out of the equation of that kiss. He'd put money on the fact that Victoria took herself right out of most equations. She dressed like wallpaper. Acted as though she couldn't remember what a good time felt like.

And he'd taken advantage of all of that.

Which he felt bad about, he really did. He remembered when he was a good guy.

But right now, the knowledge in her eyes shamed him in a different way. Because she wanted to be a part of that kiss, but she doubted his motives. Who could blame her, really?

It wasn't as if he'd taken the time to show her that despite how it might seem, he hadn't faked his desire for her.

She practically pulsed with wounded pride and touching her might get him punched in the nose, but it seemed like the right thing to do. Much to his relief and surprise, she didn't dodge his touch and when his callused fingers stroked her palm, he heard her soft exhale, as if she was trying to hide how ruffled she was.

If he hadn't botched everything already, he might have put her hand to his chest so she could feel the pounding of his heart. Showing her how she affected him would be easier than telling her.

But he'd already been an ass. It was time to try being a gentleman.

"I kissed you because I was scared. But I kept kissing you because I wanted to."

Her head jerked back as if he'd slapped her and she narrowed her eyes. "You can't have your job back."

"I don't want it back. I don't . . ." He shook his head once, as if arguing with himself. Silencing his uncle's voice in his head. "I don't want it back. I know I can't convince you otherwise, but that man in the arena who pushed when he should have let go, that guy's not me."

She shook her head and he touched her cheek, shocking her into stillness. "And I will never forgive myself for bullying you."

"Stop." It was a whisper and a lame one, but he'd promised himself he would listen, so he dropped her hand and stepped away.

"And I'll never forget how good you felt in my arms."
He smiled, filled with remorse and fondness. "Little Victoria Baker, all grown up."

Her mouth fell open, her pink lips damp and full, the shadows of her mouth an invitation he couldn't believe he had to resist. But he did. He had to. He was going to. Maybe.

"Victoria!" Celeste's voice took a hammer to the moment and Victoria jumped away, wrapping that sweater around her chest like a suit of armor. Her arms were so stiff, she might as well have been holding swords.

"Goodbye, Victoria, and good luck."

"You . . . you too," she whispered just as Celeste cleared the far stall. He turned away and walked down the aisle of the barn for the last time.

chapter
10

Victoria shielded her eyes from the sun and the dust as she stood on the porch and watched Eli's truck and trailer drive away.

She was like a frontierswoman. A gritty, aproned widow getting rid of the bandit who had threatened her home and her life. All she needed was a shotgun and a bonnet. Perhaps a trusty hound.

Instead she had Celeste, who in Gucci sunglasses and a turquoise head scarf that fluttered in the breeze could never be mistaken for a frontierswoman. Or a hound.

But right now Victoria could feel Celeste vibrating, no doubt dying to read her some kind of riot act for the scene she'd walked in on in the barn.

Victoria didn't owe her any explanations, though, so she kept silent and tried to ignore the vibrations.

Celeste whipped her glasses off and glared at the side of Victoria's face. Victoria studied the flight pattern of a passing bird.

"I made a promise to myself a long time ago that I wouldn't change my life because some man hurt me or pissed me off. I spent a lot of years before that turning myself inside out for a man who didn't give a shit. I need to know you're not going into this spa idea because of your power struggle with Eli."

"I'm not."

"I suppose you had a good reason to fire him."

Victoria nodded, though the edges of her righteousness had slightly wilted under the heat of his eyes. The power of his regret.

"Did he ask for his job back?"

"No. In fact, he said he didn't want it back. That it was okay."

"Which is why it looked like you were about to kiss him when I walked in? You felt bad?"

"I didn't . . . I don't feel bad. And I wasn't about to kiss him." Celeste snorted and Victoria smiled, cradling the bizarre turn of events in her hands like a firefly. "He was about to kiss me."

"There's a difference?"

Victoria turned to look at one of the most beautiful women ever put on this earth. Everything about Celeste—her skin, her lips, the clear blue of her eyes, the taut curves of her body—was fine-tuned to inspire lust and envy. She would have no idea what it felt like to be plain and forgotten. Not that Victoria was using that as an excuse for having almost *let* him kiss her. *No.* In fact, she was going to have a very stern discussion with herself later today and then she was going to surgically remove the memory of his face, all taut with lustful indecision, from her brain.

"In my life, yes."

"Do you think he was sincere? Or was he angling to get his job back?"

That was a very real possibility that Victoria wasn't interested in exploring, so she said nothing. After a moment Celeste turned away, and both of them stared off into the rolling green distance, waiting for the future to arrive.

Celeste checked her watch just as a shiny black pickup truck approached, kicking up dust into the robin's-egg blue sky.

"Amy Turnbull," Celeste said. "Right on time. Do you remember her?"

"Barely," Victoria replied. She vaguely recalled someone with red hair, an unsmiling face, and the urgent air of a woman looking for an exit.

"This is going to be a disaster."

Yet bright sunlight rained down on the land, turning it into a postcard, something so lovely it actually seemed like a crime that she hadn't thought of turning it into a spa earlier.

"Let's see what she has to say," Celeste said.

The second Amy Turnbull stepped out of the truck Celeste knew two things: she was going to be perfect for the job, and Amy was still exactly the kind of woman she hated.

The kind who never panicked like a gerbil over the skin of her neck.

Just from looking at the fifty-five-year-old woman, Celeste knew Amy had never even thought of Botox. Certainly never whitened her teeth, or considered plastic surgery.

Amy still wore her red hair in a long braid down her back like a donkey's tail. Her heavily freckled skin was as fine-grained as porcelain and practically wrinkle-free. Celeste would lay down money that Amy didn't have a wand of mascara to her name.

Amy was plain, bordering on ugly, but *she didn't care*.

Every step across the gravel and grass from her truck to the front porch was loaded with authority. With ownership.

Confidence that had nothing to do with her looks.

Celeste put her sunglasses back on just so she could roll her eyes. Faking superiority always made her feel better.

"Hello, Celeste," Amy said, coming to stand at the foot of the porch steps.

"Amy." Celeste smiled and walked down the steps to shake her hand. "It's good to see you. You remember . . ." She stumbled slightly, as she always did when it came to introducing Victoria. *My husband's bastard child* just didn't roll off the tongue like it should, but neither did *my friend.*

"Hi," Victoria said, practically levitating off the steps to greet the architect. "I'm Victoria Schulman."

"Of course, I remember you running around here as a kid." Amy's stern face split quickly into a smile. "It's good to see you, Victoria."

Ruby hurtled out the front door and down the steps to wrap the redhead in a hug. Amy looked strangled, hugely uncomfortable with the affection. Celeste could sympathize. Ruby could be likened to an untrained dog in her enthusiastic greetings. Celeste was barely kind to Ruby, yet the woman still hugged her every morning. It was disconcerting.

"It's so good to see you, Amy," Ruby said, stepping back. Amy was all kinds of awkward, running a hand down the front of her blue button-down shirt, as if wiping away Ruby's enthusiasm.

This was the woman Celeste remembered. Reserved to the point of chilly.

"You too, Ruby," Amy said, unable to make eye contact. She glanced up toward the front door as if expecting someone else to come out.

Perhaps Victoria was right—hiring Amy was going to be a nightmare. Because she wasn't just here for the work. She was here for her son.

Amy cleared her throat. "Is . . . ah . . . is Eli—"

"He's not here," Victoria said. "And he doesn't know that you're here."

"He doesn't know?" Amy trailed off, the skin beneath

her freckles growing even paler. "Then how did you find me? How did you know about me being an architect?"

Ruby raised her hand.

"Of course." Amy sagged. "I sent you my graduation announcement. I had totally forgotten about that."

"I left it in the barn for Eli to see," Ruby said. "But he never said anything."

"No. I don't suppose he did."

Amy turned slightly, staring off in the direction of Eli's house. "I thought . . ." She stopped, then shook her head once, a rueful smile on her thin lips. It was painfully obvious that she'd thought Eli was behind her invitation to Crooked Creek.

As a mother deeply and profoundly in love with her own son, Celeste felt her heart twitch in sympathy.

"So why did you ask me here?" Amy looked like the Tin Man in *The Wizard of Oz,* rusted and unable to move.

"Because . . . you're a woman," Victoria said. "And you're a smart woman. And I think probably very good at your job."

"I am. But . . . he didn't tell you about me?"

"He hasn't said anything about you. Ever."

"Of course not," she whispered, revealing a bone-deep ache and a surprising anger.

"We'll understand if you want to leave," Victoria said.

"I already did that once, didn't I?" Amy said. Her eyes were razor sharp when she turned back to look at them. Committed.

Celeste liked that. Respected that. Perhaps Amy was here to make things right, a sentiment she understood.

She glanced quickly at Victoria, the girl she'd treated so poorly.

A car door slammed shut and Celeste turned back to Amy's truck in time to watch a tall man, wiry and lean, dressed in jeans and a gray T-shirt, hitch up his pants. A simple gesture, men getting out of trucks did it all the time, but for some reason her mouth went dry at the flash of a muscled stomach and thick, veiny wrists.

He slipped a pair of sunglasses off his tousled blond hair and put them over his blue eyes, which was a crime, because those eyes were staggering. Light blue like the heart of a glacier or a flame.

And then he smiled, a heartbreaker's smile.

Her heart, spellbound by his beauty, by the earthiness of his allure, missed a beat and then scrambled to catch up.

"This is Gavin Svenson, my contractor," Amy said, and Celeste, feeling like a dirty old woman, was grateful for her sunglasses, because her cheeks were aflame.

"Hello," he said, and his voice slipped through her clothes, stroked her skin, ruffled her feathers. "Nice to meet you."

More handshakes. She tried not to look directly at him, using her sunglasses and her natural aloofness to keep her distance. But her skin registered the rough calluses at the base of all his fingers, the warmth of his palm, and her body shook itself awake like a dog from a decade-long nap.

There was an awkward pause, the kind of quiet knit together from secrets and unsaid truths and awkward denials.

What, she wondered briefly, as they all seemed to take one another's measure, *are we getting ourselves into?*

"Let's see what you've got," Amy said, and Victoria clapped her hands, breaking the strange mood.

"I feel really bad about liking her," Victoria whispered, looking through the door into the dining room where Gavin and Amy had their heads bent over their own notes and a calculator.

"Why?" Celeste asked. "She didn't leave you."

"I know, but still . . ."

"Do you think Amy is good for the job?" Ruby asked.

Victoria was sick with nerves. On the one hand, she hadn't felt this since Jacob was born, this unbearable rightness. As if God had come down and stacked the cards in her favor for once.

"I think she's perfect," Victoria answered. "But what about Eli?"

"You fired him, remember?" Celeste said.

"I know, but hiring his *mom*? I feel so guilty."

"You feel guilty about everything," Celeste said. "I just hope we like their quote." Celeste drank her tea and very pointedly did not look at Amy or Gavin. She'd been cool for the past two hours while they walked around the property.

But Victoria had learned a little something about Celeste in the last month: the cooler she got, the more excited she was. A survival mechanism, for sure.

"She doesn't look much like Eli, does she?" Victoria asked.

"Not one bit." Celeste flipped through one of Ruby's cookbooks.

"She totally thought Eli was the one to suggest her. She probably thought she was going to come up here and have some kind of mother-and-son reunion. It about broke my heart when she found out it was Ruby."

"What are you going to tell Eli if she takes this job?" Ruby asked from the sink.

Victoria chewed on her lip and then upgraded to her thumbnail. Celeste pulled her hand away. Victoria put it back.

"Why do I have to tell him anything? He doesn't work here."

Ruby hummed slightly.

"You think that's awful?"

Celeste and Ruby nodded.

"Okay. It is awful. But what do I say? *Hey, Eli, sorry I fired you. Oh, and by the way, I've hired your mom to change the ranch you love into a spa?*"

"Something like that," Ruby said.

"I can't." Victoria put her head in her hands. "I can't. Hiring her is a total mistake."

Ruby pressed a hand to her arm. "Not for Amy," she said. "She's here for her son, you can tell. And it's about damn time she tried to make what she did right."

That brought Victoria's head up. "You think that makes it okay?"

Ruby nodded. Celeste shrugged. Good Lord, the woman was no help at all!

At the dining room table, Gavin lifted his head. Victoria felt her face catch fire, embarrassed that he'd heard her gossiping. But then he smiled and she blushed all over again, because the man was too gorgeous for words. A civilized Viking.

Gavin looked down and Victoria sighed, her stomach in knots. "Gavin's eyes are amazing, aren't they?"

"I hadn't noticed," Celeste said.

"Are you blind?"

"No." She turned past a picture of salmon on spinach. Ruby had made it last night with mixed results. "I just make a point of not ogling the help."

"You are such a snob."

But considering her chill factor, a snob with the ooh-la-la's for the handsome contractor. Very interesting.

Victoria turned away from the two at the table and leaned against the breakfast counter, looking out the window at the rolling hills past the house.

The truth was, Amy was perfect for this job and Victoria was ready to get started. The longer they waited, the more ridiculous this dream of hers felt. She needed action. And what if hiring Amy was a win/win for both of them? She got her spa and resort, and Amy and Eli got to make amends.

"If Amy takes the job, I'll tell Eli," she said.

"Good girl," Celeste murmured.

A chair squeaked over the hardwood in the dining room and Victoria spun back around, trying hard not to seem too eager. But this fit seemed right. Amy had been no-nonsense but imaginative. Her ideas blended with Victoria and Celeste's and when she disagreed, she made a point of explaining why. The two hours that had passed by while they looked over the house and property had felt like time spent with friends—that had to be worth something, didn't it?

"We're going to need to go over the numbers a little more," Amy said, flipping her long red braid over her shoulder as she stepped into the kitchen. "But we have a preliminary figure."

Victoria took a deep breath, bracing herself. "I can take it."

Amy and Gavin shared a smile. "Your initial budget is three quarters of a million, right?"

"Eight hundred and fifty thousand," Celeste corrected. "With a rolling monthly income of two thousand."

"Well, that will handle the demo, plumbing, electrical, and much of the new framing, but for the kind of finish that the two of you want for the spa—"

"Need," Victoria pointed out and then glanced over at Celeste, who nodded. "The finish is a pretty key part of the equation and we don't want to scrimp. We know our budget is short, but we don't know how much."

"That's what I gathered," Amy said. "And I agree, wholeheartedly. But you're going to need another half a million."

"Dollars?" Ruby gasped.

"At least," Gavin added.

Victoria was doing her best dying fish imitation and luckily Celeste stepped in.

"Thank you very much for coming out," she said while standing.

"That would mean me taking a huge cut on my end," Amy said quickly, as if sensing she was getting herded out the door. "You're not going to find someone who will do this job any cheaper."

"Or better," Gavin added.

"Why?" Victoria asked. "Why did you take a cut?"

Amy glanced around the kitchen, her freckles bright orange against her pale skin.

"I think . . . I think you probably know the answer to that."

Amy's eyes, green like her son's, watched Victoria with a look of defiance. And shame.

"Frankly, the situation with Eli is one of the draw-backs to hiring you," Victoria said. "It complicates everything."

"I want this job and you wouldn't have called me out here if you weren't interested in me," Amy said. "As for my relationship with Eli . . . well, if you hire us, I'll be the one to tell him. Not you. He deserves to hear it from me. And after that, if it's a problem, we'll discuss it."

"That . . ." Victoria glanced over at Celeste and Ruby. "That sounds reasonable."

"Of course it does." Amy slipped her glasses back into her shirt pocket. "I'll fax you my official quote tonight."

Amy left and, after an apologetic smile, Gavin fol-lowed.

"A half million?" Ruby asked in the stillness they'd left behind. "You're going to need my boob money."

Victoria shook her head. "You're doing enough, Ruby. I'm not taking your savings."

"I knew we didn't have enough," Celeste said. "I

mean, I was shocked by the cold numbers, but we want top-of-the-line fixtures. We want granite and oak and glass. And that's where the money starts to add up."

Ruby sighed. "How are we going to get that money?"

"Luc." Victoria shrugged. "We have to ask him."

"Not unless it's a last resort," Celeste said.

"Well, like you said, there's not a bank in the world that will lend me money."

"What about what's left of the cattle?" Celeste asked.

"I have no idea how much they're worth."

"And the six horses left in the barn?"

Victoria shrugged, totally clueless. They could have a fortune out there for all she knew.

"Sounds like you need to go talk to Eli and find out what he left us with."

chapter
11

The five o'clock sun was an oven, and the cotton of Eli's shirt stuck to the skin of his chest and back as if a bucket of water had been poured over his head. He untucked the hem and a hot breeze flew up over his body.

Soda snoozed in the shade of the barn, smart dog.

Eli had finished the last section of the fence on the far paddock and, rolling out the sore muscles of his shoulders, he opened the gate to the smaller paddock closer to the barn.

"Heeyah!" he yelled, waving his hat, inspiring Darling and Patience to kick up dust on the way into their new home. They gave the space a good run, and he was glad he'd added a few extra feet. The horses would appreciate it, and when it came time to break some ponies, this paddock would be the best place to do it.

Satisfied, starving, and dirtier than ten men, he ducked back into the barn and opened the tiny beat-up fridge he had set up there. He was planning on turning the barn into an office, but at the moment it only looked like a hardware store, filled with boxes of shingles, roofing hammers, and nails.

For a moment his shoulders, already tired and sore, dipped under the weight of all the work he still had to do, but he wanted to celebrate finishing the paddock, so he ignored the wood and nails and unfinished stall doors and grabbed a beer.

Back outside, he hooked his boot heel up on the fence he'd spent the better part of the day building and raised his bottle to Patience and Darling, who were drinking from the trough in the corner.

The beer was icy cold down his throat.

"Eli?"

He choked, snorting beer up through his nose, where it burned and made his eyes water.

"Victoria," he gasped, turning to face the last person in the world he'd expected to show up on his land. But there she was in the glittering end of daylight. Her pretty hair was pulled back in a ponytail and she wore jeans and a white T-shirt.

It seemed like a costume, as if she was trying on a new look, and for a moment he wanted to tell her how cute she was. "I didn't hear you drive up."

"I walked over."

He glanced down at her feet, expecting to see bloody stumps in those silly red shoes, but instead she wore a pair of beat-up tennis shoes.

"That's quite a walk," he muttered, taking in the sweat running down her neck, vanishing into the loose collar of her shirt. He imagined it traveling down the curve of her breast, vanishing into the lacy edge of a bra.

"Yeah. I had some things to think about. You . . . ah . . . got another one of those?" She pointed to the beer.

Am I suffering from heat stroke? he wondered. *A one-swallow-of-beer-induced hallucination?* Because there was no way Victoria Schulman was here in tennis shoes and a sweaty T-shirt asking for a beer.

"Eli?"

"Sure," he muttered. "Just a second."

The cool of the barn felt good on his hot body, and he pressed the cold bottle against his forehead before twisting off the cap and heading back out to face this strange incarnation of his nemesis.

"Thanks," she murmured. She took the beer from his hand and then rolled it across the bare skin of her neck and chest that was revealed by the deep V of her shirt.

Embarrassed by the sudden turn of his thoughts, he looked away when her nipples got hard and she closed her eyes with a sigh.

What the hell was going on?

"I haven't been here in years," she finally said, looking around. "I'd forgotten how pretty it was."

"Yeah, well, my family saved the best property." He shot her a sideways glance before taking another drink. "You can't have it."

"Are you . . . joking with me?" She blinked, wide-eyed, as if channeling a very strange Mae West.

"I'm drinking. Don't get used to it."

"You've done a lot of work."

"A lot of work needed to be done. Still does. But the horses have a place to run and sleep, so we're halfway there."

She turned and looked over his shoulder at the house, sitting squat and square. "The house looks great. So different from what I remember."

He nodded and took another sip.

"Remember the last time I was here?" Her eyes were bright, the memory clearly a good one in her books, which was surprising considering how beat up she got. "That day you were trying to teach me to jump. God, I was fifteen."

He pulled his hat down farther over his eyes, reluctant to waltz down memory lane. This was his first fine mood in a long time, and there was nothing like the past to put an end to it.

"It was a long time ago," she whispered, slowly picking at the gold foil edge of the beer bottle's label.

The woman practically bled feelings. She was an open wound of emotion. And usually he could ignore that shit better than horse manure, but that T-shirt, those sweaty bits of hair against the elegant length of her neck—they did him in.

"You were a fast learner," he muttered.

Her laugh was throaty. A different woman's laugh. And his blood responded, running thick through his veins. "That's not true. I was a good faller, maybe. An excellent fraidy-cat."

"You were game."

Those big blue eyes of hers blinked at him and then she straightened, preening under his faint praise. "Game," she repeated. "I'll take it."

Her throat bobbed as she drank, taking big swallows of the beer. He should have given her water; that beer would hit her hard.

"You out here all by yourself?" she asked.

He nodded.

"You don't . . . you don't get lonely?"

"Nope." He stared at her, his meaning more than clear, and she blushed and looked away. That would teach her to ask questions.

"What are you doing here?" he asked and she jerked, beer spilling over her lips.

"A girl can't be neighborly?" She wiped her lips with the sleeve of her shirt. It was like watching the queen pick her nose.

"Not when she fired that neighbor."

"Eli . . . I'm sorry things ended that way."

"You did the right thing. Don't ruin it by apologizing."

The sun dipped below the leafy tops of the cottonwoods and a breeze kicked up from the west, bringing some relief. He finished his beer, balancing the empty bottle on the fence, trying not to look at her.

"I asked around, and I'll sell you that equipment for ten thousand dollars."

"What?"

"That's fair."

"Yeah, if it wasn't at least five years old. I'll give you eight."

"You stuck your tongue down my throat, Eli."

He laughed at the balls on her, trying to blackmail him with that kiss. "You liked it, Tori." Her neck went red, her eyes wide, and he decided he liked that nickname. Tori. "We both know it. That horse is dead."

She looked as though she wanted to be offended, opened her mouth as if to give him the gears, but he arched an eyebrow at her.

"Fine, but you can have it tomorrow, if you want it. That has to count for something."

It did. And he had stuck his tongue down her throat, so he figured he owed her an extra thousand for that.

"Fine. Nine. And I'll pick it up in a couple weeks. I need to make some space in the barn."

She nodded, her hair blowing off her face, and he realized the pink of her cheeks wasn't just from the heat. She had a sunburn. It made her look young. Slightly irresponsible.

Weird how exciting that was to him.

"And the horses you left behind. I'm wondering if you want them? Two thousand a head."

He tilted his head back, smelling something fishy in the air. She was underselling those horses—not by much, but by enough to let him know she needed to sell. "I don't want them," he said, and then quickly reconsidered. "No, I'll take Lucky, for half that."

"Lucky?" she asked. "She's deaf. Those others are good horses."

"Geldings. Mares past their good bearing years. No good to me."

"Crap," she muttered. She braced her hands against the fence and hung her head for a second, the beer bottle dangling between her fingers.

Covered in dirt and sweat, looking slightly beaten by circumstance, he couldn't believe it, but she looked like a rancher. Like her father's daughter.

She looked, actually, like that fifteen-year-old who hadn't been able to jump a horse over a fence to save her life, but hell if she didn't always get right back up in the saddle.

He never should have doubted her.

"Tori—?"

"What's this 'Tori' business?"

"You need a nickname. Whose clothes are you wearing?"

She glanced down at her shirt and jeans as if surprised to see them on her body. "Mine. Why?"

"I've never seen you in jeans."

"My husband hated jeans."

"He's dead, isn't he?"

Her lips, so pink and damp from the beer, were surprisingly erotic. Particularly under those eyes that pierced right through his skin. The combination was deadly.

"Yes."

"Then I guess what he hated doesn't matter much anymore."

Her smile was all kinds of sad. "It's not that easy; the past has a way of sticking around. You know that."

That truth had driven him right up until Victoria had fired his ass. His past had slept with him and eaten with him. It had pushed him into being a man he couldn't stand to look at in the mirror—and that she somehow not only understood that, but had experienced it herself, made him light-headed.

Made him wonder if he was looking at a mirage, because this person beside him—in dusty clothes, sweat cooling on the pale skin of her neck and throat, her body relaxed against the fence he had built—this seemed to be the real her.

Or maybe he just wanted it to be.

"Besides, I couldn't walk over here in a skirt, could I?"

"No, you couldn't. Now, why don't you tell me what's going on?"

"I think it's pretty obvious. I need money."

"You've got those cattle. Fifty head will get you about fifty thousand dollars, give or take."

"That's not enough."

His eyes opened wide and he lifted his beer for another sip to hide his surprise, then swore when he remembered it was empty. "Fifty thousand is enough for a lot of things."

"I need five hundred thousand."

He whistled long and low. "Is this . . . is this about what your husband did? The Ponzi thing?"

She shook her head, staring up past the cottonwoods where the sky was turning blue with shadows. "I keep getting surprised when people know about that."

"Even we get the news way out here."

"It's not that . . ." She went back to fiddling with the label on her bottle. He remembered an old girlfriend telling him that peeling labels off beers was a sign of sexual frustration. He'd let her relieve that sexual tension back at her apartment in a very satisfying, gymnastically inclined way.

Maybe it was true, because he'd never seen a more sexually frustrated person in his life than Victoria Schulman. It would be fun . . . it would be a fucking privilege to relieve that frustration.

But that is not the point, Turnbull, he reminded himself, watching the woman wrestle with bigger demons than unrelieved horniness.

"After the initial storm wore off—the media left us alone and people no longer showed up on my doorstep to scream at me . . . actually, after we no longer had a doorstep anymore," she laughed sadly, "Jacob and I got out of New York, and everything—Joel, the Ponzi scheme, the suicide—all of it became so personal. It was just me. Alone. Trying to deal with it. Trying to protect Jacob from it. From all the things our friends were saying. Trying . . . trying to make it right."

"Friends?"

"Trust me, I use the term loosely."

"You shouldn't have had to take all that on alone. Your brother—"

"Was wonderful to us. He took us in. He came down here with me even though he hated the idea. I couldn't ask him to take on any more than that."

"But that's what family does."

"You really believe that?"

He thought of his parents, his Uncle John, who supported him only when he did what Uncle John wanted.

"I don't know," he said truthfully.

He wished he could touch her, ease some of that load she carried on the thin bones of her shoulders. But he didn't know how to do that, how to touch a woman without it being about sex. So he kept his hands to himself and listened as hard as he could. Ignoring his instincts.

"So if it's not about the Ponzi thing, what do you need that money for?"

She laughed. "I'll tell you, but . . . you're not going to like it."

"You're an authority on me?"

"I don't have to be an authority to know this is going to piss you off. Royally."

Not bothered in the slightest by her predictions, he grinned and leaned back against the fence. "I don't know, I'm in a pretty good mood these days. You better tell me and let me be the judge."

Victoria tilted her beer to her lips and took two big swallows, draining the bottle. She held it up so the amber glass caught the light.

"I'm going to need another one of these."

Eli was quite a host. He came back with two more beers, a hard-backed chair, a folded aluminum lounge chair, and a square packet wrapped in tinfoil. He set down the wooden chair, worn smooth from generations of bottoms, and kicked open the lounge chair, revealing three vinyl strips across the bottom that were torn through and a dead mouse carcass.

"I'm not sitting there," she told him.

He kicked the dead mouse away with his boot and settled himself down carefully into the chair's broken embrace.

They both held their breath, and when it didn't collapse, he grinned and handed her a beer, and then opened the tinfoil to reveal a gooey peanut butter and jelly sandwich. He tore it into two and handed her half. The larger half.

"What a sweetheart," Victoria laughed, sitting down in the wooden chair and stretching out her legs, sandwich and beer in hand.

The flash of his smile kick-started her heart and she had to look away, setting the sandwich down on her leg so she could open her beer.

She felt like a glutton, taking this hospitality while she

could, because he'd yank it all away if he knew she was thinking about hiring Amy. Hell, he'd probably yank it all away the second she told him about turning the ranch into a spa.

But she couldn't quite stop herself. It was as if Eli were someone else—not quite a stranger, but definitely not the man he'd been at the ranch these last few months.

Eli's half of the sandwich disappeared in two bites and as he chewed he tipped his hat back off his forehead and crossed his dirty boots at the ankle. In this big cowboy on a broken lawn lounger, she could finally see that boy she'd known. She could see his shyness and his valor.

"You seem . . . happy, Eli." She handed him her half of the sandwich and he accepted it with a nod, a grin that made her heart pound.

"You can't distract me, Tori. Tell me what's going on."

Victoria wished she didn't have to tell him what she was doing with the ranch. She wished this moment could just keep going, this camaraderie between them. The smile on his face that was warmer than the breeze rustling through the grasses past the paddock.

Ah well, she thought. *Might as well get it over with.*

"I'm turning the ranch into a luxury resort and spa."

He stared blank-faced at her and then howled with laughter. The chair listed sideways in the sand and he jerked his feet down onto the dirt to keep himself upright while he laughed his ass off.

"All right, all right," she muttered when he took off his hat and slapped his leg with it. "It's not that funny."

"A luxury *what*?"

"Spa and resort."

"Like massages?"

"Among other things."

"Then it is that funny. Have you lost your mind? That place is the ugliest . . ."

"The money is for the remodel."

He blinked at her. His smile faded into a thin-lipped frown and she watched as it all sunk in, his handsome face going dark.

"You're not joking."

She shook her head and braced herself for some name-calling. Some vicious finger-pointing. Part of her hoped for another brutal kiss, but she slipped a muzzle on that part.

Instead he stood. Paced for a moment, as if looking for a place to curl up and give birth to his fit. But then he braced his hands against the splintered wood of the fence and hung his head between them.

Staring at his ass was inappropriate. She totally knew that. But part of her wanted to write a letter of appreciation to the Wrangler Denim Company, because *honestly* . . .

Swearing, he kicked at the dirt, pushing up clouds of dust that blew back into her face.

Her back felt like it would break under the pressure. She wasn't going to change her mind, but she fully realized how much this had to hurt him. What a bitter pill this had to be to swallow.

"Eli—"

"I want to buy that land across the river," he said, gesturing toward the fields across the creek two hundred yards away.

"It's leased—"

"I'll hold the lease."

"That's not worth five hundred thousand dollars."

Finally, he turned, everything about him level. Straight. He wasn't going to lose his temper or call her names. Apparently, he was going to do business with her.

"I'm not offering you five hundred thousand. I'm offering you ten grand for the land across the river."

"I'll sell you more land."

"I don't want more land."

She gaped at him. "I thought . . . I thought getting back all the land was the whole point of your life."

"Not anymore. The acres across the river will do. I can grow my own hay crop after the lease runs out." He looked suddenly puzzled. "What are you thinking, Tori? A luxury resort and spa at the Crooked Creek does not have a snowball's chance in hell of being a success."

Her instinct was to stiffen. To cross her arms over her chest and sniff with disdain, to walk away with her head held high, to let him know that not only was he horribly misguided, but she also didn't care what he thought about her. And then, of course, she would stay awake all night wondering if maybe he was right.

Maybe it was the beer. Or the tight and foreign caress of her old blue jeans on her legs, or just possibly that she knew exactly how right she was and no man, particularly not this one, was going to convince her, even for a moment, otherwise. So, instead of getting affronted, she laughed. At him.

He bristled right up like a porcupine.

"I never pegged you for a resort and spa authority," she said.

"I'm not."

"Then how do you know?"

"Because it's a ranch!"

"Not anymore. Remember? You took care of that."

Victoria had never been in touch with her feminine power. She wasn't one for wiles. Had no idea how to be provocative. But a hot electrical power filled her, from her feet through her legs and belly, centering in her breast.

Slowly, she stood and as if he could see the change in her, the power she was generating, his Adam's apple bobbed, and his arms flexed under the rolled-up sleeves of his gray shirt as he made fists with his hands.

The muscles in his forearms corded up, the veins standing out against the skin, and there was a small explosion in her belly at the sight. He was such a man. Big and dirty. Strong. Raw. And he spoke to the untapped domain of her womanhood. Fireworks of desire shimmered through her body as she stepped toward him.

"I happen to be an authority, Eli. And I can tell you without a shadow of a doubt that this resort will be a success. As long as I can get the money to have it done right."

"Why?" he asked as currents ran between them, slowly building speed and strength until the world fell away and it was just them in the twilight with this unreasonable connection. "Convince me."

"This land is beautiful. Wild and raw. Dynamic. Virile, in a way." She was close, too close probably, but she'd been pushed here by a wind she didn't want to fight. And she could see his heart pounding hard under a quarter-sized bit of skin in his brown neck. She wanted to lick him. Taste the skin over his blood.

"And women like that sort of thing, but from a safe distance. Behind glass. Under control." Yes. Oh Lord, yes. She wanted to control this wild, virile man in front of her. "They want to experience something unpredictable, while being cared for. While being petted and stroked and made to feel beautiful and womanly."

He blinked. "You're . . . you're talking about a spa, right?"

No! she wanted to scream. *I'm talking about sex! Wild, crazy sex. With you!*

"The Crooked Creek Ranch will offer the best of both

worlds. The luxurious and the rustic, in one beautiful place. Celeste is on board. Ruby will be the chef. We're interviewing architects. It's going to be a success."

His smile was crooked and charming. "Sounds like you've got yourself a vision. A crazy one, but a vision nonetheless." She nodded, oddly proud of herself. It was a new emotion for her, and it threw her off balance. "Good for you, Tori. I mean it."

Ah, hell, now she felt like crying.

He took off his hat and slung it over the fence post. His brown hair was matted down with sweat and he pushed his hands through it, making it stand up. It should have made him look ridiculous. It should have poured a big old bucket of cold water on those fires between her legs, but instead she just wanted to run her hands through his hair, cup his head in her hands, hold him still while she kissed him the way he'd kissed her.

If she were another kind of woman she might have hugged him, just put her arms around him and let him take it from there. But she wasn't another kind of woman, she was Victoria Schulman, and she was never sure of her welcome. Never sure if reaching out would get her slapped in the face. And this man . . . he had plenty of reasons to slap her in the face. She'd fired him, after all, from the only job he'd ever had.

Eli licked his lips, his green eyes glowing in the growing twilight. Her skin expanded, every inch aware of his gaze. His proximity, the delicious nearness of him.

"Is that the only reason you came here?"

She knew what he was asking. Her heart pounded in her chest, but she couldn't make herself respond. Owning this moment, her own desire, was too much and she wanted—needed—him to push her into it. To convince her she was safe.

"You want me to kiss you again, Tori?"

Say something, she urged her dumb lips, her stupid brain. But she was drunk off two beers and him. Off the twilight and the fit of the jeans and the breeze that teased her nipples.

"I know you do, Tori. I can see it."

She crossed her arms over her chest, embarrassed by her body's wantonness.

His lip lifted in a smile that was so sexy her clothes nearly burned off. He was every matinee idol who got paid too much money to be pretty. He was every muscle-bound construction worker who'd never whistled at her. Every cool coffee barista who flirted with all the other women at Starbucks but never her. He was Eli Turnbull, whom she'd thought wicked, salacious, debauched thoughts about while touching herself.

"It's in your eyes." He reached for her. "It's right here."

His rough fingers grazed the skin of her neck, and she gasped as his touch ricocheted through her, pinging off skin and bone, muscle and blood, until her body was lit up like a pinball machine.

"Yes." Her voice was a dry gasp, so she tried again, louder. "Yes." Too loud. She wasn't at a political rally. "I want you to kiss me."

The silence burned and sizzled. "I botched it last time," he said.

"It's forgiven. Well, maybe not forgiven. You were out of line, but—"

"You liked it. It felt good, didn't it, to be forced to feel something. To be out of control."

How was it possible he wasn't touching her? His words were making her crazy, her body climbing toward climax as if he had his hand down her pants. She was past putting words together—her hands were locked around her body so she wouldn't go flying apart into the heavens—so she nodded. Willing him to take it from there. To make her feel something again. More, this time. To not leave her to finish it on her own.

"If you want that again"—he ducked slightly, looking right into her eyes—"you have to kiss me. I won't . . . I won't bully you again. And I have to know we're on the same page."

Now, that was something of a cold shower. Her arms dropped to her sides.

"If that's too much for you to own up to, Victoria, then you should head on back home. Because I can't always be the bad guy so you don't have to admit you like getting dirty."

He had her pegged, right down to her cowardly underwear.

"How do I know this isn't a trick?" she asked, swallowing what little was left of her pride. "To get back at me for firing you?"

His heart broke for her, it really did. She was beautiful and she had no idea.

And at the same time he wished he had ten minutes alone in a room with her husband before the coward had taken the easy way out.

"Look at me, Victoria," he breathed, his arms at his sides, his erection pushing hard against the zipper of his jeans. She had to be blind or innocent not to see how his body was reacting to her.

Her dropped-jaw look of astonishment, the way her eyes darted from his crotch to the sky over his head, would have made him laugh if he wasn't sure it would run her off.

"Trust me. Hell, trust yourself. You're beautiful. You're sexy. And I want you like crazy. But . . . I have to know—"

She launched herself against him, her arms around his neck, her legs around his waist. Her sweet little tongue in his mouth.

He laughed before pushing his hands into her hair, holding her still for his kiss, but she wasn't having any of that. There was no holding this woman still; he fell back against the fence, groaning when the sweet balance of her weight fell against his erection. He arched back hard into her and she gasped.

He'd never been kissed like this, like he was water and she was dying of thirst, and he felt control slipping from between his fingers.

"Tori," he breathed, bending his knees slightly to take her weight so he could slide his hand between them, over the curve of her breast. She shuddered against him, her nipple hard in his fingers, a pebble he rolled with his thumb and forefinger, and she stopped devouring him for long enough to cry out against his lips.

The T-shirt she wore was a curse, fighting him as he tried to get beneath it to the smooth, hot silk of her skin. He couldn't get any leverage. Couldn't hold her and touch her and kiss her all at the same time.

He pulled back.

"No." She kissed him again and he went with it, because she felt so good against him. But then the need to touch her made him crazy again and he lifted her away.

"We need to . . ." He shook his head, distracted by her pink lips, the cloudy look in her sapphire eyes.

"Go inside."

Yes! His body roared. *Inside!* But his head was a little confused. A few steps behind. For some reason, he felt like he should argue.

"Are you . . . sure?"

Looping her arms around his neck, she smiled at him. "You have no idea how sure I am. Hurry, Eli. Before this feeling goes away."

He kept his eyes open as she kissed him, looking past her hair as he walked toward the barn, praying for a total lack of gopher holes.

This was some kind of luck, having Victoria Schulman in his arms, ready to sell him the land across the lake. And he wasn't a man used to luck. Happiness put an edge on his desire, made it raw and sharp. Painful almost, cutting and hacking at his control.

His boots scraped on the stone floor of the stable and his eyes were slow to adjust to the sudden darkness. He tripped, righted himself, and turned left to the would-be office, so that he could put her down on the mini-fridge.

"You better have a condom in here," she whispered into his ear before taking the lobe in her teeth.

"Damn it." He didn't lift her, just grabbed her hand and pulled her off the fridge and through the stable toward his truck.

"What . . . ?" She stopped and pointed at the house. "I don't want to drive anywhere."

"Condoms are in my truck." Her eyebrows rose. "It's . . ." The back of his neck itched, his skin shrank down to nothing. "I don't have women at my house."

"So you have them in your truck?" she squealed, pulling against his hand. "You are totally emotionally stunted."

"So?"

This was him. And he couldn't change it and didn't want to.

"That's so hot to me."

She took off for the truck and he had to jog to keep up with her.

"You're a little messed up, aren't you?" he asked, and she laughed.

"You have no idea." She yanked open the passenger-seat door and hoisted herself inside, and he ran a hand over the curve of her ass as she climbed in.

"You should wear jeans more often," he murmured, admiring her curves. Admiring everything about her—the way her hair poured over her shoulder like a night sky, the way her eyes lit up like stars. The way her smile turned her into a siren.

"And you should get in here."

chapter

12

This was her, Victoria Schulman, acting the vixen and she couldn't believe it. Couldn't believe how much fun it was. How liberating. This was something that happened to other people. Sex in a truck.

She licked her lips and he was on her so fast it was like being hit by a linebacker. A train. He filled the cab, pushing her into the fabric and vinyl of the seat. And she loved it. She loved it so much she laughed as he kissed her. She purred and groaned as he slid his hands up under her shirt, pulling it over her head.

She'd gained some weight and most of it had gone into her breasts and she was very aware of how nice they looked in her white demi-bra. Perhaps, subconsciously, she had picked that bra when she was getting ready to walk over here. But she was happy that he seemed to agree, cupping her breasts with his hands, licking the upper curves.

Oh Lord, the scruff on his chin scratched her soft skin, and it was so ridiculously manly. So carnal, she felt heat and moisture pool between her legs. Sweat gathered under her hair and she wondered, with a giddy thrill, if they were going to steam up the windows.

"Do you want to go inside?" He stared down at her breasts as if he were asking them the question.

"No . . . ahh!" He bit her nipples. Through her bra. And then he sucked. Hard. And it was as if there were coils between her breasts and her brain and the deep ache between her legs. And as he sucked her those coils glowed red hot.

I'm going to come, she thought, lost in this storm. *Like this.* Right now, if only she could open her legs so he could rest that wonderful erection against her. That was all she needed, something hard . . . right there.

But he was heavy and she couldn't move, and a sob rose in her throat.

"Come on, Eli," she whispered and he leaned up, resting his weight on his elbows by her ears.

The smile on his face made her nervous.

"You need a second?" he asked, blowing a little kiss against the corner of her lips. Struggling, she turned, tried to lure him in for another one of those long, slow soul kisses the man was so wickedly good at. But he was elusive. An elusive devil.

"You want to slow down?"

"No."

"Ah, speed up?"

"Yes." He didn't do anything. Just stared down at her and she lifted her head to try to kiss him, and when he dodged her she chomped her teeth at him.

His low laughter rumbled against her chest.

Fine, she thought and slid her hand between them, until the hard length of him beneath his jeans was in her hand. He groaned, pushing that erection into her palm.

She squeezed, licked her lips, and he groaned, resting his forehead against hers. "Maybe I need a second," he whispered.

"No!"

All of the sex she'd had over the years—not all that much, but enough—had been on her husband's schedule. Joel had even decided when they should get pregnant, coming to her like clockwork in the middle of her cycle. How many times had she wished he would linger, taking a minute to make sure she was ready, or that she was having a good time.

All of those little disappointments and missed opportunities, they all coalesced into a selfish need to have this now. Her way.

Her fingers undid his fly and slipped into his briefs until she felt his skin, so hot, so soft against hers. The spongy head of his penis jerked against her touch and she felt the small beads of moisture leaking from him.

"Now."

He swore under his breath, pulling something from the glove box, while she tortured both of them with her hands down his pants, tracing the fragile veins, finding the heavy sac, the wiry pubic hair. Thrilling in all of it. Delighting in him.

Roughly, he pushed her hands away, shoved his jeans past his hips, and rolled the condom down.

All of her fantasies crowded her brain, clamoring to be chosen, and she opened her mouth to tell him she wanted to be taken from behind. She'd always thought that would be so sexy, but he, red-faced and barely in control, pushed her legs apart, lifting her thighs around his hips.

"You want this?"

She nodded, speechless from the look of him, the wildness of him. Her body rushed to prepare a welcome as he jerked her pants down one leg. She tried to help him, kicking off her shoes, but he didn't need much help. He was pretty much a one-man sex machine. The windows were past foggy and the smell in the cab was decidedly earthy.

He licked his hand—oh, so vulgar—and touched her core, his fingers slipping across her wet, hot flesh. He groaned like a man on the rack and then, before she could prepare herself, he thrust inside her.

She screamed.

"Oh God, tell me that's a good scream." He rested his slippery, sweaty forehead against her breasts. He kissed one nipple, licked it, panting against her skin.

"So good." She wiggled her hips, urging him. "Please. I'm so close. I'm so—"

Those eyes of his were magnetic and she could only stare at him, into him, while he slowly slid out of her and then thrust back in. Harder than before. She could feel him in the back of her throat.

"Eli—"

"Shhhh."

The truck was so small, a cocoon. He couldn't move far, but he shifted his hips, thrusting forward and easing back in a slow grinding rhythm that her body adored. Her body ate it up.

He cupped her head in his hands, his fingers pulling at her hair, the pain an ecstatic counterpoint to the pleasure of her body. His thumbs touched her lips and she opened her teeth to taste him, the salty pad of his thumb, her tongue exploring the coarseness of his skin.

"Suck," he breathed.

Her body contracted at the word, the look in his eyes, so feral. Clinging to control, she opened her mouth to let him in.

He growled his pleasure, his approval.

Her body was waking up to every single difference between imagining this man between her legs and the raw reality, between the lonely pleasure she brought herself and the wilderness he was driving her toward. And then, as if she weren't feeling enough, he leaned down and in time with his next thrust, pulled her nipple into his mouth.

She exploded. A thousand pieces of Victoria Schulman, like a thousand points of light, ricocheted around the cab of that truck. Her fingernails sank deep into the flesh of his hips as if she had to hold on to him or she'd lose herself in all this pleasure.

The intensity faded and reality returned in the scratch of the fabric beneath her back, the ends of Eli's hair dripping sweat down onto her cheek. The heavy rasp of his breath, the pounding of his heart against her chest.

"You all right?" he asked and she grinned up at him, so alive with pleasure, so alive with . . . life, she could barely stand it.

But the hunger wasn't gone and she was thrilled to still want him, to still feel him hard inside of her. This was her chance to live out every fantasy she'd ever had. He was going to be her own personal boy toy.

She pushed her hands against his shoulders, shifting her hips to settle him deeper. "Let's try—"

"Can't. Oh. God. Can't. Next time." He slipped his hands under her back, curling his palms over her shoulders, holding her in place while he thrust fast and hard into her body.

Surprised, she braced her hand over her head so she wouldn't get pushed right into the door. Her lingering pleasure got squashed and while he shook over her, she could only lie there and stare at those foggy windows.

Missionary position. Her mood turned slightly sour, her pleasure dimming as shades of her former life crept in.

He groaned against her neck, sucking the skin there, and she pulled away, irritated that she would have to explain a hickey to Celeste.

And that earthy smell was . . . well, it was a little gross now.

She knew in her heart she was being miserly. She'd had that beautiful orgasm. In a truck, of all things! This was the raunchiest thing she'd ever done. It wasn't his fault she expected some boy-toy antics. He didn't know.

But she couldn't, in the heart of her cooling body, say she wasn't just a little . . . disappointed.

He lifted himself away from her and she smiled brightly at him, which must have tipped him off because his eyes narrowed.

"What?" he asked.

"Nothing. That was great." She nodded. "Gold star."

"Gold . . . *what?*" He heaved himself to the other side of the truck and she moved her feet just in time so he didn't get a toe up the bum. She watched, dry-mouthed, as he pulled the condom off and tied a knot in the end.

"Tidy," she said in asinine approval.

With a long, slow breath, he pushed his longish hair back and closed his eyes. He still wore his shirt. After all that, she hadn't seen him totally naked. Disappointing.

While he seemed to take a little nap, she curled her legs up against her chest. Without taking her eyes off him, she searched around her ankle for her underwear and jeans and then slipped both up her body.

He didn't stir, and biting her lip, she tilted her head to get a better look inside the gap in his jeans, where she could barely see his penis slouched against his leg.

She wanted to put it in her mouth.

Joel had loved that in the beginning, but then as time went on, it seemed unnecessary. A too-fancy accessory on a sparse event. And as he was increasingly reluctant to reciprocate, she withheld it as some kind of power maneuver he never seemed aware of.

But this man, she wanted to lick. She wanted to suck and kiss and find all those places on his body that made him shake and groan.

He lifted his hips, pulling his pants all the way up, and she jerked her eyes away, only to find him watching her.

"Gold star?"

A blush ignited in her cheeks and, awkward to the extreme, she shrugged and looked away, fumbling with the door handle. "I should go. My son—"

He put his hand over hers, rough and slightly clammy.

She resisted the urge to curl her fingers around his, guide those fingers to the small ache that lingered between her legs.

"You should explain what's going on in your head."

"Nothing. Honestly. That was great."

He nodded sagely. "It was. But you seem . . ."

"Disappointed."

"What?" he howled, yanking his hand away.

"You asked!" she cried right back.

"I thought you were going to say uncomfortable, or maybe overwhelmed . . ."

"I'm sorry. I am. I'm totally overwhelmed. Let's just forget it—"

"Disappointed? You're kidding, right?" He shifted sideways on the seat and pulled down the back of his jeans, revealing red scratches on his back. Red scratches she had put there. With her fingernails. "You did this to me."

He hitched up his pants, flipping his shirt down like an affronted debutante. "You came, Victoria. I know you did. Unless you faked it." He seemed oddly wounded at the thought and she put her hand against his shoulder.

His hot, hard shoulder.

The skin was smooth under that shirt, she could tell. The muscles like a boulder against her fingers.

"Tori?"

"I didn't fake it. I swear. And yes, I came. I really did. It was great. I just . . . I just . . . wanted something more. Something . . ." *wicked, raunchy, dirty.* "Different."

"Like what?"

All those years of swallowing her preferences and inclinations came back to muzzle her, to crush her with humiliation. Praying he would understand, she shook her head.

But he just kept watching her. Waiting. This man who made her scream. Who made her crazy.

"Tori, we can sit here all night."

Oh. It was so hot in the truck. Like a sauna. That smelled like sex. And latex. This was ugly. Not exciting at all. And her body prickled with embarrassment at the desire that still smoldered in her belly.

And she knew, right now, if she didn't own up to how she was feeling, she would be the one in the wrong. She would be the one pushing aside everything she wanted for no good reason. Just because she was embarrassed. Because she didn't know how to ask for what she wanted.

She didn't want to be that woman anymore. Couldn't stand to be her anymore.

There was a crack in the vinyl under her leg and she dug her finger into the foam, concentrating on that instead of on him, so that she could force the words out.

"I want . . . I want to have sex against a wall. They do it in movies all the time."

"Okay."

His easy acceptance kicked open the door. Everything she'd been denied, everything she'd denied herself. It all came roaring out.

"Yeah. And maybe . . . maybe I want to be tied up. What's wrong with that?"

"Not a thing. I got rope in the barn."

"And you. I want to tie you up."

"We can discuss that."

"And I want you to talk dirty to me."

"I think I can come up with something."

"And I want to watch porn. Real porn. Not that HBO stuff. And oral sex. Not just for you. Me too."

That made him blink, and her brain was cold with all that she'd revealed and she felt more naked than she'd ever been. Her marriage had never seemed more lonely than right now. And she'd never been more ashamed of the fact that she'd been too scared to ask her husband for what she wanted, but she could ask this man, a total stranger, for the fulfillment of her most ridiculous fantasies.

The corner of his lips lifted in a knowing masculine smile that made every girlish impulse and instinct in her body scream as if The Beatles were coming to town.

"Is that all?"

"For . . . for the moment. I guess." She wasn't going to bring up the costumes.

"I should have known," he said as he opened the glove box and took out the box of condoms. He tore off one packet and then, as if having second thoughts, took the whole box and shoved them in his hip pocket.

"Known what?"

When he stepped down from the truck he circled her waist with his hands, keeping her close. There was a delicious threat in the air, a terrible danger. She pushed away from him, scrambling backwards, but he put his hands on her knees and held her close.

"You are insatiable."

He stepped closer, the snaps on his shirt touching her breasts, her nipples, and she shied away, her body twitching with delight.

Before she knew what he was doing, he'd crouched and put his shoulder in her stomach and then stood, letting her dangle down his back.

"What the hell, Eli!"

"Shut up, Tori." He swatted her butt, not hard, but hard enough that the sparks came back.

Spanking. She needed to add that to the list.

The dark thrill ignited her blood as her body bounced against his, his big, hot palm cupped around her inner thigh, his fingers cozied up between her legs.

Oh, she thought, grinning against his back. *This is going to be good.*

* * *

Eli kicked open doors and stomped across the floor until he got to his bathroom, then set her down on the white floor he'd retiled last winter.

"Take off your clothes," he said. The snaps on his own shirt came apart with loud popping sounds. He pushed open the sliding glass door to his shower and cranked the hot water.

Her face was red from being upside down, and he guessed a pretty good dose of embarrassment. Victoria Baker—he was going to stop thinking about her married name, because clearly her husband had been a prude and an idiot in addition to being a coward and a thief—had told him she wanted to be tied up.

He still couldn't believe it.

"What . . . what are we doing?" she asked, pushing her hair off her face and behind her delicate ears. She looked so young when she did that.

"Well, before I go get that rope, I need to take a shower. And I figure having sex in the shower might be on that list of yours." She stared at him as if he were speaking Japanese and his heart thumped against his rib cage. His whole body filled with affection and lust and laughter. This woman was powerful medicine and she had no idea.

"Are you making fun of me?"

He checked the water and adjusted the cold dial. "Nope."

Out of the corner of his eye he watched her chew her lip and he held his breath, wondering if she would believe him and believe in herself, but then, much to his delight, she tucked her little hands into the hem of her white T-shirt and yanked it over her head.

She was still skinny, but not nearly as bony as she'd been before. Her breasts were full, rising over the top of that pretty bra she wore, and her hips, once she shucked her pants, were soft and womanly. Her legs were long.

Her skin was white as moonlight and it looked unbelievably lovely against the black cloud of her hair.

"I thought you didn't bring women into your house."

"I don't."

"So . . . what's this?"

"Probably a mistake."

"You think?" She laughed, which made him feel better—at least they were both going into this knowing it was going to cause problems.

Because having her in his home made him want to climb out of his skin. And would no doubt bother him even more tomorrow when this fever wore off. The distance he kept between himself and the whole wide world had shrunk down to the space of this bathroom, and tomorrow he'd want that distance back.

Right now, he could feel her eyes on the bathroom tiles, the stained-glass lights. His toothbrush! His skin itched, but he hoped that if he touched her, the itch would go away. At least for the night.

"I'm probably going to have to blindfold you." He pulled down his pants and he heard her sweet gasp.

She made him feel like some kind of love god, just for having a semi-hard dick.

Steam pooled around his ankles from the open shower and he turned, holding out his arm so she could go first, and after a small hesitation, bracing herself for stepping into the unknown, she walked into the shower.

And wouldn't you know it, beneath those ugly skirts, Victoria had a beautiful ass. She started to turn, but he stepped in behind her, crowding her against the tile wall. When his chest pressed against her back she sighed and arched, the tender skin of her hips meeting the hard length of his penis.

The water pouring down over their heads made her sleek and slick, an extra pleasure to touch, so he reached his hands around to cup her breasts, toy with her nipples.

He stepped back and grabbed his penis with his hand, pushing it down so that when he stepped back against her it slid in tight against the heat between her legs. Her sharp cry of pleasure when he hit her clitoris echoed around the steamy white tiles.

The control he'd counted on while bringing her in here seemed impossible now. She was so hot to touch, so soft and sleek, and it was all he could do to hold on.

But she wanted something dirty. Something more exotic than the vanilla she'd been eating with her husband.

Smiling, he slid his hands from her breasts to her hips, where he showed her the rhythm he wanted her to use to pleasure herself.

He should have known she'd be a quick learner. Instantly, she spread her hands wider against the tiles, curling up harder against him, squeezing him between her legs every time she shifted her hips forward.

And despite having come in the truck, he felt the excitement build faster than he'd intended and he stepped away, panting, his skin as hot as the water hitting his chest.

"You've got to be kidding," she cried, turning to face him, her eyes dark with pleasure, her lips wet. Water slid down over her white breasts, gathered at her pink nipples.

For a moment he was struck dumb by his luck.

Taking advantage, her fingers curled around the rigid length of him, the water an electric lubricant as she pumped her fist. And then, because apparently after years of ignoring him God had decided to make him the luckiest man on earth, Victoria began to drop to her knees, in front of him.

"No. No." He pulled her back up, shaking his head.

"Now I know you're kidding," she murmured, leaning forward to kiss his neck. "I may not know much about sex, but even my husband liked this."

"I like it," he told her, and shifted her around so that the water hit his back and she was pressed up against the far wall. "But I gotta make up for disappointing you in the truck."

"Eli, that . . . you didn't . . ."

He gave her a little push against the tiled wall, which he knew she liked because underneath that prim exterior lay a total deviant, and then he fell to his knees in front of her. Which he would pay for in the morning, but the scent of her perfumed the steam around his head and right now he would kneel on rocks for this woman. His hands slid from her knees to her hips, finding the muscles and riding the edges with his thumbs as he slowly pressed them open. Farther, until the sable cloud between her legs parted and he saw the delicate pink of her sex.

She was panting, her rib cage lifting and falling in tiny increments, the skin of her belly and neck turning red. Her breasts trembled, those nipples so pink and hard.

But still he waited, gathering the tattered edges of his control.

"What?" she breathed and licked her lips, staring up at the ceiling. "Is . . . is there a problem?"

For the first time in his life, the answer was unequivocally no.

"Shush," he whispered. Kissing the skin of her belly, licking the small rise of her hip bone, he settled himself at the lush, perfumed heart of her. "Let me redeem myself."

chapter
13

Eli stared at the moonlight stretching across the floor of his room and listened to Victoria scurrying around, gathering her things.

There was a thump and a squeak. She swore like a sailor, and he could feel her eyes on him, gauging his stillness to see if she'd woken him up with her noise.

He sighed and shifted, pretending to still be in a sex-induced coma. But the truth was he'd been awake since the moment she'd toppled off his body and curled up along his side.

For an hour she'd dozed against him, her little snores fanning his chest, giving him goose bumps in the cool darkness, and he'd stared up at the ceiling and counted the minutes until the regrets crept back, like hungry dogs around his back door, bringing with them the long, slow suffocation that came from being with another person.

It hadn't taken very long. His arm fell asleep under her head. And his stomach growled. For a second she'd stirred, and he'd panicked at the thought of having to make some food for them. The image of her in his kitchen wearing one of his T-shirts made his blood run cold.

What would they talk about? Cows? Sex? The weather?

They had nothing in common. She was from the city, wore silly shirts, and had a son. He was a cowboy with a penchant for do-it-yourself home repairs and horses.

This was why dates ended in his truck. Or at some girl's house.

Because he hated having people in his home. He hated their eyes on his things. Making assumptions and answering questions about him they had no business even asking.

Women in particular seemed to like to make a game of him. Reading things into his silences that just weren't there. Practically guaranteeing their own disappointment.

But then Victoria had snuffled awake and her panic had filled the room with an icy chill. After a long moment, she'd snuck out of his bed, and that suited him just fine.

And now it looked like she was going to sneak out of his house too, and that was like a dream come true. The warm sheets curled around him and he let his fake sleep melt into something real.

Crap. She walked here.

His eyes popped open and he stared up at the ceiling. There was no way he could let her walk home. In the dark. At ten o'clock at night.

Could he?

Of course not. There were coyotes out there. She'd freak out and get lost, and then that would be on his conscience, too.

The toilet in the bathroom flushed and he heard her slip into the bedroom. In the shadows, she clutched her tennis shoes to her chest. It was painfully obvious in the bend of her shoulders that she'd never done this before, the walk of shame, and he didn't know how to take the sting out.

"I'll take you home." She jumped at the sound of his voice, too loud in the silence. He dragged a clean shirt and pair of jeans from his dresser and pulled them on over his tired and sore body.

She was small in the corner, her tiny white face peeking out of the cloud of black hair.

"Thanks," she murmured. He nodded as he walked past her, unable to control his discomfort. "This the part where you blindfold me?"

He stared at her, memorizing the messy details of her.

How do I tell you I don't know how to do this? How do I tell you how much I regret having you here and how much I want to do it again?

But saying that would be all kinds of stupid.

And that smile on her face, it slowly faded away. Faded to pained self-awareness.

And he couldn't make that right either.

So he walked past her, putting the night behind him.

Once they were in the truck, bouncing up the road to the ranch house, he didn't try to make it easier. Didn't bother to fill the silence with inane chatter, and he appreciated that she didn't either.

For two people who had engaged in wild monkey sex, the silence was very uncomfortable, just as God intended.

At the top of the last rise, the house appeared, all lit up like part of the Statue of Liberty's crown smashed on top of a box with two strange, snaky arms.

Victoria was delusional. No amount of money was going to make that place look good.

"It sure is ugly, isn't it?" she said.

"I hope you have a good architect."

She watched him for a moment, the glow from the house cutting patchwork across her face. Her blue eyes were unreadable.

"Me too," she finally said, looking away.

He parked in the shadows at the edge of the light in the parking area.

"Hey, Eli?"

The longing to bang his head against the steering wheel was profound.

"Do you know where your mother is?"

His head jerked sideways. "What? Why?"

"I'm just . . . wondering."

"No. God. She left when I was eight. I haven't heard from her since."

She nodded and the silence was so thick, so terrible, that he wanted to open her door and push her out. *This was the punishment he deserved for bringing her into his home. This shit was what happened when you let a woman sleep in your bed.*

"Thank you," she murmured. "For the ride."

He nodded, and his neck burned and his throat ached.

Her swallow was audible and he stared out the front window, wishing he knew how to be casual about this. Wishing he knew how to be relaxed.

"This . . . this is it?" she asked.

"What else do you want?" He sounded harsh. Mean, even, cruel after everything that had happened in the truck and shower and finally in his bedroom. But in a way, he was asking. If she told him, he might have a shot at giving it to her.

"I don't know. I've never done this before."

His shoulders slumped and he reached for a well-worn classic. "I had a good time."

She practically lunged across the seat, her lips a dry little punch to his cheek. "Me too. Thanks for the dirty stuff," she whispered, and then was gone.

He watched her bound up the stairs to the front door without once looking back, which suited him fine, because he was sitting there with a dumb-ass grin on his face that no one needed to see.

* * *

Victoria leaned against the door, her heart hammering in her chest. It had been hammering for hours. She felt like she'd run a marathon. A sex marathon.

There could be no question that Eli Turnbull was a jerk. Emotionally stunted wasn't even the half of it. He was wound so tight it was amazing his head hadn't popped off.

Good in the sack, though. Very, very good in the sack. And shower. And truck.

She giggled, lifting a hand to her lips to hold in the sound.

His cool dismissal, the casual cruelty of his goodbye, was stinging and awful in one light, but a blessing in another.

She didn't have any guilt about hiring his mother. She was right back to owing him nothing.

"Look what the cat dragged in." Ruby stepped into the hallway, carrying a Spanish romance novel and wearing a pair of turquoise rhinestone reading glasses that made her look like a cartoon cat.

"Jacob—"

"Celeste started reading him *Harry Potter* and they both fell asleep in his room."

Victoria blinked. "Celeste?"

"Said she'd been wanting to read it to him for a while."

"Jacob?"

"Am I not speaking English?"

"Sorry. That's just . . . surprising."

"Not really; the woman is crazy for the boy."

"*Celeste?*"

"You," she waved her hands around her head. "You are too busy lusting after Eli to notice."

Well, that did seem familiar. She was going to have to pay better attention. Now that the lust had been dealt with.

In fact, now that the lust had been dealt with, a lot of things were clearer.

"Did the fax come in?" she asked and Ruby nodded, pulling a piece of paper off the hall table against the wall.

It was the quote, broken down but not any different from what they'd expected. Even with the money that would come in from selling Eli the land across the river, they were still short. Celeste was going to have to call Luc. She wouldn't like it, but she'd do it.

"I'm going to call Amy Turnbull tomorrow to tell her to start demolition as soon as possible," Victoria said, the decision made with the kind of surety and rightness that she needed at this moment.

The kind of surety and rightness she'd never really experienced before. For a moment she wondered if this was how other people felt—because it wasn't just confidence. It was ownership. She was rooted in her life, in control of all the things she normally left to other people.

And it felt good.

Very, very good.

Two days later Amy, Gavin, and the crew descended on Crooked Creek Ranch. Celeste took Gavin and his demolition guys out to the farthest corner of the west wing, where the demolition was going to start, leaving Victoria and Amy to go over the schedule.

"We're going to do good work for you," Amy said, shaking Victoria's hand. For two days since that night with Eli, Victoria had been living on some kind of high. She'd felt invincible. But at Amy's touch, that invincibility popped and she felt a sudden wave of doubt, the cold chill of misgivings.

Who am I to be doing this? she thought, as if the old her, with all that baggage filled with insecurity, had suddenly shown up with the crew. *What do I really know about building a spa?*

"Are you having second thoughts?" Amy asked, and Victoria felt compelled to lie. To laugh and shake her head as though tearing down her family ranch was absolutely no big deal, but Amy's cool green eyes stopped her and her throat tied itself into a knot.

I'm totally freaking out, she thought.

"Sometimes," Amy said, sitting down on one of the stools at the kitchen counter, "the only thing to do is close your eyes and jump."

"I've never been very good at that," Victoria whispered, dropping onto the stool next to Amy. She ran her hands over the cool tiles, looking for comfort or distraction—she wasn't sure which.

"Well, then you've done the smart thing and surrounded yourself with people who are." Amy pulled her notebook from the briefcase at her feet and slapped it down on the counter.

Is that how a woman walks away from a child? Victoria thought. *She just closes her eyes and hopes for the best?*

"I was talking about Celeste," Amy said, her voice cool, as if she could hear Victoria's thoughts. "She always knew her own mind. And Ruby . . ." Amy smiled slightly and flipped open her notebook, got out her calculator. "No one can derail Ruby. Now, let's talk about our schedule."

"When are you going to tell Eli? Is that on your schedule?"

Amy slipped on the little half-glasses she wore, magnifying the spidery veins in the corners of her green eyes.

Funny, how when Victoria first met Amy, she couldn't see any resemblance between her and Eli. The more time she spent with both of them, the more she realized the similarities between the two had nothing to do with hair color and everything to do with temperament. Lone wolves, the two of them.

"Soon."

"How soon?"

"Does it matter?"

"He's buying land from me; I have a meeting with him tomorrow."

"Here?" Panic raced across Amy's face.

Victoria shook her head. "Lawyer's office. I . . . I don't like lying to him, Amy."

"Soon," she said. "Now, let's look at our demolition schedule."

Gavin lifted the sledgehammer, heaving it overhead like some kind of Viking berserker, raping and pillaging his way across the Crooked Creek Ranch.

If Celeste had to guess, she'd say he was probably forty–five years old.

Far too young for her. But she didn't let that stop her from watching him. Oh no. Nothing short of a natural disaster—and maybe not even that—could get her out of this kitchen.

His long-sleeved red T-shirt molded to the ridge of his spine and exposed the lovely fan of muscles along his back. His hair was hidden beneath a hard hat, which really was a shame—it sort of ruined the image—but Celeste's fantasy overlooked such mundane realities. Sunlight and dust glittered around him and her fantasy, all-powerful, got rid of the hard hat, the protective goggles, and then, for good measure, the shirt.

Gavin bent his knees and the tool came down with a crunch and thud to eat a huge hole into the southern wall of the living room.

She was transfixed. Compelled. Unable to stop herself from staring. From practically drooling.

Before she had fully recovered, he turned to the western wall and took a huge hole out of that one, too.

He took the plans out of his pocket, checked them, and then, one-handed, swung the sledgehammer from his hip and made a hole in the eastern wall as well.

Oh. My.

Desire coiled low in her belly. Lust ate its own tail.

He stepped out of sight and Celeste finally let go of the breath she'd been holding. This was getting ridiculous. She was at least fifteen years older than him. And he was probably married. Men like that should be gobbled up and forced to procreate.

But since he and his crew had stepped onto the property yesterday morning, she'd been walking on pins and needles, feeling uncomfortable in her own skin.

Victoria had left to meet Eli at the lawyer's office. Celeste had no idea where Ruby was—the woman who practically lived in the kitchen was nowhere to be found—so she couldn't even pick a fight to distract herself from ogling the help.

"Excuse me, Celeste?" She jerked, nearly spilling the mug of tea she'd been stirring sugar into, and turned to face the Viking . . . ah . . . Gavin, who stood there, his sledgehammer slung over his shoulder. Dust and bits of drywall speckled his red shirt, the collar pulled aside to reveal the ridge of a collarbone.

Celeste felt herself begin to blush, something she hadn't done in more than a decade. Something she thought she'd forgotten how to do.

"We're going to set up some dust barriers, but I just want to warn everyone that the dust is going to be an issue during the demolition and drywalling."

"Ah . . . thank you."

"I understand the boy has allergies—"

Celeste nodded—those dust motes that were so pretty around Gavin's head could be threatening around Jacob's.

"Yes, ah, he does. We'll . . . handle that."

His smile was big and warm across his handsome face. It was, in fact, one of the friendliest things she'd ever seen. One of the most open and welcoming gestures that had ever been extended to her, and she found herself panicking in the face of it.

Warmth seeped into his eyes as if he knew the effect of his smile, and a sudden familiarity bloomed between them.

He hadn't come over here to talk about dust or Jacob. He'd come over to talk to her. The realization filled her with anxiety. He'd probably recognized her.

"I don't want this to sound weird," he said, and she braced herself for the worst.

"But I kept a magazine with you on the cover for years."

And that was the worst.

"The *Sports Illustrated* cover?" she asked, feeling all that heat in her belly turn to ice and then to lead. The weight of her body, of her aging skin, suddenly made her wretched. She'd been forty in that shot, the oldest model to get the cover.

She'd been ogling this man who had ogled the perfection of her much younger body. Probably masturbated to the firmness of her breasts, the sleekness of her thighs, the fullness of her lips.

"Yeah." He looked sheepish, charming, really. She wanted to reach out and push back that lock of hair over his eye. Like she was his mother. "You probably get that all the time."

She could feign a certain flattered demeanor, encouraging this man and his flirtation, but instead she shrugged, lifting her tea to take a sip, letting her gaze slide past him, as if there were something more interesting just over his shoulder. She was uncannily good at pushing men away, at making them feel like fools.

Her cool reply pushed him off his stride, that smile waffling at its corners.

"I suppose you have work to do," she said, just to crush the smile and the charm and his flirtatious impulses into dust. And it worked. He stiffened, and as if he had a loudspeaker in his brain, she could hear his thoughts, like those of a hundred others before him.

What a bitch.

It wasn't the worst thing she'd been called over the years.

"I suppose I do." His gaze flinty, he turned away, swinging that sledgehammer like it was nothing and settling it over his shoulder.

As a point of pride, she sipped her tea and didn't watch him go.

"We could have done this at the ranch," Eli said, all shoulders and knees wedged into one of the stiff chairs in Randy Jenkins's waiting room. He wore what Victoria realized now was sort of his uniform, blue jeans and one of those snap-front shirts she thought only country music stars wore. This one was light blue and the snaps looked like pearls. He was so handsome, so . . . beautiful sitting in this stuffy waiting room, that she felt the absurd desire to fling open the doors and tell everyone that this gorgeous creature had had sex with her.

Three times.

"Done what?" She was distracted by his hair, by the remembered sensation of it between her fingers. Her thighs.

This morning, getting ready, she'd thought she would feel awkward seeing him again. But she didn't. She wanted to unsnap that shirt of his, find the pale skin of his shoulders and back so she could kiss the constellations of freckles that gathered there.

"Signed these papers."

No, we couldn't, she thought. *Not with your mom there.*

"I'm just trying to keep everything aboveboard," she said, primly crossing her legs and smoothing the hem of the blue skirt she wore over her knees. Thinking she'd need it, she'd put on her best armor this morning, the last of the Chanel skirts that still fit her and her favorite St. John's blouse—red, with a high collar and a ruffle around her wrists.

She felt like Queen Elizabeth in this shirt.

Eli cleared his throat and stared at the clock, and she examined every cuticle on her right hand while watching him very carefully out of the corner of her eye.

Oddly, she didn't take his silence, his reluctance to talk, personally. It was obvious he kept his distance with everyone. Just as it was obvious that he felt far more uncomfortable and awkward than she did. She didn't know what it was that made him so unsure.

When she and Joel had first gotten married, the sudden change in social circles had been dizzying and she'd spent months quietly sitting in the elegant and constantly redecorated living rooms of the women she was supposed to be friends with.

She'd been paralyzed by nerves, awkward to the extreme. And all those women had looked at her out of the corner of their eyes and whispered behind their palms that they didn't understand what Joel saw in the little mouse.

But everything had changed when she'd started channeling Celeste. She'd adopted the imperial mannerisms that had made her childhood such torture: the tilt of her head, the arch of her eyebrow.

And over time, she'd been accepted into that cannibalistic group, had become their leader by virtue of her husband's money and the cool snobbery she'd perfected.

Clearly, Eli had no such role model. He sat there oozing discomfort.

Thinking about those years, those people, made her melancholy. All too aware of the time she'd wasted cultivating connections and relationships that had been made of smoke and poison.

This man in front of her, the things they'd done, the way he made her feel—she couldn't pin a name on any of it, couldn't point at it and say "that's love" or "that's friendship," but it was real. Complicated, sure, but it had been the real her in that truck and in his bed. She hadn't been pretending to be someone else.

Real in a way she'd forgotten about. Real in a way she never thought she'd have outside of her son and brother.

"You look like a nun in that shirt," he muttered.

"So?"

"So, you're not."

She laughed. "Are you saying I should dress . . ." The waiting room was empty; Gladys, Randy's secretary, was sealed back in the copy room, but Victoria still whispered. "Like a slut?"

The idea had some appeal. With these new boobs of hers . . . she should show them off. Joel was long gone, and his opinions on what she wore no longer mattered.

"You should dress like a woman." Across the waiting room, those green eyes of his undressed her, pulled away the silk and the skirt, the plain underwear she wore, to find her skin. The tender places only he knew about.

Her body reacted, heating in acquiescence, and she realized what she needed armor against was this. This knowledge he had of her. And the way he could pull her apart with just one look. One word.

She opened her mouth to tell him it was no business of

his, but the door to Randy's office opened at the same time.

"Randy will see you now," Gladys said, unsmiling. As if being a legal secretary was grim, life-or-death stuff.

"Great," she said and practically jumped out of her chair.

Eli walked out of Randy's office an hour later, his pockets a little emptier, but his life so full he wanted to shout with joy.

He had all the land he needed. Everything was coming together in a way he'd never even considered possible, wedged as he'd been in his role of family savior.

And this woman beside him, searching for the parking stub in her giant suitcase of a purse, had been the unwilling key to it all.

His gratitude was expressionless; he had no way to tell her what she'd done when she'd fired him and freed him from that self-sacrificing role.

"Thank you," he murmured as they approached the elevator that would take them down to the parking garage. He'd parked his truck next to the old Cadillac her father used to drive.

She laughed, still digging through her purse. "All I did was sell you some land." She pushed a pair of sunglasses into her hair, revealing the curve of her cheeks, the fullness of her lips, and his gratitude turned into an arousal, a lust so sharp he hurt with it. They stepped into the hush of the elevator. "So, thank—"

The elevator doors shut and he stepped up against her, crowding her in the corner.

"What—oh." She gasped as he arched slowly against her. The purse fell from her fingers and she braced herself against his arms.

She was as aroused as he was, as susceptible to this

strange fire between them, and that made him hotter, harder.

He didn't kiss her, difficult as that was, trying to think of something slightly dirty he could do to her in appreciation.

"What are you wearing under that skirt?" he whispered as the elevator hurtled them down down down.

"Underwear."

Underwear? Honestly, she needed a better vocabulary. "Give them to me."

"What?"

"Take them off and give them to me."

"But—"

"Before those doors open, Tori, and I do something worse."

Her trembling lips parted, her eyes so dilated it was a wonder she could see past her desire. Carefully, daintily, like the princess she used to be, she reached up under those ugly clothes and slipped down a pair of white cotton panties.

Never in his life had white cotton been such a turn-on.

He tucked them in his pocket just as the door dinged open to reveal two men in business suits. They nodded, smiled at Tori, and a green-eyed monster roared in his chest, hating their eyes on her. He grabbed her bag, holding it over his swollen crotch, and took her gently by the elbow, leading her out of the elevator and across the parking lot to their vehicles.

After fishing her keys out of the bottomless pit she carried, he opened her driver-side door and helped her in. Threw her purse in the passenger seat.

"What . . . are we doing?"

He kissed her, holding himself in check because he wasn't going to have sex with her here. Too many people, and even if that was on her list of harmless perversions, he realized he didn't like the idea of sharing this side of Tori with anyone else.

But he would give her something else to cross off that list.

"Touch yourself," he whispered against her lips. "While I watch."

She gasped, and he—showing superhuman control if he did say so himself—shut the door. His attention split between her and making sure no one else was around, he watched, dry-mouthed, as she eased her skirt up her legs and slid her hand between them.

This is crazy, she thought, so turned on by his eyes through the glass. So turned on by what she knew he could see. So turned on by doing this in a public place. She was on fire with all of it, and seconds after her fingers touched the swollen heat between her legs, she exploded, her gasps and cries echoing through the empty car.

Feeling both powerless and powerful at the same time, she glanced through the window at Eli. His eyes glowed, his chest heaved, and she grabbed the door handle to open it, to get out or pull him in, whatever it took to touch him. But he put his hand against the window, keeping the door closed. His eyes shifted over the roof of her car and she heard tires coming. Another car, and she partially froze with horror.

His smile when he looked back down at her put her at ease—for some reason she knew he wouldn't have let her do that if someone else was watching. As if he unconsciously knew where her lines were drawn.

And suddenly this moment, separated by glass and steel, was more intimate than anything they'd done two nights before. She lifted her hand to the window, where his hand was still pressed, pink and flat.

Touch deferred, she thought.

"Drive safe," she heard him say, muffled through the glass.

He walked around his truck and got in. She watched him start it, then brace his hand across the back of the bench seat to turn around. When he saw her watching, he lifted his fingers in a wave and pulled away.

With her underwear in his pocket.

A week later and Victoria couldn't take it anymore. Every time she heard a truck roll over the gravel outside she was convinced it was Eli, and she just about had a heart attack.

Thursday morning Victoria saw Amy's truck pull into the parking area and she raced out the front door to catch her.

"Amy!" Victoria skidded to a halt just as Amy turned to face her. "You have to tell him. You have to tell Eli you're here."

"I will," Amy sighed.

"I've heard that for a week." All she could think about was his hand against that glass window, the way he gave her everything she wanted before she knew she wanted it. And the way he looked at her while he did it.

And she was *lying* to him. It made her sick thinking about it.

"What am I supposed to say to him, Victoria?" Amy asked.

"I don't care anymore." She bounced on her toes. "I just want you to tell him."

"Every day I wake up and I think, today is the day I'm just going to drive down there and let it happen. And then I get here and I realize all over again how . . ." She shook her head. "How much he must hate me. How much I deserve to have him hate me."

"You're chicken?"

Amy's lips lifted in a tired smile. "Bawk bawk."

This whole situation would be easier if Victoria didn't like Amy. It wasn't just the good work she was doing and the work ethic she possessed. The woman was funny and smart—in a different life, they might have been friends. Maybe they were. Victoria didn't know anymore, the whole damn thing was such a mess.

"But don't you think you need to do something?"

Before I have a heart attack. Before he finds out I'm lying to him and hates me as much as he hates you?

"I am doing something. I'm getting you a deal on your hot tubs."

Jacob stepped out the front door, carrying his shoes. He waved at Victoria with his whole arm. Seven years old and he loved her with his entire body. Eli had probably once loved Amy that way.

With that thought, the world shifted.

"Do you have other kids?" Victoria asked, leaning against the hot metal door of Amy's truck. Jacob sat down to put on his shoes.

Instead of answering, Amy uncorked her blueprint case and unrolled the fragile blue paper across the front of her truck, weighing down the edges with tape measures.

"I guess that's none of my business."

"You're right."

"How about other family?"

"You're not going to let this go, are you?"

"Just making conversation with my trusted architect." She grinned, and Amy took off her glasses as though she were laying down arms, surrendering her sword.

"No, I don't have any other kids. Gavin started working for me when he was pretty young, and he's about the closest I have to family now."

"That's too bad. Eli could use a little brother or sister."

"You say that like he's eight."

"In a lot of ways he is." *And whose fault is that?* She didn't say the words, but they were there, between them. Amy's face went still, as loud a sign of pain as a scream, and Victoria hardened her heart.

Jacob ran down the steps, grinning at her, his big backpack flopping against his back. Her heart hurt with love for him. And she couldn't do this anymore. She couldn't continue to lie to Eli, who had already gotten hurt more than anyone should.

"You have one more day, Amy. You tell Eli, or I will."

Eli opened the brown bag and spread the food out across his father's hospital table. Uncle John grabbed his grease-stained paper carton of fried rice and a plastic spoon and sat back in his chair.

His dad's bed was empty; the old man was getting physical therapy down the hall.

"You're looking awful dressed up for a Thursday night," Eli said, taking in his uncle's clean red shirt with its pearl buttons. His good white Stetson sat on the table by the window.

"Just got back from Galveston. Had to impress some folks." He waggled his bushy eyebrows and Eli smiled.

"How was your meeting?" Eli sat down in a chair next to his father's bed and cracked open his carton of lo mein.

Green onions again, crap! How many times does a guy have to ask for no onions?

"Good. We're gonna start drilling outside of Galveston at the end of October. I'll be down there a chunk of time. Till the New Year, at least."

They ate quietly for a few minutes, Uncle John using

that spoon as a shovel and showering his shirt with rice and bits of egg.

For some stupid reason, Eli could not stop thinking about Victoria. Not just the sex, though that had kept him preoccupied for over a week. But the way she'd described that damn spa. The way she saw it.

Victoria had a vision and it impressed the hell out of him.

Or maybe it was the sex; he couldn't tell anymore.

Either way, he couldn't stop thinking about her.

But as he picked aside the mini-corn-cob things he hated, he thought about that money she needed. He could tell Uncle John that Victoria wanted to sell him five hundred thousand dollars' worth of land and John would hand that money over without blinking.

But Eli didn't want that land. Not anymore. A month of being his own man and he was happier than he'd been in years. Hell, maybe his whole life.

"What's on your mind, Eli?" John asked, watching him across Mark's empty hospital bed.

"Victoria sold me that land across the river."

John put down the Chinese food. "I thought you said she wasn't ever going to sell you any land."

"Guess I was wrong."

"She going to sell you any more?"

Eli shook his head. "I got all the land I need."

John stared at him for a moment and then swore under his breath. Eli tried not to let it get to him. He'd let his father down enough over the years—it was about time his uncle started getting disappointed in him, too.

They ate for a while in silence, waiting for Mark to be brought back, watching the shadows grow across the room.

"Heard something crazy the other day," John said.

Eli grunted around a mouth full of noodles.

"There's some work being done over at the Crooked Creek. Big work."

Eli's heart pounded once, hard in his chest. Lying to his uncle was new to him, and not easy. So, instead of revealing his knowledge, he kept his mouth full and shrugged.

"You know anything about that?"

"I got fired," he said after he swallowed. Sorting through the noodles for a piece of chicken became very important. Paramount in his life. "Not much reason to go back."

He thought of Victoria in the car looking up at him, her hand pressed to the window. He'd felt her through the glass and steel. He tucked the memory away someplace safe, where his uncle's knowing eyes would never find it.

"I suppose not," Uncle John said. "That woman, that whole family, is trouble, son. You remember that."

"Don't worry." He smiled into his lo mein. "I remember plenty."

By Friday, the brunt of the demolition had been done. The whole west wing of the house—the dining room, den, living room, TV room, and four unused bedrooms— had been stripped down to studs.

Victoria and Amy walked through the space, delineating rooms and walls.

"We'll have a men's locker room here." Victoria pivoted in a small corner. "Women's over there, with showers and a steam room."

"Five treatment rooms," Amy added, pointing along the wide hallway where the bedrooms had been. "If you want to add that other room, then we'll need to take down the far wall." It was a decision that needed to be made, and Victoria wished that Celeste were here. She had a better gut for the questions that would impact the future, not just their bank account.

"No," she said, hoping she wouldn't regret it. "I think we're good with five."

Amy nodded as if the decision had been a wise one, and Victoria felt better.

"I'm going to need more money," Amy said.

"I know." Victoria sighed. "I'll talk to Celeste." Celeste had wanted to put off calling Luc until it was completely necessary. And they'd reached that point.

"I can't believe how fast you guys did this," Victoria said, stepping through what used to be the dining room wall.

"Tearing it down is easy," Amy said. "Tomorrow we'll get the frame up, and after that, the trades will come in to rewire and plumb. That process is going to take a lot longer, and it's going to seem like nothing is getting done, but you have to trust the process."

Amy arched a ginger eyebrow and Victoria nodded like a good student. "Trust the process, got it. But when you say a while . . . what exactly are you talking about?"

"A project this size, all our guys on it, it's going to be six to eight weeks. It's going to get trickier with your saunas and mud baths."

"Okay, but you still think we'll be all right for the New Year's opening?"

"It's the beginning of October now, so if everything goes according to plan, we should be okay."

Everything had gone so well, Victoria didn't even want to think about the plan not working. Plans were already in motion for the opening-night party.

"What could go wrong?" she asked.

"Tori!" a voice yelled from the front door, and Victoria's heart stopped in her chest. Only one person called her that. Icy prickles of panic ran over her skin, settling in her bones.

"Who is that?" Amy asked.

In an instant Victoria lost her illusions. The lies she'd told herself to keep the guilt at bay vanished and she smacked headfirst into what a huge mistake she'd made by not telling Eli about Amy. Believing foolishly that Amy would do as she said and that Victoria didn't owe Eli the truth was about to destroy them all.

"Your son," she whispered, and Amy's face went white.

chapter
14

Eli pushed aside the plastic sheeting and stepped into the kitchen, just as Victoria stepped in from what used to be the dining room.

Truthfully, he felt foolish being here. Not that he didn't have logical reasons, but the real reason had nothing to do with logic—he wanted to see her.

And because of that he found it hard to look at her, choosing instead to take careful note of the studs revealed by all the demolition.

"You didn't waste any time, did you?" He kicked at a nail in the pine subflooring and couldn't believe that it had only been a month since he'd been in here. So much had changed.

"What are you doing here?"

He blinked at her tone, surprised by her panic. Especially since he'd been so excited to see her. "I'm picking up the breeding equipment."

She stepped forward, her arms extended as if he were a spooked cow and she needed to herd him out of danger. Which was weird, but he got distracted by those jeans she was wearing again. And a green T-shirt that made her blue eyes glow.

"How about you let me deliver it to you?" She smiled, but it was false—everything about her seemed false—a light turned up too bright. "Tonight."

"You need a truck," he said, sidestepping her outstretched arm, suspicious. The woman was a terrible liar. "Why don't you show me around real quick? Let me see this vision of yours."

Her look was so pained, so horrified, that he instinctively reached out to touch her, to smooth the panic on her face, but she grabbed his hand, squeezing his fingers. "What's going on, Tori?"

When she closed her eyes, he was struck by the absurd impulse to brush his lips over the feathery lashes, the thin blue veins in her eyelids.

"I've been a coward."

He laughed, and her eyes opened.

"I think you've been pretty gutsy." He kissed her knuckles, reeling her in so he could get to those eyelashes. "What you did in the car isn't for the faint of heart."

There was movement behind Tori, and another person entered the kitchen. A tall woman in canvas work pants with a long red braid over her shoulder. He stepped back, sheepish. Tori didn't want to make out with some guy in front of a contractor. "Sorry," he muttered. "Why don't we go on outside."

He turned his back on the woman, but Tori didn't move. She stared up at him as if waiting for something to happen. Something bad.

"Eli?" The woman, the redhead, spoke and Eli stopped, his body, his blood and muscles, the bones that held him up, all twitching at the sound. Like a memory. A half-forgotten dream.

Eli? Time to come in for dinner.

Eli? Can you come over and help me with this horse?

Eli? Who is my favorite little boy?

No, he thought, pushing away the thought, the dark demon, *that's crazy.*

"I'm so sorry," Tori whispered beside him and the ground under his feet went soft. His knees buckled and he put a hand up against what was left of a kitchen wall.

Don't be sorry. He resisted the tide, fought with every muscle the pull of the truth. *Don't. Don't do this to me. Don't let this be happening.*

"Look at me, Eli," the woman said. "Please . . . just . . . look at me."

Stiffly, his body uncooperative, his brain in cloudy denial, he turned to face the woman. The stranger. With red hair.

And his eyes.

"No." He said it this time. The word falling into the silence of the room, shattering it into a thousand pieces that cut and tore at him.

His mother. That was his mother right there.

Forcing himself to feel nothing, to close down and block off whatever reaction was happening in his brain, he turned on his heel and walked out the way he'd come in. Dimly, through the wild open roar in his head, he heard Tori follow him and behind that, he heard the heavier footsteps of his mother.

His mother. What the hell?

He stepped onto the porch, the sun so bright the world went white, and for a moment he stumbled, lost in the landscape. And Victoria's hand held him, braced him against the sensation of falling.

"Eli—"

He shook her off, pushed her away, and took the steps down toward his truck two at a time.

"Stop, please, Eli." Tori's voice clung to him, pulled at his clothes, his pride, what remained of his control.

Eli kept walking, the chrome of the truck's door handle hot in his hand.

"Eli. I'm sorry." Another voice, his mother's voice, cut through the distance, through his skull, and the scream escaped. The anger ignited and blazed out of control.

The cruelty of her being here spun him around and he ran back up the steps, right toward her, unsure for a wild moment of what he was going to do. He knew what he wanted to do, how he wanted to shake her. Scream at her.

But he stopped inches from her, confronted by the familiarity of her face, aged but the same. Those eyes, the freckles, the sad set to her mouth. It was her. His mother.

"I don't know why you're here—"

"Because of you," she said quickly, definitively, as if she'd only been waiting for the chance to say those words. "I'm here for you."

His skin crawled at the thought. "I don't want anything to do with you."

When she started to shake her head, he pointed his finger at her, barely controlling the wild impulse to poke her as hard as he could. He wanted to hurt her. This woman who once used to kiss him good night, who taught him how to whistle and ride a bike and lay tile.

Who broke his heart into so many pieces he still couldn't find half of them.

"Stay away from me. I mean it. You are nothing to me." Her lips went white, but those eyes of hers, like looking in the mirror, stayed dry. Defiant. All but telling him she would do what she wanted.

He turned to Victoria. Nothing dry about her. Tears flowed from her eyes. "You knew who she was?" he asked through numb lips. Slowly, tears making fresh tracks down the snow of her cheeks, she nodded.

Bile soured his stomach, flooded him with disgust. And he wished it was all directed at her, the liar, but mostly he was disgusted with himself. He had thought, like an idiot, that Tori was safe. That this *thing* between them was without risk. That there was no way she could hurt him.

But holy shit, how much more sparse did his life need to get so he wouldn't be betrayed by the few people left in it?

Because he'd liked Tori. He'd liked her. Liked who he was with her.

And she hadn't just lied to him. She'd lied to him about his *mother*.

He drove away from the ranch, directionless. Unable to go to his home, the one he'd shared with his mother for eight years, unable to see all the changes he'd made in an effort to chase her ghost from the walls.

The memories he'd tried to forget, that he'd torn down and sanded and repainted, that he'd fixed up and cleaned, were there, unbidden. Unwanted. And he was just a boy, suddenly, lost and grieving. Wondering what he'd done that was so wrong that his mother had left him behind. Wondering why he was so unloveable that she hadn't chosen to take him with her.

By rote, unconscious of the decision, he found himself on the road leading to The Elms, his father's nursing home. The shell of his father—the familiarity of his face, his voice—pulled him here like a magnet, even though he knew the father he needed wasn't in that building. Wasn't in the body in that bed.

And really, never had been.

But with his aloneness making him feel foreign in his own skin, making him itch and ache with everything he wanted to forget, he got out of his truck and went inside to sit beside the father who didn't even know who he was.

Victoria watched Eli's truck kick up dust as he sped away from the ranch, the air still smoking from his pain, acrid and terrible.

"Well," Amy sighed, blowing out a big breath. She put a hand to her stomach, her throat, and then, as if forcing herself to be okay, as if swallowing whatever emotion had surfaced at the sight of her son, she turned to Victo-

ria, her face placid. Her eyes clear. "That could have
been worse."

"How?" Victoria gasped.

"I . . ." Amy stopped, shook her head. Her composure
gone, she looked like those pictures of people standing
in the wreckage of their homes after a tornado. "I don't
know."

That Victoria had been a part of this made her sick,
made her wish she could go back in time and scream a
warning to him: *Don't trust me. I'll hurt you so badly
and you'll never see it coming.*

"What do you want from him?" she asked.

"You have a son. What do you think I want?"

As if all the sand were running out of her, all the courage and determination, Amy crumpled, her hand finding
the edge of the rocking chair where she collapsed.

"I wouldn't leave my son," Victoria said. Honestly,
now she wanted to take the high road? After the damage
had been done? Where had her righteousness been last
week?

"It's easy to judge me," Amy said, a willing bull's-eye.
"I deserve it. Trust me . . ." She blinked up at the sun, as
if sending Morse code. "I know what I deserve."

"Why didn't you just tell him last week! You said you
would!" The wind kicked up, making the plastic sheeting flap around them—it sounded like a protest, and her
voice got lost in the wind.

"I know. I just . . . I just fail him, every time."

Amy shook her head, bowing it over her clenched
hands. Victoria, always unsure around these Turnbulls,
didn't reach out. She kept her hands to herself and stared
at the edge of the woman's muddy and frayed canvas
pants.

"I should have told him myself," Victoria said, shaking her head.

"Why didn't you?"

"Same reason as you. I was scared."

And she sat there, the sun beating down against her skin, the wind blowing into her eyes, waiting for the next thing, the right decision to present itself. But there was nothing except the decision she'd already made, the work that she'd committed to at the ranch. That she believed in.

Was she supposed to fire Amy? Would that make this better? Because that wasn't something she was ready to do.

Amy swore, breaking the silence, and pushed herself up out of the chair and down the steps.

"What are you doing?" Victoria asked.

"Something," Amy said, shrugging. "Anything. I can't just sit here and feel like shit. I've done that my whole life. My *whole* life. And even if he doesn't talk to me—even if he hates me—I gotta try to do the right thing for once."

An hour later, battered but calmer after watching his father sleep quietly—enviably unaware that the past had come back to haunt them—Eli left The Elms, walking past Caitlyn at the front desk.

"You all right?" she asked, that little wrinkle of concern popping up on her forehead. Her fingernails were covered in rhinestones; they were gaudy and wild, the furthest thing from what he knew of Caitlyn.

Everyone has secrets, he thought, numb all over.

When she caught him looking at her hands, she tucked her fingers away as if she didn't want him to see that side of her, the rhinestone side. As if he'd blown the password.

"I'm fine," he lied and even managed to smile. He gave her a two-finger wave and headed out into the last of the day, the sunshine pouring over his truck and the parking lot like honey.

He wished he could scoop some up in his hands, a little sweetness to chase away the sour. He wished, actually, that he could head on over to Uncle John's and get stupid drunk. Totally shit-faced.

But he didn't know what he'd say to his uncle. And if he even wanted to talk about it at all. Things were different lately with Uncle John, who acted as if Eli getting fired from Crooked Creek had been some sort of betrayal.

What he really wanted was to pretend he'd never seen that woman. That Victoria hadn't lied.

Drinking seemed like the best way to accomplish that, but the horses had to be fed.

Work, as always, needed to be done.

And he had enough booze at home to put him into a coma, if that's what he wanted.

He took the back way to his house; it was longer, but there wasn't a chance in hell he was driving past the Crooked Creek. Not for a long time.

But when he spun his truck around to the front of his property, there was a black pickup sitting where he usually parked. Boxes were loaded in the bed, along with two horse-shaped phantoms.

Standing beside the truck was his mother.

He thought about his father, a stranger in that hospital bed. The man who had raised him was, for all intents and purposes, gone from this earth. He could handle that shit. It had taken years to distance himself from the skeleton that raged at him every time he went to visit, the ghost who didn't remember him.

But he'd done it.

He'd swallowed every offense, every rock and stone of grief and regret and anger, until he felt nothing.

And he just had to do the same with the woman standing there, staring at him with his eyes.

With a craftsman's precision he sanded all of himself

away when he looked at her, every memory. He stared at her until she was a stranger, a collection of features that meant nothing to him, until finally, he could breathe again.

Carefully, aware of his temper, he turned off his truck motor and stepped out onto the gravel. He didn't say anything, just watched her. Hated her.

"Where do you want this stuff?" She uncrossed her legs and jerked her thumb back at the load in her truck.

He chewed his lips, wishing he could tell her to go to hell, but that was his equipment in there. Equipment he needed.

"I'll get it," he said through his teeth.

He opened the back of the truck, grabbing the first two boxes and taking them into that messy office of his in the barn. He came back out only to find her carrying two boxes toward him.

He grabbed them, hissing.

"Don't touch anything."

"I'm just trying—"

"Don't. Just . . ." He took a breath and walked the stuff into the barn. "Don't."

Refusing to look at her, but painfully aware of her eyes on him, he unloaded all of the boxes, dragged the phantoms out of the truck, and wobbled them over to the barn.

She followed him a few steps, lingering outside the door while he arranged what he could.

"This place looks good. You've done a lot of work here," she said, her voice unsure, which wasn't how he remembered her. Sad, yes. Never unsure. And he didn't want to remember her at all.

He grabbed his white bucket and walked right past her. Like she was dirt. Like she was nothing.

"Get the hell off my land."

* * *

God's mighty fist was punching Eli's brain. It felt like God had a grudge, the sunlight had knives.

Soda, his dog, whined, and the sound scraped the inside of his skull. Soda's cold nose bumped Eli's hand, then dug under the blanket for Eli's face, which he licked, breathing the stomach-turning scent of dog mouth all over him.

"Okay, okay." Eli sat up and waited for the world to stop spinning before attempting to stand.

Looking down at himself, he realized he'd passed out last night cradling a bottle of bourbon like a lover, with one sock, no shirt, and his pants still on.

He dumped food in Soda's bowl, getting half of it on the floor, but he didn't bother to pick it up. Soda would take care of that.

Appalled, he pulled four condoms out of his back pocket. He remembered a half-formed plan to head into town to find Caitlyn or another woman who would make him forget his life for a few minutes.

Luckily, he'd been too drunk to remember where his keys were.

After getting dressed, he braced one hand against the door so he could fish his sunglasses from the bucket of crap by the front window without falling on his face. He burped up a mouthful of fumes, grossing himself out.

This was why he didn't drink. He couldn't stand himself hungover. The smell reminded him of his dad nursing a hangover every other morning. Sitting at the breakfast table, his head cradled in his hands, while Eli finished the toast he'd made himself. Eli used to drive himself to school those mornings, his father slouched in the passenger seat, his hat pulled low over his eyes as he dozed on the twenty-minute drive into town.

Like father, like son. The bitter thought was an angry bull and he gave it free rein as he jerked open the door.

As the sunlight attacked, his skin cringed in terror and his eyes screamed in surrender.

He wanted more than anything to crawl back into the house and hide until his head stopped hating him. But the sun was up and the animals were hungry and he'd already had a stomachful of self-pity.

Halfway down the steps he smelled something different on the breeze. Something delicious and life-saving. Coffee.

The sudden awareness that he wasn't alone froze his muscles, wiped out what was left of his brain. And he could only stand there, numb. Refusing to turn around.

"Eli?"

His brain went red, his skin hot with a sudden spasm of a thousand emotions he had no interest in feeling. Anger, sure, but laced with a hurt, with a fucking betrayal, that made him murderous.

Victoria.

He thought he'd drunk the raw edges of all this misery away, but at the sound of her voice, it reappeared. Like a dead body bobbing to the surface.

chapter
15

She stood on his porch, staring him right in the eye like a dog who didn't realize she'd shit all over the carpet. She was supposed to be cowering. Groveling for his forgiveness.

But instead those legs of hers were plugged wide on the wood of his porch. His dick twitched in admiration of her guts.

Cool it, cowboy.

She took a sip of coffee from the travel mug in her hand and his brain screamed like a toddler who wanted a new toy.

The wind blew past him, and a second later Victoria's nose wrinkled.

"You've been drinking."

He didn't say anything, just stood there and wished he could lie down. She came down the steps, the cracked galoshes she wore squeaking as she walked.

"Here." She handed him the coffee and for a second he wanted to slap it out of her hands, but the hangover took over his body and he grabbed the mug. Guzzling the coffee, ignoring the cream and sugar, desperate for the caffeine.

"I brought Lucky," she said. "If you still want her?"

He glanced at her and away, unwilling to commit to this conversation, much less look at her, all serious but glimmery in the sunlight. "I paid for her," he said and took another drink of coffee.

"She's in the trailer."

Then he saw the Crooked Creek horse trailer connected to a black pickup that he recognized as Amy's.

It made him feel violated all over again, to realize the two of them were cozy enough to swap cars.

He walked over to the trailer and opened the locking mechanism. The door swung open and Lucky stomped, swishing her tail. Panicked, he knew, because she hated to travel. He slid in next to her, sidestepping up to her head to calm her.

She shook her mane at the sight of him, nosing his hand, spilling coffee over the hay at their feet.

Something happy beat back the jagged edges of his hangover. The press of her damp nose against his neck felt like comfort.

"Hey there, my sweet girl," he crooned, stroking her nose, scratching her ears, taking his time with the moment, because every other moment in his life loomed large and clumsy. "Let's go see your friends."

Wrapping one hand around the strap of her bridle, he clucked and led her back out of the trailer, shushing her when she balked and shied away.

He ignored Victoria standing there, full of expectation and questions, and led Lucky toward the barn, past the stables and then out to the paddocks, where Patience whinnied in welcome.

He put her in with Darling. The two horses ran circles with enthusiasm and he smiled, taking another swig of the coffee.

"We need to talk," Victoria said, from behind him.

The smile died on his lips. "I need to feed the horses."

It didn't take long, even though he tried to stretch it out. The feed bucket got emptied into the feed bags and he finished the coffee and finally, when he couldn't put it off any longer, he turned to face Victoria.

She wore her hair pulled back in a tight ponytail, and resistant black curls hid behind her ears, along the tender skin of her nape. Those little curls were so at odds with the flinty look in her eye.

Looking every inch a Baker, she squared her shoulders and for a moment, for a raw, visceral moment, he hated her. He loathed her for her control. For her bloodline, and for her ability, despite the crushing blows that had been dealt her, to stand there on her own two feet trying to make a fucking go of it, when he was swamped by the past. Blown over by his own life.

Crippled by what his mother had done to him.

"I know . . . I know you must have questions. About Amy."

At some point on his way through that bottle last night, he'd told himself he didn't care why she'd lied; all that mattered was that she had. She'd looked at him, submitted to his every dark whim, even perpetrated her own minor perversions, which had seemed so endearing, which he'd been so damn *grateful* to be a part of. And then she'd lied.

But in the brutal sunlight, weak from the beating the hangover had given him, he found himself wanting to follow her lies back to the source.

"Why?" he whispered, knowing if his father were here and cognizant, he'd call him a pussy.

That hard wood façade of hers cracked and the woman he thought he knew peeked out.

"Because I'm a coward. Because I thought I was doing the right thing for me, for the spa, but I should have told you. Amy said she was going to . . ."

He scoffed deep in his throat. If it was the right thing to do, he could guarantee his mother wouldn't do it.

She stepped closer and in a bizarre twist, he found

himself stepping away. Not because he was repulsed, but because suddenly, all his windows, every door was thrown open and he felt everything, sorrow and anger, melancholy and regret. And under all of it, a loneliness so profound he could barely resist the need to touch her, to pretend—for as long as it took to fuck her—that he wasn't totally alone in this world.

But she stopped, looking as if he'd slapped her.

Good, he thought, vindictive and despicable. *Good.*

"What were you scared of?"

"That you would pull away from me. After what we'd . . . done."

"You didn't tell me about my mom because you wanted to keep fucking me?"

She nodded, miserable.

Karma. He thought of every woman he'd ever lied to, every woman he'd hurt, just so he could keep on fucking her. They'd all be lining up and laughing right about now. *Son of a bitch.*

"Did you know?" he asked. "What she did?"

"Enough that I knew you'd be upset. Enough that I didn't tell you." She rattled on about Ruby having the idea to call Amy and how Amy had come to the ranch looking for him, but pretending otherwise, and how she'd taken a pay cut in order to get the job.

A pay cut? The hair on the back of his neck stood up. *Bullshit.* Why his mother was here, out of the blue, after all these years suddenly made so much sense. And the laughter, like acid, churned out of his gut.

"What's so funny?"

"You need to get another architect."

"What? Why? We've already given her a deposit."

"Because I can guarantee my mother will not finish this job. She isn't the kind of person who finishes things; she walks away."

"Eli—"

"She didn't tell me she was here, did she? Despite her promises?"

Victoria lifted her chin and he knew he was right. It would be Victoria's just desserts to get screwed by Amy, but the thought didn't bring him much satisfaction. It practically levitated him off his feet with anger.

"And there's a really, really good chance she is only here to tear that place to the ground. She hated the ranch. She'd have no interest in seeing something on this land succeed."

Including me, he thought. *Especially me.* A yawning cavern opened under his feet and he was breathless with vertigo.

"What . . ." Her hand touched his sleeve, burning through the fabric to scorch his skin. His bone. "What happened, Eli?"

There was no way he was answering that question, no way he was prying open his brain to pull out those memories, so he grabbed her hand, relishing the connection. Needing it.

Apparently she didn't need to worry about lying to him in order to keep him in her pants. Her knife could go right between his shoulder blades and it wouldn't make any difference.

He was mad at her, so filled with anger he shook with it, but he wanted her. Craved her, craved the silence and stillness she could give him. The scales in his head tipped toward relief. Toward succor. His blood began to pound in his veins, inflating his skin, filling him with something besides ghosts and cobwebs. Slowly, carefully, he tugged her closer.

Her eyes popped open and she stumbled against his chest.

"Eli? What—" He kissed her. Pressed his thirsty lips to hers. He cupped the back of her head, carefully reading her reaction through the haze of his own dumb animal lust. He could taste her surprise, but under that the sweetness of her surrender, the warmth of her welcome.

He didn't want to talk or think. He just wanted to feel and forget and let this woman take away the worst of the pain.

This was wrong. Way wrong. And Victoria was going to stop it in just a second. Any minute now, she was going to push this man and his magic mouth away.

His tongue touched the corner of her lips, sweeping inside, and she felt herself tipping toward not caring. Not caring that he used sex as a distraction.

She pushed away, not far and not with much conviction, but enough so that she could breathe. With his scruff and his bloodshot eyes, his shirt unbuttoned halfway down his muscled chest, he looked like a rogue cowboy. An outlaw.

Her blood thrilled and her imagination longed to take that little fantasy and run with it, add some subplots and costumes.

"Eli, I can't . . . I can't just sleep with you. We need to talk."

"Trust me." He kissed her neck, his hands cupping her hips, pulling her closer. "We don't."

"I can't—" She groaned, her head filled with static, as the stubble across his chin scraped her skin. She stepped away, breaking all contact so she could think. "Do you even like me? Do you . . . forgive me?"

"Does it matter?" His hand slipped over her butt, grabbing the curve with his whole palm. Oh, she loved that.

"Of course it does!"

"Fine. I forgive you."

"Stop it. Eli. Stop it." She pushed him away again. A terrible spark lit the air between them, his rage given room to burn, and she longed to step back even farther, like behind the house, to find some safety. But she'd been cowardly enough already.

"I'm so sorry, Eli. I really am. I didn't do it to hurt you."

He turned away and she grabbed his arm.

"Your mother is here," she cried, stunned by his willing obtuseness. "After twenty-seven years. I brought her here. Hired her. I like her, Eli."

"What?"

She hadn't meant to say that, but she couldn't take it back.

That did it. She felt the change in him like electricity in the air even before he turned on her, even before he stepped toward her, his eyes wild and feral.

"You *like* her?" he roared and the ground shook. "She left me, Tori. Her son. And I was a kid." He pounded his chest. "I was eight and I loved her and she just walked away and she never came back. She didn't call, she didn't write, she just vanished. And it was just me and my dad. And he didn't care. He couldn't be bothered to stay sober, or get me to school, or see me fed. And she left me with him. Like I was a dog that she didn't care about. Like I was nothing. And I missed her. I missed her so much . . ."

His voice broke and her heart broke with it.

He shook his head, once, a hard shake like that of a horse tossing aside a rider, and she knew it was over. The storm had passed, that window into him was nailed shut.

His sideways glance revealed all sorts of pain, a million shades of agony. A red flush swept up his neck.

This beautiful man didn't deserve what had been done to him. Not by his mother, and not by her.

And she knew it was wrong, and she didn't care if he hated her, if he didn't forgive her, but she was going to have sex with him. Right now. Probably in the barn. Hopefully against a wall.

She was going to hate herself for using her body to apologize, to atone for all the crimes against him, but it seemed to be the only comfort he would take.

Carefully, as if he were a wounded animal, she slid her hand up to his shoulder. Half expecting him to pull away, break the contact, she was relieved when he didn't. But he didn't look at her either; he stood there, shaking despite his stillness, staring at the dust. As if he'd been so broken he couldn't lift his head anymore, couldn't bear to see his reflection in her eyes.

She wrapped her arms around him, holding him as tight as she could.

She could feel him pulling away inside his skin and she knew somehow if he did that, he'd disappear. Vanish behind hard eyes, and harder lips. And the man who'd watched her through glass in that parking garage, the man who had sprung the lock on her every single hidden longing, would be gone forever. And that would be awful. Terrible for her.

But worse for him. Because the anger and the grief and the confusion were all still inside of him, searching for someplace to go.

And he would ignore them.

Or worse, he would find another willing body to numb the suffering he'd barely acknowledge.

And that just wouldn't do.

Whether or not he forgave her no longer mattered. Her pride was crumpled under her regret and her lust and her worry for him. She combed her fingers through his hair, gripping him hard until she heard him gasp, and then she put her teeth to his neck, with erotic care, tasting the bourbon and sweat.

His growl rumbled against her, setting off earthquakes in her body. Rough and uncontrolled, he clutched at her hips, and her body rejoiced even as her heart splintered.

"It's okay," she whispered. "It's going to be okay."

As if she weighed nothing, he cupped her butt in his hands, lifting her, carrying her toward the barn.

Everything in him was strung so tight, pulled taut until his skin seemed ready to split over his heartbeat, over his bones. And she clung to him, wrapped her arms around him, using her flesh to hold his together.

In the barn, he pushed her against the wall, and that antiseptic fantasy, that lukewarm shell of an idea, was demolished under the reality of this man. The breadth of his shoulders, the strength of his hands on her body.

He pulled away clothes—hers, his, it hardly mattered, all that mattered was getting closer. All that mattered was touching him as much as he would allow. Taking both of them to whatever limits existed between them.

She thanked God at the sound of a condom wrapper being torn open, the rough scrape of his knuckles against her core as he slid the condom on using one hand.

A miracle of dexterity. A blessing of haste. And then he was inside of her, so hard, so fast. So thick and real that she tilted her head back against the wooden wall, her mouth open in a silent scream of pleasure. Her entire body thrown open to the forces at this man's command.

And as he pounded his grief out against her, she hoped, she truly hoped, that he found some kind of relief in the violence that raged inside of him.

The cold draft on his butt forced him to move. Otherwise he would have stayed where he was, plastered against Tori, buried inside of her, his face hidden in the hair that had fallen down around her shoulders. He would hide here, in this sensation. His brain turned low, his body at peace.

But that chill was getting personal, and if he felt it, she must, too.

Carefully he pulled away, holding her up when she came off the wall like a poster that had lost its tape.

"That was way better than how it looks in the movies," she whispered against his chest, wincing as she got to her feet, and he remembered how rough he'd been. How angry and out of control. It was the arena all over again, but she had met him halfway, taken his fury and altered it into something foreign, something shared. Hard, yes, ugly and raw, heavily painted with the blackness of his grief, but it was theirs.

In a life lived alone, it was a light in the darkness, a warm glow he could never have expected and could not resist.

And that he didn't want to resist it made him panic, as though he was being held underwater. As though he couldn't breathe.

She cleared her throat and pulled away from him, taking back her arms as if they were something he'd borrowed.

Moving like she'd aged thirty years up against that wall, she slowly leaned down to pull up her pants, tucking her T-shirt into the waist, her hands shaking.

"Did I hurt you?"

She shook her head.

"Tori—"

The tears in her bright blue eyes made him feel as if his skin had been peeled away.

"You didn't hurt me, Eli. It was amazing. *You* are amazing. But you don't like me. You aren't forgiving me for lying to you and the ridiculous thing is that I don't care. I don't have any pride when it comes to you. No control. No self-respect. It's like my marriage all over again, but with sex instead of money."

He had nothing to say to that, nothing to make the shame go away.

"Nothing to say?" She used her whole arm to toss her

hair back over her head, a neat feminine trick. "How did I know?"

"What do you want me to say, Victoria? That I forgive you?"

"Yes."

"But I don't."

"Then . . . how? How can you . . ." She gestured back at the wall as though she didn't have words for what had happened between them. He didn't really either; it was like stumbling on a new species of horse. "Do that with me?"

He shrugged. His body and his heart lived in two different counties and weren't always on speaking terms.

"I'm not . . . I'm not doing that again until you forgive me." She nodded as if seconding her own motion, and he could see he was going to be outvoted here.

He stared at her, long and hard, deciding that she wasn't bluffing. Go figure. "Might not happen again."

Soda barked somewhere behind them while the bones in her face went soft for one second, as if she just couldn't hold her expression in place anymore.

"If that's the way it is," she said, "then that's the way it is."

He watched her walk away, her body filling out her clothes in a way it never had before. She seemed to be getting more solid, moving into her body to stay. It suited her, taking away all that fragility that was such a lie and replacing it with bedrock.

But forgiving her was off his map, and he didn't know how to get there from where he stood.

chapter
16

Celeste earned her first hundred-thousand-dollar check when she was sixteen. She'd come back to Montreal from New York a freshly made woman, with more money than her family had seen in three years combined. She had something called a portfolio, and she wore new clothes with a new attitude. Victorious, she swept into her family's run-down Victorian in St. Henri and slapped that check down in front of her mother.

She stood there, expecting gratitude, wonderment even. A party, at least. She'd even smuggled champagne home in her bag, envisioning how adult she'd seem when she popped the cork. How worldly. But instead her mother pushed the check back across the table and said no thanks.

Celeste remembered laughing. Remembered laughing even though her stomach felt like it had been teargassed.

"Why?" she asked.

"Because you're more than your looks, and I know this money will make you forget that."

Her mother had been wrong. She wasn't more than her looks, she was the exact sum of her parts—the blue eyes, blond hair, skin the color and texture of milk, her grown-up body and girlish face.

And the money never let her forget that.

Modeling had been good to Celeste; she'd kept her career going for longer than most of the girls she'd started with and she'd never needed to take any of her son's money. Luc had made a fortune in his own right with the NHL by the time he was twenty-five. In the end she'd accepted his expensive gifts—the car when she turned sixty. Vacations. A very ugly diamond bracelet she treasured like nothing else.

Now, however, things were different, because she *needed* his money. And calling her son to ask for it, she had a new perspective on what her mother had said to her in that shabby kitchen. Luc's career in hockey did not define him for Celeste. He was so much more than his skill on the ice, and asking him for the money he'd earned there seemed like she was putting a box around him. Agreeing that his worth was monetary.

I'm sorry, Maman, she thought.

"A spa?" The cell phone connection between Celeste and Luc was crackly, but she could hear—loud and clear—her son's skepticism. "At the ranch?"

"Trust me. It will be perfect."

"Well, if there's anyone who knows spas, it's you and Vicks."

"So, the five hundred thousand?" Celeste stared out the kitchen window at the muddy mess of the backyard, the piles of building materials covered in tarps, and tried to pretend she wasn't begging her son for money.

Luc chuckled, and the sound was fairly new. Luc had never been a *chuckler,* but his relationship with Tara Jean Sweet seemed to have turned him into a happy man she barely recognized as her driven, focused son.

"Maman, it's okay, you can have the money."

Instead of relief, instead of sighing with gratitude, she ran a hand down her throat, across her chest, trying to coax her lungs to breathe.

She wasn't in the habit of asking for things. Not since she was a young woman, pregnant and alone on this ranch, begging her husband to notice her. To spend time with her.

"Thank you."

"Maman—" Pity colored her son's voice.

"We'll see you and Tara Jean at the grand opening? We're setting the date for New Year's."

"Great idea. I'll make sure it's on the calendar. And it will take a while, but I'll get the money into the ranch account."

"Wonderful." She smiled to make the word convincing.

"Hey, Maman . . ." He dropped his voice and she could hear him moving, closing doors behind him. "We were going to wait until Tara stops freaking out, but I want to tell you—"

Please. Please. She closed her eyes and actually prayed to God. *Pregnant. Grandchildren. Please.*

"We're buying a house in Dallas."

She blinked open her eyes. It was good news, no reason to feel bad. Her son, close by. "That's fantastic news, Luc."

"Yeah. It is. We're excited. Tara's never owned a house before, so she's taking it seriously."

Celeste smiled, thinking about her son's trashy girlfriend who had more class than most women she knew.

"Does that mean you'll be getting married soon?"

"One thing at a time, Maman."

They discussed neighborhoods for a moment, and then Luc finally had to hang up.

She pressed the phone to her lips, mourning that grandchild who, for the span of ten seconds, had been so real she could feel the baby in her arms.

In a cold, naked moment of honesty, she realized she was waiting for a grandchild so she could have someone to touch. Someone to shower with affection, someone upon whom she could unleash all this love she kept frozen.

What if there were no grandchildren? What would become of her? Who . . . who would she touch? Hug? Who would hug her?

Because Celeste Baker wasn't a woman people hugged. Not without written invitation.

The clatter and bang of workmen entering the house snapped her upright, out of her mood. Gavin came in first.

He should model, she thought, though she knew he wasn't that kind of man. But his body, that long, lean, loose-legged walk, would have made him a fortune. Not to mention his eyes, and that careless flop of white-blond hair. That confidence, that delicious masculine poise . . .

Celeste looked away, opening the laptop in front of her with sweaty hands. Honestly, sweaty hands—was she sixteen?

Behind Gavin his crew fanned out through the shell of the house, setting down their tool belts and lunch boxes.

"Good morning, Celeste," Gavin said, and her mouth was dry so she just nodded, which for some reason made the dark-haired man behind Gavin smirk.

Her instincts screamed that she should run up to her room, do the work she needed to do up there, but the wireless worked best in the kitchen and she was trying to get an ad for a spa manager up on several job sites.

Ruby had also gotten this great idea to email a Dallas morning show about doing a story segment on the spa. A producer had responded to Celeste's initial email and Celeste had to get back to her.

"My guys are going to be in here."

"Fine."

"Great."

Animosity rippled through the air; all the other people in the room had to feel it too, like a low-level electrical current. Someone coughed; another man pulled the collar away from his shirt.

The dark-haired man ducked into the other room and came back with a ladder.

"Try to stay out of the lady's way, Thomas," Gavin said, but his tone said "Careful, she bites."

"Will do." Thomas grinned at her, cheeky and young like a puppy, and she found herself smiling back at him.

The website was taking forever to load, so she watched as Thomas took out some plans and spread them over what was left of the counter. Then, picking up a pencil, he began to write on the walls.

An electrician, she decided. Her father had been an electrician back in Quebec. She recognized the symbols. The small tools in his pocket.

While the little hourglass spun on her screen, and Thomas went about his business, she tried to resist the urge to seek out Gavin. But now that all the walls were gone, he was too easy to find.

His blue shirt was like a neon sign in the far corner, where he and another man were bent over another set of plans.

The man should always wear blue. It should be a law. A constitutional amendment.

"That's the plumber," Thomas said, and she realized he'd caught her staring at Gavin and the other man. "Winston."

She made a little humming sound in response, relieved to see the website working.

"He's getting married next weekend."

"Who?" Her gaze flew up, only to see Thomas smiling at her.

"Winston."

She hummed, feigning a polite interest as she started to load her information into the website that had finally decided to cooperate. After drafting the ad, she hit enter and the hourglass reappeared.

Surreptitiously, she glanced back up, watching as Gavin built imaginary walls with his arms.

"Gavin's single," Thomas said, his voice rich with knowledge.

Hourglass be damned. She stood, pushing back the stool she'd pulled up to what was left of the breakfast counter. It screeched against the tiles, and both Winston and Gavin turned to stare.

In her prime, when her flesh had brought her gold and her eyes had brought men to their knees, she could have made Thomas crawl across glass just to smell her skin. But now he laughed at her because he knew she was old and her beauty was faded and she lusted after a man far too young for her.

She didn't know who she was more angry at, Thomas for noticing or herself for being unable to hide it.

"Get back to work," she snapped, and put the laptop under her arm and went to her room to hide.

A few hours later, hunger drove Celeste out of her room and she was delighted to find the house empty of Vikings and cheeky electricians. She grabbed a yogurt from the fridge and a spoon from the drawer and went out the front door to sit in the shade of the portico to eat her lunch.

Much to her horror, her spot was taken by a wide back in a blue shirt. Gavin took a bite of sandwich and then grabbed a chip from the bag between his feet. He stared off into the distance as he chewed.

She wondered what he was thinking about so intently.

Sports, probably. A man like him. Boxing. Professional wrestling, something brutal and raw. That seemed like his sort of thing.

Trying to be dismissive didn't change her fascination. Largely because she knew herself to be a liar.

Poetry, she thought. *He could be sitting there thinking of e.e. cummings, and you're such a bitch you can't allow him any depth.*

Sometimes, honestly, she hated herself.

Trying hard not to make a sound, she eased the door open, but he must have seen movement out of the corner of his eye, because he turned and then stood, his lunch held at his side.

"Sorry," he said. The ham sandwich, with his mouth-sized bites taken out of it, seemed so vulnerable. Interrupting this man at his lunch seemed akin to finding him with his shoes off.

How, she wondered, marveling at her own sad thoughts, had she become so isolated? How was it possible that thinking about a man's feet seemed like an imposition?

He glanced down at his lunch box and then at the yogurt in her hands. "I'll get out of your way," he said.

"No, stay. Please. I can . . ." *Go inside. Hit myself over the head. Die a painful death.* "Make do." He still stood as if questioning whether she was sincere, or if he wanted to spend any more time with her.

"This is my favorite spot for lunch," she said, awkwardly trying to play nice.

"It's nice," he said. "The view is peaceful."

"That's what we're counting on," she said. "For the spa."

He nodded, then glanced down at his sandwich as if just realizing it was there. "Do you have plans for the barn?" He pointed to the roof of the barn past the greenhouse.

"Not really."

"Perfect spot for a yoga studio."

She blinked, stunned at his perception. They hadn't thought of the outer buildings, choosing to focus on the house, but the barn would be an ideal studio.

"Some windows along one wall. Re-covered pine floors."

"Are you a closet spa-goer?"

"Men can't like yoga?"

"I just didn't think someone like—" Oh dear. She stopped herself.

"A guy like me would like yoga?" His flat eyes accused her of being a snob, and he was so right she could only nod. Owning up to her own failures wasn't something she excelled at, but she tried to rise above her instincts.

He tossed his sandwich back in the crumpled bag on the step. "I need to get back to work."

She also wasn't very good at apologies. Instead, she took a bite of yogurt, stepping out of the way when he walked by her.

"Oh," he paused, right at the door, so close she could smell him. Wood and sweat, something tangy. An orange from his lunch. Her body melted at the scent. "Thomas, the electrician?"

"What about him?" she asked.

"He's got a mouth, and a wicked streak I haven't been able to beat out of him."

"You beat all your electricians?" she asked.

"Only the one who's my kid."

The yogurt got trapped in her throat and she coughed delicately until she could breathe again.

"Did he do anything out of line?" he asked.

His son? The thought was a panicked bird in her chest, bashing itself against windows, unable to find an exit. *Gavin's son knows I want Gavin.*

"No," she whispered. "He was fine."

He turned to leave. All lean strength, all muscular control, and she, suddenly loose-limbed and desperate to try to make some kind of connection, stopped him.

"Do you really do yoga?"

For a very long moment he watched her as if deciding whether to waste any more time with a woman who always seemed to insult him. She stood there and tried to look . . . nice.

His grin was sly, turning his attraction into something that was in total and full ownership of itself, something she couldn't just push away with the weak power of her snobbery, of her icy insecurity.

"No."

She smiled, really smiled, laugh lines be damned, and all those weak and tired locks she kept on her kindness and compassion, her warmth and generosity, fell to pieces.

"My ex did," he said, "and I spent a lot of money on her being able to do it in places far less beautiful than this ranch."

She nodded, processing his words. The ex part. And the part about a lot of money.

"Please," she said, gesturing to the steps he'd just vacated. "Finish your lunch. I'm sorry I was . . ."

He crooked a wicked eyebrow, his smile pure devilment.

"Unpleasant," she said instead of the word in his head, even though his word was a more apt description. "Please, sit."

"Only if you'll join me."

She took a deep breath and nodded, wondering why it took so much bravery to just sit down with the man. To just let go of the worst of herself, the old suit of armor that chafed.

"I'd be delighted."

No fucking way.

That was Eli's rationale for driving up to the ranch on Monday morning and parking his truck under the poplars just like he had for twenty years.

For a man who wanted nothing to do with the woman

who'd left him twenty-seven years ago, sitting twenty feet from where she worked was insane. He knew that.

But there was no fucking way he could sit at his home, while Amy was up here doing God knows what.

He'd tried to talk himself out of this ridiculous idea all morning long, but it was as if someone else was driving his body. The eight-year-old she had left behind was calling the shots and he was just the bag of bones moving shit around.

Victoria could take care of herself, he'd learned that firsthand, and if she didn't want to listen to his warnings about Amy, then that was on her head.

She'd fired him, after all.

And then hired his mom behind his back. And then lied about it.

He didn't owe her anything.

But somehow he couldn't stop thinking of the way she'd wrapped her arms around him, even when she knew he was furious with her. Then she'd told him everything was going to be okay and did her damndest for ten minutes to make sure it was. He remembered with a pain in his side that just wouldn't go away the way her hands had shaken as she pulled up her pants, the way her tears had sat, unfalling, in her eyes.

He couldn't forget that just a few days ago, he'd liked her. More than he'd liked another person in a long, long time.

All of this had run him out of the house this morning, because he couldn't stand by and let Amy walk out on one more thing. Even a spa he didn't care about.

So, if Victoria wasn't going to protect herself against Amy, he'd have to do it for her. He would sit there every morning and make sure Amy finished the job.

He knew Victoria took Jacob to school each morning, so while she was gone, while she couldn't come and shoo him away like a stray dog, he would sit here and make his presence known.

Let his mother know that even though she had Victoria fooled, he was on to her. And she wasn't going to walk away this time.

He got out of the truck, well aware that his mother was standing on the front porch staring at him, slack-jawed, as he took out the lawn chair from his truck bed and kicked it open in the shade of the trees.

Making himself at home, he cracked his cooler and took out a bottle of water and his breakfast—a grape jelly and creamy peanut butter sandwich. His lunch sandwich had strawberry jam and chunky peanut butter. A major distinction.

Amy glanced around, no doubt to see if anyone else was going to come down here and tell him to get lost. When no one came charging out of the house with a shotgun, she slowly, as if waiting for the ground to open under her feet, walked down the steps toward him.

"What are you doing here?" she asked, stepping into the shade. She wore a pair of men's work overalls and he tried to remember what she'd worn when he was little, but he couldn't. He'd been too young to notice.

"Watching you." He talked through a bite of sandwich.

Lines showed up between her eyes, suggesting she was angry or confused. Those he remembered. She used to walk around like that for days, never smiling, always looking like she was never sure how she got to be where she was. He remembered every single knock-knock joke he'd told her to try to make those lines go away, every single chore he'd completed without being asked. All so she might smile at him instead of frown.

"Why?"

"I'm going to make sure you don't walk away from Tori."

"I'm not walking away. I signed contracts—"

"Just like you promised Victoria you were going to tell me that you were back here?" *Just like you promised me you'd always be around? That you'd always love me? Always take care of me?*

She had the good grace to look sick at his words.

"Your promises don't mean much to me. You're a liar and a quitter." God, the words felt so good and there were a hundred more locked away, things he wanted to say to her, terrible things he wanted to call her, and he had to swallow them all back down. "I won't see you hurt her, Amy."

"You sound like your father."

He smirked and took a bite of sandwich.

At an impasse, she glanced over her shoulder at the house that was starting to change shape.

"You don't want to see this ranch in ruins?" she asked.

He crossed and uncrossed his legs, uncomfortable with the reminder of what his intentions had been before he'd been fired, of how he'd treated Victoria.

"No."

"I want to burn it to the ground."

He surged to his feet and she lifted her hand, as if that could stop him from picking her up and stuffing her in her truck. "I said that I want to, not that I will. This land, and wanting it back, has ruined a lot of Turnbulls. It nearly ruined me."

"Well, good thing you got out when you did." His sarcasm was a sword he swung as hard as he could, but she just stared at him, unbloodied. "And you're not a Turnbull," he added, just to be mean.

"I tried, Eli. For years I tried to convince your father to leave. But he wouldn't—"

"This land was his life."

"Funny, but when he married me, he said *I* was his life. And he chose this land over me."

"Well, maybe if you hadn't been so mean to him! Maybe if you'd been nice. Or happy."

He knew how unfair he was being. How cruel. Hell, he knew how his father could destroy niceness, how he could pull apart happiness until only strings remained.

But she'd left him to that and she didn't deserve his consideration.

Red splotches, matching the carrot of her hair, climbed up her neck, across her chest, obliterating freckles, burning them into nothing. Her mouth opened and shut as if she was trying to put some words together, but he just glared at her, stalwart in his bias.

"I came here thinking that you were reaching out to me."

He laughed. Right at her. Into her face. Because she had to know he would never reach out to her. But she absorbed his laughter like his injustices, like his hate, as if she were a sponge. And all he had to throw at her was water.

"And when I found out that you weren't, I wanted to pull this house apart with my bare hands. I was furious that I'd come back here only to be hurt all over again."

"*You?*" he cried.

"Do you think it was easy leaving you?"

"Yeah. I do. Because you did it."

"Eli—"

He sat, picked up his sandwich, mashing it in his hands.

"I didn't come here to fight," he said and took a bite. He didn't taste it, didn't want it, but he had to do something to keep himself from asking the questions he thought he'd outgrown. "I just want you to know that I am watching you."

"And I'm not leaving," she said, her eyes drinking him in, the way he remembered her doing, standing at his bedroom door, saying good night. "I want to see something happy on this land. Something that makes people feel good."

"Right—"

"Believe what you want, but this land has hurt enough people. I'm here for healing."

She turned, walking out from under the shade into the sunlight, with her head held high, her shoulders back, as if she were in the right.

"Bullshit!" he yelled.

But she didn't turn; she just kept walking right back to the house.

chapter
17

"*Do you think* Lucky will be happy to see me?" Jacob asked, bouncing in the passenger seat.

"Seat belt, Jacob."

"Mom, Eli's ranch is right there." He pointed out the front window of the squat house in the distance, black against the crimson sunset.

"I don't care. Wear your seat belt."

She could practically hear Jacob rolling his eyes as he pulled the belt over his shoulder.

"I do think Lucky will be happy to see you," she said, and Jacob all but glowed in the twilight. She should have done this a while ago. He'd been heartbroken when Eli had bought that horse.

It was on the tip of her tongue to ask her son if he thought Eli would be happy to see her. Not that he would have an answer, and she knew better than to ask. But she felt as though she was wandering into unchartered waters with only her son to protect her, and he was distracted by a deaf horse.

Celeste had told her that Eli had been coming to the house every morning for a week. He'd sit there, eating a sandwich and glowering, yelling things at the crew. And then he'd leave before Victoria returned from dropping Jacob off at school.

Today, one of the young electricians had almost started

a fight with him until Amy and Gavin had pulled the kid away.

It was time to face the lion in its den. Enough of being scared of him, scared of her own lack of control.

She was here to call Eli off, and she'd brought Jacob so that she'd keep her clothes on.

The truck was barely in park before Jacob was out the door and hurtling across the dry grass toward the house. But the house was dark and she turned just as Eli stepped out of the barn, wiping his hands on a towel slung over his shoulder.

His hat shaded his eyes from the last of the daylight, but not so his mouth, and the magic light that glowed all over his lips was like a neon sign saying "Kiss Here."

She reached for the buttons on her cardigan, unhappy to find only the cold metal zipper of the sweatshirt she'd borrowed from Ruby. All of her old clothes—her armor—were getting too small. It wasn't just her boobs growing anymore. Gaining weight was great, but she could use a little cashmere right about now to remind her to keep her hands to herself.

One glance at him and she wanted him. Wanted those lips on hers. That mouth on her body. And as she watched, his lips curved, surrounded by a day's growth of beard, as if he knew exactly what her wicked mind was thinking.

Seven days since she'd last seen him, and it was like he'd just peeled her off the barn wall a second ago.

"Eli!" Jacob yelled, jumping off the side of the porch. Eli jerked sideways at the sound, and he barely managed to catch Jacob as he tumbled to a halt in front of him.

"Have you fed Lucky?" the boy asked.

"Nope." He smiled down at Jacob. She'd forgotten how endearing the man was with her son, how out of his depth but game. She blinked, remembering when he'd said the same thing about her.

"Can I do it?" Jacob asked, bouncing on his feet while reaching down to scratch at his ankle where the summer's mosquito bites lingered.

Eli smiled and glanced up at her, lovely in his warmth. His surprising openness. "Come on."

She lingered at the closest paddock, watching Eli show Jacob how to feed the horses. When Jacob caught on, Eli let him take over, and he came to stand next to her, his arms slung over the top rail of the split-wood fence.

"I hope you don't mind," she said, pointing to her son, who was diligently following Eli's instructions, a pretty brown-and-white collie following him.

"Of course not."

In the silence, her body hummed and her imagination traced the edges of the distance between them, charting him like a foreign land.

"You've been coming around the ranch this week."

He said nothing, spit something over his other shoulder.

"What were you doing this morning?" she asked.

He shrugged.

Immediately exhausted by his still, deep waters, his taciturn cowboy routine, she hung her head, too tired to force him into talking.

"You're going to chase her away, Eli. Is that what you want? Because it will ruin everything for me."

He pressed his foot against the fence post and said nothing.

"I don't need a watchdog, Eli," she said. "And I don't need you starting fights with my employees."

His hand touched her skin and she jerked away. If he touched her, she would unravel, she would. She was so damn weak.

"He started a fight with me."

"Eli—"

"Look, Tori, I don't believe her, I don't trust her, and if Amy's going to be there, I'm going to be there."

"Why are you doing this? You have no stake in this ranch."

"I'm trying to protect you."

"Two months ago you were trying to ruin me."

He said nothing, both of them watching the sky, anything but each other.

"Are you saying your feelings have changed that much?" she asked.

"Christ, Tori, we . . . slept together."

She laughed, though it hurt a little to diminish what had been so special in her life. But there was no way sex in the front seat of his truck with a lonely widow was all that out of the ordinary for him. "It meant that much to you? I'm flattered. But I don't think you look at sex that way, Eli. You also had sex with me when you were furious with me."

Muscles in his jaw tensed.

"I think you're there because of her. Because . . ."

"Don't, Tori. Don't imagine things that just aren't there. She's nothing but a threat right now. To you. She's nothing to me."

Yeah, right, she thought.

"You want me to fire her?"

"Yes! God yes."

Jacob tossed rocks into the tall grass on the far side of the paddock, and the collie ran in and fished them out, setting them at his feet. Watching her son, the dog waited with such gratitude, such enthusiasm for him to throw another rock.

"No."

Eli dropped his head, thunking it against the fence.

"My husband committed suicide," she said, focusing all of her attention on the brittle grain of the wood under her hands. "And my best friend, Renee, told me that Joel married me because he knew I would just spend my life being so damn grateful that he'd even noticed me that I would never . . . even if I suspected something about how much money he was making and how fast, I wouldn't say anything, out of fear that he'd take it all away."

"Did you know? What your husband was doing?"

"I knew he was doing something," she whispered. "And I didn't do anything and that's enough, right? That's wrong. And she was right—I was a guest in my own house for years, so damn grateful just to be there."

"Your best friend sounds like a bitch."

"She was. Is. They all were. So was I. I was their leader. But she was right, and I can't . . . I've got to make the right decisions for me. For my son. My life."

"And you think Amy is the right decision?"

"I do, Eli. I'm sorry."

He shrugged. "Then I'll be under those poplars every morning."

"Don't you have better things to do? Horse-breeding things?"

"My girls aren't ready to go yet. And thanks to the land you sold me and the income it brings in, I've got some wiggle room. In fact, for the first time in my life, I've actually got money in the bank."

She snorted, letting him know what she thought of his wiggle room.

"I won't . . . you can't jeopardize this, Eli. I need her."

He stared at her. But he didn't say anything. She could get no promises from Eli Turnbull, and it pissed her off.

"Can I ask you a question?" she asked.

"Would it matter if I said no?"

"Where's your father?"

Back when she had money, she kept the heirloom jewelry passed down to her from Joel's mother in a vault at her bank. To get to it, she would have to pass through a series of armored doors with locks and keys and pass codes. An armed guard.

And all those doors and vaults and guards had just closed up tight in Eli's head.

But he reached out to her, his fingers tracing her cheekbone, and just that touch made his intentions clear.

"Do you forgive me?" she asked, her voice made out of steel and concrete, because honestly, he had to be joking.

"Do you really care?"

Her body certainly didn't. Not when the calluses of his fingers sent ripples over her skin like water after stones had been tossed in.

Luckily, her self-respect, wearing cashmere and silk and a dozen buttons she could mentally count and stroke, shored her up.

She stepped away and his mouth twisted into a grim line.

The silence wasn't comfortable, but not pained either, and she was reminded of those days in the penthouse, before Jacob—when it was just her and the housekeeper, trying to avoid each other in every room.

"The Elms, downtown," he said. "He's got Alzheimer's. Dementia. Violent . . . tendencies they call it." He shrugged, but there was nothing nonchalant about him. "Took care of him as best I could until it became obvious the man needed help full time or something was going to get burned to the ground."

"How long has he been there?"

"Seven . . . eight years, this December. Put him in at Christmas . . ." He stopped, tipping his hat low as if he couldn't bear her watching him. "That's the kind of son I am."

Oh, his heart was right there on his sleeve and she'd never expected to see it. Never expected him to show so much of himself. The desire to kiss away the worst of his guilt, the load he carried like a backpack of dead weight, was hard to resist.

"Sometimes you don't have a choice in those things."

His sigh was heavy and deep, pulled up from the bottom of his guts, full of disagreement.

"I was sixteen when I left my mom," she said, surprised to be talking about her own ancient history. "I left her to her boyfriends who didn't really care about her. The painkillers that cared even less. I tried for years . . . but in the end I had to save myself. I just stayed at boarding school, didn't come home on holidays, told her I was too busy with classes."

"I never met your mom. All those years you came down."

"She hated it here. Too boring for a woman who had to surround herself with people just so she could feel something. And with Celeste—"

"Must have been hard."

She shrugged, because he seemed to know how hard it had been. He seemed to see right into the damaged places, because those same places were damaged in him.

"I actually liked the holidays at school. It was just me and some of the housekeepers. A couple of teachers. Mr. Jennings the gardener. We played a lot of poker. I got to read all day long if I wanted, or help Mr. Jennings in the greenhouse."

She smiled. The air smelled like sun-baked grass and sweat and horses, and it was better than a glass of wine at taking care of those knots in the back of her neck. The worries that grew on them.

Or maybe it was the man next to her who did that.

She hoped not, she really did, for her own sake.

"Once I pretended to be sick, just so I could spend the day reading," he offered.

"Once?" Pretending to be sick had been her bread and butter for a lot of years.

"*The Hobbit,*" he said. "Uncle John gave it to me for my eleventh birthday and two days later, I had a hundred pages to go and just couldn't wait."

"Your Uncle John, I don't remember him."

"He steers clear of Bakers."

"Because of the land?"

Eli nodded. "John's polished that grudge to a high shine. Doesn't like the fact that I've stopped caring about getting the land back."

"Where is he now?"

"Full of questions tonight, aren't you?"

"Sorry. I . . . I didn't mean to pry."

But she did, and he knew that, and she intended to pry until he stopped letting her in, which seemed like it might happen this very moment.

It was time to go home; she'd tried to call off her guard dog and had managed to keep her clothes on. This . . . conversation was only going to make a complicated situation worse. She didn't need to like him. She already wanted him plenty.

"Jacob," she called, "it's time—"

"He's in Galveston until after Christmas," he said, winding and unwinding that towel he'd been carrying around the fence post. "When I was a kid, John was an oil rigger. He came to visit once when I was about ten. Dad had been on a three-day bender and I had done what I could with the animals and his work and school, but . . . well, Uncle John saw what was happening and didn't leave. Bought a house over in Springfield and tried to pick up the slack as much as he could."

"Thank God for him."

Eli nodded. "I do most days."

She waited a few more seconds just because she wanted to, like lingering in a bath before the water got too cold, and then she pushed herself away from the fence. "We better get—"

His hand covered hers and she gasped at the contact, the sudden heat, the roughness. All the receptors in her body were thrown wide open and she wanted to absorb him, pull him in through her skin, her nerves.

"Come back. Tonight." If his touch was desperate, his face was unreadable, a granite mask, and she knew if he'd shown the least bit of weakness, desire, lust, anything, *for her*, she would have said yes.

But right now, this need he had for her had little to do with her.

"Have you forgiven me?" He was silent, his grip on her hand hard enough to hurt, and then he let go. All the answer she needed. "I told you I wouldn't come back unless you did."

"How do you know I haven't?"

She ached to touch him, to cup that jaw in her hands, to press her lips to his, to sip the bitterness and grief from him. "Because I haven't forgiven myself."

"Hey, Eli!" Jacob came running up, the dog at his heels, and she jumped backwards about eight hundred feet, not that her son noticed. Nope, he only had eyes for the cowboy. Must run in the family. "Can I come back, help you feed the horses again at night? After school?"

"I . . . ah . . ." Eli looked over at her and she reached out for Jacob, putting her hands on his head. She needed distance from Eli, not friendly horse-feeding visits. It had been stupid to stay here, asking questions.

"I don't know, Jacob, Eli's a busy—"

"It's fine with me." Eli scratched his dog behind the ear and the dog's fool face split in a wide, happy doggy smile, his tongue hanging down to the tall grass.

Jacob cheered, the dog barked, and she mentally went back to counting those buttons on her self-control.

Back at the ranch, the moon was coming up over the house, the yellow lights leaking out through the new windows installed today. Surprisingly, Amy's truck was still there and when Victoria got out of her car, the woman emerged from the shadows.

"Amy? What are you still doing here?"

"Is he coming back?" she asked.

"Eli?" Victoria watched as Jacob trotted up the stairs, yelling for Celeste so that he could tell her every detail of feeding those horses.

"Did you tell Eli to stay away?" Amy demanded, pulling Victoria from her thoughts about Celeste's eerily good grandmother ways.

"I tried."

"Damn it, Victoria, why'd you do that?"

"What? He's causing problems, isn't he? Starting fights with your employees?"

"Thomas started it, and he'd pick a fight with a scarecrow if he thought it was looking at him funny."

Victoria tossed her hands in the air. "Well, everyone was acting like he's been sitting there like a giant pain in the butt."

"Oh, he is. Yesterday he wouldn't move his truck to let the guys delivering the two hot tubs closer to the house. We had to get everyone on the crew to carry the things right past him, while he sat there, eating a sandwich."

"So? It sounds like I tried to do everyone a favor."

Amy stared at her, her jaw looking as if she were chewing rocks. "Is he coming back?"

Too late, too wrapped up in her own head, Victoria realized what this was about: a mom being close to her son.

Amy'd had Eli, hating her, causing her nothing but grief, sitting a hundred yards away from her every morning. The closest she'd been to him in decades.

And Victoria had told him to stay away.

"If you want to see him, go see him, Amy."

"You know it's not that easy."

"Yeah, and whose fault is that?" Victoria didn't think Amy was going to walk out on her, she had enough faith in Amy's professionalism, but she totally understood why Eli would think the worst. It wasn't just that his mother had walked out on him, it was that she'd worked here for a week without going to see him. Three miles away and she couldn't bridge the distance she'd created so many years ago.

"Is he coming back?"

"Yes. He said he'll be here until you're gone."

Amy's tense face relaxed into a relieved smile. "Good. That's . . . good."

Amy walked away, back to her truck.

What the hell is wrong with all of us? Victoria wondered.

chapter
18

Celeste was usually very good with a blank slate. The fashion industry was all about blank slates. But the barn wasn't blank. It was full of cats and hay, saddles and bridles, equipment and generations of hardware. It was the opposite of blank. And she just couldn't see past the reality to the possibility.

So, she called in some help.

"Hey, Celeste," Gavin said, walking down the wide center aisle of the barn. Dust motes glittered around him, and looking directly at him was like looking into the sun. "Thomas said you were looking for me."

He tucked his thumbs inside his tool belt and leaned against a stall door. The last two weeks she'd been eating lunch with him, and his glamour was undiminished by familiarity. None of his appeal had worn away. And now she knew that beneath his surfer hair he had an artist's clever brain and a saint's generous heart. A combination that drew her in like gravity.

"We need more room," she said.

Gavin held up his hands, his laugh a deep ripple through the air. "I've been in the middle of this fight with you and Victoria too often."

"But you know I'm right." She smiled at him over her shoulder and the air popped and smoked between them. Flirting was dangerous, since it was obvious he was as attracted to her as she was to him. Or at least as attracted to the idea of her, that poster of her. But it was hard to resist the flirtation sometimes. The interest of a man like Gavin put the panicky gerbils in her heart to sleep. And she no longer cared about looking younger, because she *felt* younger.

"You're right, Celeste. You ladies need more room."

"And this barn is just sitting here. How much square footage do you think we have?"

He pulled his tape measure from his tool belt. "Hold this." He handed her the metal tab and walked away from her, the metal ribbon uncoiling between them.

She followed him around the barn, holding the tab when he asked her to, remembering the numbers he called out.

"You're a good assistant," he said, as the tape measure snapped and slithered back into the case in his hand. "If the spa business gets old, you can come work for me."

"You can't afford me."

"You don't know that," he said, chastising her. He'd gotten very comfortable calling her on her snobbery. "I might be rich."

"Fine. You can afford ten of me. How big is this barn?"

"I'd say you could get ten more rooms, between the main floor and the hayloft. Or ten more rooms and a yoga studio."

"What about the arena?"

He looked at her in a way she was utterly unfamiliar with. Men were captivated by her surface. They didn't try to figure her out; they didn't guess at her inner workings. Didn't care if she had any. But Gavin did. Gavin looked at her as if she were his favorite puzzle, and it made her feel like she had a bag over her head.

It was liberating.

"What are you thinking, Celeste?"

"I'm thinking about weddings."

His eyes went wide, and he spun on his heel to look into the dark shadows of the riding arena at the end of the hallway. "A ballroom."

"Yep."

"Absolutely. You could do it. In fact . . ." He walked down the hallway and she followed, drunk on his enthusiasm.

He pointed up. "Skylights." He spun. "Open the doorway up. Lay down some hardwood. A few windows. Maybe take out the walls between the arena and the barn and you could get a hundred people in here, easy."

It was as if he were singing her love songs.

"How much will it cost me?"

He took his time, this methodical man. He walked around, pushed on joists, paced the barn again, and she walked back out into the aisle, where it was lighter. "A hundred grand."

She blew out a long breath. That was better than she'd expected. Another call to her son would be forthcoming.

"You think Victoria will go for it?" he asked.

"No." She laughed. "Absolutely not."

"Why do I get the feeling that's not going to stop you?"

"You think it should? You said it yourself—I'm right."

He crossed his arms over his chest and leaned back against a closed stall door. "I think you and Victoria are complicated enough without you going behind her back."

Celeste fought the urge to fidget. To bite her lip, or put her hands in the back pockets of her jeans. She just stared at him and wished he weren't right.

"What's the story between the two of you?" he asked.

Immediately she turned away. They'd discussed a lot of things over their lunches. Politics. Art. The many blessings of a Starbucks drive-thru, but they hadn't talked about anything personal. At least she hadn't. But it was getting harder and harder to stop herself. To keep what was private private.

"She's not your daughter. And you don't treat her like a friend."

Celeste whirled back around, a strand of hair getting caught in her lip gloss. "She is my ex-husband's bastard daughter, born a year after my son."

"Oh . . . Celeste. I'm sorry—"

"Don't be. Honestly." She waved her hand as if she could wipe up the mess that was the Baker family. "She had the worse end of the deal."

"What do you mean?"

Oh Lord. She felt the familiar chill of her anger, of her self-directed guilt and loathing. She pulled the hair away from her icy smile. "Thank you for your help, Gavin."

He stared at her and she stared right back. And right about the time most men would walk away, Gavin tilted his head back and laughed up at the ceiling. Birds darted from their nests, startled by the sound of his howling.

She frowned at him, and still he laughed.

"Does that usually work?" he asked.

"What are you talking about?"

"Does that usually scare away all the men that want to get to know you?" He stepped closer to her, his work boots silent on the dirt and straw.

"It scared you, remember?"

He lifted a big, callused finger and she wanted that finger in her body, against her skin. "But I've seen you, Celeste." He was close now, very close. She could see the faint glimmer of his blond beard coming in, the handsome wrinkles that crinkled in the corner of his blue eyes. The smell of him, masculine and earthy with just a hint of the apple he ate every morning, curled and coiled around her and she had to open her mouth to breathe just so she could taste him.

His eyes touched every part of her face and his smile was sweet, tender, even, as if he were staring at something with sentimental value. As if he were staring at something that mattered.

"You can talk to me, Celeste. And I know you're going to hate this, but I'll say it anyway. I think you could use someone to talk to. I think you could use a friend."

"Is that what you are?" She wanted to sound sarcastic, but instead she sounded plaintive. Yearning almost.

"Yes." He was definitive. Rock-solid. "So, tell me, Celeste. Tell me about you and Victoria."

And just like that, as if she'd been standing on the edge of a cliff she wasn't even aware of, she opened her mouth and the whole sordid tale came out. Her anger with her husband; the way she'd taken it out on Victoria, punishing her for something that had never been her fault.

"Guilt won't change anything," Gavin said. "I used to feel so bad about my divorce, like if I had just tried harder Thomas would have a real family—"

"You can't save a marriage on your own, Gavin," she whispered.

"Yeah, it took me a long time to learn that." His smile was bittersweet. "But you and Victoria seem like you're on good terms now."

Her eyes burned with tears and the ache of so much sensation, so much feeling, made her gasp. "I'm so proud of her, Gavin. I'm so proud and I can't even tell her. What . . . ?"

She stopped herself before asking, *What's wrong with me?* Certainly she wasn't so much of a fool that she'd lay herself naked like that.

"Oh, babe," he sighed, and before she could stop him

or prepare herself, he pulled her into his arms. Against his chest.

The heat and strength of him was intense and she gasped, her skin, every nerve ending, thrown open to soak him in. This was dangerous, reckless.

And it certainly wasn't just friendship.

She pulled away, wiping her eyes, frantically searching for some kind of joke, something sarcastic to remind her of the distance she liked around herself.

His thumb touched her cheek, wiping away a tear, and her brain emptied out like a grocery bag turned upside down.

"You're even beautiful when you cry," he whispered.

Speechless, ruined by his kindness, she turned and ran.

Victoria pulled up in front of Eli's barn, and he stepped off the porch of his house to greet them before Jacob could even get his seat belt off.

She concentrated very hard on turning off the car, on the metal and plastic under her fingers, the kick and rattle of the engine that she never had time to get inspected. All instead of staring at him in those jeans, that long-sleeved shirt that hugged his shoulders against the cool early-November evening.

He was sex in cowboy boots, masculinity with a rock-hard jaw.

And this was her sixth excruciating visit. Her son had progressed from feeding the horses to learning how to ride. According to Eli he was a natural, and even she had to admit that he looked comfortable up on that saddle.

And Eli . . . Eli just looked good.

She couldn't take much more of this. Not without begging him to forgive her, or buying some mail-order sex toys.

Truth be told, she'd forgiven herself halfway through the second visit, mostly in the hopes that if she did, he might too, and then she could come back to his place and work out this frustration she could barely stand. She wasn't used to feeling this way, as if her skin didn't fit. As if her body wasn't her own. As if she'd do anything to get his hands on her again.

A sad state of affairs, but there you have it.

She unrolled her window and Eli leaned in, smelling of sun and sweat and man. Her body went haywire at the smell.

"Hey there," he said, that slow smile crossing his face. She wanted to lick that smile from end to end, a voyage of discovery.

Jacob unclipped his seat belt and leaned over the console, bracing his weight against her leg. She winced and tried to move his hand.

"What's going on, Eli?" he asked. "Everything all right?"

"Sure." Eli nodded. "Right as rain, but it might not be the best night for a ride."

"But . . . why?" Jacob's face was a picture of devastated boyhood.

"Well." Eli rubbed his neck, a blush visible through the golden-brown hairs of the beard he had coming in. "Nothing . . . ah . . ." He glanced at her, a purely pained, adult look. From behind the stables, horses whinnied and cried. Her eyes opened wide at the sound. It sounded . . . matey.

"It's like equine porn back there," he whispered.

No. They definitely didn't need to go watch that.

"The horses are sick," she said to her wide-eyed, innocent son.

"Yep." Eli nodded. "Sick."

Jacob's shoulders fell. "It's not forever," she murmured, kissing his head.

"But I don't want to go back to the ranch," he said. "If we go back, you and Celeste and Ruby will open up those notebooks and I'll be bored."

She didn't want to go either—coming to Eli's had given her a much-needed break from Celeste and Ruby's notebooks, Amy's calculator. Her own drive to see the spa succeed.

Eli didn't want to talk about the tiles in the change rooms or Celeste's conviction that they needed to renovate the barn. Or this *Dallas A.M.* talk show possibility.

Instead, she and Eli talked about how Jacob was doing in school, Eli's horses. Two days ago he'd given her an elegant soliloquy on the differences between creamy and chunky peanut butter. Half the time they didn't talk at all, and somehow that back paddock of his had become the most peaceful place in her life.

"Well, we can't stay here," she finally said, wishing that weren't the case.

Eli listened to Victoria give Jacob options for their evening, each more boring than the last. When she got to doing laundry, he winced, on everyone's behalf.

For two weeks now he'd been blaming his excitement about seeing the kid on the fact that he so badly wanted to sleep with Victoria. She and Jacob were a package deal.

But contemplating a night alone when he'd been planning on seeing them all week . . . well, all this privacy he'd cultivated, this solitary life, just seemed lonely.

"I've got an idea," Eli said, and Jacob perked up like Soda, who sat on the porch drooling.

Victoria eyed him as though he were trying to sell her rotten eggs.

"Eli, you don't have to—"

"What?" Jacob asked, bouncing. "What's your idea?"

"You got Ruby's peace offering?" Eli asked, and Jacob scrambled down to the floorboards and grabbed a tinfoil-wrapped plate.

Ruby, since finding out that Victoria and Jacob were coming over to Eli's most nights, had started sending him food. A way of saying she was sorry for bringing his mom back to the ranch, without ever actually having to say she was sorry.

That kind of passive-aggressive cowardice was right up his alley. He and Ruby had always understood each other.

"Brownies," Jacob said. "I helped. No nuts."

"Thank God." Eli took them through the window, his hand touching a few strands of Victoria's hair—like hot wire filaments, he was burned by them. "Anything else?"

Victoria leaned back and hauled a paper bag up from the backseat. Bottles clanged together inside.

He grabbed it and stepped away from the truck.

"Come on with me," he said.

She and Jacob shared a quick look and practically tumbled out of the truck. Jacob whistled for Soda, who bounded off the porch and then headed toward the other side of the house and the thin dirt trail that parted the wild fennel.

Jacob charged up ahead, getting in front of Eli, and then turning around and walking backwards to talk to him.

"Careful," Victoria cried.

"Mom . . . ," he groaned, rolling his eyes at Eli, who shook his head.

"Listen to your mom," he said and the boy turned around. He was always so amazed when Jacob listened to him as if he were the voice of God, made him feel as if he were playing a strange game of Simon Says.

"Where are we going?" Jacob yelled over his shoulder.

"We got a spring back here, the source of the creek that gives the ranch its name."

"Hey, I remember the spring," Victoria said.

"Is it crooked?" Jacob asked.

"Not really."

"Humph."

They walked a while, crickets bouncing off the grass around them. "Hey, Eli?" Jacob asked.

"What?"

"Amy's your mom, huh?"

He nearly dropped the bag, and he heard Victoria trip behind him.

"Yeah."

"She left you, when you were a kid?" Eli turned to glare at Victoria, who shook her head and mouthed "What was I supposed to say?"

"Yeah, she did," Eli finally answered.

"My dad left me, too." Jacob turned in the middle of the trail, the grass hitting the bottom edge of his shorts. So small, but his eyes were so old and full of things that shouldn't be there—disappointment and hurt. Resignation. The awareness that what was absent was never going to be returned.

"It sucks," Jacob said.

"Yes, it does," he agreed.

Jacob turned and kept walking. Eli didn't turn around, though it was hard. He could feel Victoria, hurting for both of them.

They burst out onto a muddy bank and stepped down to a small pebbly shoal. The clear spring was twenty feet around, surrounded by memories, glittering like fireflies in the sweet grass.

"Are we going swimming?" Jacob asked.

"It's pretty cold this time of year," Eli said, looking around as if someone was supposed to meet them. "They're not here."

"Who?" Victoria asked, slipping down the muddy slide to collide into him. The heat of her against his back was solar in its warmth. Its brightness. Even through the shirt he wore.

She stepped away, and his body felt like the far side of the moon—lonely and cold.

"Let's sit down and wait." He stepped sideways to a worn-down area and sat, putting the plate of brownies beside him, the bag of bottles between his legs.

"Hey, Jacob," he said, taking out four brown bottles and then handing him the paper bag. "See if you can find some frogs before Soda catches them all."

Jacob grabbed the bag and ran over to the water's edge, mud squishing up over his feet.

"Take off your shoes, Jacob," Victoria said. "And your socks."

Jacob rushed to do what he was told, and Eli handed her a brownie and a brown bottle.

"What are these?" she asked, looking down at the label-less glass.

"Best beer on the planet. Ruby's dad brews this in his basement. Part of her peace offering."

After her first sip, she nodded, which for no good reason made him happy.

"Remember that summer we spent down here?" she asked. "We taught you how to swim."

"You taught me how to barely not drown." There was a brownie crumb in the corner of her lip that he couldn't quite look away from.

He shoved another bite of brownie in his mouth. This was dinner, one of the better ones of the week. This cooking-for-himself garbage was going to kill him.

"That was the summer before my mom left," he said, washing down the brownie with the rest of the beer. He didn't know where these words were coming from; all of this shit he'd buried was springing up around him like gopher holes. Yesterday, he'd stood at the kitchen sink, looking out the window and eating cereal, remembering the time Amy's horse had gone into labor. The vet hadn't arrived in time and he'd sat in that barn and watched his mom pull a living, breathing foal from a frantic mare, and there hadn't been a shadow of a doubt in his mind that she was Wonder Woman.

"My folks were fighting so much I thought they were going to tear the house down," he said, because apparently he just couldn't shut up. "Drowning in the middle of this spring with you seemed safer."

He didn't want sympathy, didn't say that to garner any, and she seemed to just . . . get it.

"So I take it your breeding business is finally off the ground?" She changed the subject and he wanted to kiss her with gratitude. With gratitude and lust—a weird combination, like brownies and beer.

"I put the stallions in with the mares last night and woke up to the sweet sounds of horse love."

"Horse love. You make it sound so romantic."

He didn't even have to look at her to know she was thinking about sex. For two weeks she'd been coming out here, wanting him so badly he could smell her. He could taste her in the air between them, but she just kept saying no.

"It doesn't have to be this hard," he said, because it was hard. Some places harder than others.

"Do you forgive me?"

She was so resolved, so deeply seated in this forgiveness issue, and he didn't know how to change her mind.

He rolled the brown bottle in his hands, feeling the glass heat under his touch. At the water's edge, Soda knocked over the paper bag and it shook as the frogs inside made a bid for freedom they never thought they'd see.

For a second he found himself sympathizing with the goddamned frogs.

"What if I don't know how?" he asked. "My mom—"

"No one's saying you have to forgive her."

"Then what the hell is this sex embargo about?"

She ignored him, just kept talking, her blue eyes boring into the side of his head like a drill right into his brain. "There are some things in this world that maybe . . . maybe you just can't forgive. Your mom left you and that's pretty bad, Eli. Not a lot of people can forgive that. I can't forgive my husband for what he did to us. I can't forgive the way my friends treated us. I can't . . ." She stopped, tilting her head as if checking her shit list for more names. "Well, maybe that's it. I've forgiven my dad. I needed to if I was ever going to get over my childhood. My mom, too."

"What's that like?" He laughed, trying to make it sound like a joke, but his laughter was nothing but hot air. The joke was on him. He'd been left in this place, this black paper bag, and he didn't know how to get out of it.

"Forgiving someone? Feels good, Eli. Better than you can imagine."

"How—" He cleared his throat, wondering how the hell he got here, asking this woman how to forgive her. In what world did that make sense?

"You have to be tired of being angry," she whispered, tugging the bottle away from him. He let it go, his hands sore. He must have been squeezing it. "More tired than angry."

Right over their head, a giant bird flapped its wings. Victoria squealed and ducked, just as his two guests sent plumes of water into the air as they landed.

Two swans, like a mirage—no, like aliens from outer space, so unexpected he couldn't help but gasp even though he'd seen them here before, settled into the center of the spring, folding their wings back against their bodies. Their elegant white necks curved toward each other as if they were finishing a whispered conversation.

"Look, Mom!" Jacob pointed at the birds as though she might have missed them.

"I see them, bud," she said back. "What . . . what are they doing here?" she asked Eli.

"Showed up last fall. I guess they're migrating."

"But isn't this pretty far south?"

He shrugged. "Global warming or something. I don't know."

Soda flopped himself down on Eli's boots and Jacob came back to Victoria, wedging his little body between her legs. Eli watched the two of them, absorbing their wonder as they watched the swans paddle around their pond, unaware that they were making a home out of some place they shouldn't be. Unaware that they were a miracle.

The mornings were cooler now that it was November, so Eli set his lawn chair in the sun, his eyes on a new crew member at the Crooked Creek taping vapor barrier over the insulation.

This anger of his had grown roots, curled around his organs, his guts and spleen, causing cracks in his lungs, pushing up between his intestines.

He couldn't breathe, couldn't eat anymore; every time he opened his mouth he breathed fire and ash, burning anyone in front of him.

Victoria and Jacob had canceled their last visit. She told him they were busy, but he knew it was because of him. Because it was so hard being around him. He felt like his father, barking at anything that moved, just to vent some of the anger that was making him crazy.

"Kid!" he shouted, and the boy—honestly, it was like

child labor—looked around and then pointed at himself.

"Me?"

"You're leaving gaps so big it's gonna snow in that house."

"But . . ." He looked at the tape and the pink insulation and the gloves that were too big for him. "We're not supposed to talk to you."

"That's fine, but someone's gonna—"

"If you're going to harass my workers, why don't you just get some tape and do it yourself." Eli craned his neck to look up at the Viking dude who ran the construction site.

"Why don't *you* hire competent workers?"

"My taping guy is home with his sick wife and this is his son. He's trying to learn a trade."

"Very fucking noble."

"Yeah, and how about you, sitting out here every day making my life hell. How noble is that?"

The testosterone smelled like an electrical fire and Eli slowly uncurled from his lawn chair. His hands were already in fists, his muscles loosely coiled, ready to take that first punch.

Gavin laughed and took another step closer. The guy was a fricking giant, which made the adrenaline pound hard in Eli's veins.

Yes, the anger hissed. *Yes. This one. Let's take this one.*

"Amy's warned everyone on our crew that if anyone so much as looks cross-eyed at you, they're fired."

"You scared?"

"Of your mom? Yes. Of you, not so much."

When Eli was sixteen, he punched his father. It was a sloppy, emotional left hook that didn't do a whole lot of damage, but his father turned around and broke Eli's nose with one punch. He'd bled for days. It was the only time Mark had hit him, but the lesson had been learned.

Eli had never hit another person.

Until this moment. He pinned a vicious left hook right across the blond man's cheek, snapping his head sideways. Gavin roared, looking every inch a Norse berserker, and Eli had one moment of "what the hell have I done" before the big man wrapped his arms around his waist and took them both down into the dirt.

They knocked over the chair, then the cooler. Gavin landed a punch to Eli's gut that sent his sandwich running back up his throat, and Eli punched the side of Gavin's skull, which hurt his own hand more than it seemed to faze Gavin.

He was dimly aware of a group of guys coming to stand around them, and he managed to leverage his weight onto Gavin and heave him onto his back, only to get sprayed directly in the mouth with a blast of cold hose water.

"Git!" Ruby yelled and Eli stood up, trying to dodge the icy blast delivered by a housekeeper wearing a tie-dyed track suit. "Look at you two, is this any way to behave?"

Gavin stood up, blood and water trickling down from his hair. "I don't give a shit what's going on with you and Amy," he said, pointing a finger in Eli's face, and it was all Eli could do not to bite that finger off at the knuckle.

As if sensing his intention, Ruby sprayed him again.

"Christ, Ruby!" he yelled. "I get it. Enough!"

"Stop acting like a dog and I'll stop spraying you like one."

Gavin ran his hands through his wet hair, wincing when he touched a cut. "Stop interrupting my guys," he said. "Stop getting in the way of my work. I don't know what you think you're going to catch us doing out here, but this is my job. My life. And I'm getting pretty sick of you acting like a spoiled bitch."

Ruby blasted Gavin, who howled and leapt away. "What the hell . . . ?"

"Name-calling, Gavin. You oughta be ashamed of yourself."

Gavin shook his head, muttering about the crazy folks out here in the country as he wandered back toward the house.

"You ruined my sandwich," Eli said, putting his chair back up and dumping the water and his soggy sandwich out of the cooler.

"I'll make you another one. You're beginning to look half peanut these days."

Eli's stomach roared in anticipation of Ruby's cooking. Since being fired from the Crooked Creek, that was truly the one thing he missed without reservation.

"What are you doing out here, boy?"

"Making sure . . ." He swallowed. "Making sure she doesn't run away and ruin everything."

Ruby tossed the spray nozzle away and crossed her arms. "She already ruined everything." Eli blinked up at her. "Remember? She left you?"

"Ruby—"

"That's a shitty mom thing to do. I ain't a mom, but I know that. You don't leave your kids."

"What are you doing?"

"I'm just saying, she can't ruin anything worse than what she already ruined."

"She could ruin this . . . this spa thing you're doing."

"Like you care?"

He was about to say *Of course I do,* but Ruby lifted one of her thin eyebrows and he kept his mouth shut.

"Eli, she ain't ruining this."

"Not yet."

"Look, Eli." She pointed to the house, and then shook

her finger when he refused to look, holding what little ground he had left like a child. "Look. Those walls are going back up. And it's beautiful and solid. It's real, honey. She's doing a great job, taking real good care of us."

Reluctantly, Eli squinted over at the house, the cotton-candy-colored insulation going up. The next step after that was drywall.

If she'd been planning on leaving this place in ruins, that window of opportunity was over now. Gavin was showing that kid how to tape the vapor barrier, keeping it tight.

"So, honey, if you're gonna come around here, you need to come up with a better reason."

His face throbbed where Gavin's fist had connected and he touched his tongue to his lip, tasting blood.

"Now, why don't you come on inside and I'll make you up a proper breakfast."

Eli followed, soggy and sore. And tired.

Really, really tired of being angry.

chapter
19

"*You decided on* those tiles yet?" Gavin stepped into what would be the change rooms and instantly the room got smaller. More intimate. How that was possible with exposed pipes and the presence of five other men, Celeste wasn't sure, but that was Gavin's magic.

He turned every room into a potential bedroom.

"We're going to go—" She looked up and gaped at him. Gavin was soaking wet, a runny trickle of blood easing down past his eye from a cut on his eyebrow. "What the hell happened to you?"

He touched the eye, winced, and then used the bottom of his shirt to swipe the worst of the blood away. The skin above his belt was white, like marble. Muscled like the statue *David*. Perfection. And she went dizzy with her desire to see more of him.

He swore a blue streak. "Where the hell is the first-aid kit?"

"Come on," she said, not believing that she was actually doing this. The bathroom she shared with Victoria and Jacob was full of Spider-Man Band-Aids and Neosporin.

A bubble surrounded them, the awareness that she was leading him someplace private. That he was following, so closely she could feel the heat of him, or perhaps she was imagining that. Either way, her body loved it.

She was going to touch him—she would have to in

order to dress the cut. And she couldn't wait. She was going to take her time, milk every minute.

The lights blinked on in the bathroom and she pointed to the closed toilet without looking at him, preferring to keep her intentions in her own head for as long as she could.

Once she had everything in her hands—a cotton ball with alcohol, the little tube of Neosporin, and a Sponge-Bob SquarePants Band-Aid, she turned.

But he wasn't on the toilet. He wasn't sitting there like an obedient patient. He was standing right in front of her, a wall of masculinity, an ungovernable force.

He kicked the door shut. Her body went wet.

"Tell me right now if you don't want this," he said. The blood, the blue of his eyes, the restrained temper in his jaw—it was too much. She would regret this, the memory would embarrass her for eons, but there was no refusing.

She threw the things in her hands into the sink and met him head-on. Her arms curled around his neck, chains to keep him close. His lips touched hers and the world exploded into nothing.

All that remained was heat and a kiss more intimate than anything she'd experienced in ten years.

He stepped her backwards until the top of her hips hit the marble edge of the sink and in one delicious movement, he slid his tongue into her mouth and lifted her until she sat on the sink, her legs spread to accept the width of his hips between them.

But he didn't grind into her. He didn't shove his erection at her. He cradled her cheeks in his hands. Swept her hair from her face, then kissed her neck, her eyelids. Her mouth again.

It was tender. Reverent.

"Sorry," he murmured, and after another slow, sweet

kiss, he stepped away, helping her down from her perch. The perch she had no desire to leave.

"For what?" She knew she was staring at him, wide-eyed, like a starstruck virgin.

"I've been thinking about kissing you for a long time now, and I didn't want it to be like this. Stolen, in a bathroom, of all places." He wiped his hands through his hair and winced when the cut over his eye split and started to bleed again. "Damn it."

"Sit down," she said and gathered the things from the sink with shaking hands. Grateful as she was to have something to do, her body was still processing that kiss and she felt her cheeks burn. Between her legs she was wet. Her nipples ached.

"Close your eyes," she said, unable to stare into those eyes and keep herself in order.

"Are you mad?" he whispered, his head tipped back. She smiled down at him, only because he couldn't see her. "Have I blown it?"

"Blown what?"

"A month of lunches, Celeste. I was working toward a dinner date." He opened one eye and when she didn't drop her smile fast enough, he grinned.

"I don't . . ." date, she was going to say. But that wasn't the truth. She dated plenty. "I don't date younger men."

"Younger? Come on. By what, five years?"

"I'm sixty-three." She arched an eyebrow at him. "How old are you?"

He picked his jaw up off the floor. "It doesn't matter."

She laughed because it hurt, like waxing all the hair off her body, a wild stinging pain. She put the Band-Aid on over the cream and leaned down to kiss it, taking as much heat from his body as she could. "Of course it does."

* * *

Victoria loved walking in the front door of the ranch these days—it was like walking into a beehive. Men carrying heavy equipment. Women on phones, bossing the men around. She stepped over ladders and skids of materials and headed into the kitchen, eager to see the new appliances that had been delivered just as she was taking Jacob to school.

Ruby stood in the center of her kingdom, a queen in tye-dyed yoga pants. A pair of legs in denim and cowboy boots stuck out from behind the new six-burner professional-grade stove.

"Look, Victoria," Ruby said, "it's the mother ship."

She ran her hands across the sterling-silver dials. "So shiny!"

The terra-cotta tiles had been laid and sealed a few days before and the fridge and freezer had already been hooked up. The deep stainless-steel sink and new dishwasher still sat in boxes just inside the sliding glass doors. The counter had been replaced with stainless-steel worktables.

"I didn't think Gavin was going to have any guys to spare for this today," she said.

"I got my own guy," Ruby said, her eyes twinkling over her reading glasses.

"I heard that." To Victoria's surprise, those legs belonged to Eli. He shimmied out from behind the stove. "There you go, Ruby."

She felt foolish, gaping at him, but it was sort of like finding a rainbow at night. He was literally the last person she expected to see here. Helping, of all things.

She hadn't seen him since the swans. She'd canceled the last visit because she was rubbed raw by him. Rubbed raw by his crossroads, and she just needed a break from it.

"Ruby bribed me with food." He reached over to tap her jaw shut. He was sunny as a beach vacation, and she wanted to tip back her head and absorb this surprising change in him.

"What happened to your face?" Now that he was right in front of her, Victoria could see he had a big swollen lip and a cut through the corner.

"Allergic reaction," he said.

"Yeah," Ruby snorted. "To Gavin's fist."

"You fought with Gavin?" She tried not to make it sound as if it turned her on, because it was totally inappropriate that it did.

"Who fought with Gavin?" Amy walked in, and immediately Eli closed up like a fist. That beach vacation was suddenly rained out. "You? Eli? Are you—"

Eli glared at her, storm clouds rolling in across his face. This was going to be a doozy.

"Are you all right?" Amy asked her son.

"Fine. It was nothing."

She pointed to the appliances.

"Did you put in the stove?"

Eli nodded, unrolling his sleeves, refusing to look at her with all the force and intention of a tornado.

"The fridge?"

"You just plug it in."

Victoria and Ruby stood there, watching the two of them act like they were playing tennis with grenades. Eli grabbed his jacket from the counter and swung it over his shoulder, before stepping toward the sliding glass doors.

Amy slammed her clipboard down on the stove.

Here it comes, Victoria thought, wanting to dive behind the counter.

"This isn't going to work," Amy said, and Eli turned around. "I can't have my guys working like this. Two of them are talking about leaving. You're fighting with my foreman. And I thought—"

"You'd show up after twenty-seven years and we'd magically make up?" he asked, and Victoria winced.

"No. I don't expect us to make up. I don't expect you to forgive me, but I thought it would be worth it, just to have you here."

"How is that working out for you?"

"It's not. None of this is working."

"Wait a second," Victoria said, not liking the way this was going. "The renovation is working pretty great."

"I'll go," Amy said, not even looking at Ruby or Victoria. She only had eyes for her son, putting all of their fates in his angry hands.

Victoria fumed. This was exactly what she'd feared would happen with Eli sitting outside the ranch like a damn pest—he was chasing Amy away.

"Leave the ranch?" he asked, his eyes opening wide as if this were the last thing he'd expected.

"If that's what you want," Amy agreed with a solemn nod.

"I'll sue you, Amy," Victoria breathed. "I mean, I'll have to. You can't . . . you can't just leave."

"I should never have come," Amy said, looking every minute of her age and then some. "This was a mistake. I'll give you back the rest of the deposit, I'll recommend another contractor, maybe Gavin will stay—"

"It's fine," Eli said.

Victoria took in a shaking breath, because he wasn't looking at his mother, he was staring right at her with the kind of focus and intention reserved for dark deeds against walls and in trucks. "I'm tired of sitting out there every damn day. Stay. Finish the job. For Victoria."

Amy nodded. Eli turned to Victoria, his intent incendiary. "I'll see you tonight," Eli said. Not a question.

Her body understood what was happening before her

brain clued in. It wasn't until he was out the door that she realized she'd be going to his ranch tonight.

Without her son.

The air she pulled into her lungs was hot and damp, and it tasted of sweat and sex. She pushed the pillow that kept flopping over her head off the side of the bed and braced her hands against the wall. Her hips pushed back, meeting Eli's slow, steady thrust, and when he pulled back, she moaned, nearly crying, trying to follow his body with hers.

"Slow," he breathed in her ear. His heavy chest, muscled and slick with sweat, settled against her back and the sensation of being covered, of being dominated by this big man, turned the dial up on her excitement.

"Please," she gasped. "Come on. Please." She tossed her head, her hair falling over her face, and he put his lips to her shoulder, that place where neck met body, where a cluster of nerves lived and breathed, waiting for his attention.

She groaned, curled up against him, the thick, heavy length of him inside of her pinning her to the bed.

"You're so beautiful," he whispered, and that was it. She couldn't take it anymore. She might not be as strong as him, but the frustration of the last few weeks had given her power.

Rocking her hips forward she squeezed her legs together, clamping him inside of her, and he groaned. She did it again. And again. Gathering speed and rhythm until the friction made her see stars.

His hand landed on her hip, his thumb against the flesh of her bottom. Gaining leverage where she could, she could feel him reacting to her, feel him giving up his control. Losing it altogether, holding himself in place so she could work him. Work both of them.

"So good," he breathed against her ear and she felt him rest his forehead on the center of her back, craning his neck so he could watch, and that made her crazy.

The orgasm started slow, curling through her body, gathering sensation from every limb, every nerve ending, until she was suffused with light, with lust and excitement and passion, and then when she couldn't take it anymore, when it started to hurt, Eli groaned, "Come with me."

And she splintered apart, raining down on this bed and this lonely ranch and the night outside as glitter, until Eli rolled her over, pulling her into his arms, and put her back together. Arm here, leg here. Pounding heart at the center of it all.

"You're right," he breathed against her forehead. "Forgiveness feels great."

She laughed, soundless, because her voice was still missing, but her body shook against his and she could feel his smile against her cheek.

As the sweat cooled on her body and goose bumps cropped up across her skin, Eli reached down to get blankets, but she stopped him.

"I have to go," she said. "Jacob—"

"Are you sure?"

She laughed, despite the fact that it hurt a little to play this game with him. Being casual was new to her, and she didn't yet have the appropriate calluses. "Don't pretend you're not relieved," she said, reaching down beside the bed for her underwear.

He sat up in the bed, his muscles silvered in the moonlight that came in through the window. He was all shadows and light, his muscles so beautiful, his face so sweet. "I'm glad you came over," he whispered.

"Me too," she whispered back, smiling at him through her hair as she pulled up her jeans. She tossed her hair over her shoulder and looked down at him. Studied him.

The weeds of her doubts finding room to grow, despite everything they'd done in the last hour.

"I really . . . I can't believe you've really forgiven me."

"I've done some seriously shitty things in my life, Tori," he said, scratching at his chest. "And some of the shittiest were to you. You didn't owe me anything. The fact that we'd had sex just complicated things. You did the right thing for you."

"What . . . what about now?" she asked, pointing to the bed. "Does this complicate things?"

"Probably," he said. "But I'm ready to risk some complications."

chapter
20

Eli was very susceptible to bribery. He wasn't proud of it. The morning after Victoria had come over, Ruby called and asked him to hook up her sink and dishwasher.

All the soreness in his body, the pinpricks of pain along his neck and back where Victoria had sunk her nails, blazed at the thought of seeing her so soon.

But his mind thought all that excitement was a bad idea. "Don't you have a bunch of people there whose job it is to get that shit to work for you?"

"They're all busy. Gavin's telling me the dishwasher isn't a priority until next week."

"Well, then I figure—"

"Food for a week," she said, "so you don't have to keep eating those sad little sandwiches."

His stomach roared with its vote and he just couldn't say no. Sometimes he thought if he saw another jar of peanut butter he just might cry. "Tamales?"

"Of course."

"Damn it. Give me a few hours. And make sure Amy and that Gavin guy aren't around."

Which is how he happened to be on his back, trying to hook the dishwasher up to the water line behind a stack of boxes and stainless-steel appliances, when Victoria, Celeste, and Ruby came in and started arguing.

And it sounded like an old argument.

"How many times do I have to say no to this?" Victoria cried. He felt like he needed to come out of hiding, in case this was an argument Victoria didn't want him hearing.

"You don't," Celeste said. "You don't have to say no at all."

"We don't have the money," Victoria said, "to renovate that barn. We just paid for all that damn advertising! The *New York Times* Travel Section isn't exactly cheap, Celeste."

"You're being shortsighted again."

"Fine, you want to ask Luc for more cash?"

"I will."

"A couple months ago asking Luc was a last resort."

"I'm not saying I'll like doing it, but it's the right thing to do, Victoria."

Victoria muttered something he couldn't hear.

"What about those friends of yours in New York?" Celeste asked. "Have you invited them to the grand opening?"

The silence in the room was the loudest he'd ever heard and he held his breath, now praying that he didn't get found.

"I will."

"You've been saying that for weeks. We agreed that those women are our core demographic."

"I said I will." Victoria's voice was full of all kinds of steel and he admired that about her. That paisley-covered mouse had grown into a lioness. "We need to talk about this *Dallas A.M.* thing. Madelyn Cornish called—"

"She actually called?" Ruby asked, and Eli smiled. Ruby loved her a.m. talk shows. "Madelyn Cornish? What's she like?"

"She's nice, but they're pushing hard for a date we can do a spot on her show, and I—"

"Let me handle it," Ruby said. "I . . . I want to handle this."

There was a pause, and he could imagine Victoria and Celeste looking at each other. "Knock yourself out, Ruby," Celeste said, but she sounded angry.

"Celeste," Victoria asked, her voice softer. "What's wrong? You seem so—"

"Nothing's wrong," Celeste said.

"Is this about Gavin?" Victoria asked, and instead of an answer he heard footsteps walking out the door.

"I'd take that as a yes," Ruby said.

"Me too," Victoria agreed.

Victoria made herself wait four days before taking Jacob out to see Eli and the horses. Four long days and even longer nights. She didn't know what kind of magic that man had, but the second she saw him it was as if no time had passed and her body was right back on that bed.

"Any of your mares pregnant?" she asked, when he came to stand beside her at the fence after helping Jacob find the hose so that he could fill the plastic troughs in the corners of the paddocks.

"Too early to tell," he said, tipping his hat back, watching her with a focus and intent she found utterly unnerving.

"What?" She smiled, feeling herself blush, like the sixteen-year-old she never got a chance to be. Was he remembering everything she remembered? The feel of his hand on her breast, the lick of his tongue on her belly, the way—

"I was in the kitchen the other day."

She coughed, pulling herself away from the dirty movies in her head.

"New peanut butter and jelly recipe?"

"Your kitchen. I overheard you and Celeste." She felt

the smile fade from her face and she turned away, staring blindly at her son.

"Eavesdropping? That's a little beneath you, isn't it?"

"At first I was just scared. You women yelling like that—" He whistled, and she tried not to smile. Perhaps she would have hidden, too.

"What do you need the money for?" he asked.

"You can't really care about this?" she said, giving him an out, hoping he'd take it.

"I can. I do."

She stayed silent out of self-preservation. They'd blurred so many lines already, she didn't need to like this man any more. To need him any more than she did. She'd tried to put all of that needy, weak woman crap behind her.

"Tell you what," he said, shifting so his body blocked her son from view, curling around her slightly. "You tell me what you need that money for and tonight when you come back here . . . I'll get out the rope."

Her bark of a laugh, so unfeminine, echoed around the field. Horses turned, shook out their manes.

"Are you trying to blackmail me with sex?"

"Is it working?"

Yes. Very much, yes.

"Celeste wants to renovate the barn and arena so we have more space. A ballroom. She seems to think we could make a fortune in weddings."

"You don't agree?"

"I totally agree, but we just don't have the budget right now. We can do it in a few years, once things take off."

He nodded. "Seems wise."

Never in her life had she been called wise. She liked it. A lot. "Thanks. But she's going to go and get the money from Luc—I know she is."

"If Luc's got enough money, why is that a problem?"

"Because we've already borrowed a huge amount of

money from him and I don't want to keep running to my brother every time I need something. The spa was supposed to be about me standing on my own two feet, and how is that supposed to happen with my brother paying for everything?"

"What about those friends of yours?" he asked. "You gonna call them?"

"When pigs fly," she whispered, bitterness boiling up in her throat like vomit. "They'd come in a heartbeat. Pay whatever I asked them too, and tell every single one of their friends where they were going to go—"

"Sounds like the kind of people a spa could use."

She glared at him. "That's what Celeste said after she called all of her bitchy model friends and invited them. But my friends . . . those cannibalistic—" She shook her head, so angry she couldn't find the right words to describe the terribleness of those women.

"Asshats?"

That brought her up short and he shrugged. "I've always liked that word. *Asshat.* Sounds good."

How was she laughing? How could she stand here, filled with the sourness of her animosity, and laugh?

"You shouldn't invite the asshats," he said. "No matter what Celeste says. It's got to be bad for business."

An emotion too similar to gratitude welled up behind her heart and she welcomed it with resignation. It was her lot in life to be grateful, to be on the receiving end of someone else's generosity. She wondered what she gave Eli in return. Or her brother. Celeste.

All of the people who helped her, did they see how one-sided their relationship with her truly was?

Eli stepped away, letting the world back between them. "I was going to show Jacob some of that ultrasound—"

"Wait a second, I have a question."

He smiled, settled back in, a sexual light filling his eyes. "What do I get for answering?"

This was a dangerous game. Totally reckless; her son was just yards away. Her brain was screaming warnings, but his eyes . . . that body. Those hands that knew just what to do with her weak and willing flesh.

"Tonight," she whispered, leaning toward him slightly, channeling all the vixen/sex goddess she could while wearing cracked galoshes. "I want to put you in my mouth."

His Adam's apple bobbed, his mouth opened and shut, and she felt such power at her fingertips.

"What's . . . what's your question?" His voice was guttural, sexy and dark, and her body responded. Night could not come quick enough.

"Why were you in my kitchen?" She smiled, drunk on her power. Her fingertips touched his collar, the heat of his skin beneath.

"Ruby bribed me with food to put in her dishwasher."

Ah, didn't that just kill a girl's inner diva! She pulled her fingers away, but he grabbed them, pressing her hand to his chest, where she felt the pounding of his heart underneath his shirt.

"And I wanted to see you."

Celeste had so far done a very good job of ignoring Gavin. It had been a mistake to cultivate this relationship. Luckily, the awareness her body had of his made him easy to avoid. Every time the fine hair on the back of her neck started to vibrate, she found a pressing need to be anywhere but where she was.

Thomas, on the other hand, was not so easy to shake off.

"You want to check out the lights in the change rooms?" he asked, leaning against the door to the kitchen, his black T-shirt striped with dust. Skinny and dark-haired, he didn't look anything like Gavin.

She wondered what his mother looked like, what kind of women Gavin usually chose when he wasn't trying to make time with sixty-three-year-old former models.

"You're done?" she asked, surprised. He'd started cutting holes for the recessed lights yesterday.

"When you hire the best . . . ," he said with a grin.

She'd long ago stopped trying to be distant with Thomas. He made it impossible. He told her dirty jokes, for crying out loud. No one told Celeste Baker dirty jokes.

"Go on in," he said, gesturing for her to head in first. He stood by the light switch. "I want you to have the full effect."

"You're good, Thomas," she said, glancing over her shoulder at him. "But they're just lights."

It was dark in the windowless room, and as she turned the corner away from the door it got even darker.

"Okay," she yelled, and warm yellow lights illuminated the room from behind the subtly elegant brown sconces.

The pot lights overhead flickered on, staying dim, giving the room an intimate, sophisticated glow.

She turned slowly, taking it all in. "I may have to eat my words—" She stopped. There, in the middle of the room, between the first bank of lockers and the whirlpool and sauna, was a sheet of plywood propped up over two sawhorses.

A plastic water bottle had been stuffed with mums and zinnias from Ruby's garden, and two wrapped Subway sandwiches sat on either side.

"Thomas!" she yelled just as someone behind her did the same thing.

"Where the hell are you, Thomas?" Gavin walked around the corner, gleaming like copper and gold in the low lights.

Her stomach, her womb, clenched hard at the sight of him.

He glanced down at the sandwiches. The flowers.

"Did you do this?" His blue eyes were so bright with hope and excitement under the glitter of his lashes. His smile spoke directly to her sex, whispered secrets her body loved.

"This?" she asked, too loud, too crisp. "No. Lord, no."

He turned away, nodding as if agreeing that it was a ridiculous idea, and she realized how awful she sounded.

"That didn't come out right," she said.

"I don't care how old you are."

"That's because you have no idea what I have to do to look like this. Trust me, five years from now—"

He shrugged, his lips twisted into a cruel knot. "I don't care about five years from now."

"I do."

Suddenly he was right in front of her and he was angry. Not the icy anger from weeks before; this time he burned like the hottest part of a fire. As if everything inside of him was being torched. "I was ready to go slow, let you get used to the idea, but you win. I'm out, Celeste. Enjoy your fucking old age."

The pain was actually quite stunning. Like being blinded.

He turned on his heel, his big, broad back leaving the warm glow of light his son had prepared.

For a week now Victoria had been coming out to Eli's house after her son was asleep. A week of lying in this bed. In his house. And he couldn't quite get over how unbothered he was.

He wouldn't go so far as to say it felt natural, but it was comfortable, her shoes sitting beside his front door, her sweater slung over the back of his kitchen chair.

Her warm, soft body in his bed.

It was the second week in November, and the days were flying by in anticipation of the nights they spent together.

He sat up against the headboard and stroked her back. "You ever notice how the quiet's not as quiet when there are two people?" he asked.

"Is that your way of asking me to leave?" She pushed herself up on her elbows, her breasts cradled in the white sheets of his bed, like lovely eggs in a nest.

He kissed her shoulder. "No."

"Excellent, because I have a favor—"

Good God, the woman was persistent! "The answer is still no. No costumes, Tori. Leave a man some dignity—"

"It's not costumes, but I still think you'd make a hot Wild West sheriff."

"Well, sheriff, that's different. You said sheik or some other shit last time."

She kissed him, and her laughter tasted like peaches and candy and everything delicious. The soft weight of her breasts felt even sweeter. He eased himself down in the sheets, bringing her with him. *Once more,* he thought. *Just once more before she leaves.*

But she sat back, pulling her body away from his, leaving nothing but cold air. She wrapped the sheets around herself. "I'm serious."

"I can see that."

He sat up, pulling the blanket across his lap.

"We're painting next week."

Eli nodded. One thing he could say about his mother and that Gavin guy—they worked fast.

"Celeste is going to a hotel in Springfield." Eli waited, wondering what this had to do with him. Victoria suddenly became very interested in the stitching on the seam of the sheets. "I . . . ah . . . I can't really afford that."

"You need money?"

She winced, looking at him from under her dark lashes.

He loved those lashes. The way they rested on her cheeks like fans while she slept. They were so long, they cast shadows in certain light. "I was hoping for a place to stay. For . . . Jacob and me."

It took him a second to realize what she was asking, and she just stared at him until the shoe dropped and he laughed.

"You're kidding, right?"

She sucked in a quick breath, turning her face away.

Uh-oh. Not kidding.

"I just . . . you want to stay here? With Jacob?"

"Never mind." She shot a bright smile over her shoulder while she reached down to the floor for her underwear. The long, pale length of her back was exposed by the sheet and it was rigid.

He put his hand on her spine and she stiffened away from him. "It was dumb . . . to ask. I know how weird—"

"Sure."

Her brow furrowed as if she were trying to translate his word into ancient Greek. "Sure what? We . . . can stay, or it's weird to ask?"

"You can stay."

Other women might have squealed. A couple of them in his past would have started planning weddings, stopped taking their birth control pills. But not Victoria. She eyed him skeptically, clutching that sheet tighter across her chest, as if waiting for his second thoughts.

"You sure?"

"Yeah, I got that guest room. The bed's pretty soft, but I figure he'll be okay for a few nights."

Her smile made him ache, made his chest feel too tight.

"I can't . . . I won't sleep with you while we're here. I don't want to have to explain—"

That Mom's acting the slut. He didn't blame her.

"I mean, he knows I'm not going to . . . you know . . ." She trailed off into an agonized silence.

"I don't. I have no clue what you're talking about."

"He knows I'm never getting married."

The word *married* made his chest even tighter.

"It's the guest room, not a proposal."

"I know . . . but I don't want you to think I'm embarrassed or . . ." Her eyes became very serious, her whole body tense with meaning. "Anything. About you."

"Anything" meant in love. Message received. He wasn't "anything" with her either.

"It's the guest room, Tori. And I didn't think you'd be sleeping with me while your son was only a few feet away."

"Okay. I know. Sorry."

He leaned over and kissed her lips, puffy and swollen from their kisses earlier in the night.

"Thank you," she whispered against his mouth. "I know how hard this is for you."

It wasn't. Not really. Not as impossible as it would have been a few months ago. But somehow revealing that to her would be revealing too much to both of them. And she was looking at him as if she knew that, as if she could read what he was feeling better than he could read it himself, and that was an imposition.

He wasn't ready to look at what has happening in his heart. He had no interest in analyzing what it meant that they could stay.

It felt . . . good. And that was more than enough for him. More than he'd ever thought he'd have.

So he leaned back against the headboard and ran his hand down the muscles of his stomach until he held his erect dick in his palm.

"You really ought to make it worth my while."

It took her a second. He could see that she wanted to discuss the situation, figure out how her staying here might change things, but he stroked himself, pushing the sheet down so she could get a good look, and that was enough.

She flung off the covers and crawled across his small bed with the sheets he'd washed just for her. *What is happening to me?* he wondered. If those women he'd screwed in his truck, the ones he'd never let see his home, much less his bed, could see him now they wouldn't recognize him.

He didn't recognize himself.

chapter
21

On Monday, Eli closed the door on the back room, his childhood bedroom. He should have bought a new mattress—the ancient double was no better than a hammock. He'd be lucky if Jacob and Victoria didn't leave here with broken backs.

He paced into the kitchen and glanced up at the old clock above the sink. Seven o'clock. Tori had said they'd come by after dinner. What time did they eat?

He'd bought ice cream at the grocery store, which wasn't all that different from what he usually did. But he'd also bought those cheap cones that fell apart half the time. And some ham instead of peanut butter. And a jug of milk. Kids need milk.

Outside it was getting dark, twilight pushing its purple edge toward his door. No sign of the Cadillac.

Cleaning up last night, it had taken him a half hour to find his remote control. Then he'd realized that he'd stopped paying the cable bill and they'd shut it off. So. Nothing but news and Mexican soap operas. He hoped the kid spoke Spanish.

This was going to be a disaster. He could feel it already. Tense and pissed off, he stomped from room to room, counting all the ways he was being imposed upon. And all the ways he was doomed to make a fool of himself.

Ice cream cones, what bullshit.

Maybe . . . maybe he'd just hang out in the barn. Let

them have the house, so he wouldn't have to see them.
That would be better. Actually, maybe he'd go get that
hotel room . . .

The utterly foreign bong of his doorbell broke the silence and he jumped at the sound. A wild knocking followed, and then he heard Tori's quiet voice muffled by
the wood.

Fucking disaster, he thought, stomping across the
floor to throw open the door.

"Eli!" Jacob cried, his black curls airborne as he
jumped into the house. "We brought movies and pop-
corn and Ruby packed some dinner for you. She said
you were starving to death. I said I was too, so she
packed more of those brownies. Awesome, huh?"

Jacob destroyed the silence of his house. Smashed the
stillness. Eli watched him ping-pong from room to
room, in and out of doors, off tables and chairs that had
been there so long Eli never even noticed them.

"Have you seen *Monsters Vs. Aliens?* It's a little lame,
but there's this funny part with a huge robot. And a
giant moth shoots stuff out its nose. That's cool. Is that
a branding iron? Why is it on your wall?"

His house was transformed by the boy. The dark corners he hadn't been able to sand or renovate out, the
sadness that lingered like stains on the linoleum, were
lifted away.

Not even as a kid did he think of his house as a place
where people were happy. But this kid walked around
like it was Disneyland.

"Ruby packed enough food for an army," Tori said,
setting two big bags down beside her. "Can I . . . can I
put it away?"

Appreciation that she would ask, that she was aware
of the growing pains currently crackling and aching
through his chest, allowed him to nod, and she stepped
into his kitchen.

As if she belonged there, she opened the refrigerator door and started putting away food. The white light hit her face, not doing her any favors, but it didn't matter.

He wasn't any different than his house. Alone and lonely, out of habit, a choice made long ago. He never thought of happiness anymore.

Until her.

"I'm glad . . ." Man, it was hard to get it out. The words weren't more than a whisper. A rasp squeezed past an emotion he didn't comprehend. He couldn't grasp the size and shape, the strange parameters, of this boulder on his chest.

"I'm sorry, Eli. Jacob, can you keep it down for one second?" She grinned at Eli. "He's excited. I'm sorry, what did you say?"

The words alone were lame. So he stepped across his floor, high-fiving Jacob, because the boy never seemed to get enough of that kind of stuff, and stood in front of Tori.

She looked a little panicked that he might kiss her right there in front of her son, and that was what he'd planned on doing, but her palpable worry quashed his plans.

"I'm glad you're here," he said, in a voice that was surprisingly strong.

"Stop it," Eli muttered, giving Patience a shove with his elbow. She was gumming his hair, pulling it while he ran the ultrasound wand over her belly.

If the indignant nature of her snort was anything to go by, Patience wasn't fond of the cold jelly on her stomach, so, giving in to the inevitable, he let his horse chew on his hair.

Come on, he thought, using his shoulder to press the

earphone closer to his ear. *Come on, comeoncomeon-comeoncomeon.*

And there it was: the faint echo of another heartbeat. Pregnant.

He rested his forehead right over the sound of that heartbeat and thought about crying. Just a little.

"Hey, little guy," he whispered.

"Eli?"

Shit.

He leaned back out of the stall to look down the long center aisle, surprised to see Celeste walking through his barn in a pair of tight jeans tucked into high brown boots.

She made his barn look like one of those fashion shows. Lord, she was a beautiful woman. Scary, too.

Quickly, he pushed off the earphones, gave Patience a pat on the rump, and smoothed back his hair. Couldn't meet Celeste with horse spit in his hair.

"Hey, Celeste, if you're looking for Victoria, she took Jacob to school."

Her smile was cool and classy, like the expression of one of those women in the black-and-white movies. He could actually feel the dirt on his boots.

"I'm actually not looking for Victoria. I'm looking for you."

"Me?" He grabbed the bandana out of his pocket and wiped the lubricating jelly he'd used on Patience off his hands. "What can I do for you?"

"I've got a car full of cats."

"Cats?"

She held up her hands covered in bandages. "Barn cats, vicious little beasts. We're starting work on the barn and those damn cats need a home. They're yours if you want them."

He'd never seen Celeste like this. Rattled, a little dirty. It was charming. Humanizing.

"I'll take the cats," he said.

"Good, it was that or the river."

He smiled at her bullshit—at least he hoped it was bullshit—and followed her back out to her car.

"You finally convinced Victoria to renovate the barn?"

"Her problem is the money, and I can get the money."

"You've talked to your son?"

"Not yet, but I will."

She opened the back door of her car and the three barn cats jumped under the front seats.

Celeste growled and lunged toward them as if she were going to pull them out by their tails. He put a hand to her arm and stepped in.

He whistled and clucked his tongue, and all but CJ, the big tabby, leapt out of the car to curl around his boots.

"CJ, sweetie, come on out."

"You're like the cat whisperer or something," Celeste muttered.

"I've been pouring their kibble most of their lives."

"You really are a cowboy, aren't you?"

That had to be one of those rhetorical questions, so he didn't answer. It took a few more minutes of sweet talk, but CJ finally crept out from under the driver's seat.

"I'm going to have to give my car a flea bath, aren't I?"

Eli chuckled. "The cats are clean," he said, leaning down to scratch CJ under the flea collar he was fairly religious about. He spent so much time in barns, it was in his best interest to keep the animals free of fleas.

"Well, that's some good news." Celeste smiled. "We haven't seen you around the ranch lately," she said, digging her keys out of her pocket.

"Not much reason, I suppose."

"Now that Victoria is here?"

The November wind was cool as it blew through his

stable. Just as cool as the look in Celeste's eye. He tucked the rag back in his pocket.

"What are you asking me, Celeste?"

"A few months ago you were trying to ruin her. And now you've got her sleeping in your home."

He felt the heat seep up over his throat, but it was anger, not embarrassment. "You think I'm planning to hurt her?"

"I don't know what you're planning."

"She's an adult, Celeste, and I don't think this is your business."

"Yes." She bristled, all five feet nine inches of imperial model. She was formidable; he wasn't going to lie. "It is, because I care about her and the woman has zero sense of self-preservation, and I just want to make sure she's not going to get hurt again. That man over the summer—"

"You're not comparing me to that Dennis guy?" he asked, stunned that anyone would lump him in the same boat as that sleaze-bag con artist.

"No. But you could hurt her, just the same."

"I'm not . . . I don't want to hurt her." He didn't know what else to say past that—it was as if he stood at the edge of a big fog and his flashlight was out of batteries.

Celeste nodded as if that answer was agreeable.

"Victoria said she invited you to Thanksgiving, but you said no."

"I spend the holiday with my father."

"Are you sure it's not because your mother will be there?"

He wished he had his hat on so he could pull it down to that low spot right over his eyes and he wouldn't have to look at her. "Look, I'm pretty busy, Celeste, so if there's nothing else—"

Celeste's forehead wrinkled as she studied him, as if he were a calculus problem she just couldn't figure out.

"I'm sorry," she finally said, running a hand over her forehead, erasing those wrinkles as if they had never existed. Neat trick. "I shouldn't have brought her up."

Damn right.

"Well, thanks for taking the cats."

"No problem."

Celeste turned to go and he stopped her, putting a hand on her arm, and she turned back to him with her eyebrows raised.

"How . . . how much is the barn renovation costing you?"

"Why?"

It wasn't easy, reaching out in this way, putting himself in all kinds of weird emotional and business danger. It wasn't the way he liked to live, but the way he liked to live was lonely. And he was tired of that.

"I'd like to invest."

"In the spa?" Celeste lifted her sunglasses off her eyes. He nodded.

"The barn renovation is a hundred thousand dollars."

That was a little less than what he had in the bank left over from the sale of the Angus herd.

"You believe in the spa?"

"I believe in Victoria."

Celeste melted, all that cold ice she surrounded herself with just vanished, and he was struck dumb by how freaking otherworldly beautiful she was, and by how real she seemed at this moment. Every other time he saw her, it felt like he'd be able to put his hand right through her if he worked up the balls to touch her.

Not so right now. She was flesh and bone, and honest to God, she looked like she could use a hug.

"She's a lucky woman," Celeste said.

"I'm the lucky one."

* * *

Victoria came running through the house to set two bottles of champagne on the counter. Jacob followed, carrying his book bag and the papier-mâché moon Eli had helped him make.

"What's going on? I swear to God I broke every speed limit on my way back here," she panted. Honestly, she needed to get a gym membership or something. The sprint from her car had her winded.

Ruby grabbed the champagne and wrestled the cork out, until it popped. Her nut-brown face was shiny, her eyes red-rimmed as if she'd been crying. But her smile indicated that they had been happy tears.

"Someone tell me what the hell is going on here, before I have a heart attack," Victoria said, staring straight into Celeste's smug and smiling face.

"Let the woman pour, Victoria."

"I swear, Celeste, I will—"

"Can I have some champagne?" Jacob asked, climbing up onto one of the stools.

"No," Victoria said, just as Celeste said, "Yes."

"Trust me, Victoria, this is a truly special occasion."

Ruby poured bubbly up to the brim in four glasses and then filled a fifth only halfway.

"Who is the other glass for?" Victoria asked as Ruby handed all the crystal out.

"Me," Eli said, coming through the back door. "I think. Sorry I'm late."

Her mouth went dry at the sight of him. Three days she'd been living in that man's house. Three amazing days. Two very, very long nights of staring up at the ceiling in his guest room, wondering why the hell it mattered if Jacob knew she was having a relationship with Eli or not.

Maybe Jacob wouldn't even figure it out.

But then she thought of trying to have that conversation with her son, about how she and Eli weren't real.

Weren't going to turn into a family. How did she explain that she was just having fun to a seven-year-old who looked at Eli like he was part cowboy, part Superman, and all hero?

Eli winked at her, sending her heart into ecstatic pre-pubescent sighs, and then glanced down at Jacob, who was holding his champagne glass like it was gold. "Whoa, we're breaking out the good stuff!"

"Will someone please tell me what's going on?" she demanded.

There was a moment of hushed silence before Ruby exploded. "Me first! Madelyn Cornish is coming to our opening-night party! And I've booked the segment on her show for March, but the segment isn't going to be about the ranch. It's going to be about me!"

"Ruby—" Celeste groaned.

"The producer said 'kitchen.' I am the kitchen."

Celeste shrugged in concession.

"That's amazing!" Victoria cried, wrapping her arms around Ruby's neck. "Great job, Ruby—"

"That's not all," Celeste said in a little singsong voice. "We sold out for opening weekend. All eight rooms! We have twenty guests."

"What?" Victoria couldn't feel her feet. She clutched the edge of the counter for support.

"And there's a waiting list."

She blinked, as Ruby nodded in rapid agreement.

"Those ads!" Victoria cried. "Those ads in the *New York Times* worked." The photography, the prime space. The website. It had been worth it.

"And then some," Ruby agreed.

"We need to renovate the barn," Celeste said, and Victoria put her glass down on the counter, all of her joy colliding with the ceiling and going splat.

"You already talked to Luc?"

Celeste shook her head. "We have an independent investor."

"Who?" Victoria asked.

Eli raised his hand. "Me."

Victoria was never the smartest kid in the class, but looking at Eli and Celeste, she started to connect the dots. And when they all came together, she glared at Celeste.

"Don't be pissy, Victoria." Celeste pointed her champagne glass at her. "But when we got this big reservation, I knew we needed to get to work on that barn."

"I'm not pissy, I'm angry that you talked to Eli." Champagne sloshed over her hand when she put the glass down. "Without talking to me first."

"I approached Celeste," Eli said.

"Why didn't you approach me?" Victoria asked.

"It was sort of spur-of-the-moment." He shrugged as if it were no big deal, and Victoria had to breathe through the anger.

"Why are you so mad?" Ruby asked.

Because he's my lover! she wanted to scream. *Because things are confusing enough. Because I like him and he likes me and there has to be some separation in my life.*

"Can you give us a second?" Eli asked.

"Can I take this with me?" Jacob whispered, holding on to his champagne glass. Celeste nodded and shuffled him out the door, followed by Ruby.

"What's got you so upset?" Eli touched the tips of her hair where they fell against her ratty polo shirt. She was wearing more of Ruby's castoffs. Honestly, if her friends from New York could see her now!

"You don't believe in this project." It wasn't why she was upset, but that hardly seemed to matter; she spit it at him anyway.

"I believe in *you*."

"I don't . . ." She took a big breath and looked him in the eye. "I don't want to need you."

He started slightly as if she'd poked him where it hurt, and she wanted to rush in with an apology, but she had to hold her ground somewhere. She wanted him, liked him, desired him, respected him—it had to stop there, otherwise she'd be right back to where she was with her husband. Needing a man who didn't need her. Grateful for what he gave her, for what she could never return. "Okay. You want me to take back the money?"

She knew she couldn't. Celeste was right. He was right. Everyone was right about that damn barn. "Why . . . why are you giving us this money?"

Eli took off his hat, setting it carefully on the counter next to the champagne, and rubbed his hand over his face, through his hair. "Because I have it." His eyes were weary, so weary, and she wanted to touch him as if it were the middle of the night in his dark, dark bedroom. "All I've been able to offer people most of my life is shit, because that's all I've had. And I want to offer you something more."

"You've given me enough, Eli."

That seemed to make him mad, his anger filling out his chest, the whole room, and she stepped back.

"You mean when I tied you up? When I told you to suck my cock? That's enough for you?"

She blushed so hard she got dizzy, tongue-tied. "Yes . . . I mean, no. I just . . . I don't expect more."

"Is that your way of telling me I shouldn't expect more from you?"

The silence buzzed like a swarm of angry bees.

"What . . . what are you saying?" This couldn't be happening. Couldn't be happening. Did he . . . love her? Eli? Was that possible?

"Look at you, so scared. Forget it, Tori. The money is yours."

"Eli . . . I'm not looking for another relationship . . . my husband—"

"Is dead. Dead. And that woman you were when you were married to him—she's dead, too. And if it's just sex between us, that's fine. My mistake for thinking there was something more."

For a moment her brain scrambled, everything flipping over and then back. This man led a solitary life. The only connections he allowed himself were shallow ones. Sex in his truck. No women in his house. He was a fortress, and she hadn't even realized she'd stormed the gates.

He'd probably let her in farther than he'd let anyone in since his mother had left him. And she'd just kept hammering away at every door he put up, every lock he put on, until he'd had no choice but to open up.

"Do you . . . love me?"

His dry chuckle hurt like a match across her chest. "What do I know about love, Tori? Nothing. I like you. A lot. And I just wanted to share in something good. That's all."

"I'm sorry . . . I don't know what—"

"Now you're pissing me off."

"I like you too, Eli. A lot." She smiled up at him until finally he smiled back at her, his hand curving around her waist.

"Then say thank you," he whispered against her lips. "And take the money."

"Why in the world couldn't they get more comfortable chairs in this place?" Eli asked, searching for some spot on the hard-backed chair beside his father's bed that wouldn't make his ass go numb.

"Most people bring in their own furniture," Caitlyn said, not looking up from the chart she was scribbling on. Her fingernails were red, with little dragons painted on them. So intricate, he wanted to get a better look, but she kept her distance. "Comfortable chairs, pictures, blankets. Homey stuff."

Eli looked around the blank and bare room. The way it had to be for his dad to keep any kind of equilibrium.

His ass was just going to have to stay numb.

"They also bring their own Thanksgiving dinner," she said, nodding at the turkey and congealed gravy on the plastic plates from the cafeteria.

"Yeah, well, I'm not much of a cook."

He was fully aware of how sad this scene was, sitting here with his unconscious father while Victoria, Jacob, and everyone else dined on Ruby's no-doubt-delicious dinner.

Victoria had invited him, but he'd declined.

Things were getting complicated. The painting at the ranch was over, but Victoria and Jacob were still at his house. There was an unspoken agreement between them that it was okay for Jacob and Victoria to stay.

His silent house was full, all the time, with chatter and laughter and video game beeps and cell phones ringing. At night, Jacob had nightmares and Eli stood outside the door of that guest room listening to Victoria whisper to him, calming his scared, little-boy tears.

Last night Victoria had climbed into Eli's bed and he knew it was because of the investment he'd made, the conversation they'd had a few days ago about his feelings.

Gratitude and something like pity had been in her eyes. Which had pissed him off.

He ran a hand over his neck, across his cheek, feeling the scrape of his beard. He was embarrassed by how he had used her. Flipping her onto her stomach so he didn't have to look in her eyes. Putting his hand over her mouth when she started to scream, making her come until she begged him to stop.

Afterward she'd asked him again to come to Thanksgiving dinner with her family, and he'd told her to leave his room.

Not his finest hour.

"What about you?" he asked Caitlyn. "Working on Thanksgiving. Is someone keeping a plate warm for you?"

"I'm, ah . . . I'm back with Jimmy," Caitlyn said, her smile shy but sweet. "He stopped drinking. We're going over to his family's place tonight."

"That's great," Eli said, and she glanced up, clearly surprised by his earnestness. "I'm serious, you deserve some good stuff, Caitlyn. You really do."

Those little dragons on her fingernails winked in the sunlight as if in agreement.

"What's . . ." He pointed at her hands. "What's the story with your nails?"

"Oh." She laughed, curling her hands into fists in embarrassment. "My sister and I are taking some classes to get a part-time job. You know, nails and things. We're trying to save a little money."

Nails and things. Spa stuff.

"There a lot of jobs around here for that?" he asked.

"Not really," she said. "We'd have to drive to Dallas."

"You hear about what's happening over at Crooked Creek?"

She laughed. "Everyone's heard about it. A spa?"

"Go apply."

"No." She shook her head. "I haven't even graduated. They probably want someone . . ."

"Just like you. Apply."

She blinked at him, as if unsure of what to do with this version of him. As if some other animal had taken his place. God, he thought, had he been so bad to her?

The wariness on her face said it all.

The answer was yes. To her, he'd been awful.

"I'll put in a word for you. A recommendation."

"Okay," she said, that smile coming back, the one that had drawn him to her in the first place. The smile that made her great at her job, that would make her great at the spa. "That's great. Thanks."

He nodded, and the two of them stayed in that room—more comfortable together than they'd ever been when they were involved.

"He's awfully calm today," Eli said, pointing to his father, who was sleeping quietly in the bed, his sheets and pajamas unruffled, so unlike the mess he usually made of things, thrashing around and swearing at people.

"He's been doing great lately," Caitlyn agreed. "Ever since Amy started coming around."

The back of his head hit the wall behind him, and his brain splattered everywhere.

"*Amy?*" he whispered.

"Yeah." Caitlyn continued as if she hadn't totally gutted him. "Showed up a few weeks ago, saying she wanted to see what her money was buying."

chapter
22

The oak-and-glass door of the Crooked Creek was paper under his fist—Eli practically tore through it, stepping into the foyer of the ranch like he was ready to take it down.

Tori came sliding to a halt outside the kitchen door. She was back to wearing her fancy, ugly clothes, a satiny purple shirt and black skirt. The smell of turkey and pie and happiness wafted out around her. "Christ, Eli, you scared the crap out of me."

"Where the hell is she?" he demanded, and Victoria jumped. He was scaring her and he didn't know how to stop it. This was a train with no brakes.

"Wh . . . who?"

"My mother!"

"I'm here." Amy stepped in behind Victoria. She was dressed up, in a pair of gray slacks and a red shirt that clashed with her hair, all for Thanksgiving dinner. Victoria had told him she was invited, but it still burned to know that she was welcome here.

"You've been to visit my dad."

Amy nodded, so composed. So together. He'd had a horse like her once that he had to put down because she had cancer in her mouth, and when he gave her the needle of succinylcholine, she looked him right in the eye. Full of pain and dying a terrible death, she had still been all defiance—she had practically dared him to do it.

And it had just about killed him.

"Yes. I've been to visit him five or six times now."

"You have no right!"

"I have every right," she countered. "I pay for that room in that place you put him."

"No." Eli shook his head. "No, that's not true."

"It sure is, Eli. Your Uncle John called me a few years ago and I've been paying ever since."

It was as though the room had shrunk; the whole world was too small and he was totally disoriented. Claustrophobic. "Why . . . why would he lie?"

"You have to ask him."

"But why are you paying?" None of this made sense—Uncle John lying to him, his mom forking over big money to care for the man she'd left.

"Because I shirked a lot of responsibilities when I left, Eli. I know you don't think I know that, but I do. I wanted to make one thing right. John gave me that chance."

"So you choose to pay for your husband's nursing home?" He laughed. "That's what you pick? Sending a check? Great job, Mom—way to own up to your mistakes."

He couldn't stand it anymore. He couldn't be in this place one more second breathing the same air as her. Everything he swore he'd never feel again, everything he swore he'd never ask, was so close to the surface, right there for everyone to see.

He turned and left, walking out the front door. The sunlight was bright, the air cold; the trees were turning bright yellow and red, as if they were on fire, and none of it mattered.

"What can I do, Eli?" Amy followed him out onto the porch. "You want me to stop. I'll stop—"

"I want you to—" He shook his head, doing everything he could to swallow the question. Everything he could to strangle the eight-year-old boy inside of him who was dying for answers.

A hand touched his back, full of static and electricity, and he knew it wasn't Victoria, so he spun, knocking that hand away so hard it had to hurt. But Amy just stood there, looking at him.

"Ask me," she whispered, as if she knew that the questions were burning the insides of his mouth.

"Why?"

"Because he was hurting me so bad it felt like I was dying." The words tumbled out on a river of breath. "Because I knew if I stayed one more minute—"

"No." Oh God, it hurt. It hurt so much. "Why didn't you . . . ?"

"Wh . . . what?"

"Why didn't you take me with you?"

That shell around her cracked wide open and he could feel her pain, her incredulous agony. Her shoulders caved and for a moment, one breathless still moment, he wondered if she was going to fall at his feet. But then she lifted her watery green eyes. There was too much hurt in those eyes, just like that horse he'd had to put down. "It . . . it never occurred to me that you would want to go. I was moving to a one-bedroom apartment in the middle of the city. I couldn't imagine taking you away from the land or the horses. How could I take you away from everything you loved, everything that made you who you were? I couldn't imagine taking you from . . . from him. You were always . . . his. From the beginning, as a baby, you . . . you wanted to be with him, all the time. I'd hold you in my arms and you'd scream for him. You were your father's son."

"But you never tried."

"I did. And I could have tried harder, I know. But your father got custody and he wouldn't let me back on the land. I tried to get you to visit, honey—" She reached for him and he flinched away. She dropped that hand, clutching it in her other one as if holding it back. "Summers. Christmas. Your father . . ."

"Said no." Of course he did. She'd left him.

"I imagined . . . that it was you saying no. That I'd hurt you so much, you were punishing me."

He remembered one summer, cleaning out the stalls in the early June heat. His father coming into the barn and watching him for a long time. "You want to go see her?" he'd asked.

"Who?"

"Your mother."

By then he'd been twelve. Uncle John was there. The land. His horse. The rock of his grudge. He'd shaken his head and his father had walked away. She was never brought up again.

"I admit that it got easier to let you go," she whispered. "In my head. I told myself that you hated me. That you and your father—"

"Were barely surviving? That he was punishing me for everything you did? That my life was a total hell, because of you?"

He wished he didn't see her pain, wished he was blind and dumb to it, but her agony was a force of nature, undeniable as it filled the yard, lifted the sky, pushed away clouds.

"I thought you'd both be happier with me gone. You were your father's son." Her voice cracked as a sob pushed through, but she swallowed it quickly, as though it never happened. "I'm sorry. I'm so sorry."

He stepped backwards, lifting his gaze until he saw the whole ranch.

The land that he'd loved because he had nothing else in his life to care for. He thought of his uncle, of a reckoning he didn't know how to handle.

And he thought of his father. Locked in his hate. In the past. Frozen solid in a wall of grief and bitterness.

The sun was shining. How odd. But it wasn't really just shining, it was falling to the earth in great beams, like those pictures on the front of church bulletins.

Like God was saying something.

Victoria stood on the porch, that purple blouse of hers gleaming like a gem. Her level, midnight eyes were on him and him alone. He could feel her worry about him. Her sympathy. He thought of the sex last night, how angry he'd been that she would turn away his feelings.

He was his father's son. Punishing the woman he . . . loved. Oh hell, really? Loved. He pressed on all those feelings, gauging their depth and temperature, and all he knew was that he'd never felt this way before about a person. Never wanted so badly to share his life with someone. The good, the bad, the whatever.

And he'd punished her last night because she didn't love him back.

His father's son.

And he didn't want to be anything like that man.

Under the power of some foreign motor, he crossed the lawn, walking right past his mother, who lifted her head to watch him go. He stopped at the bottom of the steps, staring up at Victoria.

She didn't love him; he knew that. But she cared, and that was enough right now. That was more than he'd ever had. And he had to do this, if he was ever going to get rid of the lonely life his parents had saddled on his back.

"I love you."

She gasped. Her eyes went wide and slowly filled with fear.

Pain sliced through him, sizzling along his veins, but he kept going, throwing off the weight he'd been carrying for so damn long. "I know that's not what you want, but . . . I am not my father's son. And . . . I love you."

Looking at her silent freak-out was more than he could take so he turned and headed back to his truck.

Back to his home.

Alone.

She went at dusk, her headlights eating up the shadows, bouncing through the darkness. She was iron-clad, driving to his house. Utterly resolved.

This . . . affair had gone on long enough. What was supposed to be fun, just good old dirty fun, had turned into a mess.

Love? A wild arm of frenzied panic slipped through the cracks of her resolve. She batted it away. There would be no thinking about love. At the beginning, she had loved her husband and it had made her weak and blind, needy and ruined.

She pulled up to his house, surprised to see it dark. Happy, actually. Relieved that no one appeared to be home. She didn't want to see him. Didn't want to confront this love of his.

What. A. Coward.

Fine, she was a coward, but that didn't change the fact that she hadn't signed up for this. She'd signed up for kinky sex with an emotional cripple.

She didn't want to be loved.

Carefully, she put her hand to her neck, feeling the wild thrumming of her heart. Everything in her was running at a staccato rhythm, hard and disjointed; she could barely put two thoughts together.

Before she totally chickened out, she opened her car door and quietly shut it. She hurried up the stairs, only to run right into his legs, stretched out in the shadows under the porch roof.

He sat tipped back in a chair, his hands clasped across his lean belly.

His eyes stripped her. Stripped her of clothes, of skin, of that damn resolve she needed.

Those eyes knew her inside and out.

And still loved her, she thought with what felt like wonder. With what felt like hope and longing.

"I'm getting our stuff," she said, wishing she sounded stronger.

He nodded.

She didn't wait. She practically ran inside, shoving Jacob's video games and clothes into the bags she'd left open at the foot of the bed they'd been using. Toothbrushes, brushes, the little bit of makeup she still wore were scattered across his bathroom counter.

Messy, she thought, feeling fragmented, broken in about twenty different places. *We're so messy. We just made ourselves at home here. What a mistake.*

Using her arms, she just swept the whole disaster into a bag and then swung it over her shoulder. If they left anything, it wasn't important.

Why did she feel like crying? she wondered. Why did this hurt so much?

She stepped out onto the porch, where he hadn't moved. He sat there staring out at his land, the dust and rocks and trees that had made up his life.

"I have everything."

He didn't say anything, and her nerves were stretched so thin. So tight.

Walk, she told herself. *Just walk. Don't say anything. Don't try to make this better; you'll only make it worse.*

"You know," she said, rejecting her own sound advice. He was slightly behind her and she stared at the worn toe of his boot, the silver dull in the moonlight. She felt his eyes on her back, the nape of her neck, that place he loved to bite. "You don't really love me."

"I don't?"

"No. No. It's just, you feel comfortable with me. You like me."

"Is that it?"

"Yes. You'd feel this way about anyone you let into your life like this. You—"

The chair scraped against the wood and clattered to the ground. She jumped as she felt him behind her, so close his breath touched her neck, her cheek. He was so angry she could feel it coming off his body like heat. "Don't sell yourself short, Tori," he breathed.

"I'm . . . I'm not. I'm just, you know, trying . . ."

"I love you because you're smart; because you're tough. You're the most game person I've ever met. You're brave like no one I've ever known, and you try so damn hard all the time to be kind. You're a good mother to that boy of yours. Makes me want to have a dozen kids with you, watch you love them all. You're funny, even when you're trying not to be. Underneath those ugly clothes you like to wear you're a total pervert. You make me want to change the world for you. You make me want to forgive my mom, even when it's impossible. You open me up, Tori. Christ, listen to me, I've never said so many words in a row in my life. You cracked me right down the middle. And I love you."

Stars were coming out in the darkest part of the sky, an ancient compass leading the lost home. She blinked back tears, staring at those stars as hard as she could, looking for her way out of the darkness.

"And I know you're scared. I know you've got plenty of reasons to be. I know you've got love all tangled up with need in your head. I know you don't think you're tough enough to know the difference between the two. But you are. Love won't make you weak again, Tori. I don't know if you really loved your husband, and I don't know if he really loved you. But you have to know that

I'd never hurt you like that. I'd never make you ashamed of anything you felt for me. I'd never leave you alone and defenseless and scared."

Softly, barely, he touched her hair, and she flinched as if he'd held a knife to her throat. She heard him suck in his breath, wounded or surprised by her reaction. She didn't know which, didn't want to stick around to find out.

Down the stairs she flew, turning only when she felt the distance between them. Clutching her bags to her chest, she shook her head at him.

She opened her mouth to tell him that he would get over her. That this was . . . temporary, but her resolve broke, shattered, and when she opened her mouth she said, "I'm scared."

He nodded as if he understood, and he did, she knew he did. He'd been scared, and look at how brave he'd been earlier today. Telling her he loved her in front of all those people.

That kind of bravery was a mystery. A wonder of the world, and she did not have it. She never had.

"What . . . what if I don't love you?" she said, because she had to tell him, had to give him a glimpse of the pain coming his way. The pain he was asking for in loving her. "I don't have love in me anymore. I can't trust this feeling you have for me. Not after Joel."

"That's okay." He pulled the bags from her hands, breaking her kung-fu death grip as if it were nothing, and set them on the ground, where they slumped against her legs like loyal dogs. "You can be scared to love me. I get it, it's scary. And I'm in no hurry." His smile was so sweet, the sweetest thing she'd ever seen. "But don't be scared to let me love you."

She resisted as best she could, holding herself apart from that smile, the temptation of his touch, the utter beguilement of his words. He loved her? It seemed impossible.

Slowly, inch by inch, she leaned against his chest, his heart beating so hard against her ear, and it felt good. Like home. Like those stars had been pointing to him all along.

She squeezed her eyes shut. "I warned you," she whispered.

He didn't bother to answer, he kicked the bags away and swung her up in his arms. His kiss was reverent and just a touch wild, as if he couldn't believe his luck, as if he had something to prove, and she clasped his head in her hands and kissed him back.

I'm going to break your heart, she thought.

"Thanks, Sabrina," Celeste said, taking the file from the young brunette they'd hired from Dallas to be their spa manager.

"We've got four women to interview," Sabrina said, managing to be both efficient and friendly, two of the big reasons she and Victoria had hired her. That she looked like a healthier Angelina Jolie didn't hurt. "We can start up again after Ruby and Victoria finish interviewing the kitchen staff."

Celeste opened the front door, letting in the cool fall air, the sounds of construction on the barn. Opening week was a month away and progress was right on schedule. When guests arrived on the twenty-sixth of December, this place was going to be perfect. "Sounds good. I'm just going to have some lunch," she said.

"I'll come find you when we're ready."

Celeste shut the door and turned to find a skinny back sitting on the front step, sharp shoulder blades pressed against his black shirt, so different from the back she longed to see.

"Sabrina is so hot," Thomas said, part of his meatball sub smeared across his face. This twenty-two-year-old man boy still needed a mother. Celeste handed him a napkin as she sat down.

"Sabrina," she eyed him carefully, "is not for you."

"Tell that to Sabrina," he said with a goofy waggle of his eyebrows. He wiped his face and used his foot to push a sandwich bag over toward her.

A six-inch meatball on flatbread with cheese. It smelled like her mother's terrible cooking, heavily processed and filled with fat and calories and chemicals. Delicious.

"No thank you," she said, pushing it back at him with her toe. Every day they did this. He offered her one of his sandwiches and she rejected it, choosing the same strawberry yogurt she'd been eating for lunch for the last twenty years.

She didn't even know what her body would do if she ate a sub like that.

Love it, she thought recklessly. *Rejoice. Sing hallelujah.*

"Hey, Celeste." Thomas squinted up at the sun sitting practically on top of the barn. A solar rooster. "I'm really sorry about the other day. That thing with my dad—"

The yogurt turned to glue in her mouth.

"It was a stupid idea, the flowers and everything. It's just . . . the way he talked about you and looked at you, I thought . . ." His sigh was not the sigh of a twenty-two-year-old kid, and she wished she were the kind of woman who could talk with her mouth full, because she'd tell him to shut up. Shut up and not worry. "Well, I thought he just needed some help asking you out."

"Thomas, it was sweet, the flowers and sandwiches, it was very sweet."

"But he didn't stay."

"That had nothing to do with you."

"My mom did such a number on him—"

"I don't think it had much to do with your mother either. I think . . ." She put down the yogurt, the four bites in her stomach starting a protest rally. "I'm just too old for him."

Just too cold. Too mean. Too angry.

"Old? Come on, you're what, fifty?"

"I'm sixty-three."

"So?" He didn't even pause, bless his heart.

"So, I could be your grandmother."

"But not his. He's fifty."

Oh Lord, she was thirteen years older than him. *Thirteen.*

"And you're hot." Thomas nodded eagerly, as if it weren't just slightly inappropriate that he'd said that.

"And your father is not interested."

"But he is—"

She stood up, thinking about that kiss, the reverence of his hands on her flesh, and how she'd pushed that away. For good. "Trust me."

chapter
23

"You sure . . ." Victoria ran a hand over the big belt buckle she wore. Her last pair of pants from her old life had finally split on Christmas morning, and Ruby and Celeste had just about thrown a party.

And then they took her shopping.

"This doesn't look ridiculous?" she asked. The jeans she wore were dark and very tight, tucked into a pair of boots. She wore one of Eli's belt buckles with a bright red tank top tucked into it.

Over the top of the whole outfit she wore a loose black sweater, longer at the front, almost down to her knees. A pair of dangly earrings swung from her ears.

Eli had whistled when he'd seen her, kissed her cheek, and told her how beautiful she looked. But he'd also said that when she split those pants. The man was no judge of fashion.

For four weeks now, she'd been pushing away his tenderness, his affection. And the pile of everything she was rejecting was growing so big in the corner of her life where she'd shoved it, she was going to have to deal with it at some point. Address it before it crushed her.

But she didn't know how.

"You look great," Celeste said, without looking up from their opening-week schematic.

"I don't look like me."

"Part of the reason you look great."

"Should we be so casual?"

Celeste looked up at her, her blue eyes bright, the white tunic she wore over slim black pants making her look eons younger than Victoria felt. "We should be ourselves."

"So a freaked-out ball of nerves?"

"Look at this place, Victoria," Celeste said. "Shut your mouth and look."

They stood behind the small desk they'd put into the foyer, beneath the skylight Gavin had made out of the portico. Sunlight flooded the room, and from where she stood she could see the lovely open-air dining room with its windows and pine walls. The fireplace in the lounge crackled, piping out warmth and the smell of a hickory fire. Through the door to her left were five state-of-the-art treatment rooms, and two change rooms with whirlpools and eucalyptus steam rooms.

The door to her right led to eight suites, with thousand-thread-count sheets, views of the property, and complimentary bottles of wine, just waiting to be opened.

Celeste, Victoria, and Jacob were living in the suite of rooms above the kitchen.

Behind them, the kitchen hummed with staff, with Ruby, with the smells of delicious food being prepared.

Everything was perfect. Totally perfect.

"Why am I so nervous?"

"You'd be an idiot not to be nervous."

"You don't seem nervous."

"Years of practice."

"I think I'm going to be sick."

Celeste made a note of something on the schematic and then lifted the small wicker wastebasket from under the desk and put it on top.

"Celeste." Victoria put her hand over the all-holy schematic, forcing Celeste to look up at her. "If this fails, I'm so sorry."

"Fails?" Much to Victoria's surprise, Celeste put down

the schematic and grabbed her arms, running her hands down to her cold, numb fingers. "We're in this together. All the way."

For years Victoria had avoided this woman's gaze, knowing that she'd see all too clearly how Celeste felt about her and it wouldn't be good. But not now. Those eyes were full of warmth . . . for her.

"I should have said this years ago, but I'm proud of you. You're . . ." Celeste melted slightly, her cold angles softening, and she ran a hand over the younger woman's hair as if she were a child with a skinned knee. Victoria soaked the attention in, gobbled it up, took every moment of warmth she could from this woman, surprised by how much she needed it. How much it meant to her. "You're the daughter I never had and always wanted."

So strange, the power of those words, how they reordered the past, shuffled memories like a deck of cards. Oddly, Victoria would have thought that she was past trying to gain this woman's approval.

And here it was, when she needed it most.

"Thank you, Celeste. For everything. I don't know what I would have done without you."

"You would have been fine," Celeste said. "Look at how far you've come since this summer. You're a survivor. One of the best I've ever seen."

It was a strange compliment, like Eli calling her game, but she would take it.

"I am," she agreed.

"You are. Now fix your eye makeup. The first guests should be here any minute."

"Right. Okay." She pulled out the little mirror from the desk drawer, which was right next to the manicure kit, comb, and package of Kleenex that Celeste had thought were invaluable.

"I think you made the right decision sending Jacob off to camp," Celeste said.

"It's only until Wednesday."

"Still, we should have our feet under us by then."

Holy raccoon eyes. She used the Kleenex as best she could and as she tilted the mirror, she got a good look at herself. Her cheeks were fuller than they'd been in years, her eyes brighter. Her lips had lost that pinched look, perhaps under Eli's kisses.

"Eli looks good on you," Celeste murmured, still looking through her paperwork, but a coy smile hovered over her lips.

Victoria shut the compact and Celeste looked up at the hard click.

"Why didn't you get married after you left Lyle? You were so young and beautiful . . . I mean, you were probably asked, weren't you?" Victoria asked.

"I was. And . . . I had relationships, but when things got too serious I walked away."

"Why?" she breathed.

Celeste shrugged, looking girlish. Honest. "Because I was scared. Scared of giving someone that much power over me again. Scared of being hurt. Scared of hurting someone. Love is powerful and I never knew what to do with it."

Victoria knew exactly what she meant. The feelings she had for Eli were like a loaded gun she didn't know how to use.

Celeste's blue eyes burned with understanding. "But I regret it. I regret it very much. I regret not having more children. Not having someone to share my life with, good and bad. I wish I had been braver. I wish . . ."

Victoria put her hand over Celeste's, touching the knuckles like stones under her skin. "It's not too late, you know. I've seen how you watch Gavin—"

Celeste snatched her hand back, picking up the schematic. "Well, he's gone now, isn't he?"

"But you could call him."

"We're not talking about me. We're talking about you and Eli. And frankly, we should be talking about today. We've got guests arriving in ten minutes."

Victoria pulled her hand back and touched the belt buckle at her waist. She felt, in a weird way, branded by his belt buckle.

And the feeling wasn't bad. It was nice. Good.

Maybe she just needed to be braver. Maybe she needed to stop being so damn scared. Eli was not Joel, and she was not the woman she used to be.

That woman, just like that part of her past, was gone.

"Right. So who is coming first?" In the last few weeks, with the Christmas preparations and attending to all the finishing touches on the opening-night party, she'd left the guest management to Celeste. Names, arrival times, allergies, spa treatments. Celeste took care of all those details. Victoria took care of New Year's Eve.

Never in her life had she imagined she and Celeste would make such a good team.

"Ah, this morning we've got the Rhodes, the Marrens, and . . . the Stones."

That's weird, Victoria thought, her stomach going a little queasy. "Where are they from?"

"New York. They booked online after they saw those ads in the *Times.*"

No. No . . . no way. It couldn't be . . . it just couldn't be. This was a possibility she'd never examined. Hadn't prepared for. She leaned forward to see the women's first names, but the front door opened and the cold air of winter swirled around her.

A boy stepped in first, his nose buried in a video game. He'd grown since the last time she'd seen him. His hair had been highlighted. An eight-year-old with highlighted hair. She knew only one woman who'd do that to her son.

"Kids?" Celeste muttered. "Who brings their kids to a

spa? Didn't we make it clear this wasn't a family resort?"

Behind the kid came Bill, still handsome, his face hard, his belly soft. He was talking on his cell phone, carrying a travel golf bag.

"*Golf?*" Celeste whispered, shocked.

This was Victoria's worst nightmare made real. This was a dimension of hell she'd never, ever considered. It was *This Is Your Life, Victoria Schulman,* the disaster version. The Suicide/Ponzi Scheme adaptation.

Last in the door was a petite woman with a shiny cap of dark hair. The first friend Victoria had made in her old life, the first friend to yank that friendship away when she'd needed it most.

Renee Stone smiled with all the black menace in her heart.

"Surprise, Victoria!"

After dinner that night, Celeste volunteered to take dessert out to Renee and her table. It was something they were doing with all the tables—a personal touch, which now felt like personal torture.

"You handle the other tables," Victoria said. The five other reservations were all women from the area. And they were showing signs of frustration over the table full of kids and husbands. The kids were whiney, the husbands surfing the Net on their phones, and the women were drinking too much, being too loud.

They were a cancer, and it was spreading through the dining room.

"You don't have to do this alone," Celeste said, reaching out as if to catch her.

"I'm fine," she lied, dodging her hand. Nothing could penetrate the thin veneer of ice she'd developed in order to push her body through this ordeal. And Celeste's kindness would melt it all, leave her naked and shivering, vulnerable to Renee and all that hate.

She'd stood inside the kitchen door, watching them through the crack every time a server came and went with a tray of food. But she couldn't hide forever. Sooner or later she'd need to face these women.

Victoria put the last of the mousse on the tray and let the server pick it up, leading her out of the kitchen.

Victoria paused at the door, searching through her memory bank, her inner stash of good things, for something to give her strength, something to make her smile in the face of all their animosity.

Her son's hugs, Celeste's respect—neither seemed strong enough to help her weather the ordeal ahead.

Eli saying, "I love you."

She didn't want to use that memory, didn't want to need his love, but the thought lifted her like a lifeboat and she hit the door.

"There she is," Renee said, leaning back in her chair. Her cheeks were bright, a sure sign she'd had too many martinis. Elizabeth, beside her, looked a little dazed from trying to keep up. "Our gracious proprietress."

"Hello, I hope everyone enjoyed their meal," Victoria said, with a smile that split the skin of her face as if she were a rotten tomato. She helped Tanya, the server, set the dishes down one by one in front of everyone, avoiding Bill, who always got a little grabby after having too much to drink.

"Passable," Renee said, her smile wide, her voice carrying to the other guests. "A little simple for a spa, I thought."

"Victoria," Jamie whispered, putting a hand on her arm. "I could use a little more water, if you wouldn't mind."

Renee loved that, and beside her Elizabeth snickered. "Me too," she said, slurring her words.

"Yes, water for the table." Renee spread her arm, her eyes stabbing Victoria right through the heart. "And clear some of these glasses, would you? I promise," she cooed, "we'll leave you a good tip."

She remembered Eli's touch, the heat of his breath against the nape of her neck. "Not a problem."

"I'll get it," the server murmured, and Victoria wanted to kiss her feet.

"I had no idea you had such an interesting family history, Victoria," Renee said. "When I saw your picture on the website, I tell you, it just about made me fall over. Makes me wonder if Joel knew. Could you imagine him out here, riding horses? Busting broncos?"

The men said nothing, turning stone-faced, polishing off their drinks with one swallow. These men had considered Joel a friend and he'd robbed them.

I'm sorry, she thought for the millionth time. But her apologies had never gotten her anywhere with these people.

"It was my father's ranch," she said. "The running of it was left to me in his will."

She was fudging all kinds of truth, but she wasn't about to tell these people that she was penniless and living on the ranch at her brother's behest. "And since I didn't know a single thing about raising cattle or horses, I decided that with its location and beauty it would be the perfect spa."

"Yes, you always did love spas, didn't you?" Renee asked. Victoria stared at her, longing to spitefully remind her of all the weekends they'd spent together, wrapped in towels, gossiping beside pools. She wanted to remind Renee of how at Canyon Ranch she'd cried in Victoria's arms after the miscarriages and again after her husband's affair.

Renee looked away as if finally she remembered too, and Victoria stood a little taller in her cheap boots.

"You always liked the mud," Jamie said, smiling.

"Like a pig," Elizabeth sneered.

The table froze, even the kids stared, and someone gasped.

Me, she realized, sick to her stomach. *I gasped.*

Elizabeth must have stepped over some line Renee had established, because she got the evil eye from her lord and master.

"I think perhaps Elizabeth has had enough," Renee said through her teeth to Elizabeth's husband.

Gary, who was used to this—both his wife's public drunkenness and being bossed around by Renee—sighed and gathered his sloppy wife from the table, leading her through the dining room to their room.

Victoria could feel the eye of every guest charting their progress. She could only imagine what the feedback cards would say.

"Where's Jacob?" Renee asked, and Liam finally looked up from his video game.

"He's at camp," she said.

"Sleepaway camp?" Renee asked, her plucked-to-shit eyebrows so high up on her forehead that they vanished into her bangs. "That's not like you. Aren't you worried he'll catch something?"

"He's much stronger than he was last year," she said. *And so am I. But where is that strength now? Where is it when I need it so badly?*

These women, the past they brought back, brought her to her knees.

"But still." Jamie leaned in. "Wouldn't you just feel sick if something happened?"

Yes, she thought, panic immediately running through her system like lightning. *I would. I would feel terrible. I should never have sent him. What a mistake I made!*

Her old self was waking up from whatever dream

state she'd been in, and Victoria struggled to knock her back out.

"It's fine," she said, forcing herself to remember that she actually believed that. "He's fine."

Jamie shrugged as if she had her doubts and Victoria took a deep breath, wondering where all the oxygen had gone.

"I was looking forward to a couple rounds of golf," Bill said.

She sucked a breath through her teeth. There was no golf course attached to the spa. They'd made that clear in all the promotional materials. Of course, they'd also made it clear that it was an adults-only spa.

Renee knew all too well how a spa experience could be ruined for every other guest.

"The nearest course is south quite a ways, but if you have rental cars—"

"We took a limo from the airport, Victoria," Renee said as if she were a child.

Great. Wonderful.

"That's not a problem; we'll be able to get you there."

Somehow. Three men and all their golf clubs. It would be a tight fit in the Cadillac. And they all frowned at her as if they knew that.

"Well, like I said, we're delighted you're here and if there are any problems, be sure to let me know."

She turned to leave, ready to find some dark corner to grow back her shell, but Renee grabbed her wrist, her fingernails digging into Victoria's skin.

"You don't get to have this," Renee hissed in her ear. "You don't get to walk away from what you did. I will ruin you like you ruined us."

Victoria was frozen, paralyzed by guilt and fear and the terrible reality that Renee wasn't wrong. She wasn't right, but she wasn't totally wrong.

"Is there a problem?" Celeste asked, coming to the table with a serene smile on her face, the perfect hostess.

Renee dropped Victoria's hand but the damage was done. The old wounds were opened and the poison had filled her blood.

Yes, Victoria thought, *I am the problem. I have always been the problem.*

chapter
24

Eli parked his truck out front of the ranch like he always did. Ruby's phone message had been cryptic and he'd gotten back there as fast as he could. But he'd been a hundred miles away at Los Camillos, where he'd been hired to train some rodeo studs while he waited for his mares to give birth.

Climbing up the steps, he was struck as he always was by how they'd managed to turn such an ugly building into something so arresting. So positively beautiful.

But that was the power of Victoria. Look what she'd done to him. He felt totally transformed by her. A new man stood on this porch.

At her urging, he'd called Uncle John in Galveston. Only left a message, but still, he'd reached out. Now they were playing phone tag. But he wouldn't have called in the first place without Victoria.

The front door opened and she slipped out, his belt buckle at her waist gleaming in the twilight. He liked that on her. Liked it a lot.

"Hey, babe, what's—"

"I need you to go home," she said.

He blinked. "But Ruby said there was some kind of problem—"

"There isn't."

All right, he was no Sherlock Holmes, but Tori was

acting very strange and all his instincts went on high
alert.

The word *love* hadn't been discussed again in all the
weeks they'd been practically living together, sleeping
together, and working together, but it was there on his
side and he had a strong suspicion she felt it, too.

"Are you okay?"

"Very busy. You . . . should just go on home." She
stepped down to the next step and put her hand on his
chest. Even through his shirt it felt cold. He put his hand
over hers to warm it, to touch her, to connect in some
way with this stranger in front of him.

"I want you to stay away all week."

Now he laughed. He was supposed to help them get
ready for that big party on Saturday and then, well, he
had a suit in his closet. Brand-new. And he'd been planning on stepping into that party looking pretty slick
with her on his arm.

"I'm serious."

"You're crazy. Come on, babe, tell me what's going on."

Through the open door of the ranch he heard someone call her name. Victoria stiffened.

"Just go."

"Not until you tell me why." Something was way
wrong and he wasn't leaving until he knew what it was.

"Look at you!" she cried. "You're filthy. You've got
mud on your boots, under your nails. There's . . . blood
on your shirt, Eli. You smell like shit. You can't just
walk in here like it's still your ranch."

He stepped backwards off the porch, getting some distance from her wildness. Her uncontrolled hostility.

He glanced down at his hands, the dirt he'd never
even noticed.

"Just go," she said, and then vanished back into the
house. He heard her laugh through the door and put his
hands in his pockets.

Too late to hide them, painfully unaware that he had to.

Celeste watched Victoria rest her head against the front door and was torn right down the middle. Part of her felt awful for Victoria, for the way Renee and her friends were leaching the joy right out of what should be a fabulously successful weekend.

The other part of her wanted to shake Victoria until she saw reason.

Either way, one thing was very clear. Left to her own devices, Victoria would roll over and play dead for those women, and Celeste wasn't having that.

This was her spa, too.

"All right." Celeste stepped into the foyer and Victoria jerked herself upright. "I don't know what's going on in your head but we don't have the time to figure it out."

"What are you talking about?"

Celeste faltered for a moment when Victoria turned around. This was the old Victoria, wound too tight, pinched with insecurity and worry, plagued by the world's poor opinion of her and her late husband. Bristling in defense of every single touch. No wonder she just kicked Eli off the ranch—in the face of that man's love right now, she'd splinter.

"I'm handling the New York crowd," Celeste said. "You handle the rest of the Saturday-night details."

"Celeste, they came here for me." Victoria sagged. "I can't let you—"

Celeste laughed. "Please, Victoria, no one *lets* me do anything. I don't give a shit who they're here for; they're not going to ruin this week, for any of our other guests or for you."

"I'm fine."

"You're lying." Celeste touched Victoria's rigid shoul-

der, which only got more tense under her palm. "A lot of
people who should have protected you have treated you
badly over the years, Victoria. I will no longer be one of
them. I will also not let you or anyone else jeopardize
this week. Am I being clear?"

Victoria felt she should argue. She should explain to
Celeste that the shock of seeing the women had worn off
and she was ready to get back to work, but she felt frac-
tured, burned-out. And she could not pull the pieces of
herself back together.

She was acting on fear—just look at how she'd treated
Eli. Acting like she was embarrassed of him, when in all
honesty she was embarrassed of herself. Of these old
friends of hers. Of who she used to be. She didn't want
him to see her like this, broken down by their viciousness.

He'd been startled by her words, hurt, each pointed
insult finding a home in that soft heart of his.

*Well, I certainly don't have to worry about that love
problem anymore, do I?*

Celeste was right; she wasn't making any sense. Her
every instinct was to isolate herself with Renee and the
rest of them, to push Celeste and Eli and Ruby away so
they wouldn't be affected by her failures.

And that wasn't going to work. They had a spa full of
people.

"Okay," she breathed, and inwardly she rejoiced. The
coward in her was relieved. The old her, scared and insecure, was delighted to give up control. To go right
back into hiding. "You're right, I'm . . . I'm not making
good decisions."

"Victoria!" Renee's voice echoed down the hallway,
and Victoria's stomach clenched into a thousand little
knots.

"Go," Celeste said. "Help Ruby in the kitchen; I've
got this."

Victoria nodded, and like a scared little girl, she ran away.

"What exactly do you expect me to do?" Eli asked Ruby on Wednesday morning. He wiped the cream off Patience's belly and pulled his hair away from her teeth, wincing when some caught. "She told me to stay away."

And he had for two days now. Today he was going to paint the inside of his barn.

The inside.

All so he wouldn't go charging down there like some . . . woman, demanding to know what was wrong.

"And you listened?"

"Christ!" He tossed the ultrasound wand and it clattered onto the cart. A thousand dollars' worth of equipment and he didn't give a shit. "I don't know how these things work. She asked me to stay away and was pretty damn emphatic about it. I'm just trying to do what she wants."

"Oh Lord, that woman is so turned around by those bitches, she doesn't know what she wants."

"What bitches?"

"Those friends of hers from New York—"

"Wait . . . her friends from New York came?"

"Well, you can't really call them friends."

"She wasn't going to invite them." Cannibalistic, she'd called them. They'd kicked her when she'd been as down as a person could get. They were at that ranch? Hurting her more?

"They saw the ad in the *Times*. They brought their kids. Their husbands. Golf bags. It's a disaster. Celeste is handling them at the moment. Victoria's working in the greenhouse, finishing up all the party details, but it's getting strained around the spa."

"What can I do?"

"We need someone to occupy the men and kids. Spas are no place for boys, and the whining is making everyone nuts. They need to *do* something. Get dirty."

Well, hell. It was a ranch. There was plenty of stuff that needed doing, and most of it could get a kid dirty.

He checked his watch; he'd need to call in a few guys, a couple of favors. "I need you to call your dad and get some of his beer. Pack us a lunch. I'll be there in an hour."

When Victoria got back to the ranch after picking Jacob up at camp, the front yard was a dust cloud of activity and all she could think of was how Renee was going to complain about that.

"What's going on?" Jacob asked, leaning over the dashboard.

Something terrible, no doubt. But then she saw Eli's horse trailer and his truck.

And there, up on the porch, talking to Bill, was Eli.

Her body lost its skin. Its bones. She was a puddle of goo in the front seat of her father's El Dorado. It had only been a couple days, but it had felt like years.

Eli looked so masculine up there talking to soft-handed Bill. He looked the way a man should look. A little rough, a little wild, but comfortable in his skin, his frayed denim.

I'm sorry I said those things to you, she thought. *I love the way you smell and how hard you work, and how all of that has made you the man you are.*

"Eli!" Jacob cried and flew out of the car.

Eli, her heart echoed, and she gathered herself as best she could before following her son.

"Hi there, Eli," she said, sparing a glance for Bill, whose eyes seemed a little too interested in the low V of her T-shirt. The lace edge of the camisole was supposed to be down there somewhere making things modest, but it had gotten skewed in the car.

Eli noticed Bill's attention and stood up a little straighter, his body brushing her arm, making her skin sizzle with awareness. With want.

"What's . . . what's going on?" She crossed her arms over her chest, pulling away from the contact. Eli's face was all strange, his smile on crooked or something.

"Well, I've got those fifty head of cattle up on the high pasture. I need to get them down to the low pasture, and I heard you had a bunch of men here who might be able to help."

She stared, gobsmacked. Was . . . was this a joke?

"See?" Bill pointed at Victoria's face as if that was the proof he'd been waiting for. "I told you that was ridiculous."

"I can help!" Jacob yelled. "I can totally help, can't I, Mom?"

"I want to help, too!" Liam said, and the little circle of boys that had gathered around Jacob when he got out of that car all piped up, hands in the air as if they were waiting to be chosen for the horse-riding team.

"The more help the better." Eli reached out and tousled Jacob's hair, holding his head for a second. "Missed you, bud. How was camp?"

"Great. I learned how to canoe."

"Good thing to learn. Can you teach me?"

"Yeah!"

Victoria shut her mouth, biting her tongue for composure.

"You can't just take my son horseback riding," Bill said. "He has no experience."

"Dad!" Liam groaned.

"Well, you don't, son. And I don't know who the hell this man is."

"He's our neighbor," Victoria jumped in, unwilling to

listen to one negative thing come out of this man's mouth about Eli. "And he's a good man."

Bill's shrewd eyes narrowed on Victoria. "Excuse my bluntness, but your track record suggests you don't know a good man from a crook."

You're right, she thought. *You're so right; I have no idea what I'm doing.*

And she couldn't even defend Eli, who was worth ten of Bill. That's what a mess she was, how miserly her spirit.

Eli's brows slammed down tight on his eyes and Victoria put her hand over his arm. The last thing she needed was for him to try defending her honor.

"Do you think I would do anything to put my son in danger?" she asked.

After a tense moment, Bill shook his head.

"It's a nice safe trail up to the pasture, and the hands, Phil and Jerry, will do most of the work. Your boys will just need to hold on," Eli said. "And if you don't believe me, perhaps you should accompany your son."

"Yeah!" Liam cried, and Victoria knew how starved these boys were for their fathers. The same way her son had been starved for his father, desperate with hunger for his time. For his attention. For scraps of affection. "Come on, Dad. Come. It will be awesome."

It would take a heartless bastard to ignore the appeal in Liam's eyes. Bill was a lot of things, but heartless wasn't one of them. He smiled into his son's beaming face.

"All right. Let me get Gary and Robert, and we'll meet you back out here in ten minutes."

"You'll need sweatshirts or something," Eli said. "It's cold up there."

Everyone ran into the house and Victoria turned to face him. Her heart, her body, her everything panted for him.

"What are you doing, Eli?" she asked.

"Well, Ruby said things were going pretty rough over here and since I've got a stake in this thing succeeding, I figured I ought to pull my weight."

After all the things she'd said to him. After the way she'd treated him. Gratitude nearly choked her.

"Thank you."

He looked into her eyes the way he always did, as if he were taking inventory of her heart, seeing what she needed. "You're welcome."

He touched her cheek and she sighed into his hand, took a moment with his touch, feeling all her shelves get restocked, all her broken pieces get reassembled.

She caught sight of Renee at the door and stepped away, her cheeks on fire.

"Sorry to interrupt," Renee said, malicious delight coating her words.

"You're not interrupting anything," Victoria said clearly.

"I haven't seen you here before." Renee held out a limp hand toward Eli, her tennis bracelet practically falling off her thin wrist. "Who are you?"

God bless him, Eli didn't take her hand. "Help," he said, unsmiling, as if he knew this was the source of Victoria's trouble. Men liked Renee upon seeing her, she glittered under their attention like a diamond, but not Eli. He just stared at her with distaste.

"You're the one taking the boys out?" she asked. "Some kind of trail ride?"

She made *trail ride* sound like it was a trip through the sewage treatment plant. Eli nodded.

"Do you want me to sign a waiver of some kind, or insurance . . . a permission slip?" she asked, her eyebrow arched at Victoria. "It's not that we don't trust you . . ."

But she didn't. And why would she?

Victoria felt every one of her husband's failures like
stones against her body, most of which she deserved.

And she wondered if Eli could feel her failures the way
she did, a physical pain he had nothing to do with and
had done nothing to warrant.

She was so relieved when Celeste showed up.

"Come on inside, Renee," Celeste said, opening the
door. "We'll get this all squared away."

Once Eli got the men away from the ranch and confis-
cated their damned cell phones, things got . . . pleasant.
The sun was bright, the air cool. It was a good thing
he'd borrowed those extra horses and dogs. He'd been
hoping the fathers would come, but he'd known it
wasn't a sure thing.

The dogs ran ahead of the horses as if they couldn't
believe their luck to be out on a day like this. The boys
were sort of like that too, preening under their fathers'
attention.

The fathers, though—they handled their sons as
though they were sticks of dynamite or talking frogs or
some other kind of scary mystery. They kept looking at
the boys like they'd never seen them before, like they'd
just popped up riding alongside them.

Bill, as if to compensate for his insecurities, started
acting like John Wayne, as if he'd been born on a horse.
Which had made it so gratifying when Lucky had shied
away from him, making him stumble as he mounted.

Lucky did not suffer fools.

But the man had calmed down some and was pointing
out a hawk making high circles in the blue sky. Liam, his
son, was a nice boy. He kept his wonder-filled eyes fixed
on his dad in case he vanished.

Eli remembered being a kid and feeling that way, before things got so bad. His mother had been right: he'd

been his father's boy all along. Following the old man around like a dog looking for a treat, a scratch behind the ears, anything.

The realization was a sour one. Sad.

"You got a plan here?" Jerry asked as he rode up next to him, frowning at the line of people making their way up to the pasture. Jerry would not have been Eli's first choice for this kind of work—the man was as sour as a crab apple, but he'd been available. "I mean, the dogs can get those cattle down to the low pasture before this crowd even gets up there."

Eli glanced at the sun and then back at the ranch. They had another hour ahead of them, two hours if they came back at this same pace.

"We'll go up and have lunch." Ruby had given him bags of food, which he'd strapped on Phineas's back. The beer was in a cooler bag on top. It was his ace in the hole. "Come on back after."

"Biggest waste of time I've ever seen," Jerry grumbled, riding ahead to where one of the kids had dropped his reins and his father was about to fall off his horse getting them back.

"This is fun, Eli," Jacob said, beaming like a bag of lightbulbs as Eli rode up next to him.

"You think so?"

"Totally."

"These . . . ah . . . these boys being nice to you?" Eli didn't want to put too fine a point on his feelings, but he would leave a kid out here all night if he so much as looked at Jacob funny.

"They're fine. I don't think they know . . . you know . . . what my dad did."

Eli squinted into the sun, knowing without a shadow of a doubt that Tori would hate for him to talk to Jacob about the Ponzi scheme, but his feelings for the two of them overrode her fears. And he had to figure out what was going on here. Why she was hiding herself away.

"Do you know what your father did?"

"He stole from a lot of people and then killed himself. Everyone got really mad at my mom, like it was her fault and she had to try to make things right."

He remembered how Tori had told him months ago that she'd been a guest in her own home. How in some ways she'd suspected what her husband had been up to, and that her suspicions and her failure to act on them had been reason enough for her to take everyone's punishment.

And man, wasn't history repeating itself.

It didn't take a genius to see that Renee and her crowd were here with whips in hand and Tori was hiding away because she thought she deserved to be their whipping post.

And he had the sinking feeling that he wasn't going to be able to convince her otherwise.

chapter
25

The moon hung big and fat over the greenhouse, where Eli found Victoria sitting in Tara Jean's old office chair among the party supplies they'd stored in here for Saturday night. The moon filled the place with icy white light, making things look different, playing with his perceptions.

Eli put a bottle of beer down on the desk.

"Thought you might need a drink," he whispered, wishing he could kiss away every line on her face, every sadness in her eyes.

"Way ahead of you," she murmured, lifting up a tumbler a quarter filled with amber liquid.

"The trail ride went well," he said, pulling up an old stool and sitting on the edge of it. He kept a wide berth, sensing the land mines around her.

"I heard."

"Some of the other guests came over and asked if they could do it tomorrow."

"Thank you," she said. "Thank you for coming back after what I said to you. I was so out of line—"

"I understand."

"Really?" she asked.

"Everyone freaks out sometimes, Tori. It's okay."

"I don't deserve that," she whispered. "I don't deserve you."

Now, this was getting troubling, because the woman

he loved was slipping away and if he didn't find a way
to stop it, he'd lose her.

"I'll tell you what you don't deserve. You don't deserve to be sitting on the sidelines while everyone else is
out there working on your vision."

"I'm working," she snapped. Her eyes crackled and
he rejoiced at the glimmer of the Victoria he knew and
loved. If only he could tease more of that out, get rid of
this ghost that plagued her.

"You're hiding."

"It's for the best, Eli. For everyone."

"How in the world is you hiding in here for the best?"

"Because I was screwing everything up! That's . . .
that's what I do, Eli. I fail."

It hurt him to see her so twisted around, pulled sideways by these people being here. "Kick them out."

"Don't be ridiculous."

"I'm serious. You don't need them. They're ruining
this experience for you."

"They're paying guests."

"They're asshats, remember? You don't owe them
anything!"

Something ignited in her eyes and she sat up straighter.
She sat all the way up. "I knew he was doing something
wrong, he was making too much money, too easily—"

"Hindsight is twenty/twenty, Tori. Give yourself a
break."

"I don't get a break, Eli! I don't deserve one."

"Bullshit." He flew across the room, fed up with this
nonsense. Standing over her, he felt himself pulled in
two by hope and worry. "That is the most self-sacrificing
nonsense I have ever heard in my life. And I know
self-sacrificing. I know it really well, spent most of my
life doing it. And you know where it gets you? Alone.
Fired, actually. And so damn sick of yourself you can't
stand it anymore."

He pulled her up from the chair, feeling all her wires pulled too tight. "You know," he smiled, "I realize now why you kept your legs crossed until I forgave you."

"Because I did something awful to you—"

"Because all you think about is forgiveness. Because you're obsessed with guilt. So you married an asshole who stole from people and made your life miserable. It's not your fault. Get over it so you can move on with your life."

"That's really easy for you to say."

"Yep. You know what's hard for me to say? My mom left me when I was eight with a drunk dad who didn't love me half as much as I loved him. And that's not my fault."

She blinked at him, her eyes old in her face, her body small in his hands. "I'm really, really good at handling the shit life hands out, Tori. I'm an A student in managing it. But before you, that's all I had. And you brought me into this life of yours, your son and this wild idea, and it was all so good. It was happy, and I want it back, not just for me, but for you. You deserve to be happy, you've worked hard for it. So don't let those people take it away from you. Don't let them push you aside."

He knew she didn't believe him—he could feel it in her body, in the distance between them that he couldn't stand—so he pulled her closer, as close as he could, until he felt her heartbeat against his.

Her glass went down on the table with a small thunk and she wrapped her arms around his neck, pulling his lips to hers. She tasted like grief, like desperation, like a woman with her fingers in all the cracks, and part of him wanted to leave, wanted to get to higher ground, because the woman kissing him didn't love him the way he loved her.

Or didn't have the courage to claim it.

And he couldn't save her.

Still, he wrapped his arms around her with a groan, lifting her against his body, pressing her against the erection at his hips. She sighed and wiggled closer, splitting her legs to wrap them around his waist.

Yes, he thought, something dark and needy rising in his blood. If she wouldn't have him any other way, she'd have him like this. He took three steps toward the wall, pressing her there, holding her with his hips, and she groaned, throwing her head back.

He kissed her neck, his hands cupping her breasts, filling his palms with the beauty and reality of her. She arched against him, throwing gasoline on this reckless fire between them.

He fumbled with his pants, with hers, pushing aside fabric until he felt the heat of her, sank his fingers into the wet of her.

Her frantic breaths burned his skin, filled his head until all he heard was their heartbeats. Pushing down his pants, he shifted his hips and thrust into her.

She pushed against his shoulders, finding leverage to move her hips against him, up every time he pushed in, and the friction was hot, too hot, and it felt so good, the kind of heat he could live in.

His orgasm barreled down on him.

He gripped her hips harder, shifting her so he hit her clit with every thrust and he felt her frenzy rise, her agonized pleasure. And he managed to hold off until he knew she was coming, her body locked around his, her mouth open in a scream.

He erupted, pouring himself into her. All his love. All his worry. All his fear that she'd never love him back.

They stood there, chests heaving, bodies stuck to the wall. He closed his eyes and wished things were different.

"If . . . if you don't love me, Victoria, I gotta walk away. I thought I could love you enough for the two of us. But if you won't even stand up for yourself, when are you ever going to stand up for me? For us?"

He kissed her neck, felt her shake against him, unsure if it was the cold or tears or fear that locked her muscles.

"I'll help out here the next few days, but then . . . maybe I need to go."

Say something, he thought, pressing his head to hers, as if he could force the words out of her.

"I'm sorry, Eli," she breathed.

His skin, his chest pulled flat, and he couldn't suck in a breath. Couldn't pull away from this pain—he had to just ride it out, like that strawberry mare down in Mexico. He held on and let himself get hurt.

Finally, he pulled away, tucking himself into his pants, trying not to feel the slick heat of her on his body.

Something felt wrong.

Yeah, idiot, he thought, *it's your heart breaking.*

But then reality stampeded back and his hands froze on his pants.

Shit.

"I didn't use a condom."

chapter
26

Victoria, looking like a ghost, like a shadow of herself, stepped into the kitchen on Saturday morning and slid the party planning binder onto the stainless-steel counter.

Celeste had thought when she volunteered to take on the soulless monsters that were Victoria's old friends from New York that Victoria would agree, that within a day she'd realize what a fool she was to let these women get the better of her and she'd come out swinging, setting things right, and Celeste could stop pretending to care about Renee's every little problem.

But it was Saturday and it hadn't happened.

Things around this ranch had only gotten worse. And it wasn't because she was waiting on Renee and her unquenchable thirst. Victoria didn't look like a woman who ran a spa, she looked like a woman in desperate need of one.

And Eli, well, it was plenty obvious the poor man was nursing a broken heart; luckily, it just made that stoic cowboy persona he had going for him more attractive. Those women from New York were infatuated.

She wondered what Victoria would do if Celeste told her about what Renee said about Eli's butt.

"A little lipstick wouldn't kill you," Celeste said, trying to get a rise out of the girl, but Victoria just ignored her.

"Are we ready for the party tonight?" Ruby asked, wiping her hands off on a towel.

"No, actually," Victoria said. "We've got Eli leading a trail ride up to the North Pasture with most of the guests and most of the hands. Celeste—"

"Is being treated like a dog by your snobby friends. Honestly, Victoria, what did you ever see in them?" Celeste said, sipping her tea.

"They were all that was available, I suppose," she said, flipping open the binder. "With everyone so busy, we're going to need a few more hands. Some muscle to set up for the party."

"Luc—" Celeste said.

"He and Tara had to catch a later flight from Toronto. They won't be here until tonight."

"Who are you going to call?" Ruby asked.

"Gavin," Celeste said, caught off guard that she couldn't pretend she hadn't missed him. That she hadn't thought about him a hundred times a day.

"Do you want me to call him?" Victoria asked. "Or do you want to?"

Me! Me!

"Why would I want to?" Celeste asked, arching a perfectly trained eyebrow.

Ruby muttered something in Spanish and turned back around to the sink and the carrots she was peeling.

"I just thought you might."

Celeste tilted her head. "And what do you think about Eli?"

Victoria flinched.

Ah, Celeste thought, *a reaction.*

"It was never going to work out between us," Victoria said, pushing her hair behind her ears like a nervous thirteen-year-old girl.

"Did he know that?" Celeste asked.

Victoria cleared her throat. "He does now."

Celeste's heart hurt for Eli, who'd been suckered in by the chimera of the person Victoria had become these last few months, having no idea that under pressure, the strong, independent woman would disappear like a popped bubble.

"You're a coward," Celeste said.

"Yes, I am. It's the one thing I'm good at." Victoria picked up her binder, tucking it under her arm. "I have to go pick up liquor. Call Gavin. We need him."

And with that, she left.

Celeste stared out the bright blue square of window over the sink and calmed her racing heart. She had a reason to call Gavin. An excuse. And after the stress of the last week, the gerbils weren't just panicked, they were manic. And she'd gotten used to it. It was as if that gerbil she'd been afraid of had moved into her brain, procreated, and built a gerbil city.

"I'm starved," Celeste said and Ruby spun, her face alight. "Really, really hungry. Honestly, I've never been this hungry."

"Well, I have just what you need."

Ten minutes later Ruby slid a bowl of something fragrant and warm in front of her and without a second thought, without even looking at what she was eating, Celeste dug in.

Cheese. Eggs. Sour cream. Delicious.

She glanced down and realized it was exactly the same thing she'd given to Victoria months ago when the woman began taking over the ranch.

Courage food, apparently.

She was going to call Gavin. She wanted to call Gavin. She ached to hear the sound of his voice, even if it was telling her to get lost.

Celeste put a little hot sauce on the eggs and thought

about what she was going to say: *Gavin, can you please come back here? Gavin, I need you. I'll pay you whatever you want—just . . . please . . . help me.*

Holding her breath, she picked up her cell phone and hit the speed dial that went right to Gavin's cell.

"Gavin Svenson."

"Hi . . . ah, Gavin?" She closed her eyes, wished herself in a deep dark hole with nothing but eggs and cheese and no cell phones.

"That's me."

"It's Celeste."

"Hi." She tried to read warmth in that voice, but it was impossible. He was an arctic ice cap. At night. "Everything all right?"

"No. Well, I mean, yes. There aren't any problems with the spa, except . . . I need your help."

"Mine?"

"Yes." Watching Ruby's back at the sink she explained the situation as best she could without getting too detailed. "I know it's beneath your pay scale, but I'm desperate and there's no one here to help me set up for this party and . . . I need you."

He was silent for a moment and then he chuckled, the warm sound bouncing through the air waves to slide down her back like the stroke of a finger. "How in the world can I say no? Celeste Baker needs me."

She closed her eyes, clinging to the strange intimacy. "Is it safe to say that I need Thomas, too?"

I do. I do. I need you both. She was so damn tired of her cold life. Her loneliness that no amount of friendship with Ruby and Victoria could fill.

"We'll clear off our schedules and get there in two hours."

Celeste hung up. Those gerbils were drunk on champagne, doing silly things in her stomach, making a mess of her ordered life.

"The cavalry's coming," she said, trying to appear as composed as possible. But one glace at Ruby's face and Celeste knew she wasn't buying it for a minute.

"Girl, you in a heap of trouble."

And wasn't that the truth. On so many levels.

At three in the afternoon on Saturday, Eli collapsed into one of the wooden deck chairs on the front porch. He wasn't going to move for a week. Not one week. His feet hurt. His back was killing him, and he hadn't talked so much . . . ever. In his life. About useless shit.

Small talk.

Three days since the greenhouse. Three days of Victoria not looking at him.

Luckily, he'd been working himself to the bone for her and was too damn tired to be worried or sad. But, oddly enough, he still had plenty of energy to be pissed off.

She could be pregnant, right now, with his baby, a baby he couldn't want more, and she still didn't have the courage to lift her head. To look him in the eye and say "We're in this together."

The front door opened, and much to Eli's surprise Gavin, the Viking contractor, walked out, his son behind him. Eli felt oddly compelled to hide, but Gavin had already noticed him, sitting in the shade of the porch.

"Go on and get the rest of the lights, Thomas," Gavin said, and much to Eli's horror, the older man started walking toward Eli.

Thomas shot Eli a poisonous look from his dark eyes and hit the steps to do what his father had asked.

He really hoped Gavin wasn't interested in fighting, because the shape he was in, Eli was just going to sit there and get punched.

"You look beat." Gavin leaned up against the railing, stretching his legs out like he was getting ready for a good chat.

Eli nodded.

"Quite a scene around here," Gavin said. "Heard you've been busy."

"What are you doing here?" Eli asked. What little small talk he'd been born with had been used up.

"Helping Celeste set up for that big party tonight."

Eli groaned, planting his hands on the arms of his chair, trying to coax his muscles into a standing position. He'd totally forgotten about the party. Celeste and Victoria must be frantic.

Or not. He couldn't tell a single thing about Victoria anymore.

"I got it, man," Gavin said, holding out his hand. "Thomas and I can set up tables. Hang the lights."

"Not quite your job description." Eli sagged back into his chair with relief.

"Yeah, well." Gavin looked at the front door as though he expected his life to come walking through it. "Celeste called; I couldn't say no."

Celeste? And Gavin? Eli would have smiled if his mouth wasn't sore from all the talking. Good for them. "Well, thanks."

Gavin stood, that smile fading, replaced by something worried. "I'm sorry about that fight—"

"I started it." Eli lifted his hand and let it flop back in his lap. "I was an ass."

"Yeah, but I'd been wanting to hit you for a long time. And not just because of the shit you were pulling in the yard." He ran a hand across the white railing as if admiring his own craftsmanship. "Your mom is my friend. The best one I've got, and it sucked watching her get hurt like that."

Maybe he was just too tired to fight, or maybe he didn't care anymore. Either way, all the protestations—about how badly she'd hurt him—died on his tongue.

"I imagine it did."

"She's excited about coming out tonight. She wouldn't say so, but she is."

Eli was done with conversation. He'd hit his limit and he couldn't lie and say he was excited to see her. So he said nothing, and after a moment Gavin nodded and walked down the steps to his truck to help his son gather up armfuls of white Christmas lights.

A few minutes later, Jacob came out and Eli groaned. "No more hikes, buddy. No football games. No trips to see the swans. I'm beat."

Jacob's jeans had a hole in the knee and he was covered in dust and dirt and suspicious brown smears from the baseball game in the high pasture. All the kids were, even some of the dads. Eli was too tired to care whether or not that mattered.

It was going to take an hour just to get this kid cleaned up for the party.

Jacob climbed onto the side arm of his wooden seat, leaning against Eli's shoulder, tucking his feet in between Eli's legs, like he'd been doing it all his life.

And Eli shifted and slid, lifted his arm to put it around the boy's back so he didn't fall off the chair. It wasn't comfortable, but he wouldn't change it.

For a moment he allowed himself to think about a kid of his own. A baby, growing right now in Victoria's belly.

But then he pushed the thought away, because it was too sharp to touch, his longing too painful to bear.

"Thirsty?" Like an angel of mercy Jacob handed him a blue, ice-cold juice box. Not his drink of choice, but beggars can't be choosers, and the fruit punch was a blast of sugar and flavor. He slurped it down, twisting the straw to get the juice in the corners.

"Go get some more of those, would you?" Eli asked, handing back the empty box, the straw cockeyed.

"All out." Jacob sighed heavily, and Eli rubbed the knobs of the boy's spine through his long-sleeved T-shirt.

"What's wrong, kiddo?"

"My mom is acting funny."

"I didn't notice." He tried not to be sarcastic, but there was just so much ugliness inside of him right now.

"Will you go talk to her? Make her act normal." The boy's eyes were very powerful and it was hard to say no, but in the end, his heart was as sore as the rest of his body. He tucked his arm around the boy again.

"Sorry, buddy," he said. "She's . . . she's got to do this one on her own."

He had done everything he could. The rest was up to her.

"You ready?" Thomas asked and Celeste smiled, despite the hurricane of nerves in her stomach. She didn't really have time for this, but she'd been unable to say no to Thomas's excitement.

"You're good, Thomas," she said, keeping her eyes shut as requested, "but they're just lights."

"Not anymore they're not," Gavin whispered, standing beside her.

"Pull the switch," Thomas said in his best Dr. Frankenstein voice and Celeste felt warmth on her face, sensed light from behind her eyelids.

Gavin's hand was a warm breeze across the skin of her shoulders and back.

"Open your eyes," he whispered, and she did, looking right up into his Nordic blue eyes, the fierce features of his face. So handsome, her hand actually lifted to touch him.

"What do you think?" he asked, set against a blinking world of fairy lights. A galaxy of stars. White lights of all sizes filled the ceiling, reflected across the windows and into the darkness of the night outside.

"It's magical," she said. Better than she'd dreamed it could be.

"Never underestimate the power of white twinkle lights," Thomas said, coming to stand beside them.

The rented cocktail tables were set up along the windows, draped in white linen, candles flickering on each of them. The buffet tables were set up. White-gloved waiters were getting their final instructions from Ruby, who wore an apron over a completely age-inappropriate red flamenco-style dress.

They'd gone ten rounds over that dress and in the end Celeste had thrown up her hands. The woman would do what she wanted; she always did.

Guests were going to arrive within two hours. Everything was perfect.

Except Victoria.

Celeste wasn't even sure where she was at this point.

"Wow, Maman!" Her son's voice sent her spinning around, her heart in her throat.

"Luc!" she cried, climbing the steps to put her arms around her giant former-NHL-star son.

"Her son is Luc Baker?" Thomas asked, and Gavin shushed him.

Beside Luc was Tara Jean Sweet, his girlfriend, who was looking at the changes in the ranch with her mouth hanging open.

"Celeste," she sighed. "Look at what you've done to this place! It's amazing. I don't . . . I don't even recognize it."

"I don't even recognize *you*," Celeste said, kissing the

girl's cheeks. When she first met her, Tara had worn leather skirts no bigger than Band-Aids with more attitude than one girl should have access to. Now she wore a silver cocktail dress that managed to be just the right side of respectable, but only just.

"Where's Vicks?" Luc asked, his sharp eyes scanning the room, searching through the hired staff for signs of his sister.

"Maybe you can find her," Celeste sighed.

"Is she lost?" Luc's dark brows clashed over his eyes.

"You can say that again."

Getting ready for this party, Eli had the bad feeling that he was getting dressed for his own funeral. He was putting on a suit and a tie just so Victoria could finish the job she was doing on his heart.

He'd hung around the ranch as long as he could, waiting for her, convincing himself that she was working through her feelings, getting her shit together so she could come over to him and say, "You know what, Eli, you're right. I love you."

But for some reason, sitting in his truck hours later, watching fancy people in fancy clothes walk in the front door of the Crooked Creek Ranch, his gut was telling him she was just too scared.

And in the end, he was going to have to walk away, because he had spent most of his life with a father who didn't love him enough. And he wasn't signing up for that shit again.

A small knock on his window spooked him and he jumped.

It was Amy, her long red hair piled up on her head.

"Sorry," she mouthed, her smile shy.

His heart hammering, he opened the door and slid out

of his truck. "You look handsome," she said. The look in her eyes was all mother and it made him nervous, uncomfortable.

"Thanks." He pulled on his collar, totally adrift. Utterly uncomfortable. "My shoes hurt."

"Mine too." She lifted the skirt of her navy dress with sequins at the waist that glittered in the light from the ranch. Her shoes were pointy. Very uncomfortable-looking. He stared at them instead of staring back at her. "Should we . . . should we go in?"

Together. That's what she was thinking and he couldn't stand her hope. Couldn't stand her spending the rest of the night reading extra meaning into any exchange they might have.

"I don't . . ." He blew out a long breath. "I don't know if I can ever forgive you. So you gotta stop waiting for that. You gotta stop . . . watching me like it's the next thing I might say." He wondered if he looked at Victoria like that. He probably did. He felt as though he'd been waiting to hear her say she loved him all his life.

Her face closed down and she nodded, as subdued as the dress she wore. "I know, I'm sorry. I don't mean to make you uncomfortable. I'm just . . . happy to be here."

"At the Crooked Creek? That's gotta be a first," he laughed, though it wasn't all that funny.

She smiled too, lifting the thin strap of her purse higher on her shoulder. "It is. Look, Eli, I know I'm too late to be your mom. And it's ridiculous to think we might be friends, but . . . I just want to know you. Know who you are. And maybe in time you might want to know me. That's all."

That's all. Lord, months ago that would have seemed impossible. Maybe it still was. But with the renovation Victoria had done on his heart, nothing was what it had once been.

"I'll see you in there," she said, stepping away, her head held high, and why the hell not. She'd done the best she could. Maybe not in the past, but right now she was trying her hardest. Even he could see that.

"Hold up, Amy," he said. "I hate walking into these things alone."

chapter
27

In hindsight, the fact that Jacob got so sick after Joel's suicide had allowed Victoria to compartmentalize. She hadn't been forced to deal with her husband's death because her son was busy fighting for his life. And over time, compartmentalizing became her greatest skill. Her one big achievement.

And she was putting it to good use with Eli and this party.

She didn't have to think about how she was hurting him, or how she might be pregnant, because right now she had to wrap prosciutto around melon.

It was important, this melon. It was crucial.

It required every ounce of her energy because she could feel her worry and her panic and her pain over Eli pushing hard against the compartments she'd put them in.

She hoped Ruby had an endless supply of melon and prosciutto.

"Have you talked to Madelyn Cornish?" Celeste asked, stepping into the kitchen with an empty tray.

"No, not yet. Is she looking for me?"

"Yeah, she's out there talking to Senator Phillips, so you've got some time. Ruby, Luc's hockey friends are here, so let's double the trays going out."

"Got it," Ruby said, opening her double-wide fridge to pull out more food.

Victoria took off the apron Ruby had given her and

handed it to Celeste. Her black dress was sleeveless and tight, which had made her nervous, given all of the weight she'd gained, but it utterly changed the way she saw her own body.

In this dress she was curvy. Voluptuous, almost.

She'd bought the dress thinking about Eli, about how he'd love it. How he'd corner her in some dark room and slide his hands up under the skirt . . .

Well, she thought bitterly, *you've taken care of that, haven't you?*

Sick of herself, she opened the kitchen doors and stepped into the full swing of her party. Hoping that the noise and heat and energy would fill her with some kind of emotion, something she could cling to, besides this vast nothingness that was drowning her.

Sixty guests mingled about—local friends they'd made and guests from the resort, along with Luc's hockey friends, looking like a tribe of giants among the regular folks. Tara Jean had invited some people she knew from her leather design business. Higher-ups at Nordstrom and a couple of artists from Dallas, who gave the party a bohemian flair.

You did this, she thought, trying to force herself to feel something. Pride. Worry. Anything.

She just felt numb.

She asked one of the servers if he'd seen the stunning *Dallas A.M.* talk show host, and he directed her to the lounge.

At the door, holding a beer, stood one of the most terrifying men in America. Billy Wilkins. Billy had played hockey with Luc and was his very best friend.

He was huge—his shaved head plugged into wide shoulders that tapered down to a lean waist and long legs. Any beauty in his body was destroyed by the scar at the corner of his lip, which made a crooked path across his cheek to the bottom of his jaw. It pulled his lip sideways when he smiled, making him look like he was in pain.

Or about to murder someone.

His nose had been broken into a messy knob in the middle of his face. But his eyes were warm and when she looked into those brown eyes, she saw the sweet boy he once must have been.

"Hey, Vicks," he said, using Luc's nickname for her. "Quite a shindig you got here."

"Thank you, Billy." Affection filled her. Billy, for all of his rough edges, was a sweetheart. He used to flirt with her, awkward as that was—but then, he flirted with everything in a skirt.

Imagine that confidence, she thought. *Imagine that strength.*

She'd had it, just a few days ago. Standing in the foyer with Celeste, she'd felt so good about herself, but now it was all gone. And she didn't know how to get it back.

"I'm so glad you could make it."

"Well, I'm in Dallas now, playing for the Mavericks, so I'm practically in the neighborhood."

"Then I hope we see you around some more."

He laughed. "I'm not much for facials and stuff."

And wasn't that the truth.

"Victoria!" a voice behind them cried, and both Victoria and Billy turned to see Madelyn Cornish practically running down the hall toward them. Beside her Billy sucked in a breath, and Victoria guessed it was because the woman was so breathtakingly beautiful. Not in that perfect way of Celeste's, but in the messy, wild way of gypsies. Her brown hair curled extravagantly around her dark eyes and full red lips. A gauzy, sparkly scarf trailed behind her like pixie dust.

"Jesus Christ," Billy muttered.

At the same time Madelyn Cornish stopped in her

tracks, that wide smile draining slowly from her face. Her brown eyes locked on Billy.

"Hi, Maddy," Billy whispered.

And after a long, speechless moment, Maddy turned around and ran the other way.

"What . . . was that?" Victoria asked.

"My ex-wife," he muttered.

Celeste opened the desk drawer in the foyer and pulled out the small stash of safety pins.

"We'll fix it, don't worry," she told Caitlyn, who was holding up the bodice of her lovely but clearly cheap blue dress, her face red with shame.

"I can't believe that happened," Caitlyn whispered. "Do you think anyone saw?"

"Probably." Celeste smiled at the girl's duress, stabbing the pin through the thick seam at the back of the strap. "But what's a little wardrobe malfunction at a party?"

"You wanted tonight to be so elegant, and I go and flash everyone—"

Celeste cupped the girl's shoulders. "Everything is lovely, including you. I think we should be paying you extra for having to put up with some of our guests."

Caitlyn shrugged. "Trust me, compared to my other job, these women are pretty easy."

Caitlyn left the foyer and Celeste returned the safety pins to the drawer. Through the open doorway, she saw Gavin, who was holding a glass of tonic water, deep in conversation with the producer for that a.m. talk show. As if he could feel her looking at him, he glanced up and met her eyes, and the slow, sweet smile that crossed his face was the most erotic thing she'd experienced in a long, long time.

The front door banged open and Celeste whirled

around to see a big man wearing a white cowboy hat and a messy suit standing in the threshold of her spa.

"Well, look at this here," he said, his pale blue eyes wide. "I hardly recognize the place."

He was too loud, too big, and she knew people from the party would be glancing over.

She smiled, slipping right into disaster-control mode, and slid out from behind her desk to shut the door behind him. The man's eyes touched every part of her. Her silver hair, her bare shoulders and neck—revealed by the draped fabric of her plum dress. Her breasts. Her legs.

His interest was unmistakable.

"Well, you certainly class up the place, don't you?" he asked, dropping his voice.

Her smile was cold, practiced a million times over the years on men just like him. "This is a private party, sir. I think perhaps you might be in the wrong spot."

"Something sure as hell is wrong here, but it ain't me."

"Celeste?" It was Gavin, standing at her back, her knight in a red silk tie. "Everything all right?"

"Not really," the man said, staring at Gavin in the knowing way of an ape sizing up another ape. "I could use a drink. You a waiter?"

Gavin stepped forward, but Celeste put her hand out. "Perhaps, if you could just tell us who you are, and what you're looking for here, we could sort this out."

"You are a cool one. I like that in a woman." The man's eyes explored the modest cleavage revealed by her dress as if he were a sherpa and lives depended on his knowledge of the terrain. Gavin all but growled behind her, which was sexy in one respect and utterly unnecessary in another.

"Sir," she snapped, and the man's face, familiar somehow, lifted to hers.

"I'm John Turnbull. And I'm looking for my nephew."

* * *

Victoria was having no luck finding Madelyn Cornish. Most women would go and hide in the bathroom after a run-in like that, but the women's rooms were all empty. The dark corners of the back porch were also deserted.

Great, she thought, throwing her hands up in the moonlight. *Just great.* A big break like this and her brother's buddy ruins it.

Not that she should blame him.

Poor guy, he up and left, too—grabbed his coat and just walked out the door.

Well, no sense in trying to find a woman who had no interest in being found. She turned, heading for the screen doors leading into the kitchen, only to find Eli standing there, his hands tucked into the pockets of his handsome black suit.

Time lost its momentum and rolled to a stop.

"I've never seen you in a suit," she said, because it was the stupidest thing to say and about all she was capable of.

"Bought it special." His honesty was piercing and she ran her hand down the front of her dress, feeling for blood. "You look beautiful," he whispered.

"Thank you."

"You . . . ah . . ." He rubbed a hand across the back of his neck. "You feel all right?" His green eyes looked sideways at her and she felt him drinking her in.

Her laughter was a pained gust of air. "Are you asking if I'm pregnant?" His jaw tightened and he dropped his hand. "It's only been three days. It's a little early to tell."

He nodded as if he knew that, or as if he was gathering up speed to spit something out, and she braced herself, unsure of what was to come. "I want you to know, if you are pregnant, I want to be there. I mean, I want to be involved with the kid. A lot."

Tears stung her eyes. Of course he would, and why did

he have to make it sound like he wanted nothing to do with her?

Because you're a coward, remember? A coward who won't fight for him.

The sliding glass door opened with a gasp and a whoosh and Ruby appeared behind Eli, her scarlet dress a splash of color in the night.

"We've got a problem," she said.

"Madelyn?" Victoria asked, already moving forward.

"No." Ruby's eyes fixed on Eli. "Your uncle is here."

Eli's face went white in the moonlight, the bones of his skull pressing against his skin, making him look like a different man. Angry and worried. Worn down.

And very, very much alone.

"Eli—" Victoria held out a hand to him, but without looking at her, as if he knew she would be no help to him, he walked back into the house.

She'd pushed him away that night in the greenhouse, too scared to hold on to him, too scared to try, too lost to even know how.

That man had stood by her side for months now—he'd invested in her vision. Unleashed her inner deviant. Told her he loved her.

And now he was going to go face the demons of his past headfirst—without her. He'd never had anyone fight for him. Stick up for him. Protect him. All the people that should have loved him had betrayed him.

And the realization that she was just the latest person to let him down destroyed her. Shamed her right down to her core, where the pain changed her. Reorganized her fear and her worry and her doubts.

All of those terrible things she'd gotten so used to, that had made her blind to the beauty around her, were pushed away by something so much stronger. Something so much bigger.

The night reeled around her, shoved off its moorings

for a moment, and when it settled, the world was new. Different.

How stupid she'd been to think love was a choice! As if she could deny it and it would go away. Watching him walk away from her had cracked her right down the middle. All of her compartments had burst.

And she was awash, flooded, overrun with love.

I love him.

And it wasn't the love she'd had for Joel; it wasn't weak and scary. It didn't make less of her. It made more of her. It made everything she felt for Eli—the gratitude and the worry, the lust and the desire to protect—into something noble. Into something beautiful.

In the vacuum he left behind, she felt the different parts of herself come together as something new. Her past, her present, the person she wanted to be—they no longer existed in isolation or conflict.

She could be scared and brave and worried and confident and grateful and generous—because he loved her for who she was.

No part of her was shameful. Least of all her love for him.

She had built this place. It had taken courage and grit and strength, and it had taken love. From Celeste and Ruby and Eli. And those people were counting on her, just as she counted on them. It was circular and right. She was blessed by the people in her life and she'd . . . she'd let her fear rob her of too much to let it take that, too.

And right now, the man she loved needed help. Needed someone by his side. And she might be too late, but she wasn't going to let him go without a fight.

Without a second thought she followed her heart, and her man, inside.

Eli followed his uncle's magnetic pull into the front foyer, where a small crowd had gathered. Eli didn't know what he expected to feel or think upon seeing his uncle after all this time, after all that had happened to him.

But at the sight of that big white hat he felt like an eight-year-old boy who needed help. And the only man who had given it to him was his uncle.

"Look here." John's big voice was too rough, too loud for the backdrop of cocktail party chatter. "There's my boy, looking fine, too. Eli, you clean up real nice."

Celeste and Gavin, who were clearly trying to keep the man contained, stepped back and he got a good look at his uncle. The man might be smiling, but his eyes were pure rattlesnake. Uncle John was pissed.

Yeah, well, so am I, he reminded himself. *He lied about paying for Dad's hospital. For years he let me feel indebted to him for that.*

"You've got barbecue sauce on your collar," he pointed out.

That smile got hard real quick. "Drove up from Galveston and stopped at your place. Surprised you weren't there."

"I'm here." He held his arms out.

"Yeah, I see that. Real comfortable in the home of the family that robbed us for generations."

Eli said nothing. Just stared at his uncle, who stared right back.

Someone stepped up behind Eli. Victoria—he knew it by the way his skin reacted, the way he instinctively knew to step sideways, blocking her from Uncle John's sight.

But she stepped forward, right into the middle of things. "Is there a problem here?" she asked.

"I got it, Tori—"

"Tori!" Uncle John boomed. More people gathered into the foyer. Renee, Bill, their merry gang of asshats.

"Tell me what you're doing here, Eli," John asked, looking truly baffled. Truly heartbroken.

"He's an investor in the Crooked Creek Resort and Spa," Victoria said, and Eli shut his eyes, swearing under his breath. *Now she gets brave.*

"Investor? Eli, tell me she's lying. Tell me you did not *invest* your money with Joel Schulman's ex-wife. Hasn't she ruined enough lives? Taken enough money?"

"Yes," Renee hissed, breaking her husband's hold on her wrist. "She has. She has ruined everyone's life."

Jesus Christ. Could this get any worse?

chapter
28

Everyone was talking at once, a wild hum of noise. Eli was trying to get his uncle to leave. Celeste was trying to get both of them to stay.

"How many lives do you have to ruin?" Renee hissed in Victoria's ear, like a mosquito she couldn't swat away. "I'm so glad I'm here to watch you get your due—"

"Stop it!" Victoria cried, and the room fell silent as if she'd shot off a gun. "You," she turned to Renee. "I've had enough of you and your viciousness. I am sorry my husband stole from you. I am sorry I cannot bleed enough to give you back what you lost, but I am done trying. I want you off my property by tomorrow morning."

"You're kicking us out?"

"I can't do anything more for you, Renee. I've made my reparations—"

"You've made nothing!" Renee cried. "You knew what he was doing—"

Bill stepped forward and put his hands on Renee's shoulders; she strained away, but he held on. "Enough, Renee," he whispered. "We all knew. In hindsight . . ." He glanced around at the stricken faces of all of Victoria's old friends, and the knowledge and guilt that was in their eyes. "We knew that Joel was up to something, and you've got to stop punishing Victoria. It wasn't her fault."

Damn straight!

"How can you say that?" Renee asked, turning burning eyes on her husband. "We lost everything . . ."

"Not everything." He touched her cheek, his smile full of apology and reproach. Renee, however, wasn't buying it. She shook her head, her shoulders stiff, and finally Bill pulled her against his chest. After a moment he glanced up at Victoria and then Eli. "You've been wonderful to us. This place . . . what you've done here . . . it's wonderful, and we're sorry if we took away from any of that this week."

Renee buried her head in her husband's suit jacket. Victoria glanced sideways at Eli, who only nodded once. His cowboy way of saying all was forgiven.

"Thank you, Bill," she whispered. Bill led Renee away and the rest of them scattered. Without their leader, they had lost their venom. With them out of the room, Victoria focused on Eli.

"Well done," he murmured, and she felt a wild, bright beam of hope.

"Better late than never," she said, attempting a smile.

"Perhaps," Celeste said, reaching for John's arm, "we can give them a moment alone." Celeste was the perfect hostess in any situation, even this one, for which there was no Miss Manners advice. Love for Celeste, who had to be the strangest mother figure a woman ever had, filled Victoria.

"It's okay, Celeste," Victoria said. "Why don't you go see to our other guests."

Celeste blinked, her mouth opened to protest.

"I don't need you to protect me," Victoria said. "Not anymore. But I will always love you for trying."

Celeste glanced meaningfully at John, who was decidedly red around his too-tight collar. "I just want to help," she said.

"I know."

"Then let me." Victoria should have known Celeste wouldn't relinquish control so easily.

"Gavin?" Victoria said, and as if he'd been waiting for the chance to cart Celeste off someplace, Gavin read her mind.

"I'm on it," he said, and looking more like a Viking than he ever had, he grabbed Celeste's hand and pulled her away, kicking open the door to the treatment rooms. John stared after them like his new lollipop had been stolen.

"What's happening here?" he asked.

"I believe we're being managed, Uncle John," Eli said, crossing his arms over his chest and smiling as if he was enjoying the show.

Amy stepped out of the hallway into the foyer, and Uncle John stiffened as if he'd seen a ghost. "Hello, John," she said.

"What the hell are you doing here?" he demanded, his face going red. He looked at Eli. "What is she doing here?"

"She's the architect," Victoria said.

"Victoria hired your mother?" John asked Eli. "And you invested in this circus? Christ, son, I would never have stayed in Galveston if I'd known you were going to lose your mind."

"Don't insult him," Victoria said, stepping closer to John, who pushed back his hat and laughed. "I'm serious. He's not a joke. He's a man, and a good one."

John looked at Eli. "You said Victoria was a mouse. A . . . a scarecrow. A pushover."

Eli shrugged. "Looks like I was wrong."

"Why didn't you tell Eli that Amy was paying for his father's care?" Victoria asked John.

"Is that what she told you?" John asked, pointing a finger at Amy. "This woman left you—"

"I know what she did," Eli said. "Better than anyone. But you lied to me, Uncle John. Why?"

"Because she oughta pay for something!" John cried.

"I think she's paid enough," Victoria said.

"What the hell do you know about anything?" John asked. She tried to resist the urge to duck behind Eli, because John was big and getting angrier by the second.

"All of it," Eli answered John's question, standing beside Victoria without touching her. "Victoria knows everything, and she's right." Eli turned and nodded at Amy, who stood pale and stalwart against the backdrop of the party behind her. "My mom's paid enough."

Amy's eyes filled with tears but she didn't say anything— just stood there, pulsing with emotion—and Victoria wasn't sure she could love Eli any more than she did at this moment.

"I never thought I'd see the day," John said, all kinds of judgment in his voice, and Victoria wanted to take Eli's hand to show him he wasn't alone, but he stepped forward, out of her reach.

"I never thought you'd lie to me, Uncle John. All these years you let me believe you were paying for Dad's care and I felt so indebted to you. And all these years you knew where my mother was and you never bothered to tell me."

"I didn't think you'd care."

"Well, I do."

The silence pounded in the foyer and Victoria stepped toward the door, her heels clicking loud against the stone tiles.

"I think you should leave," she said and opened the front door.

John ignored her, staring daggers into Eli, and she wrapped her hand around his arm.

John grabbed her fingers, so hard and quick that she gasped, more in surprise than pain. "And I think you should mind—"

Eli, his jaw tight, his eyes murderous, shoved John out

the door, following him over the transom as the older man tripped slightly.

"You don't put your hands on her," Eli said, following his uncle across the porch as the older man stumbled backwards down the steps. "Ever."

"Eli, I only wanted this land for you. For your birthright," John said from the bottom of the stairs, his face bleached with moonlight and regret.

Eli nodded toward the full parking area. "Get in your truck and go on home. I'll find you when I can stomach looking at you."

John seemed to know when he was beat, and he pulled his hat down low before turning and winding his way through the trucks to his own.

"Thank you, Eli," Amy said quietly from the door behind them.

Eli turned—his shirt, teeth, and eyes bone white in the moonlight. So handsome that Victoria ached looking at him. He reached for Amy's hand, gathering her fingers into his own like a bouquet. Amy gasped slightly, staring at their joined hands as if she'd stop believing it if she stopped seeing it.

Finally, Amy laughed a little, gusty and girlish. Awkward, she patted Eli's hand before dropping it and stepping back inside the house.

"I'll leave you two alone." Amy quietly shut the door behind her, and then it was just Eli and Victoria standing in the moonlight.

"He hurt you?" he asked, his hands in his pockets, his eyes watching the taillights on his uncle's departing truck.

She shook her head. This porch, this ranch had grown so familiar to her over the last few months. She knew the view from where she was standing better than she remembered what had been outside her penthouse window. But standing here with Eli, who wasn't looking at her, made it all seem terrifyingly unfamiliar.

What if I am too late? she wondered. *What if he's realized what a mistake it would be to love me?*

"Startled me mostly."

"I'm sorry."

"It's not your fault."

He sighed, hard and deep through his nose, and then he turned to watch her. His face was utterly unreadable.

"You put on quite a show in there," he said. "I've never had a woman fight for me like that. Never had *anyone* fight for me like that."

There were a thousand things she should have said, starting with *I'm sorry no one has ever fought for you, because you deserve to be protected and cared for and battled over.*

Instead she smiled like a fool and said, "Glad you liked it."

"Well now, I wouldn't go that far," he said, turning to face her fully, his hands in his pockets, his head tilted slightly as if he was trying to see her a little more clearly. Her heart took a cold bath in his words and hope faltered. "Why'd you do it, Tori?"

Gavin led Celeste into the first massage room he came to and shut the door behind them.

"What the hell are you doing?" she howled, pointing toward the door and the scene beyond it. "I need to help her."

"I thought she was doing fine on her own."

She tried to step around him but he got in her way. Exasperated, and trembling with fear and excitement and the dense, wonderful awareness of how alone they were right now, she plunked her hands on her hips. "That's my party out there."

"Why did you call me today?" he asked.

The change of subject threw her off and she backed up against the massage table.

"I needed help. I told you. The lights."

"Right. You needed an electrician and a carpenter to hang Christmas lights."

She took a deep breath. "Fine," she said. "I . . . wanted you here."

"Why?"

"Because you worked so hard—"

He shook his head, his grin so sly and knowing that her body got damp just from being in the same room.

"Can I tell you what I think?" he asked, stepping toward her slightly. "I think you called me because you missed me. Because you wanted to see me."

"You're right," she admitted, leaning against the massage table, because her legs were shaking. She crossed her arms over her chest, balling her hands up under her arms, making sure they understood that there would be no more touching, even though that place on her arm where he'd touched her still burned. "You're a good friend."

To her utter shock, he started taking off his coat, pulling at his tie. He leaned against the door and toed off his shoes, and when that was done, he locked the door.

"What are you doing?"

"What I should have done the day I met you."

"Making a fool of yourself?" Oh, she turned her nose up good with that one. It would take a better man—

He laughed. He unbuttoned his shirt, revealing the muscled perfection of his ivory chest. Her mouth went dry, her core went wet, and all of this was a mess.

"I don't know what you think you're doing, but I want to leave." She laid it on thick, hiding behind the imperial bitchiness that had gotten her through some of the worst moments of her life, this one right up on the list.

"Really?" he asked, stepping toward her, his eyebrows

raised, his lips curled into a predatory smile. "You don't know what I'm doing?"

"No, I—" He turned her around, just flipped her right over until she was braced against the massage table and his hands were lowering the zipper on her dress.

"I'm staking my claim, Celeste," he said and kissed the skin revealed by the splitting zipper. "I don't give a shit how old you are." He leaned against her, and she felt his erection against her hips and hung her head, lost in the sudden upswell of desire. "But it clearly bothered you and I . . . I wanted to give you the distance you seemed to need, but I was wrong. I was wrong to let you push me away."

The dress slipped off her shoulders, catching on her hips momentarily before falling to the floor, leaving her in a black bra and panties.

"Oh God, Celeste, you're so beautiful," he groaned, kissing her spine, her neck, the side of her face, and she found deep inside of herself the strength to push him away, to turn and face him with her imperfections. The crepey skin and spider veins, the fat around her middle, the sagging breasts that looked fine in a bra—but when she took this puppy off, watch out.

"Are you looking at me?" she asked, running a hand down her body. "Or are you seeing that cover?"

"What . . . ?" It took him a moment, distracted as he seemed to be by her breasts in the black lace. "That magazine I kept for so long?" he asked. "That's what you're worried about?"

She didn't say anything, refused to fish for compliments, for assurances that he wasn't going to fuck her and think of the old her.

"That woman wasn't real, Celeste," he said, his blue eyes warm, his smile sweet. "Not like you. Look, I'm . . . stubborn. And moody. Loyal to a fault. I make a bunch of money and never spend it. I have a son who thrives on causing trouble and I need someone real by my side. Someone tough and strong and passionate and smart. That woman in the poster—she was beautiful, no doubt about it. But you are what I need. You are what I want. And I don't care how old I am, or you are. I want you."

"But thirteen years, Gavin. I'll be an old woman and you'll still—"

"Want you." He held her hand. "We have no idea what the future will bring, Celeste. But we could kill what we have right now worrying about it, and I don't want to do that. I don't want to waste another minute I could be spending with you."

That gerbil in her brain fought a good fight for a second, pitching a fit, sending adrenaline and panic out through her veins until the need to run was almost overwhelming. But then she looked at Gavin, really looked at him, and she made a choice. Easy as that.

She wasn't going to push this man away.

And just like that the gerbil packed its bags and left, and the silence was . . . sweet. The panic was gone, and— for the first time in a long time—she found herself alone with her reality. She didn't have anything to prove anymore. Not to herself. Not to her dead ex-husband. Not to her parents. To no one.

She only had to please herself, and that was easy enough. The man in front of her looked more than equal to the task, on every level.

She and Victoria had planned for this room to be soothing and they'd set it up for the party. Plum walls, myrrh incense burning in a cup, the piped-in sounds of chanting monks.

But somehow, those monks . . . they sounded like sex.

And the plum walls were the color of sex.

And myrrh was definitely the smell of sex.

And Gavin in front of her, his white-blond hair and handsome face, his body, those smooth muscles, the dip and swell of his arms and shoulders . . . he looked like the future.

"I want you, too," she said.

Gavin's arms came around her, strong and gentle, and his lips touched hers. Unbelievably, she found herself laughing. Giggling at first, against his lips, but then she was really laughing, fighting for air, leaning against him for support.

"I'm trying not to get offended here, Celeste."

"I'm sorry, truly." She tried to hold in the laughter, but ended up snorting. Her. Celeste Baker, snorting. "I'm just so happy."

Gavin smiled, chuckled a little, laughed. His hands slipped into her hair, holding her head, ruining her classic upsweep, and it didn't matter. Nothing mattered but him and the happiness he gave her.

"Me too, Celeste." He pressed sweet kisses against her jaw, along her cheek, and that laughter changed in her chest, became something breathless and full of wonder.

Her hands learned the textures of him, the contours, while her tongue learned the taste of her very own Viking.

chapter
29

In a heartbeat Victoria realized what Eli was doing. He was giving her nothing. Which was roughly the equivalent of what she'd given him for the last few months. And into that great void he'd tossed all his love and affection and respect. He'd opened himself up, body and soul, for a woman who'd told him she would only hurt him.

"You're the bravest man I know," she said, amazed anew at his strength.

"On with it, Tori."

She grinned, so in love she felt like she might split at the seams, her volume increased by the never-ending flood of her feelings for this man.

"I love you."

Of all the reactions she had expected, narrowing his eyes at her as if she might be lying hadn't even been on the list.

"I do. I'm serious."

"I don't want your guilt, or your sacrifice—"

"Well, too bad!" she cried. "You've got it. Look, clearly, I have some sort of . . . complex. What do you want—my mother was a mess, my dad was an asshole, I married a crook. I have issues, Eli. That doesn't mean I don't love you. Because I do. And I'm a coward. Life is scary to me most of the time and I work really hard at being brave, but sometimes I'm going to fail. That doesn't change my feelings for you."

"You didn't seem so scared in there." He jerked his thumb back toward the house.

"I know, right? I was awesome," she cried, and he smiled and the night became her paradise. Her heaven. All she needed was this man, her family in that house somewhere behind her, and a future with all of them. "You deserve to have someone fight for you," she whispered, her fingertips finding his sleeve, the edge of his dark jacket. The fabric was so soft, very fine. He'd probably spent more money on this one suit than on his entire wardrobe for a year. For her. And she'd almost blown it.

"I need you, Eli, for the days when I'm not brave. For when I'm feeling guilty for something I have no business blaming myself for." She felt as if the box inside of her where she kept all of her needs, all of the demands she was scared to make of people, was being torn apart and she couldn't shut up. "I need you to keep me from worrying. To keep me from coddling Jacob. I need you to make me laugh and to show me swans and to make me feel sexy and beautiful. And I need to do that for you—I need to show you how wonderful you are, how honorable and smart and generous. So generous, Eli. You are a miracle in my life. In everyone's life. I need to see you with my son and feel my heart grow too big for my chest." She put her hand over her stomach, suddenly wishing she was pregnant. Suddenly wanting it so bad she could barely breathe.

"Tori—" He reached for her, as if he was scared she was going to fall over, and she grabbed his hands, put them around her waist, held him there so he couldn't leave.

"I'm a mess, I know it. But you have a home with me, wherever I am. You said you only give people shit, but that's not true. You bring me so much happiness. So much peace. You make me proud, Eli. Proud to know you. Proud to call you mine. Because I need you to be mine. And I need to be yours."

This stoic, silent cowboy stared down at her, unreadable. Now she was getting unnerved.

"Please," she whispered. "Please say something."

"I like that."

"What?"

"That part about being yours. And you being mine."

The relief was like losing her body, like lifting right on out of herself, out of her clothes and skin. And climbing right inside of his.

"I love you," she whispered, wrapping her arms around his neck. "I love you so much."

"I didn't . . ." He stopped and she pulled away, watching tears fill his beautiful green eyes. "I didn't know I could be this happy."

"It's only going to get better." She wrapped her arms around his chest, pulling him flush against her body so she could feel his heart beat against hers. The two of them in perfect rhythm.

"How do you know?" he whispered against her hair. She leaned back.

"Didn't you see me in there?" she asked. "I'm a force to be reckoned with. If I say we're happy, we're happy."

His quiet chuckle warmed the night, seeped into her skin, and curled through her, filling her with an almost unbearable sense of *right*.

"This was meant to be," he said, as if he'd read her heart. And maybe he had.

"Sure as hell took a long time." She kissed his jaw, following a path of her choosing to his lips.

"You were worth the wait," he said and sealed her lips with his.

epilogue

"Don't be scared," Eli said, crouching down in front of Jacob. He loosened the silly tie Victoria had insisted the boy wear.

"I'm not scared." Eli was still getting used to the trust in the boy's eyes. The hero worship. Truth was, he lived in fear of betraying it somehow. Of not being the man Jacob saw. Turnbull men were good at that.

But Victoria kept telling him to relax, that Jacob loved Eli for Eli, just like she did. But that was all a first for him, so everyone had to be patient.

And they were. Victoria and Jacob were so good to him. A gift he tried to repay every day.

"All right," he said, pushing back a curl that had fallen over the boy's eyes. "That's good."

"I'm scared," Eli whispered to Victoria over Jacob's head. "I'm totally freaking out."

"It will be okay." She kissed his lips, patted his cheek, and then linked her arm through his, reaching out her hand for Jacob's and somehow managing to propel them all across the sun-baked asphalt toward the front door of The Elms. "Come on, we've made it this far."

He'd wanted to wait until they were married before bringing them here. Somehow being able to call Victoria his wife when he introduced her to the old man seemed important.

And she'd wanted to wait to get married until after

she'd made it through the first trimester, so she wouldn't throw up on her way down the aisle.

And then their little ceremony had just kept growing. Celeste kept making lists. Gavin had to build a gazebo. Eli had to have a long talk with his uncle before deciding whether or not to invite him. In the end, Uncle John was there and Amy had been too, and she stood in the front row beaming with happiness. Victoria's brother, Luc, gave her away, and Celeste and Tara Jean were two of the most beautiful bridesmaids ever to carry a bouquet.

Jacob had stood between Eli and Victoria during the ceremony, holding their hands as the minister made them a family before God and witnesses.

So, here they were, freshly married, four months pregnant, and he was about to introduce his new family to his old family.

"Hi, Caitlyn!" Jacob cried as they walked through the front door of The Elms.

"Hi, guys." Caitlyn looked up from the front desk and smiled, that peaceful, reassuring smile that made her such an asset. Such a friend.

"He's been a bit restless," she said and winced.

Eli stopped, but Victoria pushed him forward. "We've put this off long enough."

The hallway leading down to his dad's room was the longest it had ever been. The lights were too bright and his boots were too loud and he wanted to stop. He wanted to turn back. This was unnecessary—at best, his father wouldn't even know what was happening and at worst, well, he didn't want to have to think of the orderlies holding his father down mid-fit while Jacob and Victoria watched.

"No backing down now, cowboy," Victoria muttered, pushing him forward.

Right. No backing down. Not with this woman at his back.

Though last week he had needed to force her out of bed for an interview with Madelyn Cornish.

That was marriage, he guessed. Partnership. The support went both ways.

The door to his father's room was cracked and it opened without a sound under his hand. He peeked his head around to see the old man sleeping. His pajamas were twisted up around his body, and the sheets were sliding off the bed.

"Give me a second," he whispered to Jacob and Victoria, and he ducked inside to straighten the sheets and the pajamas.

"Behave yourself," he whispered in his father's ear, and then stepped over to open the door. "Come . . . ah, come on in."

The room was crowded as Victoria and Jacob filed in, and Eli wiped his suddenly very wet hands down his jeans to dry them off.

"Is he dead?" Jacob whispered, his eyes wide with horror.

"No," Eli laughed. "Just sleeping. He sleeps a lot."

"Can he hear us?" Jacob asked.

"Caitlyn says he can."

"Oh." Jacob scratched his nose and then took one quick step over to the bed. "Hey, Grandpa," he shouted and then jumped back.

Eli breathed deep through his mouth, blinking to get the sting out of his eyes.

"Hello, Mark," Victoria said, leaning down toward the bed. "I'm Victoria, your son's wife."

Mark stirred on the bed and Eli held his breath, but after a moment the old man settled.

"I think he farted," Jacob whispered. Victoria's look was so quelling Eli snorted back a laugh, unwilling to get his own share of her wrath, but when Victoria wasn't looking he winked at Jacob.

"Hey, Dad," Eli whispered, standing where he usually did, his legs pressed against the collapsed metal railings of the bed. He pulled Mark's pajama collar away from where it was gathered at his neck. "I want you to meet my family. Victoria, and our boy." He glanced over, smiling at the two of them standing on the other side of the bed. "His name is Jacob. He's got a good hand with the horses. You'd like him. And Victoria . . . well, she'd terrify you. But she's a strong woman. The strongest."

Mark kept sleeping, his chest rising and falling in shallow arcs. Eli took a deep breath. "And we're having a baby. In October. Victoria thinks it's a girl, something about having an ugly pregnancy, but that's a lie. She's the most beautiful woman I've ever seen."

If this were a movie Mark would have opened his eyes. Or squeezed Eli's hand, but he just lay there, silent. Sleeping.

"I'm happy, Dad. And I don't know if you ever felt this way, but I hope you did. I wish . . ." He stopped right there, because there was no sense in wishing on the past. It was over.

And his future was right here, right now, and he'd never seen anything more perfect.

"I'll see you next week, Dad," he said.

"We'll all see you next week," Victoria said, and then Eli gathered his family up, pulling his wife under his arm, his son against his hip, and walked out, into the bright day waiting for him.

*Did Billy's run-in with Madelyn Cornish
intrigue you?*

*You won't want to miss the story of how
this one-time couple is thrown together
by unexpected circumstances.*

Read on for a sneak peek of
This Can't Be Love!

Billy Wilkins sat on the bench bone-dry. He might as well have been wearing slippers. A freaking robe. All he could do was sit there and watch the second-rate team he'd been traded to give away their shot at the playoffs.

If the coaches weren't going to play him, the skates, the pads, the stick in his hand—all of it—was totally useless. Worthless. Just like him.

"Yank Leserd!" he shouted over the screaming in the Bendor arena. "He's done. That's the fourth goal he's let in in five minutes."

But Coach Hornsby wasn't listening. He never listened to what Billy yelled during the games, whether the advice was good or not, didn't matter. Hornsby wouldn't even look at him, much less reply.

But that was Coach Hornsby. Stubborn, righteous, and probably deaf.

Billy waved off the water bottle one of the trainers held up. No need to hydrate. He hadn't even broken a sweat tonight.

And what was worse, worse than the dry pads, the clear visor, the body he'd recuperated back into prime shape only to have it sit unused on the bench, was that he didn't care. He didn't care that the coach didn't hear him. Didn't care that the kid in the net was totally overwhelmed and the Mavericks' rally to get into the playoffs was going to die a pitiful death right here. Right now.

"If you stopped being an asshole, he might listen to you," Jan Fforde, their injured first-string goalie said, his consonants blunted by his Swedish accent.

"Not much chance of that." Whether Billy was talking about being an asshole or their coach listening to him, he wasn't sure. Being an asshole was his way of life, it's why hockey teams for over fifteen years had been paying his way. The sport needed assholes and Billy was the best. Used to be anyway.

Until he landed in Dallas, with a coach who preached respect and integrity.

Someone should have told Hornsby that respect and integrity didn't win games. Didn't turn momentum. A good fight did that. Let Billy get out there and drop gloves with that big Renegade center, Churo, and then the game would turn around. The crowd that booed them would cheer.

The Renegades, who were *killing* the Mavericks on their own ice, would have blood on their faces and they'd know the Mavericks went down swinging.

The Mavericks' top line—O'Neill, Blake, and Grotosky—surged back into Renegade ice, skating their hearts out. Blake wound up and hammered a slap shot that ricocheted off the post. A mob in front of the goal scrambled for the puck and everyone on the bench stood, screaming. A goal right now would tie up the game and they'd have a shot in overtime.

"Come on!" Billy whispered, willing his fight into

those young guys out there with the fast legs and the strong arms and barely managed talent, "come—"

The buzzer silenced the crowd for a moment and then the few Boston Renegades fans in the arena roared.

The Mavericks were out.

Disheartened, silent, the team skated back toward the bench, knocking fists, defeat riding their young shoulders. This team had fought longer and harder than anyone expected, keeping the playoff dream alive for a community that barely cared. Despite losing tonight, they'd fought like demons.

Hornsby was silent. Billy could think of a thousand better coaches. His grandma for one. And she was dead.

"Good effort, guys," Billy said, slapping shoulders. His teammates grunted, unsmiling.

Blake, their captain, finally led the team into center ice to shake hands. Billy stood at the end, the only guy besides Fforde without ice time. Without the sweat and blood and heaving lungs of battle. For a second the grief nearly took out his knees, that his career was going to end this way was such a sucker punch, he could barely breathe through the pain.

As he shook hands with the other team, about to go into the first round of the playoffs and get slaughtered by the defending champions, not a single Renegade looked in his face. It was salt in the wound.

Billy Wilkins, second-round draft pick fifteen years ago, was a non-fucking-issue.

Might as well be dead.

Bullshit, he thought and his temper roared through

him in a brush fire, burning lesser emotions into dust. Everything about this was bullshit.

Churo, the freakish Russian giant, was the last guy in line. As he skated past, barely touching Billy's outstretched hand, Billy—a good foot shorter and thirty pounds lighter, but blessed with a temper that leveled every playing field—coldcocked him. Snapped the big man's head back so hard Billy could see his third-world dental work.

For a moment, Churo wobbled in his skates, and Billy braced himself to be crushed, but then Churo went down on the ice with a thud.

The arena roared, the sound music to Billy's cauliflower ears.

Victory was sweet but short. Grisolm, the hardworking Renegade captain, landed a right hook across Billy's face. Billy swung back, feeling the satisfying pop of nose cartilage under his fist. Someone wrapped him up, using his kidney as a punching bag. But out of the corner of his eye he saw the Mavericks skating back from the dressing rooms, dropping gloves and sticks, throwing off helmets, all that defeat melting into raw bloodlust.

Billy smiled before someone punched the back of his head and bells rang in his skull.

Hitting Churo was dirty. A cheap shot after the game was over, the sports journalists would go crazy. No doubt Billy would get suspended. That pussy Hornsby would probably send him to counseling or some shit.

But he didn't care. As the melee continued, his face getting punished, his knuckles splitting against the ice and helmets and pads, he didn't care about what was going to happen when this fight was over. Because, for guys like Billy Wilkins, there would always be another fight.

An hour later, after the mob scene with the press in the locker room, he sat in front of Hornsby's desk, showered and changed, Kleenex shoved up his nose to stop the blood from dripping on the collar of his shirt.

Billy arranged the ice packs on his knuckles while the coach paced the hardwood floors behind him.

Coming up in the minors, half Billy's coaches had been not just old-school hockey, but old-school *Eastern Bloc* hockey. Giant men with forests of hair in their ears, who kept bottles of vodka in their desks and after a fight like Billy just caused would have bought him a steak dinner. And a hooker.

His first coach in the NHL, Bleu St. Georges, a French-Canadian force of nature, would have told the press that he was embarrassed and that steps would be taken to reprimand Billy. But behind the locker room door, he would have shaken Billy's hand and applauded him for knowing how to give a beaten team back their pride.

But over the last fifteen years the league had changed. The last five especially. All this talk of taking the fighting out of the sport? These were not friendly times for guys like Billy.

Outside the big window to his left, the crowd, the few hundred stalwart hockey fans left in Dallas, stood on the sidewalk, hailing cabs, putting away their playoff excitement until next year.

Suckers, he thought. This team wouldn't get any closer to the cup next year, or the year after. Front office called it "rebuilding." Billy called it "being a shitty team."

"What were you thinking?" Hornsby asked. Billy would have rolled his eyes if they didn't hurt so bad. "You're suspended, you know that, right? You'll be out at least the first four games of next season. Maybe more. The GM wants to trade you."

"How is that any different than the end of this season?" Billy asked past his fat, cracked lip.

Hornsby stopped pacing and the silence changed, got all loaded, like Billy had fallen into Hornsby's trap. Billy pressed his bruised knuckles, the ice pack between them, up to his lip, wishing he'd kept his mouth shut.

"You don't like sitting on the bench?" Hornsby asked questions like he was a six-foot-four, slightly balding Oprah.

"I don't like watching my team lose."

"And you think you would have stopped that?"

"Yes."

"By what? Fighting?"

"Maybe."

Hornsby sat down behind his desk, a sleek metal and glass table he kept annoyingly clean. Desks were supposed to be cluttered, covered in coffee cups and scouting reports. Hornsby clearly didn't read the NHL coach handbook.

"You know why I wanted you here?" Hornsby asked, adjusting his glasses up over the bump of his broken nose. That broken nose saved him. Billy didn't like the guy, but he'd never be able to trust him if it weren't for that nose. Men who'd never had their nose broken shouldn't lead men who barely had cartilage left in their face. It was a rule.

But then the guy went and ruined that broken nose with turtlenecks. Tonight it was a black one, under a gray coat. Made him look like a sissy.

"I have no idea, man," Billy said, twisting the toilet paper higher into his nose.

"I wanted a leader. Some experience on a young team."

"Yeah, well, put me on the ice and I'll lead the shit out of these guys."

"No, Billy. You'll fight. You'll shoot your mouth off, you'll piss everyone off."

"Sometimes that's what a team needs."

"Sure. Sometimes. But what I need all the time is someone to use their brain, show these kids how to play their way out of a 3–1 deficit."

Blood trickled down the back of Billy's throat and he coughed it up, leaned forward and spit it into the garbage beside his feet. He'd learned at a very early age how to walk the very fine line between rude and insult, between disgusting someone and getting the crap kicked out of himself. And spitting blood into Hornsby's fancy garbage can rode that line pretty hard.

He looked up right into Hornsby's eyes so the guy could make no fucking mistake and said: "I'm not that guy."

"You used to be."

Billy laughed and wondered when. Because he'd missed it, entirely.

"I've watched you, Billy. And you know, you

used to play like a high scorer with thug tendencies and then somehow over the years that balance changed—"

Oh Jesus. This Oprah shit had to stop. He stood up. "You want me to pay a fine or something for starting that fight? Do some community crap?"

"I want you to grow up and be the player I need."

"I've got one year left on my contract, Hornsby. My body is beat to shit, and frankly, I don't like you. I don't like Dallas. I don't like being here. Keep me on the bench next year, let the General Manager trade me, do whatever you want, but I am who I am. Nothing's changing that now."

"That's too bad, Billy." Hornsby folded his hands over his lean stomach. "Most players wouldn't want to go out that way."

Billy's temper snarled and spat and the urge to tip the desk right over was a tough one to control, especially since he wasn't used to trying to control anything. "We done?"

"You live in tunnel vision, Billy. And until you realize that everything's not about you—"

"Are we done?"

Hornsby sighed. "Yep."

Billy stood, turned, his kidneys throbbing, his eye swollen, and walked out of the office. The concrete hallways under and around the arena were still full of staff. Most of Hornsby's minions shook their heads as they passed him, like they were just so disappointed in him, they could barely stand it.

Billy smiled real wide at all of them.

Mike Blake stepped out of the PT room, his eye swollen shut and already going black. Even with the eye, he was still a good-looking kid. Farm raised somewhere in the hinterlands of Canada, Blake had the blond hair and blue eyes that women were interested in, and a cocky smile that sealed the deal.

Blake never went home alone.

"Hey, man," Blake said, stopping in the doorway to button up his shirt, he had to tilt his head sideways to see the buttons out of that busted-up eye. "How's the nose?"

"Fine." Billy yanked the Kleenex out of his nostrils, balling them up in his fist. "How about the eye?"

"Doc said I need to have it checked out when the swelling goes down."

"Ah, shit, man, that's not right."

Blake laughed. "I'll live. That fight was the best part of the whole damn season. Hornsby give you a hard time?"

Billy shrugged.

"Look, we're heading over to Crowbar tonight, it'd be—" Billy rejected the idea, shaking his head, before Blake could get it out. "Come on, man, the guys—"

"Don't need another fight." And that's what he felt like right now, the anxiety spinning his guts into a ball wanted to put fist to face one more time.

"I don't know about that. But you should come."

"Thanks, Blake. But I'm just gonna head home." He honestly wished the kid would stop asking him to go out with the guys, he was so tired of refusing, made him feel old. In fact, the only thing that would make him feel older would be actually going to the damn clubs.

He said goodbye and made his way back to the locker room to grab his stuff. Security had cleared out

the press a while ago, but somehow he wasn't surprised to find Dominick Murphy lingering around.

"Thought I smelled something bad," Billy said,
grabbing his stuff from the locker. The insult was a
weak one, he just didn't have it in him to try and
match wits with Dom.

The air was thick with the slightly nacho chip odor
of sweaty hockey pads. The equipment manager had
the fans going, but modern technology just hadn't
solved the problem of stinky hockey gear.

"It's your jock," Dominick said, sitting on the
bench in front of Fforde's locker.

Billy's lip curled despite his best intentions. It was
hard not to like Dominick.

"I've given you my quote."

"What did Hornsby say? Is he fining you?"

"He's buying me a steak dinner."

"Somehow I doubt it."

Billy sighed and pulled his duffle bag up over
his shoulder. His kidneys didn't like the twist of his
spine but he managed to swallow a wince. Dominick
watched him through thick glasses, his salt-and-
pepper hair was looking a lot more salty these days,
and his beer belly had a good thirty years' experience.

Dominick was freelance, a hired pen, usually for
Sports Illustrated, sometimes *Esquire* or *Rolling Stone.*
As far as sports journalists went, they didn't get any
better than Dominick. He could make you look like a
hero in less than ten words. Of course, he could pub-
lically castrate you just as fast.

And for some reason, the guy liked Billy.

Maybe because they were both dinosaurs. And dinosaurs had to stick together.

"You want to get a drink?" Dom asked. "Tell me a little more about that fight?"

"I'd rather let the Renegades have another shot at my kidneys."

Dom smiled and heaved himself to his feet. That beer belly could pass for a pregnancy from the side. Truly a commitment to poor health.

"I'll take it easy on you, Billy."

Billy didn't think much about feelings. Except anger. Anger he made a study of. He was a professor of rage. The rest of them he ignored. Tonight it was hard, though, pretending not to feel anything about the sad state of his life.

Which was the only reason he opened his mouth and asked: "Why you so interested in me? Lots of guys go out the way I do, injured and old, sitting on a bench. Why you want to buy me drinks?"

"Because the best fighter in the league gets traded to a coach who leads the charge for change in the NHL. Hornsby has supported every anti-fighting rule that the league recommends."

"So?"

"So? What's he supposed to do with you?"

Hornsby was probably up there right now cleaning out his garbage can, wondering the same damn thing.

"Nothing," Billy said and it was so much the truth it depressed him. He waved goodbye to Dominick over his shoulder, relieved that Dom was gentleman enough to let Billy go without further hounding.

The season was over. No early morning training to keep him honest anymore. The off-season stretched in front of him, pleasantly empty. His boat down in

Padre was gassed up and ready to go. He'd finally teach his buddy Luc how to fish. Tomorrow he'd do that. Tonight demanded something . . . darker.

"I need a drink," he muttered.

He thought about picking up a woman. Someone soft, with skin that smelled sweet. Someone who would whisper all the right things in his ear. He tugged on his ear, his fingers brushing the thick ridge of scar tissue that ran from his earlobe, across his cheek, to his lip, where it curled, twisting his lip into an ever-present snarl.

There were certain kinds of women who liked the scar. Who had expectations of what sex would be like with a man like him. And usually he could go with that particular flow. But playing the marauder in bed was getting old.

He thought of Maddy out there in the city somewhere. And the thought of her, her shocked face in the spa eight months ago, was the match to the worst of his instincts.

Punching open the door to the player's parking garage connected to the arena, the wet heat of the Dallas night wrapped around him like a slimy towel, his white shirt immediately stuck to him. Fforde kept making fun of him for buying such cheap clothes. With his salary he could buy the kind of material that would never stick to him, no matter how hot it got. But he didn't give a shit about clothes.

What do you give a shit about? He could practically hear Hornsby's voice.

Screw it, he thought, walking across the parking area to his Audi and opening his cell phone.

"Sabine?" he said when the woman picked up. He

could hear a heavy bassline in the background. People yelling.

Puck Bunnies. Lord, he was too old for this.

"What's up?" he asked.

"We're celebrating," she cried. "I got a promotion!"

"Congratulations," he said. He had no idea what her job was, or where she worked. He didn't care.

"Can you be at my place in fifteen minutes," he said. She agreed, which he knew she would, celebration or not, and he hung up. His blood thickened as he thought about her body, of what she would let him do to her. How she wanted him to use her. And if he was bored and slightly sickened by it all—well, too bad.

He was Billy Wilkins and this was his life.